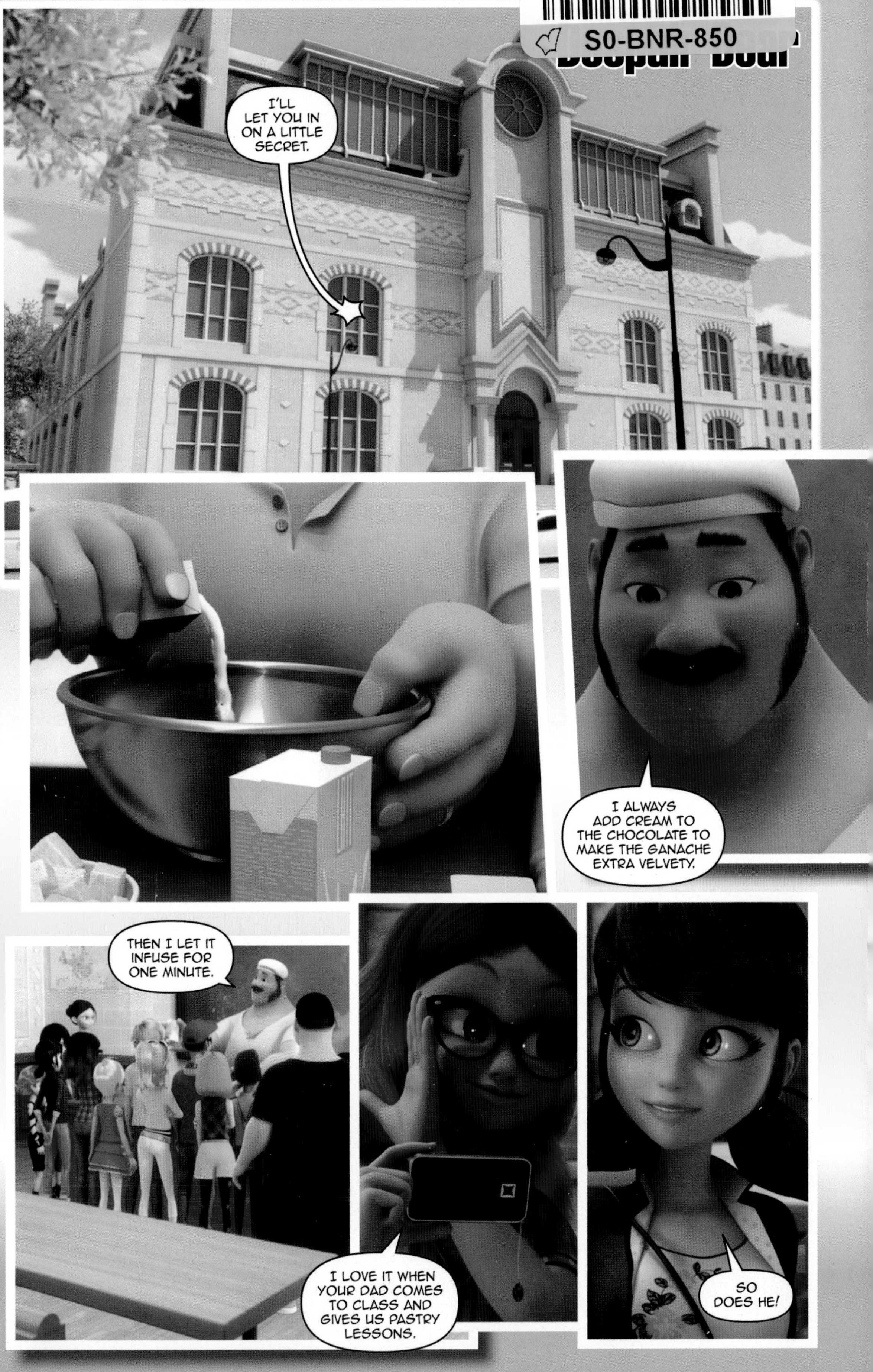
I'LL LET YOU IN ON A LITTLE SECRET.
I ALWAYS ADD CREAM TO THE CHOCOLATE TO MAKE THE GANACHE EXTRA VELVETY.
THEN I LET IT INFUSE FOR ONE MINUTE.
I LOVE IT WHEN YOUR DAD COMES TO CLASS AND GIVES US PASTRY LESSONS.
SO DOES HE!

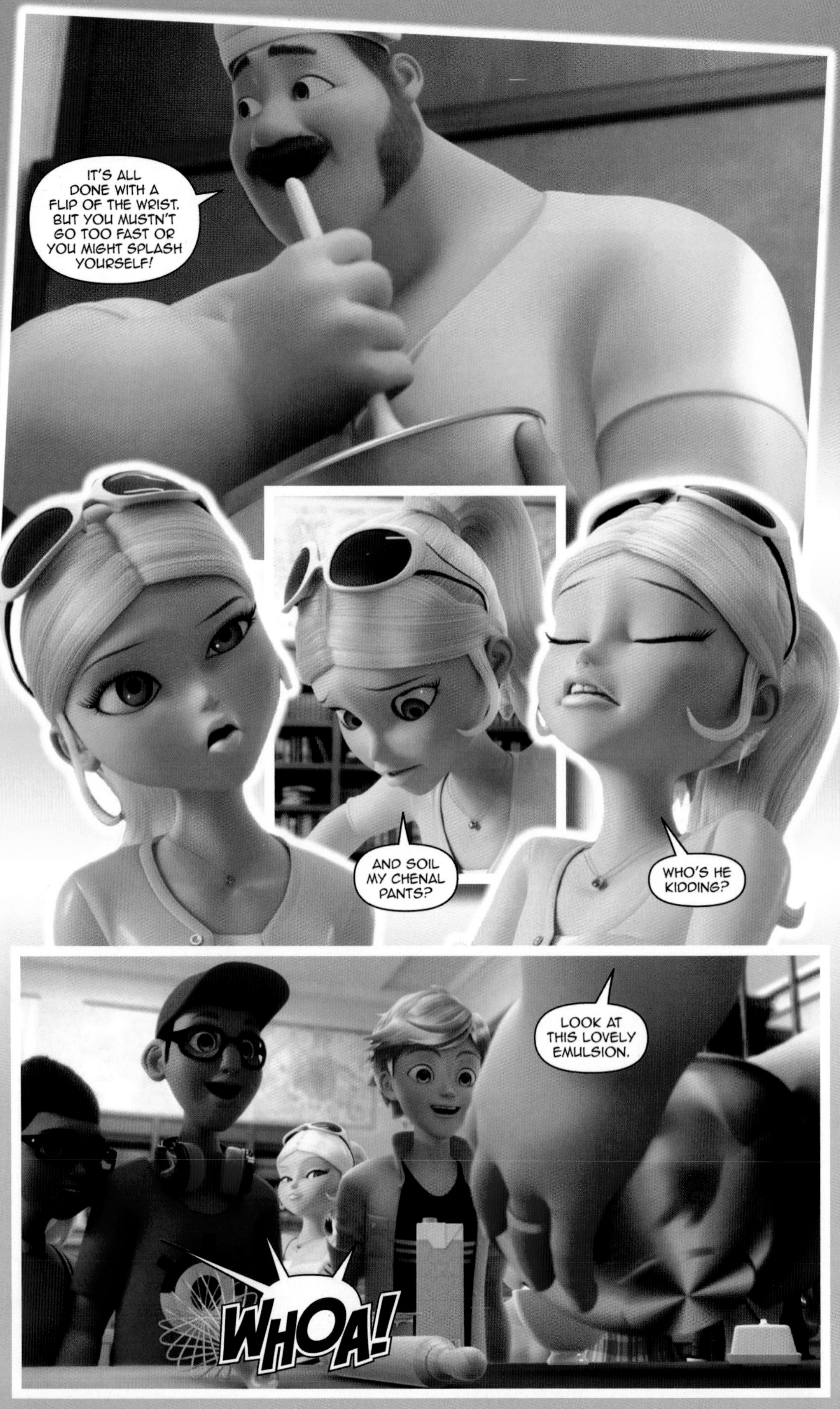
IT'S ALL DONE WITH A FLIP OF THE WRIST. BUT YOU MUSTN'T GO TOO FAST OR YOU MIGHT SPLASH YOURSELF!
AND SOIL MY CHENAL PANTS?
WHO'S HE KIDDING?
LOOK AT THIS LOVELY EMULSION.
WHOA!

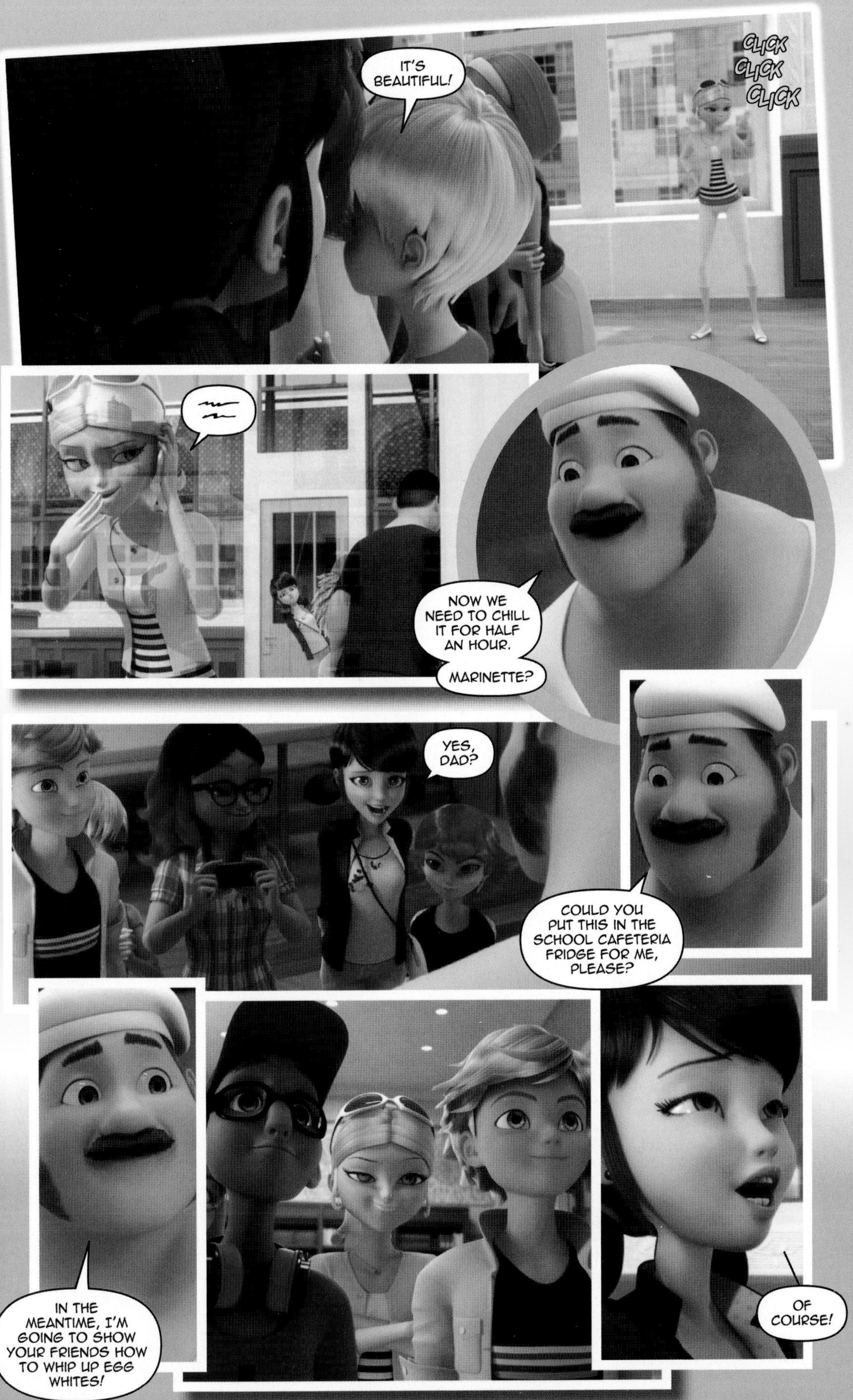
IT'S BEAUTIFUL!
CLICK CLICK CLICK
NOW WE NEED TO CHILL IT FOR HALF AN HOUR.
MARINETTE?
YES, DAD?
COULD YOU PUT THIS IN THE SCHOOL CAFETERIA FRIDGE FOR ME, PLEASE?
OF COURSE!
IN THE MEANTIME, I'M GOING TO SHOW YOUR FRIENDS HOW TO WHIP UP EGG WHITES!

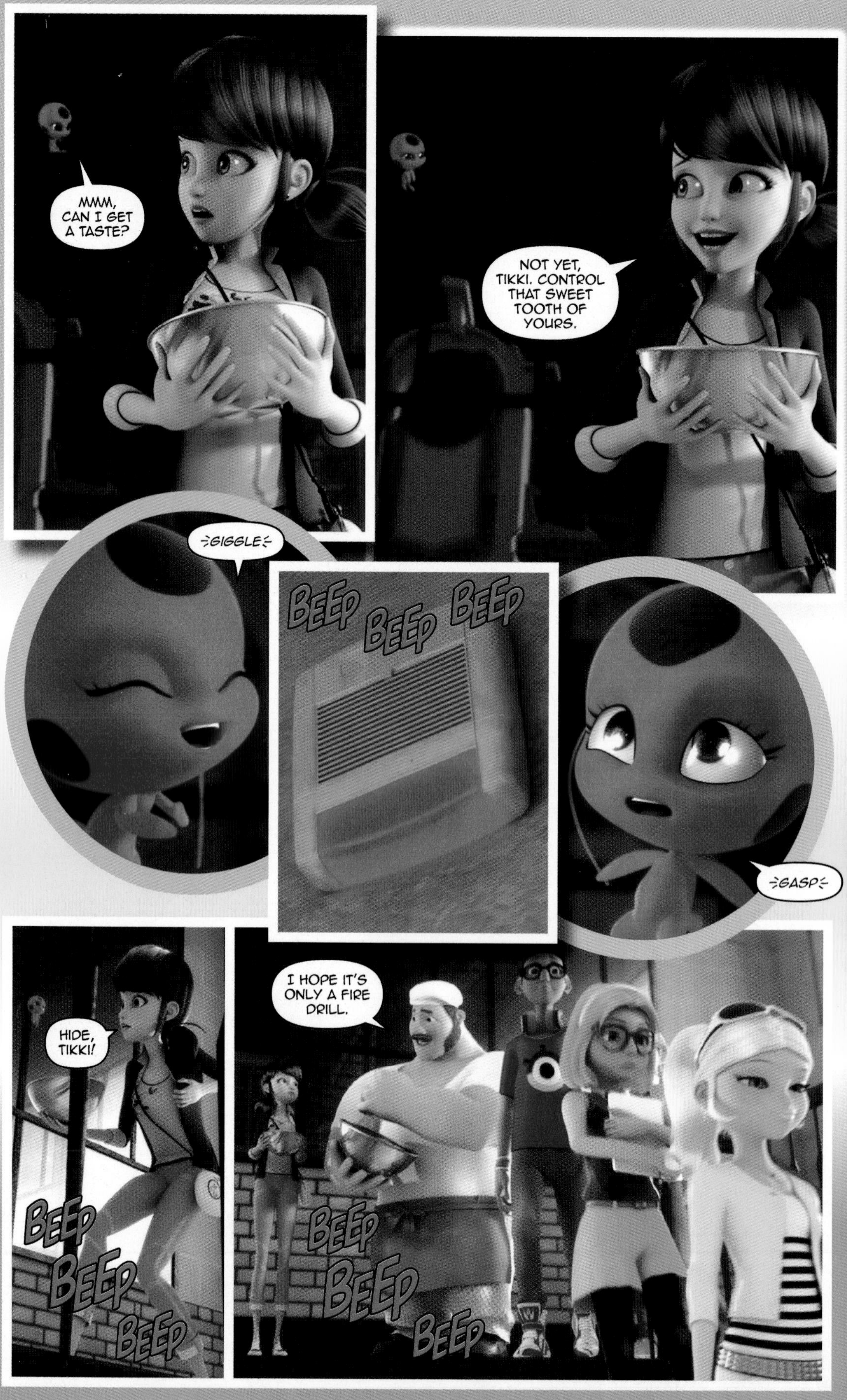
MMM, CAN I GET A TASTE?
NOT YET, TIKKI. CONTROL THAT SWEET TOOTH OF YOURS.
GIGGLE
BEEP BEEP BEEP
GASP
HIDE, TIKKI!
BEEP BEEP BEEP
I HOPE IT'S ONLY A FIRE DRILL.
BEEP BEEP BEEP

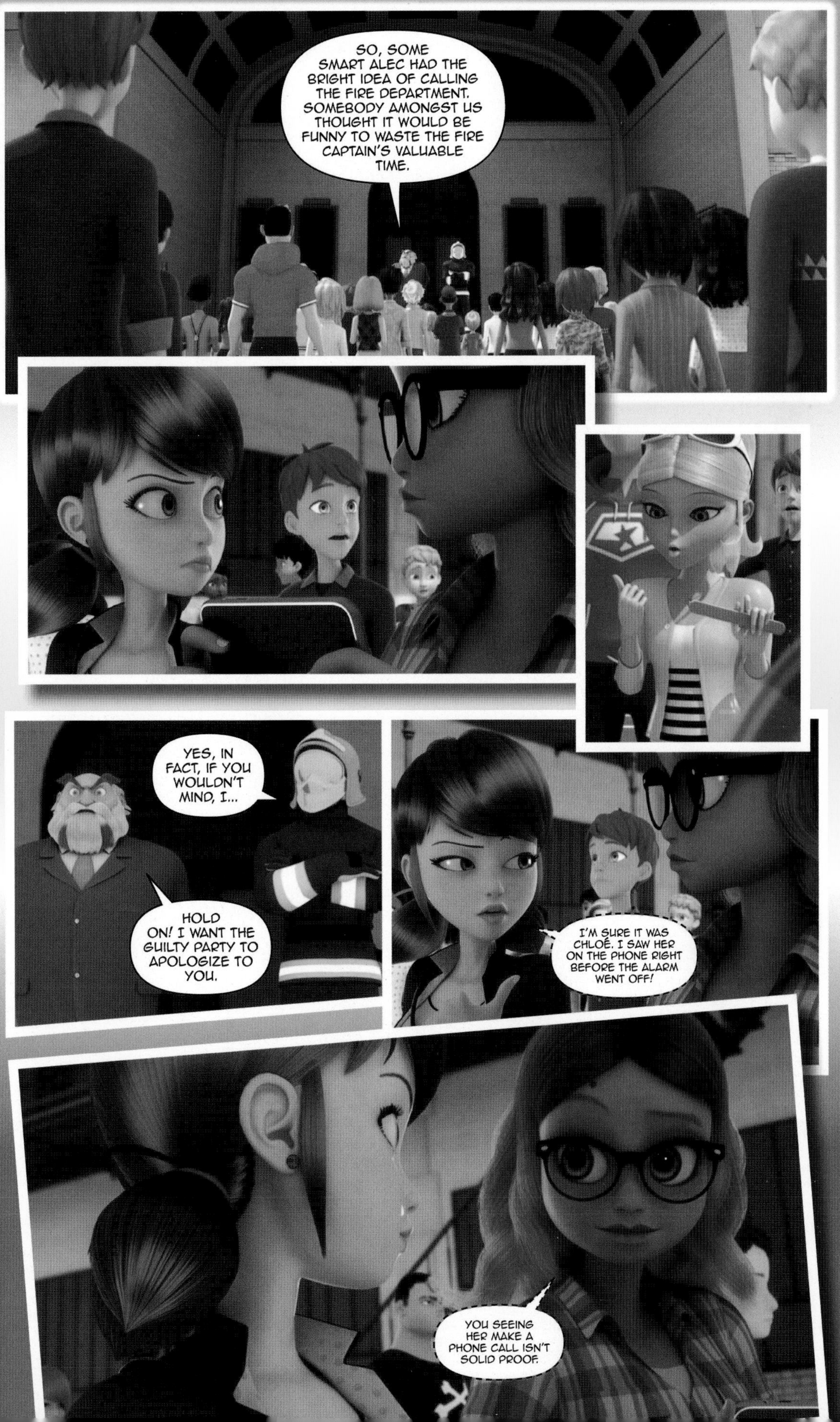
SO, SOME SMART ALEC HAD THE BRIGHT IDEA OF CALLING THE FIRE DEPARTMENT. SOMEBODY AMONGST US THOUGHT IT WOULD BE FUNNY TO WASTE THE FIRE CAPTAIN'S VALUABLE TIME.
YES, IN FACT, IF YOU WOULDN'T MIND, I...
HOLD ON! I WANT THE GUILTY PARTY TO APOLOGIZE TO YOU.
I'M SURE IT WAS CHLOÉ. I SAW HER ON THE PHONE RIGHT BEFORE THE ALARM WENT OFF!
YOU SEEING HER MAKE A PHONE CALL ISN'T SOLID PROOF.

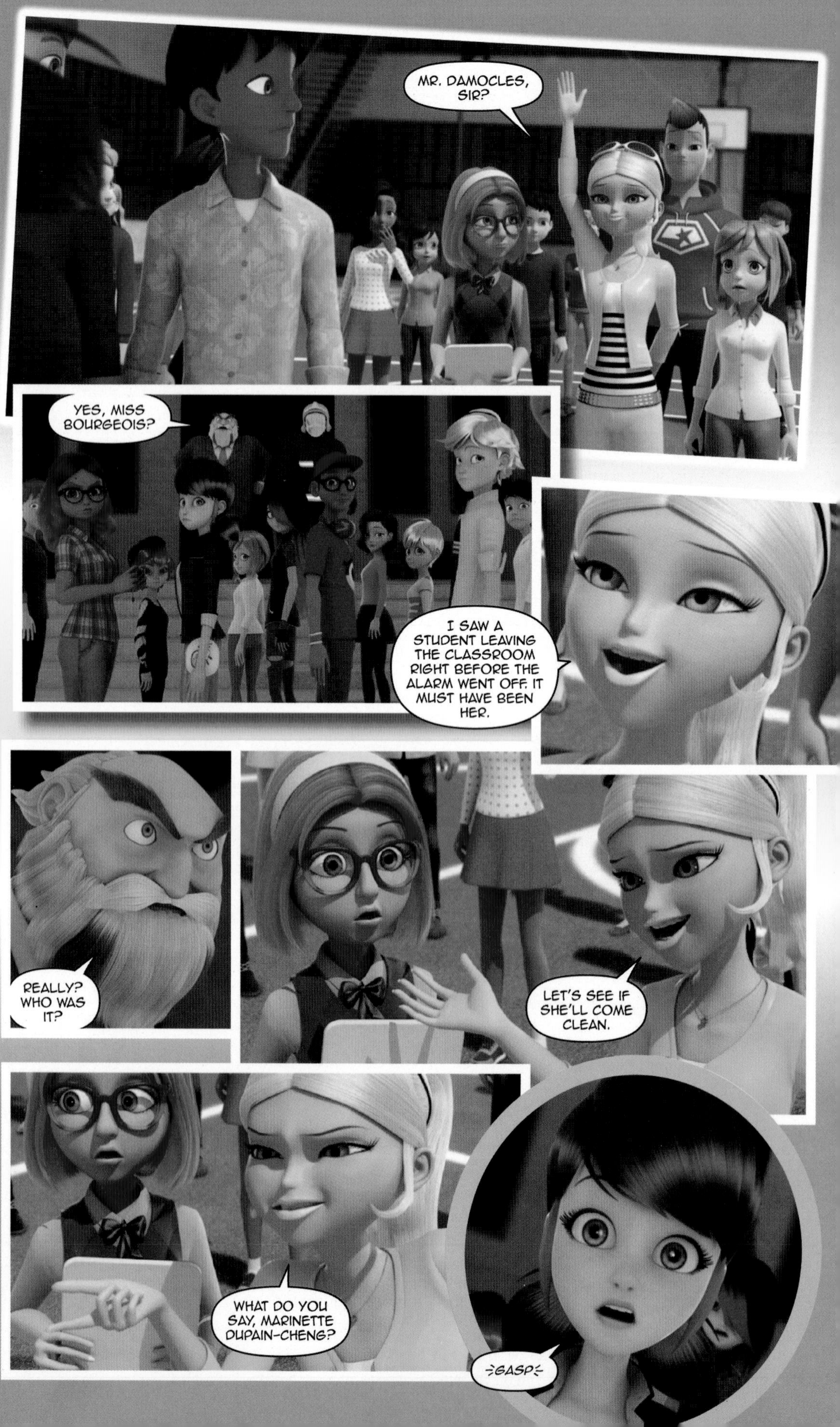
MR. DAMOCLES, SIR?
YES, MISS BOURGEOIS?
I SAW A STUDENT LEAVING THE CLASSROOM RIGHT BEFORE THE ALARM WENT OFF. IT MUST HAVE BEEN HER.
REALLY? WHO WAS IT?
LET'S SEE IF SHE'LL COME CLEAN.
WHAT DO YOU SAY, MARINETTE DUPAIN-CHENG?
GASP

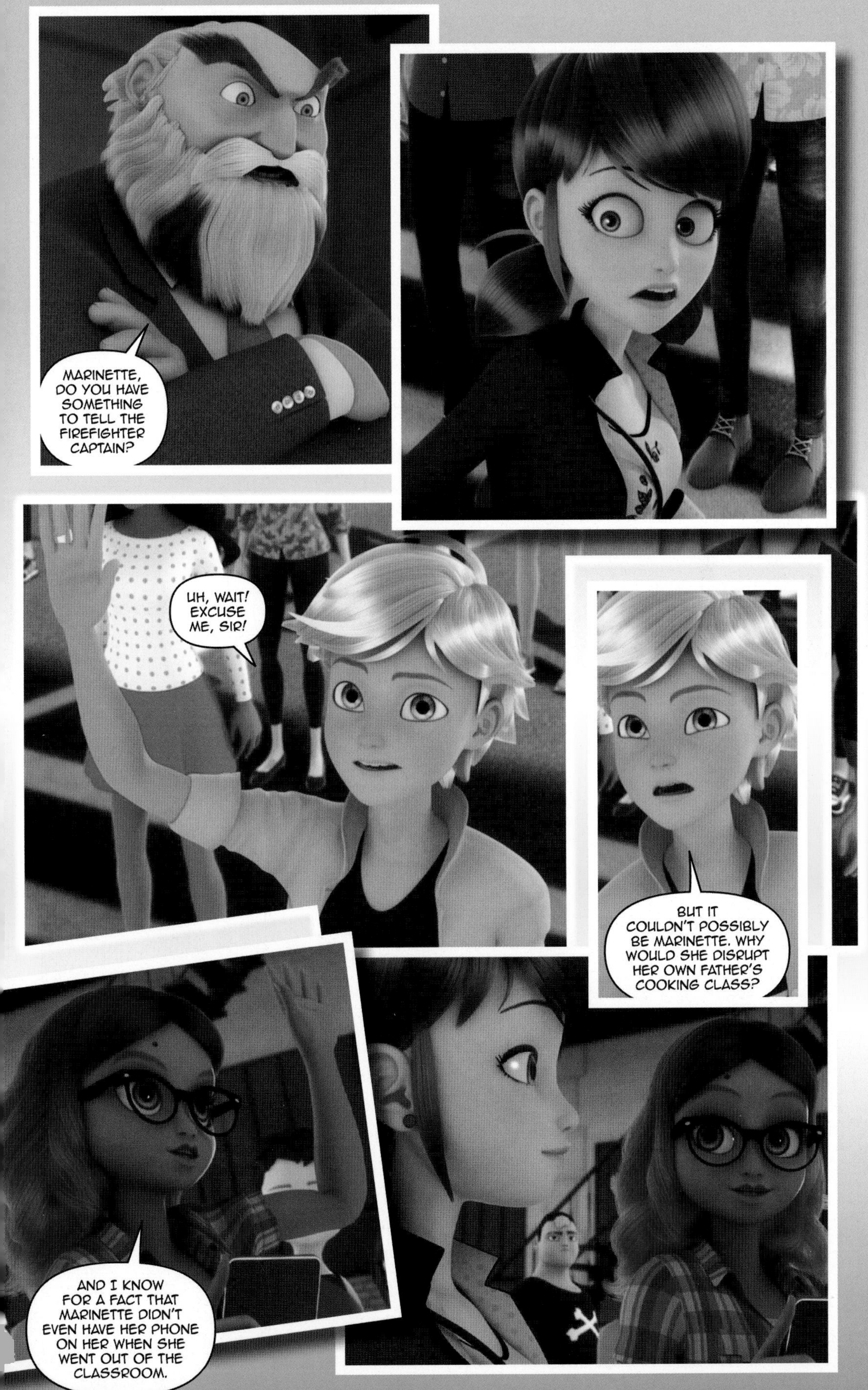
MARINETTE, DO YOU HAVE SOMETHING TO TELL THE FIREFIGHTER CAPTAIN?
UH, WAIT! EXCUSE ME, SIR!
BUT IT COULDN'T POSSIBLY BE MARINETTE. WHY WOULD SHE DISRUPT HER OWN FATHER'S COOKING CLASS?
AND I KNOW FOR A FACT THAT MARINETTE DIDN'T EVEN HAVE HER PHONE ON HER WHEN SHE WENT OUT OF THE CLASSROOM.

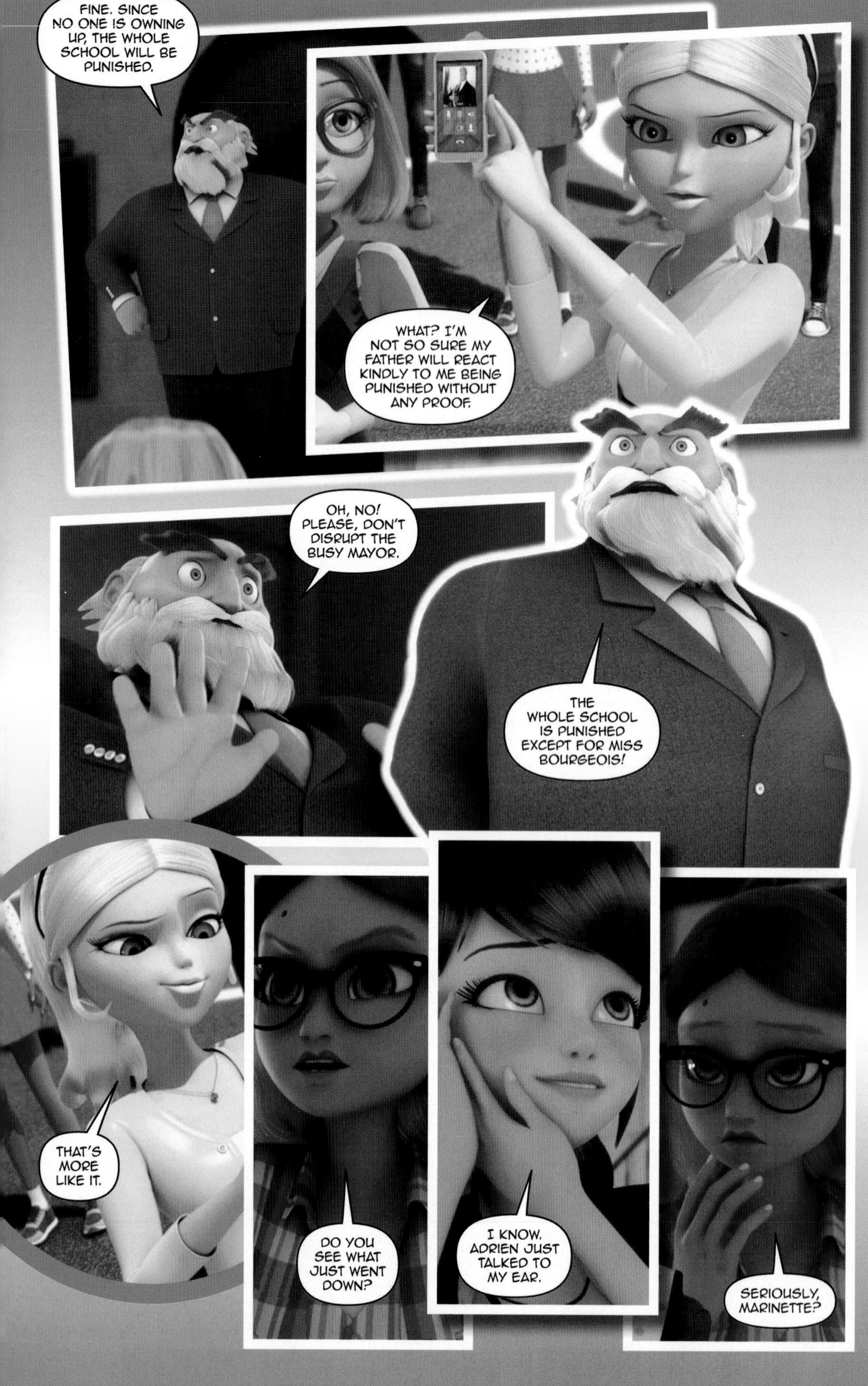
FINE. SINCE NO ONE IS OWNING UP, THE WHOLE SCHOOL WILL BE PUNISHED.
WHAT? I'M NOT SO SURE MY FATHER WILL REACT KINDLY TO ME BEING PUNISHED WITHOUT ANY PROOF.
OH, NO! PLEASE, DON'T DISRUPT THE BUSY MAYOR.
THE WHOLE SCHOOL IS PUNISHED EXCEPT FOR MISS BOURGEOIS!
THAT'S MORE LIKE IT.
DO YOU SEE WHAT JUST WENT DOWN?
I KNOW. ADRIEN JUST TALKED TO MY EAR.
SERIOUSLY, MARINETTE?

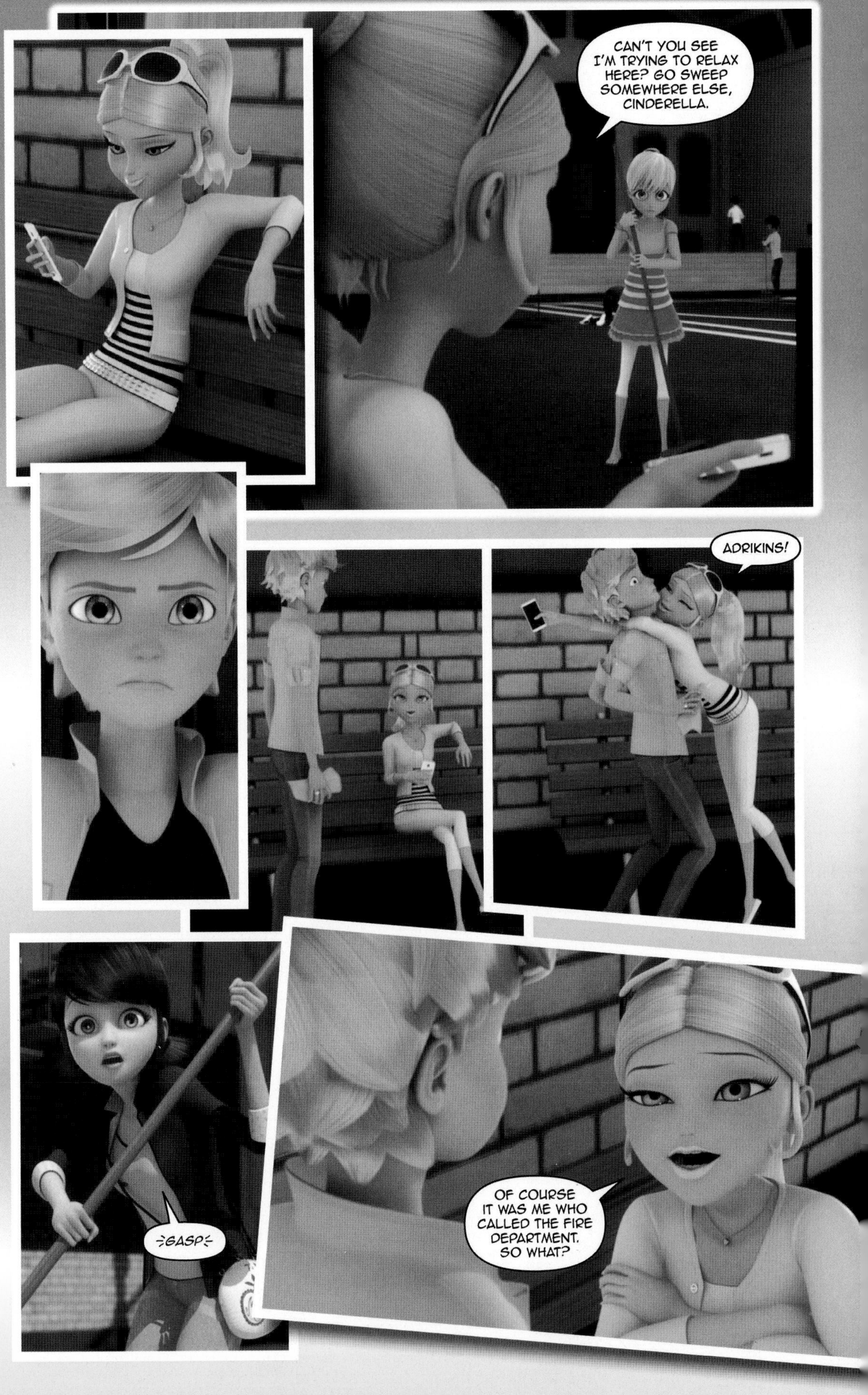
CAN'T YOU SEE I'M TRYING TO RELAX HERE? GO SWEEP SOMEWHERE ELSE, CINDERELLA.
ADRIKINS!
GASP
OF COURSE IT WAS ME WHO CALLED THE FIRE DEPARTMENT. SO WHAT?

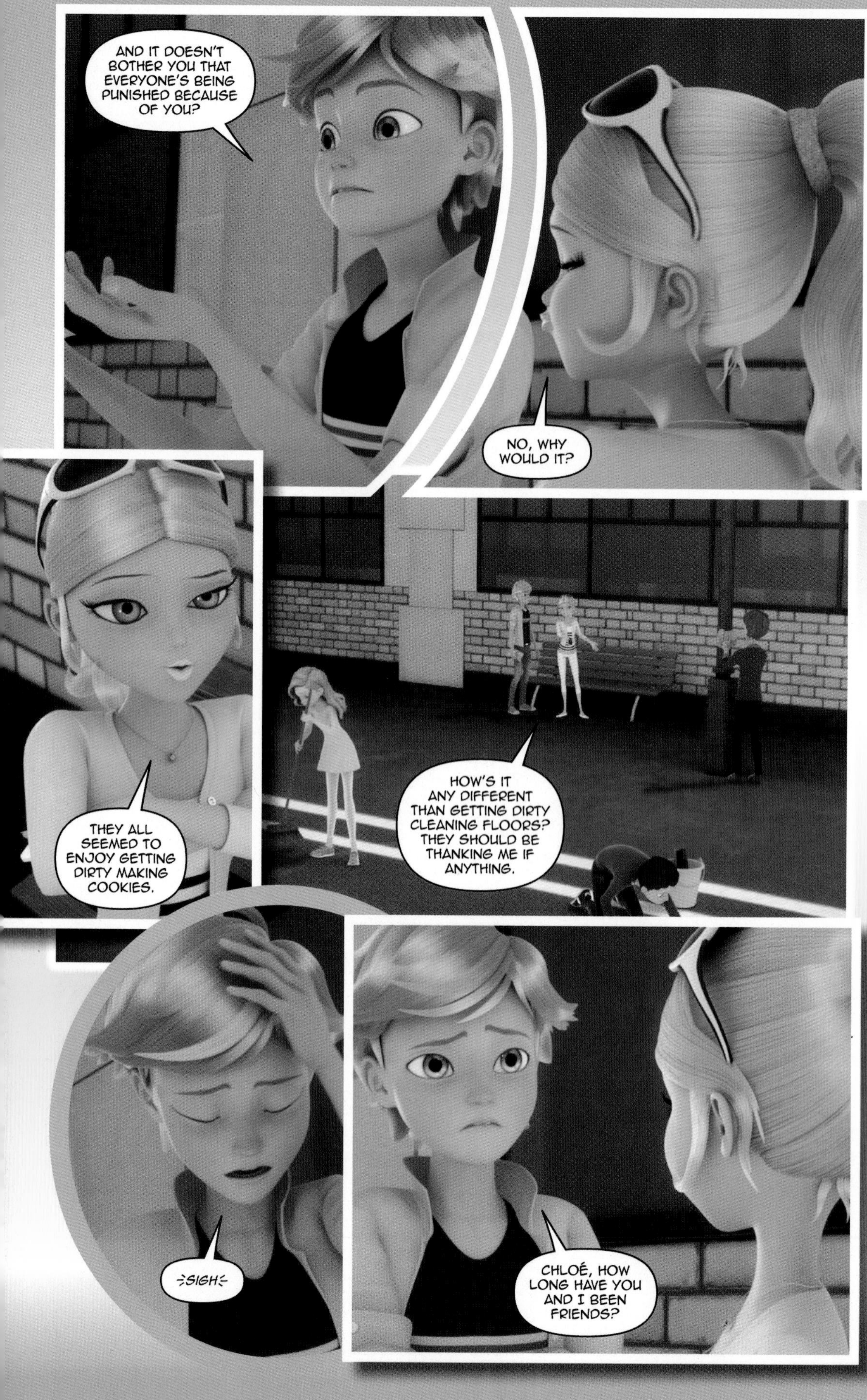
AND IT DOESN'T BOTHER YOU THAT EVERYONE'S BEING PUNISHED BECAUSE OF YOU?
NO, WHY WOULD IT?
THEY ALL SEEMED TO ENJOY GETTING DIRTY MAKING COOKIES.
HOW'S IT ANY DIFFERENT THAN GETTING DIRTY CLEANING FLOORS? THEY SHOULD BE THANKING ME IF ANYTHING.
SIGH
CHLOÉ, HOW LONG HAVE YOU AND I BEEN FRIENDS?

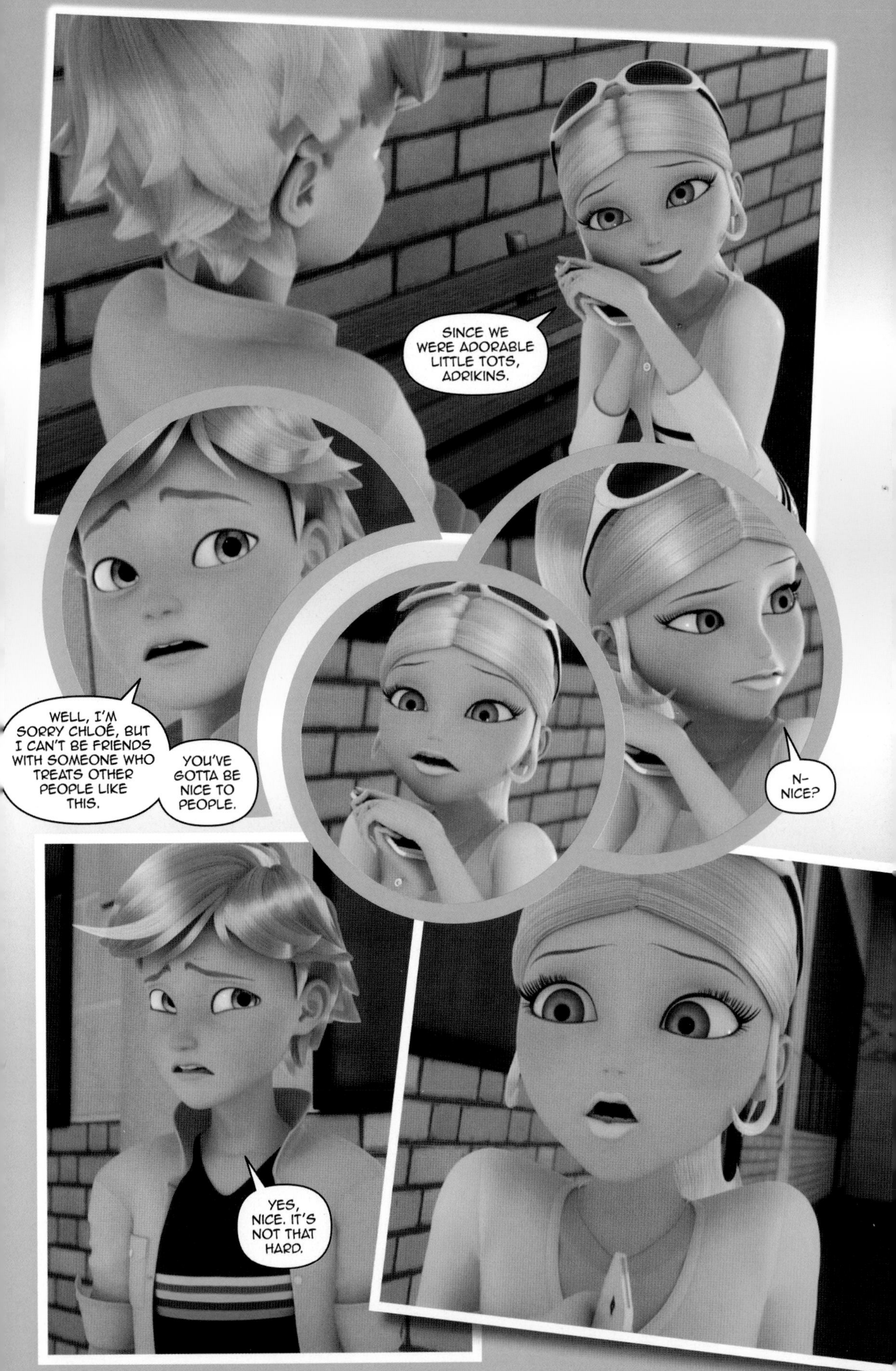
SINCE WE WERE ADORABLE LITTLE TOTS, ADRIKINS.
WELL, I'M SORRY CHLOÉ, BUT I CAN'T BE FRIENDS WITH SOMEONE WHO TREATS OTHER PEOPLE LIKE THIS.
YOU'VE GOTTA BE NICE TO PEOPLE.
N– NICE?
YES, NICE. IT'S NOT THAT HARD.

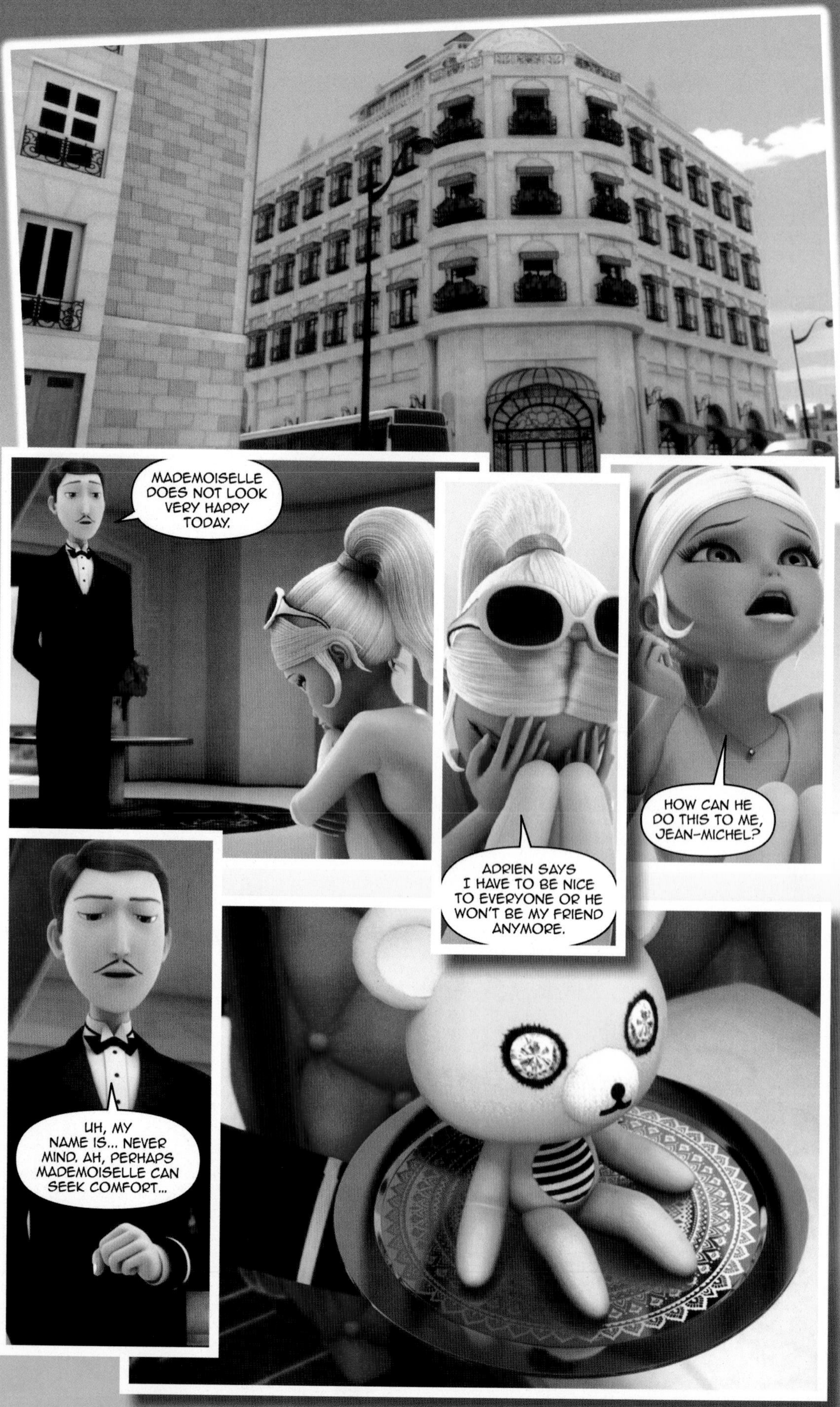
MADEMOISELLE DOES NOT LOOK VERY HAPPY TODAY.
ADRIEN SAYS I HAVE TO BE NICE TO EVERYONE OR HE WON'T BE MY FRIEND ANYMORE.
HOW CAN HE DO THIS TO ME, JEAN-MICHEL?
UH, MY NAME IS... NEVER MIND. AH, PERHAPS MADEMOISELLE CAN SEEK COMFORT...

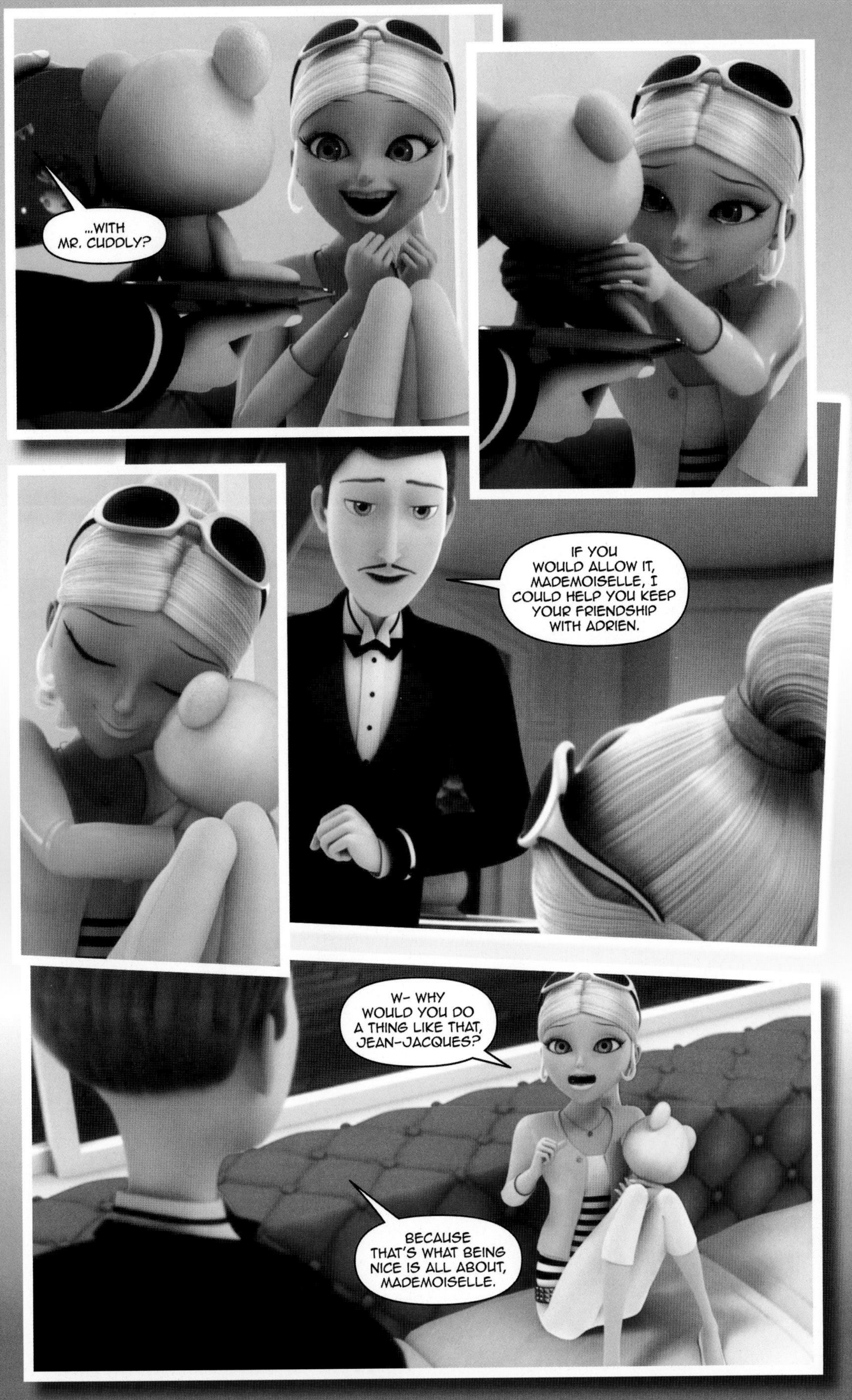
...WITH MR. CUDDLY?
IF YOU WOULD ALLOW IT, MADEMOISELLE, I COULD HELP YOU KEEP YOUR FRIENDSHIP WITH ADRIEN.
W- WHY WOULD YOU DO A THING LIKE THAT, JEAN-JACQUES?
BECAUSE THAT'S WHAT BEING NICE IS ALL ABOUT, MADEMOISELLE.

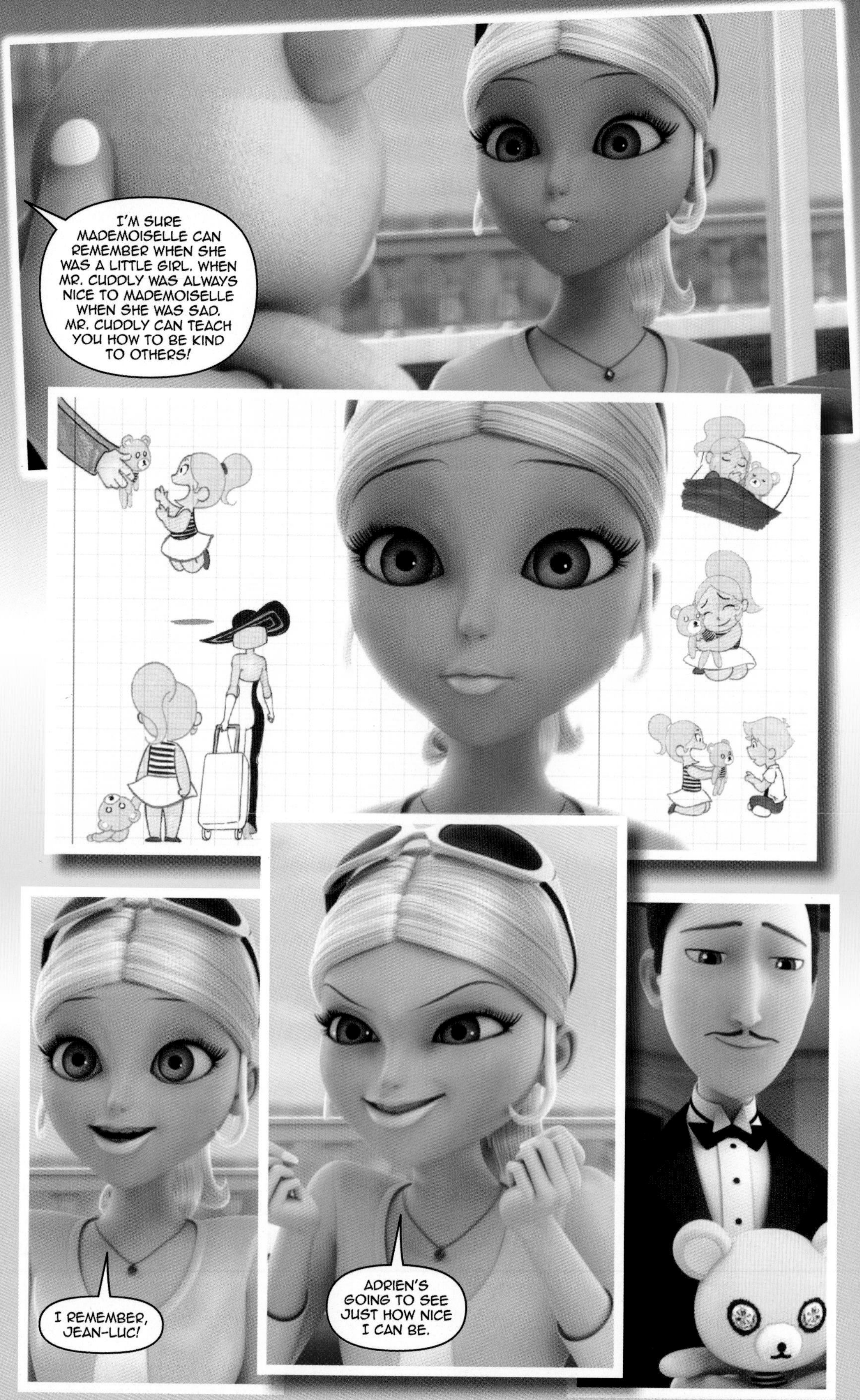
I'M SURE MADEMOISELLE CAN REMEMBER WHEN SHE WAS A LITTLE GIRL. WHEN MR. CUDDLY WAS ALWAYS NICE TO MADEMOISELLE WHEN SHE WAS SAD. MR. CUDDLY CAN TEACH YOU HOW TO BE KIND TO OTHERS!
I REMEMBER, JEAN-LUC!
ADRIEN'S GOING TO SEE JUST HOW NICE I CAN BE.

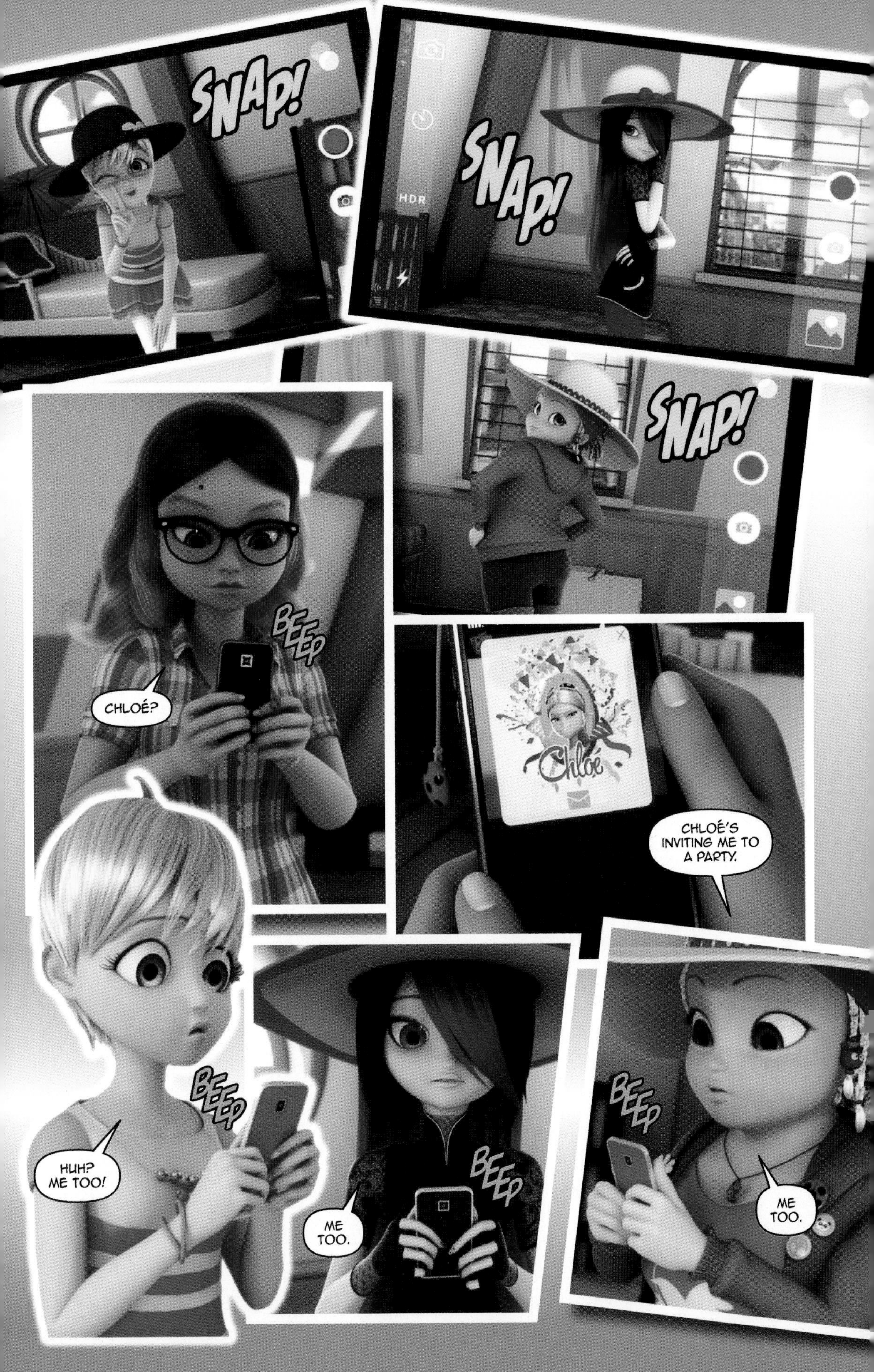
SNAP!
HDR
SNAP!
SNAP!
BEEP
CHLOÉ?
Chloé
CHLOÉ'S INVITING ME TO A PARTY.
BEEP
HUH? ME TOO!
BEEP
ME TOO.
BEEP
ME TOO.

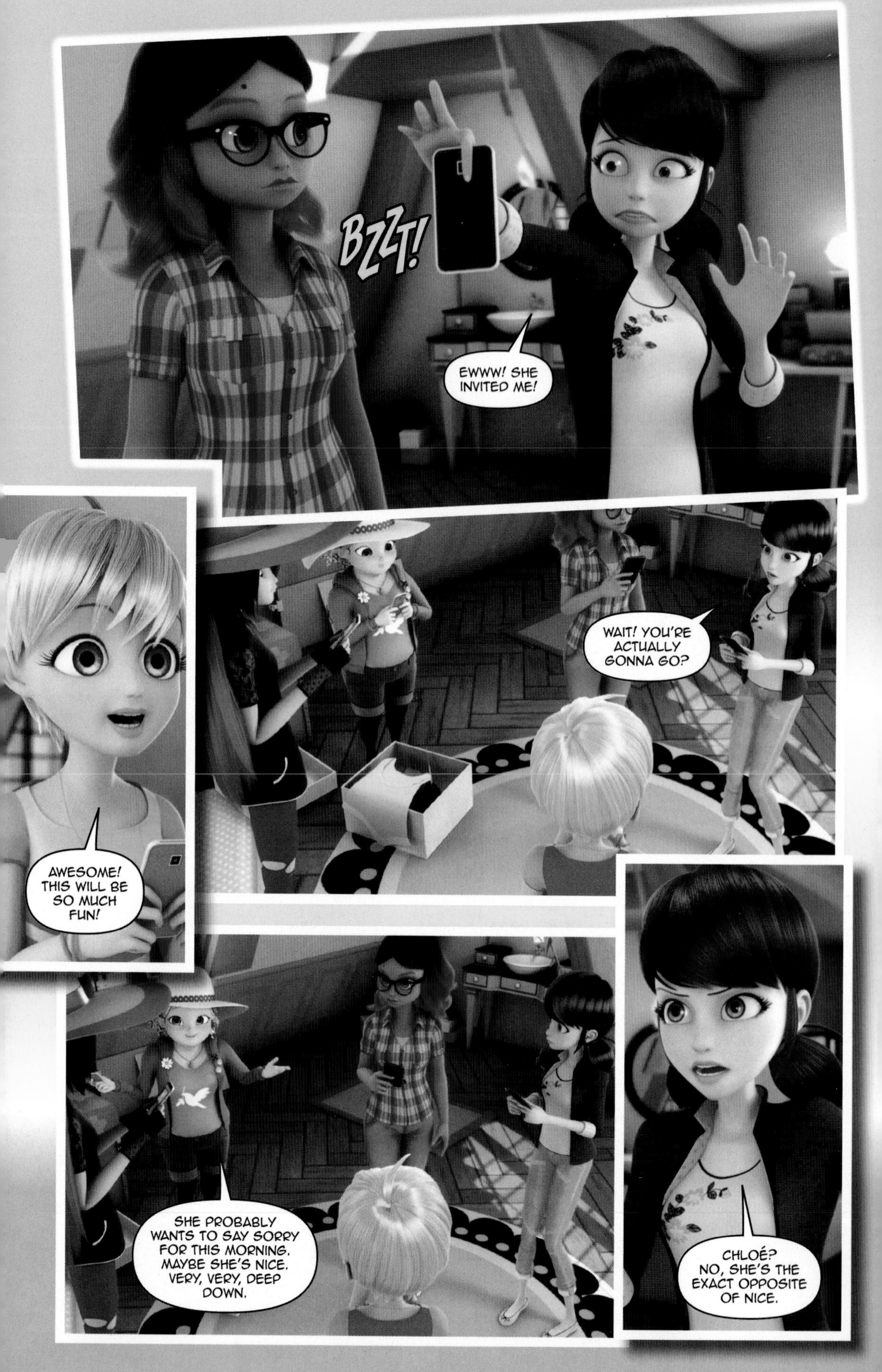
BZZT!
EWWW! SHE INVITED ME!
AWESOME! THIS WILL BE SO MUCH FUN!
WAIT! YOU'RE ACTUALLY GONNA GO?
SHE PROBABLY WANTS TO SAY SORRY FOR THIS MORNING. MAYBE SHE'S NICE. VERY, VERY, DEEP DOWN.
CHLOÉ? NO, SHE'S THE EXACT OPPOSITE OF NICE.

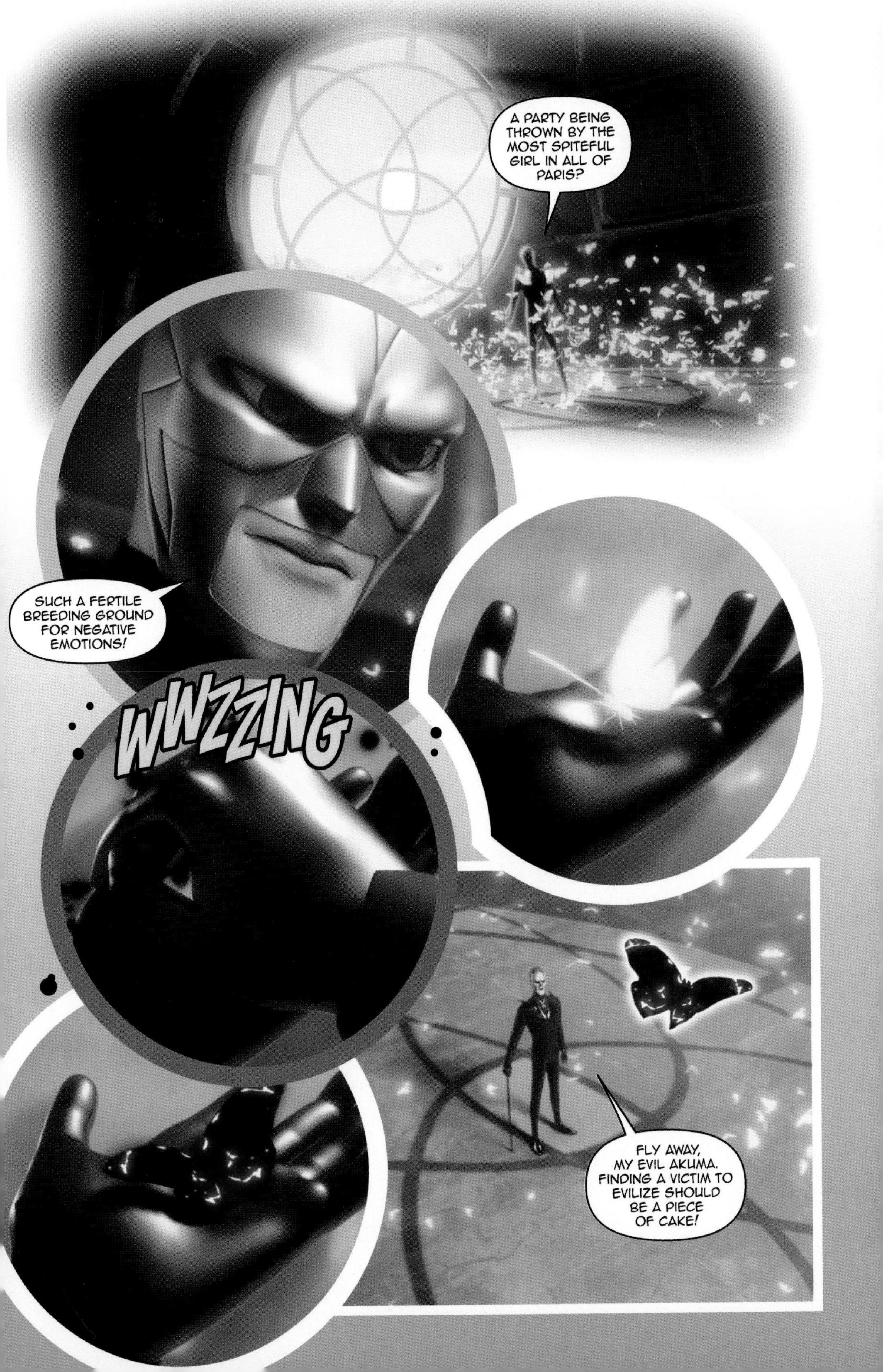
A PARTY BEING THROWN BY THE MOST SPITEFUL GIRL IN ALL OF PARIS?
SUCH A FERTILE BREEDING GROUND FOR NEGATIVE EMOTIONS!
WWZZING
FLY AWAY, MY EVIL AKUMA. FINDING A VICTIM TO EVILIZE SHOULD BE A PIECE OF CAKE!

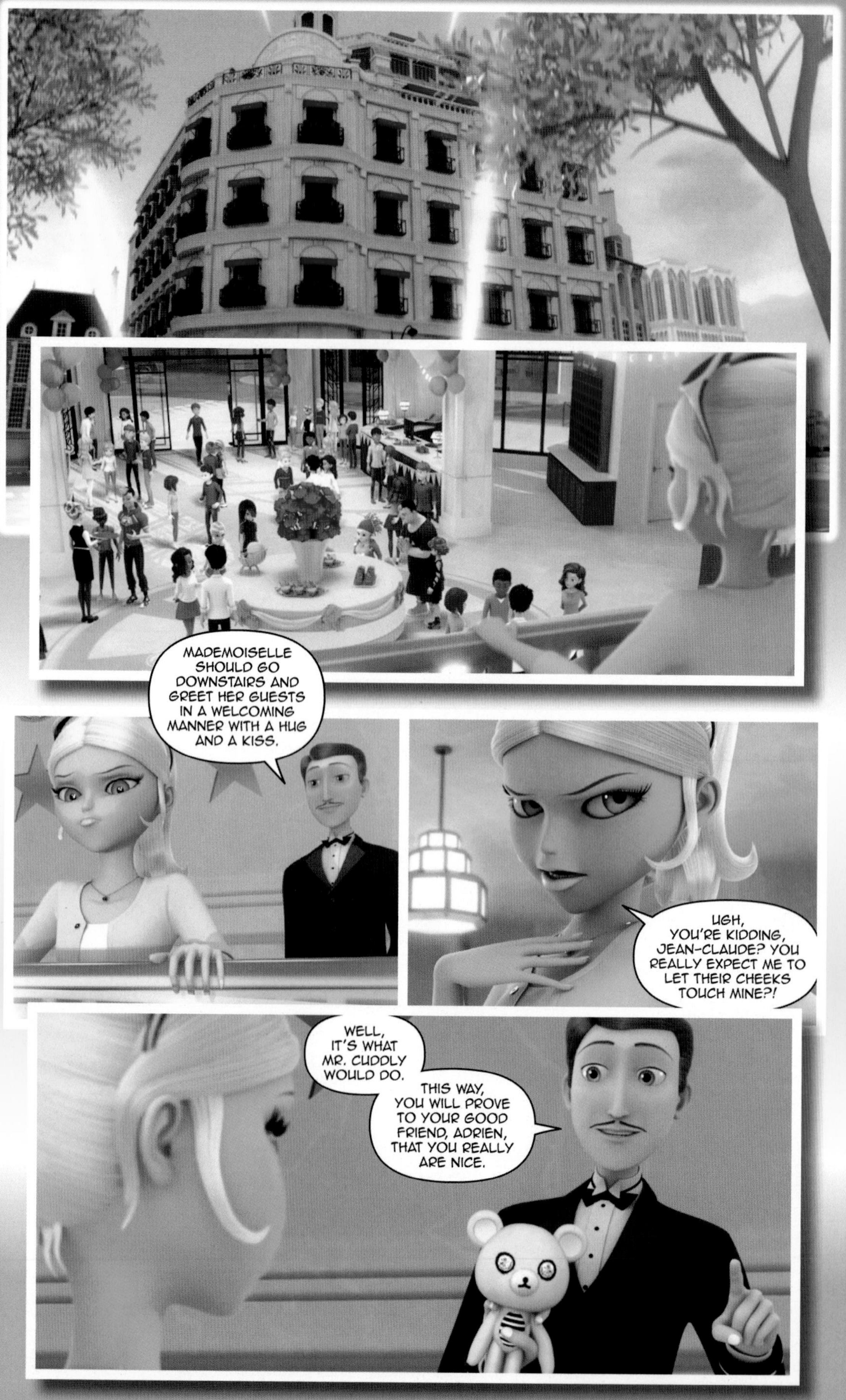
MADEMOISELLE SHOULD GO DOWNSTAIRS AND GREET HER GUESTS IN A WELCOMING MANNER WITH A HUG AND A KISS.
UGH, YOU'RE KIDDING, JEAN-CLAUDE? YOU REALLY EXPECT ME TO LET THEIR CHEEKS TOUCH MINE?!
WELL, IT'S WHAT MR. CUDDLY WOULD DO.
THIS WAY, YOU WILL PROVE TO YOUR GOOD FRIEND, ADRIEN, THAT YOU REALLY ARE NICE.

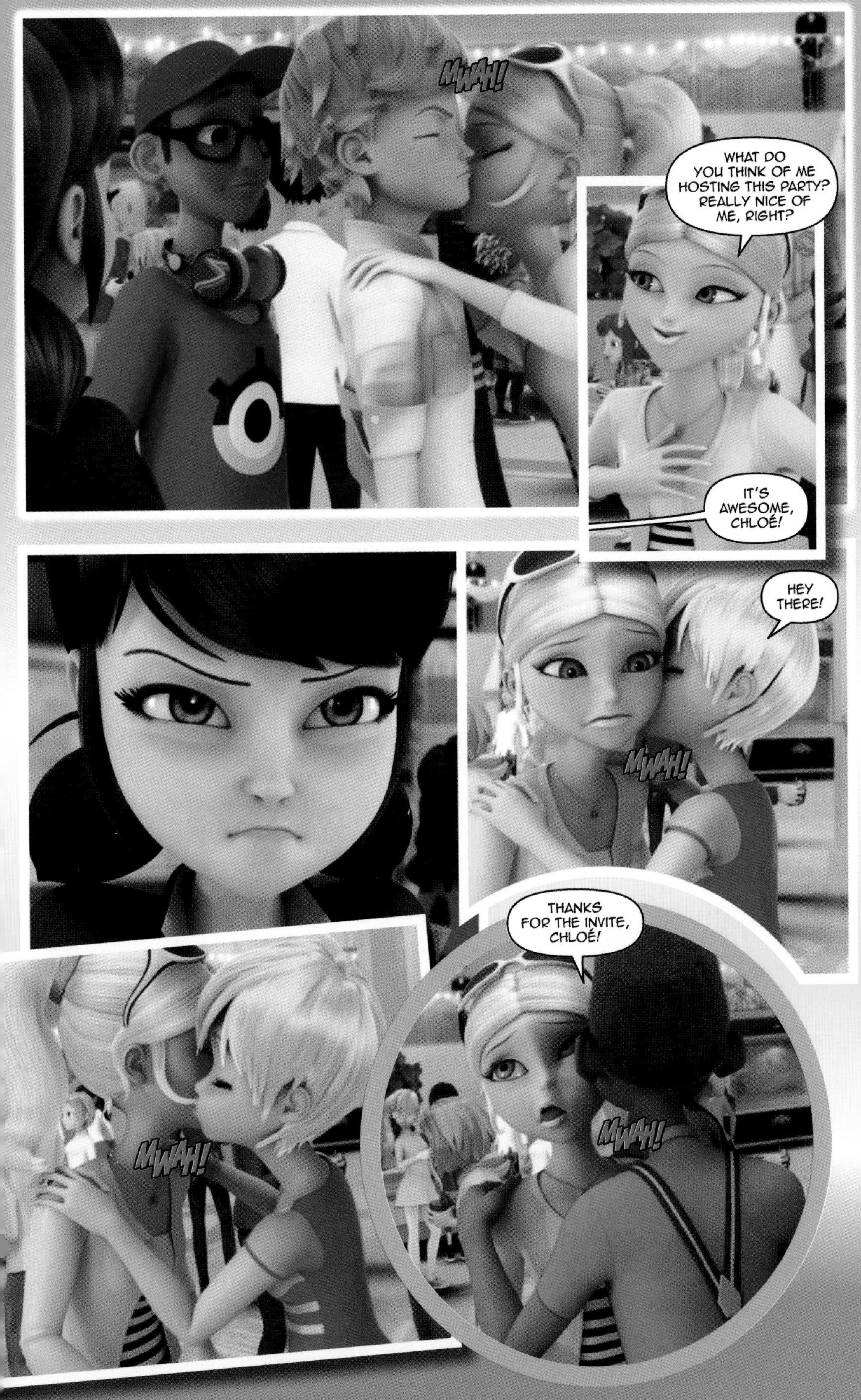
MWAH!
WHAT DO YOU THINK OF ME HOSTING THIS PARTY? REALLY NICE OF ME, RIGHT?
IT'S AWESOME, CHLOÉ!
HEY THERE!
MWAH!
MWAH!
THANKS FOR THE INVITE, CHLOÉ!
MWAH!

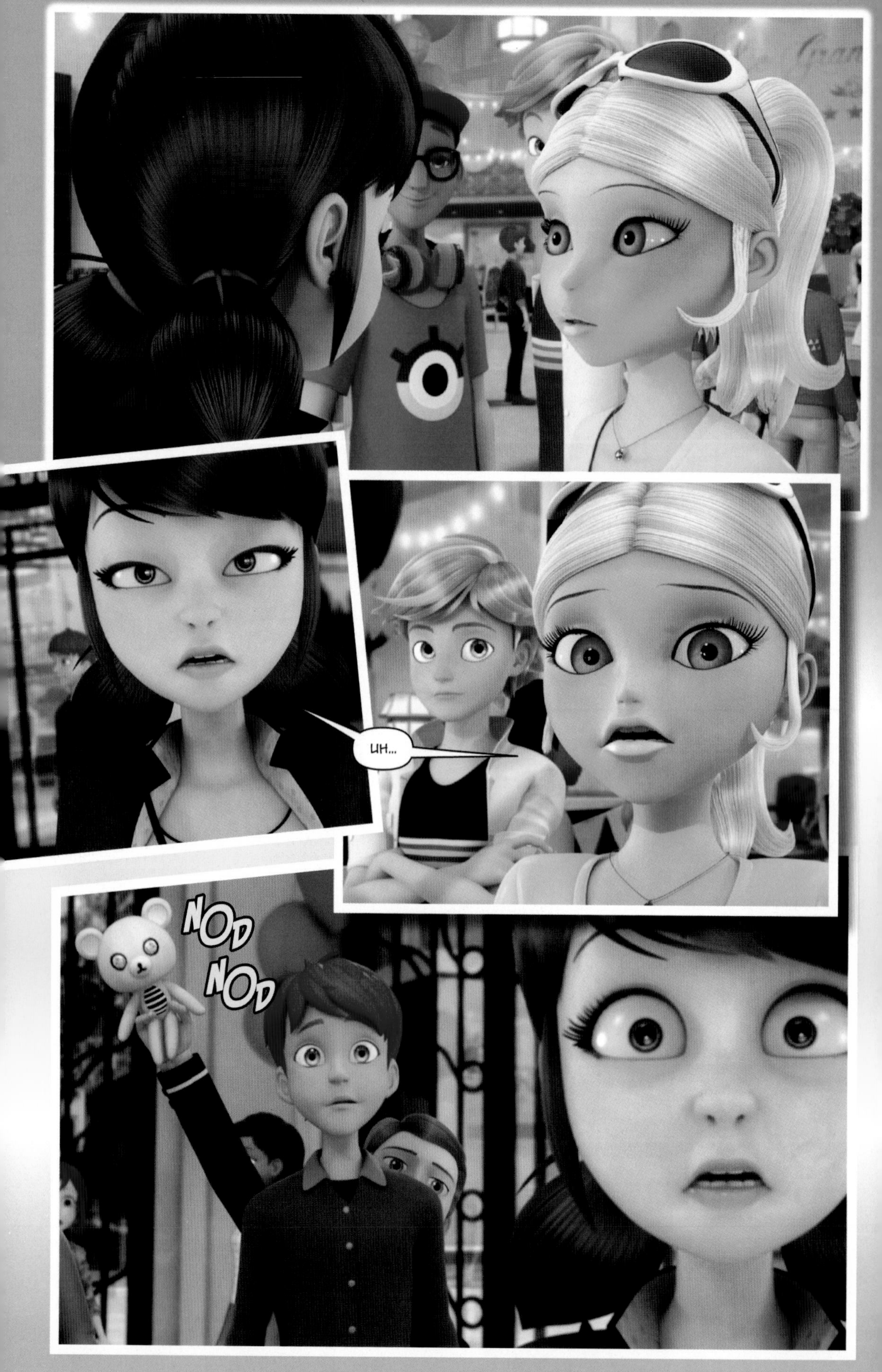
UH...
NOD
NOD

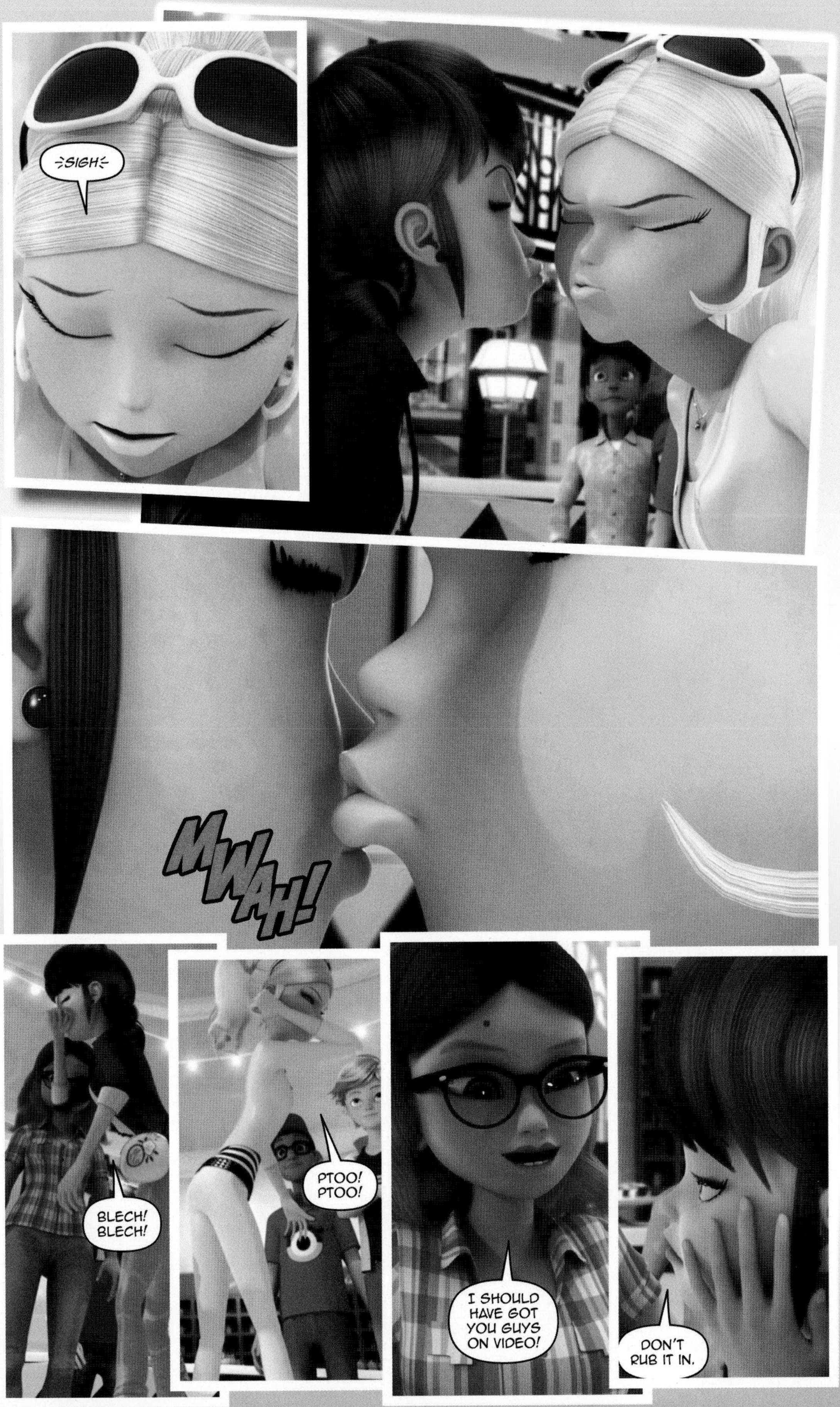

SIGH
MWAH!
BLECH! BLECH!
PTOO! PTOO!
I SHOULD HAVE GOT YOU GUYS ON VIDEO!
DON'T RUB IT IN.

I DID IT. ADRIEN SEEMS HAPPY. ARE WE DONE NOW?

IF I MAY BE SO BOLD, IN ORDER TO REAFFIRM ADRIEN OF HER KINDNESS, MADEMOISELLE MIGHT GO AND CHECK THAT HER GUESTS ARE HAVING A GOOD TIME.

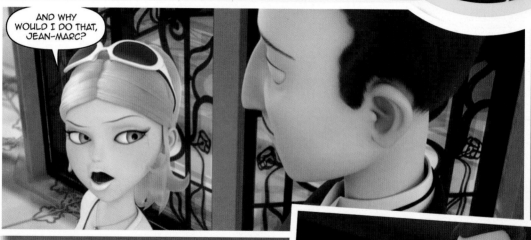

AND WHY WOULD I DO THAT, JEAN-MARC?

BECAUSE THAT'S WHAT MR. CUDDLY WOULD DO!

ALRIGHT, FINE! I GET IT.

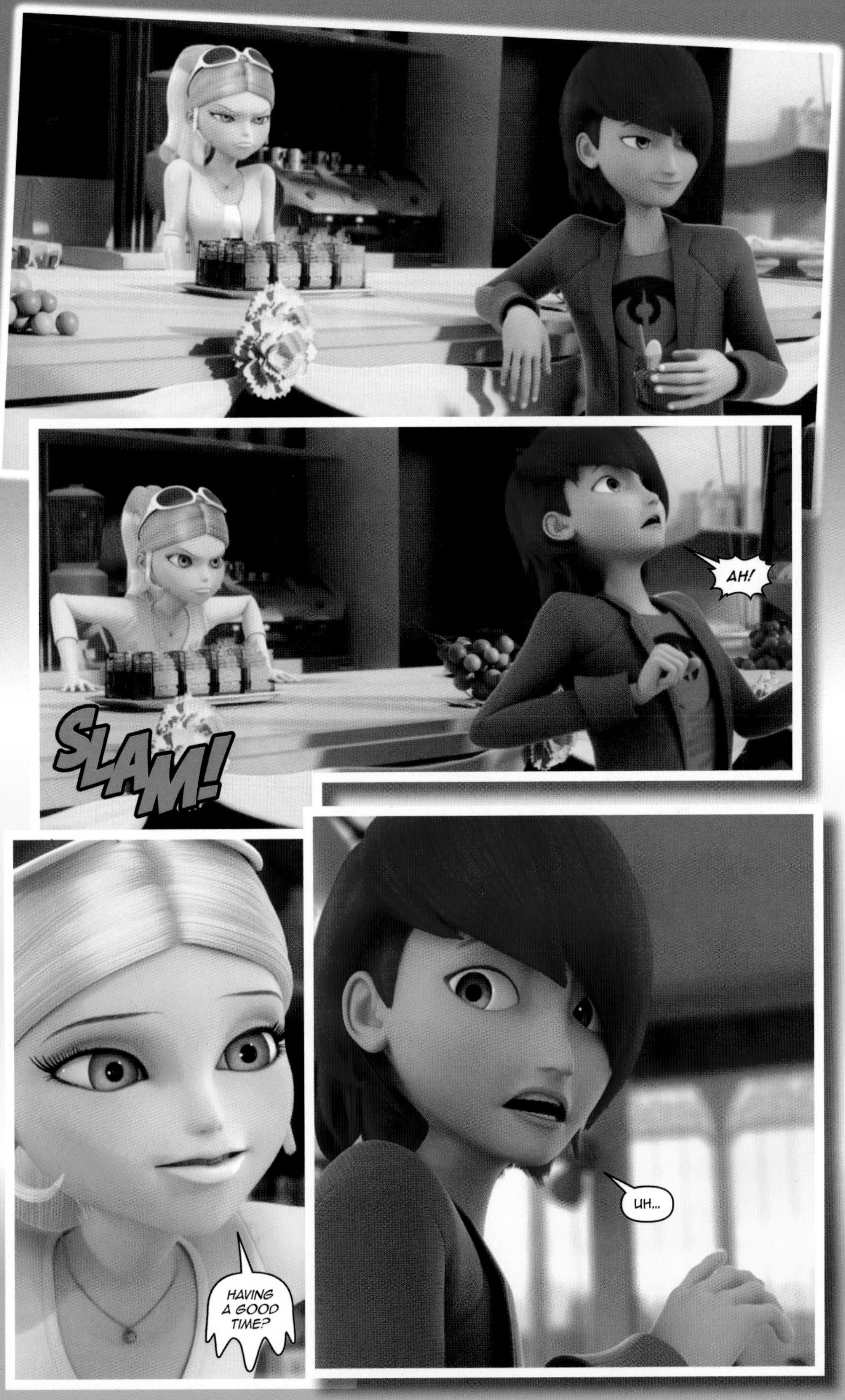
AH!
SLAM!
HAVING A GOOD TIME?
UH...

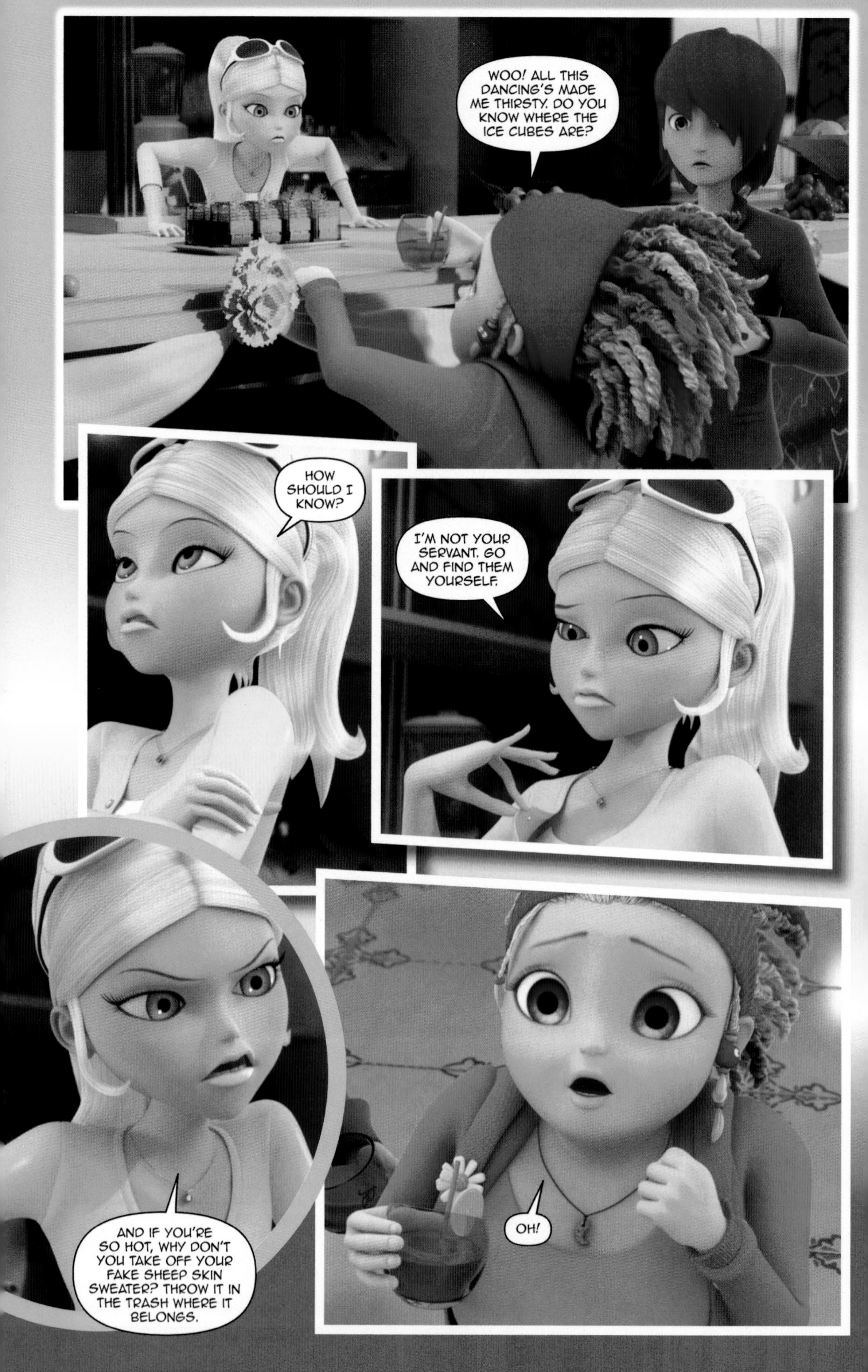
WOO! ALL THIS DANCING'S MADE ME THIRSTY. DO YOU KNOW WHERE THE ICE CUBES ARE?
HOW SHOULD I KNOW?
I'M NOT YOUR SERVANT. GO AND FIND THEM YOURSELF.
AND IF YOU'RE SO HOT, WHY DON'T YOU TAKE OFF YOUR FAKE SHEEP SKIN SWEATER? THROW IT IN THE TRASH WHERE IT BELONGS.
OH!

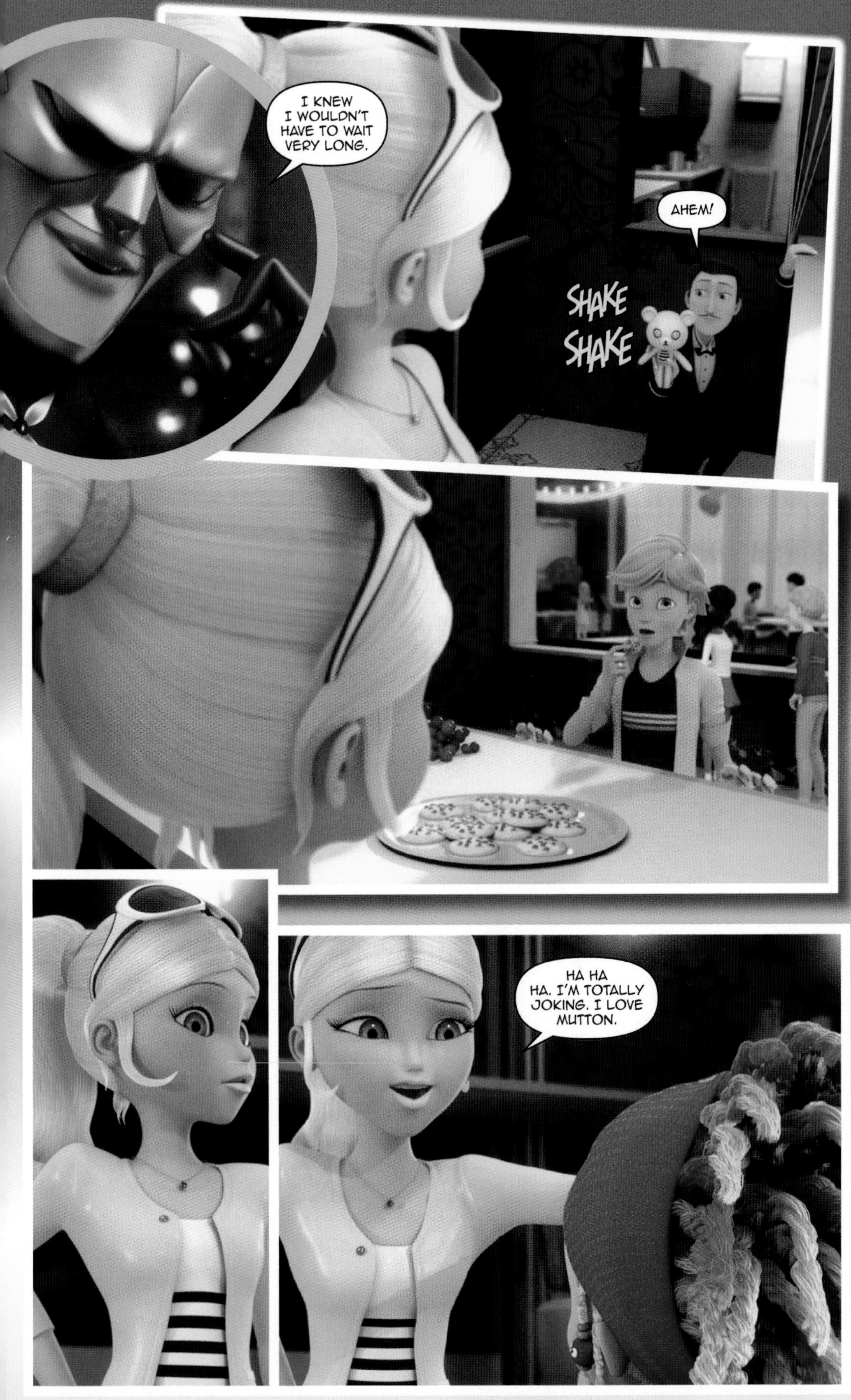
I KNEW I WOULDN'T HAVE TO WAIT VERY LONG.
AHEM!
SHAKE SHAKE
HA HA HA. I'M TOTALLY JOKING. I LOVE MUTTON.

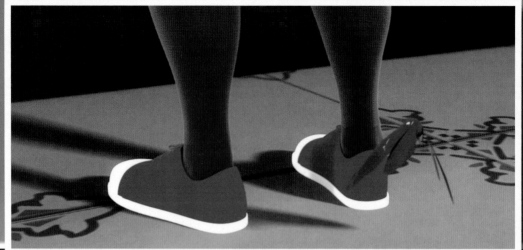

I'LL GET YOU THOSE ICE CUBES.

WHAT ARE YOU DOING, MISS BOURGEOIS? WHERE'S THAT NATURAL CRUELTY I'M COUNTING ON?

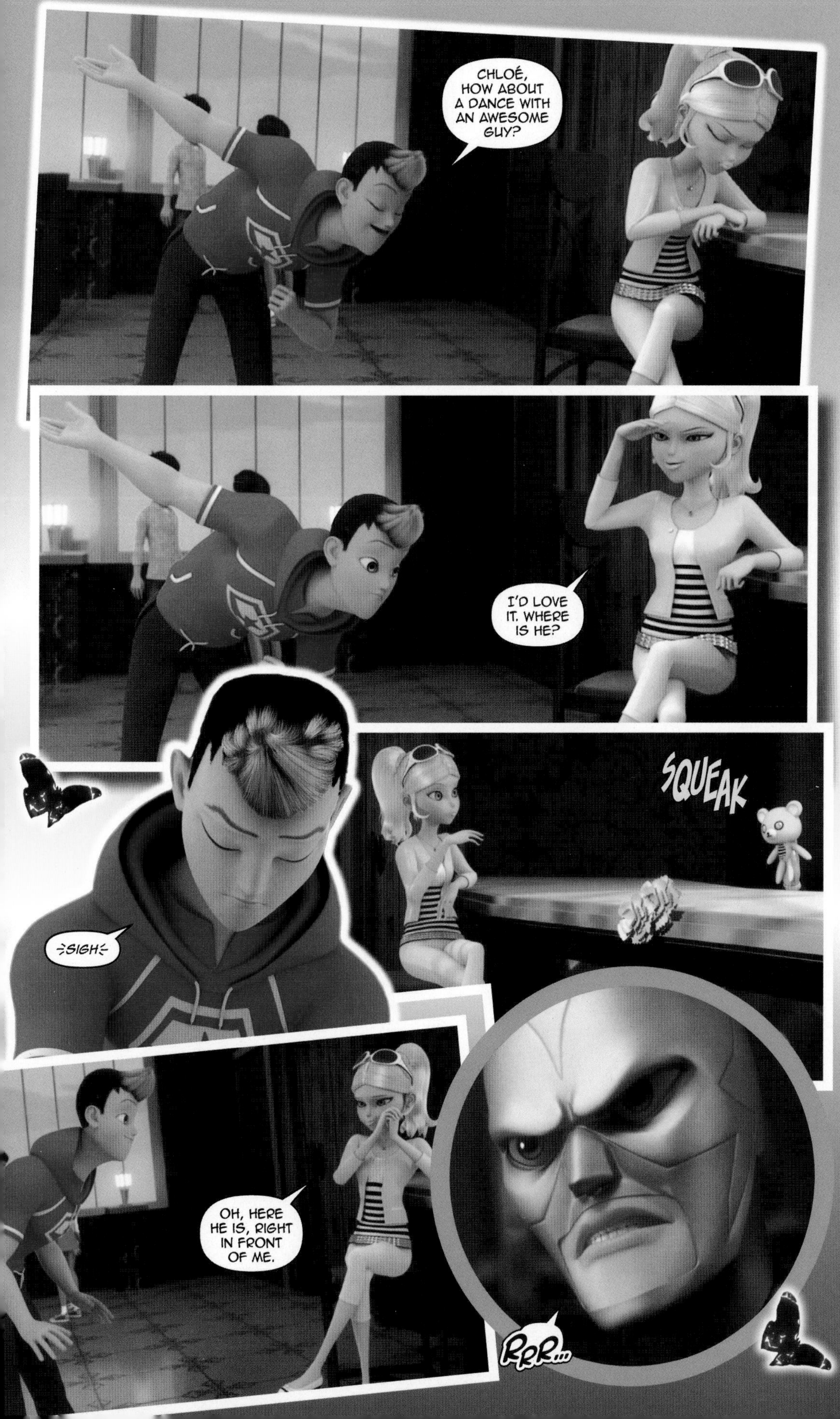
CHLOÉ, HOW ABOUT A DANCE WITH AN AWESOME GUY?
I'D LOVE IT. WHERE IS HE?
SIGH
SQUEAK
OH, HERE HE IS, RIGHT IN FRONT OF ME.
RRR...

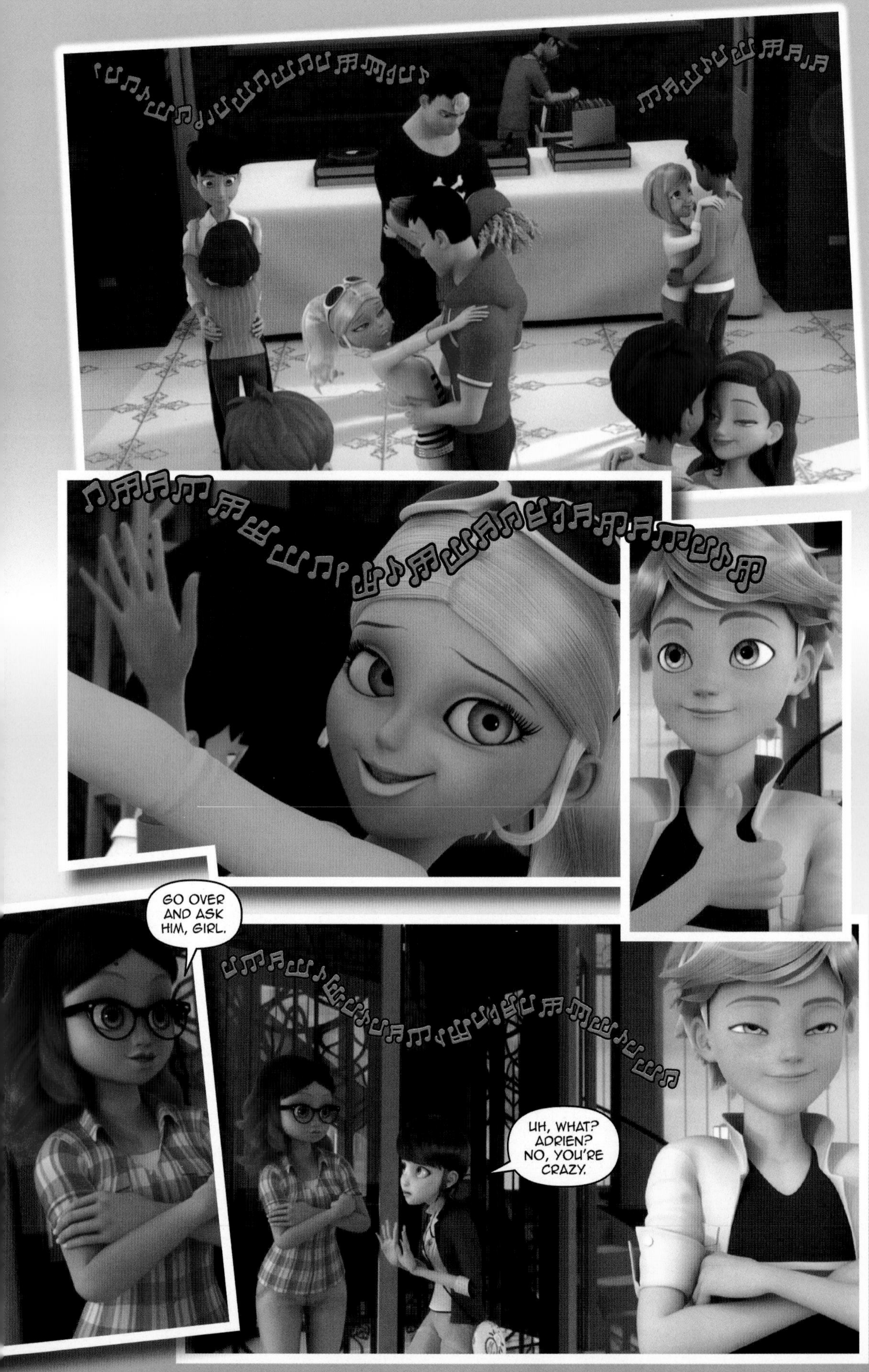
GO OVER AND ASK HIM, GIRL.
UH, WHAT? ADRIEN? NO, YOU'RE CRAZY.

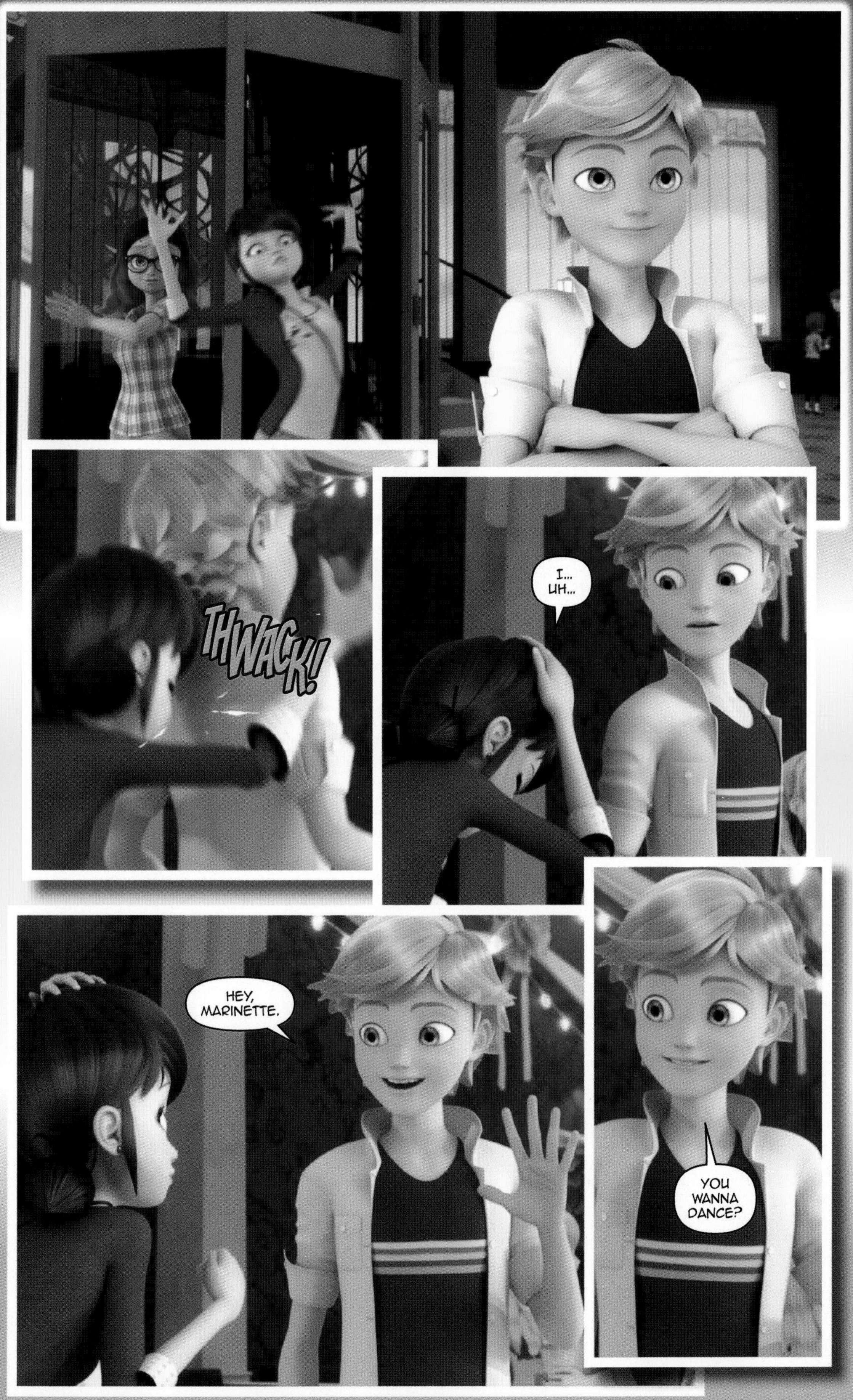
THWACK!
I... UH...
HEY, MARINETTE.
YOU WANNA DANCE?

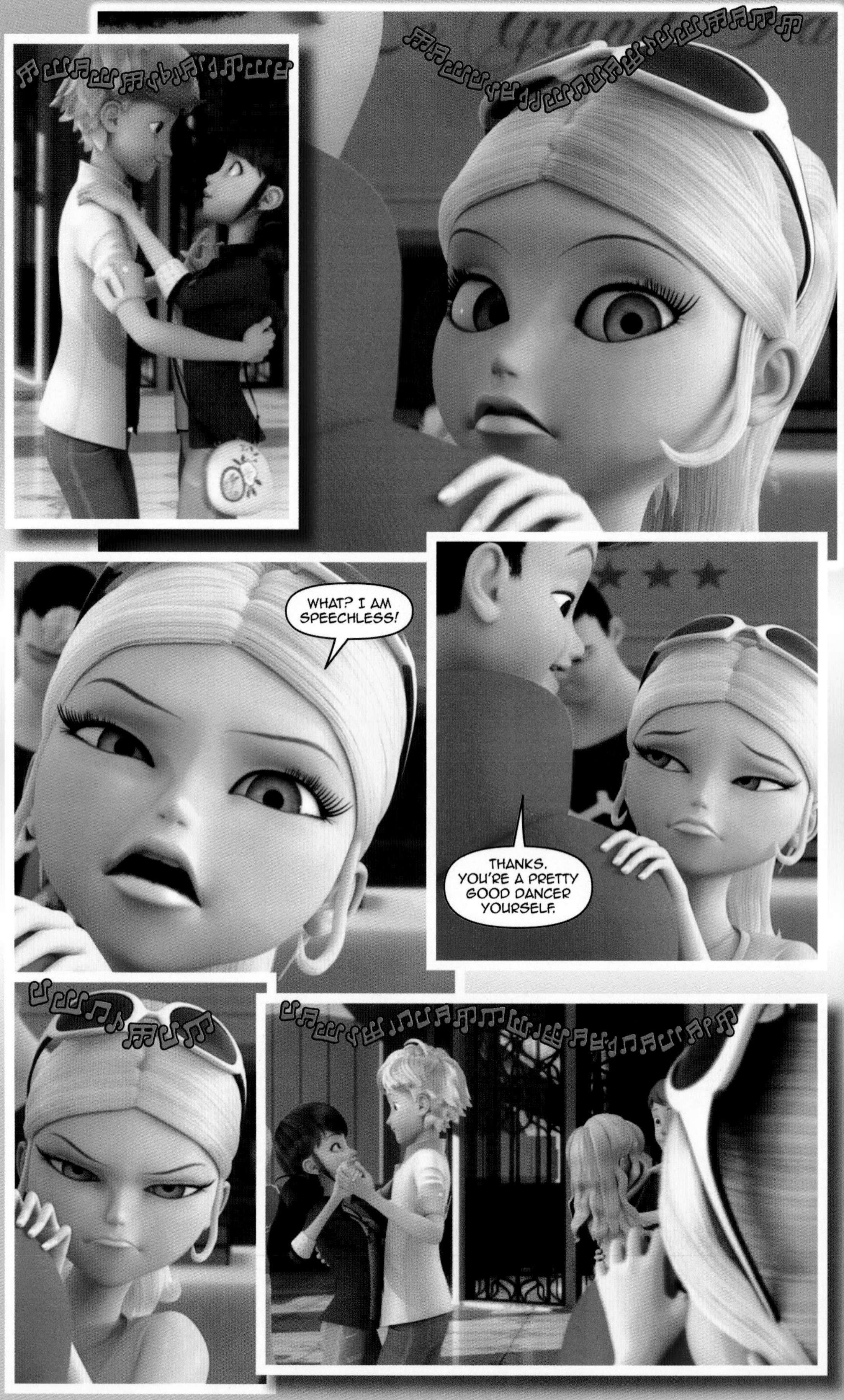
WHAT? I AM SPEECHLESS!
THANKS. YOU'RE A PRETTY GOOD DANCER YOURSELF.

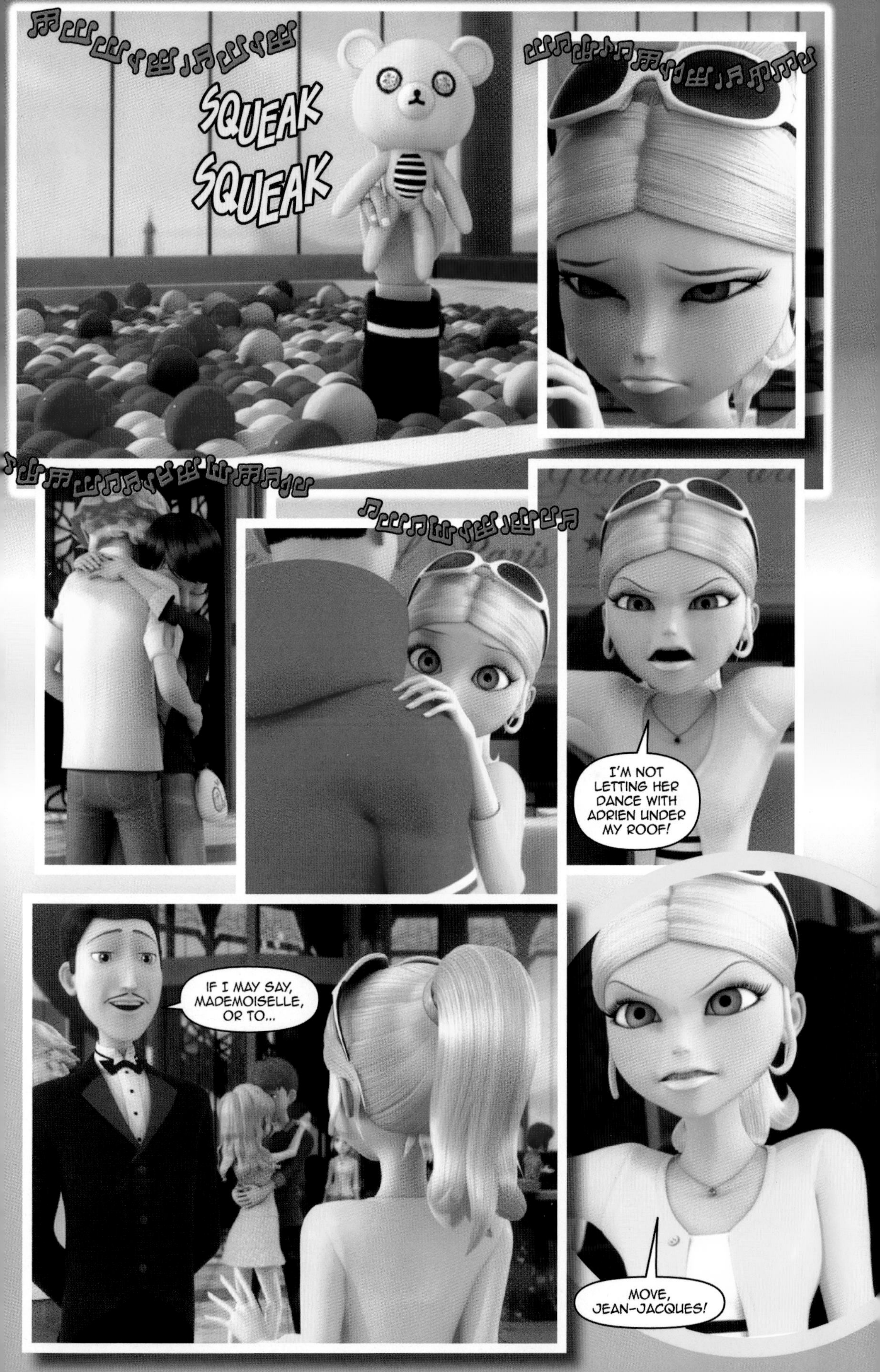
SQUEAK
SQUEAK
I'M NOT LETTING HER DANCE WITH ADRIEN UNDER MY ROOF!
IF I MAY SAY, MADEMOISELLE, OR TO...
MOVE, JEAN-JACQUES!

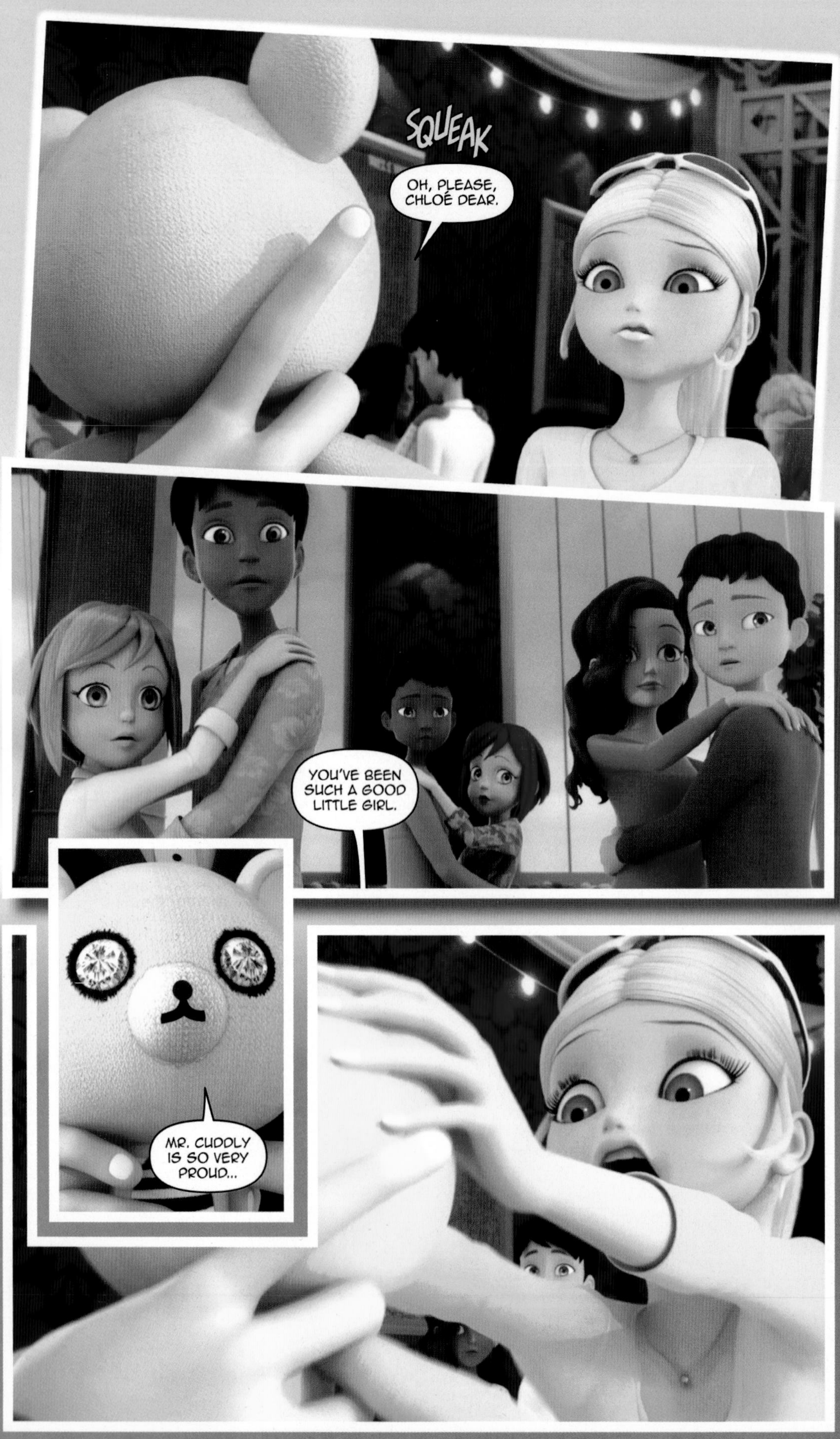
SQUEAK
OH, PLEASE, CHLOÉ DEAR.
YOU'VE BEEN SUCH A GOOD LITTLE GIRL.
MR. CUDDLY IS SO VERY PROUD...

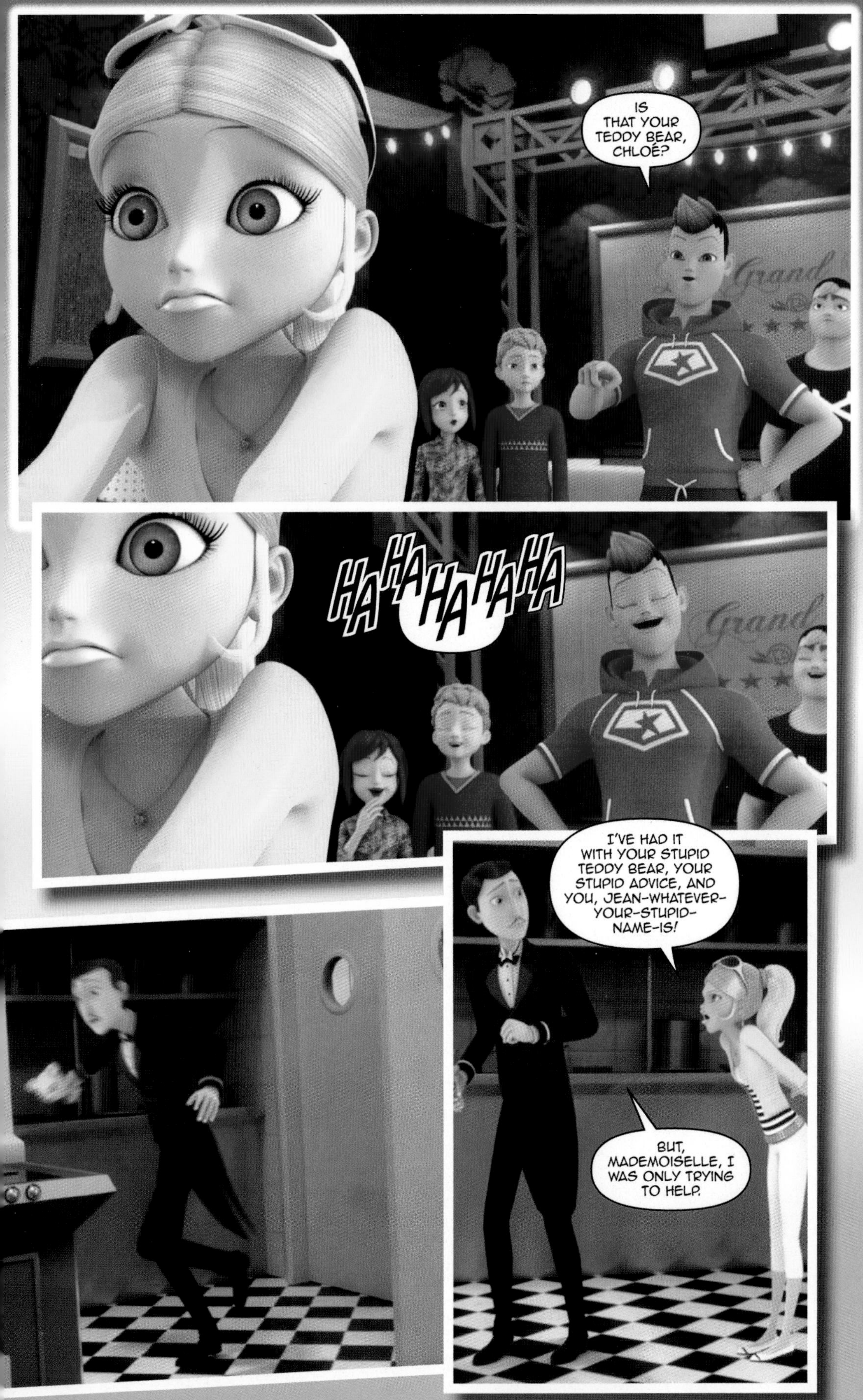
IS THAT YOUR TEDDY BEAR, CHLOÉ?
HAHAHAHAHAHA
I'VE HAD IT WITH YOUR STUPID TEDDY BEAR, YOUR STUPID ADVICE, AND YOU, JEAN-WHATEVER-YOUR-STUPID-NAME-IS!
BUT, MADEMOISELLE, I WAS ONLY TRYING TO HELP.

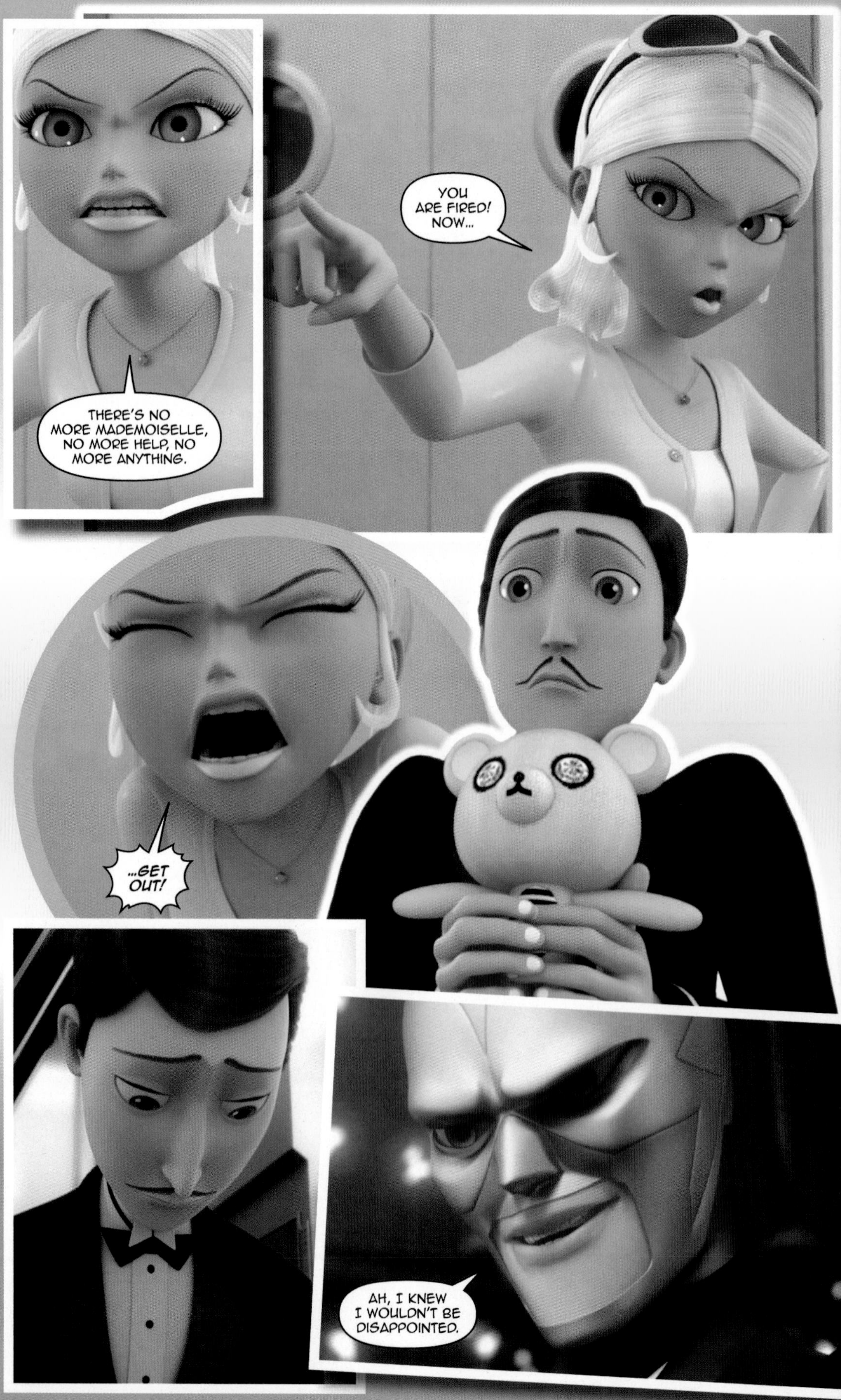
THERE'S NO MORE MADEMOISELLE, NO MORE HELP, NO MORE ANYTHING.
YOU ARE FIRED! NOW...
...GET OUT!
AH, I KNEW I WOULDN'T BE DISAPPOINTED.

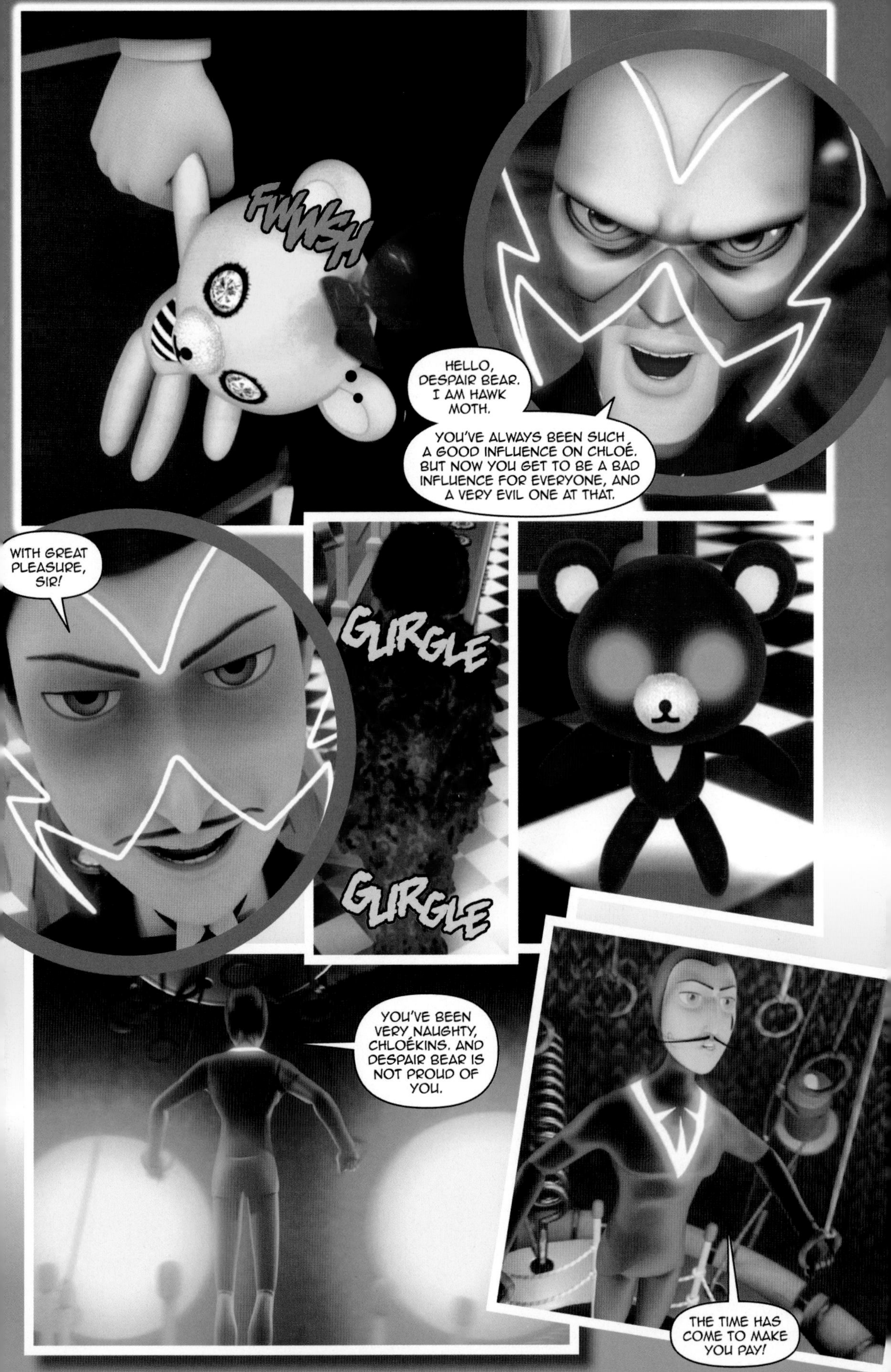
FWWSH
HELLO, DESPAIR BEAR. I AM HAWK MOTH.
YOU'VE ALWAYS BEEN SUCH A GOOD INFLUENCE ON CHLOÉ. BUT NOW YOU GET TO BE A BAD INFLUENCE FOR EVERYONE, AND A VERY EVIL ONE AT THAT.
WITH GREAT PLEASURE, SIR!
GURGLE
GURGLE
YOU'VE BEEN VERY NAUGHTY, CHLOÉKINS. AND DESPAIR BEAR IS NOT PROUD OF YOU.
THE TIME HAS COME TO MAKE YOU PAY!

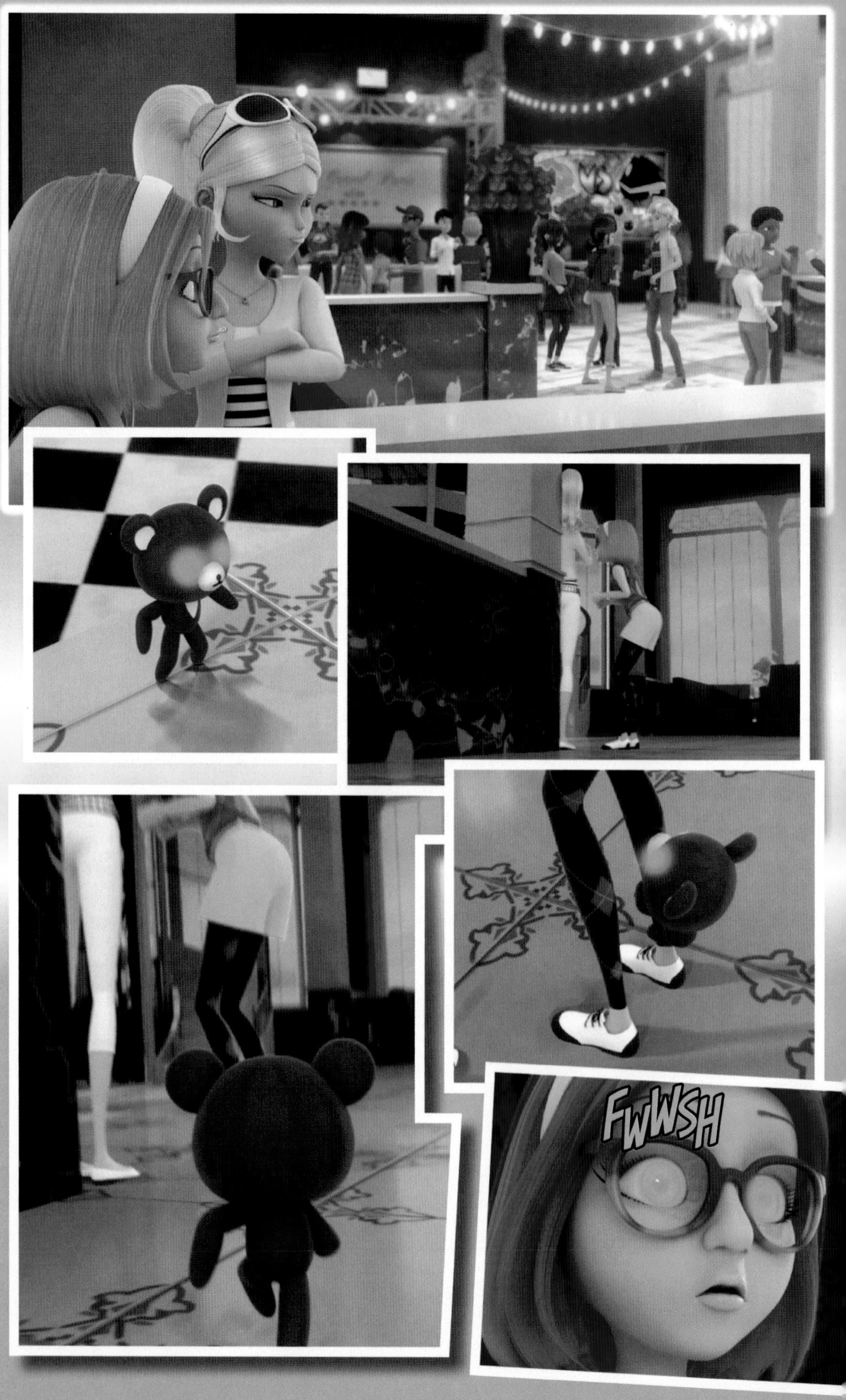
FWWSH

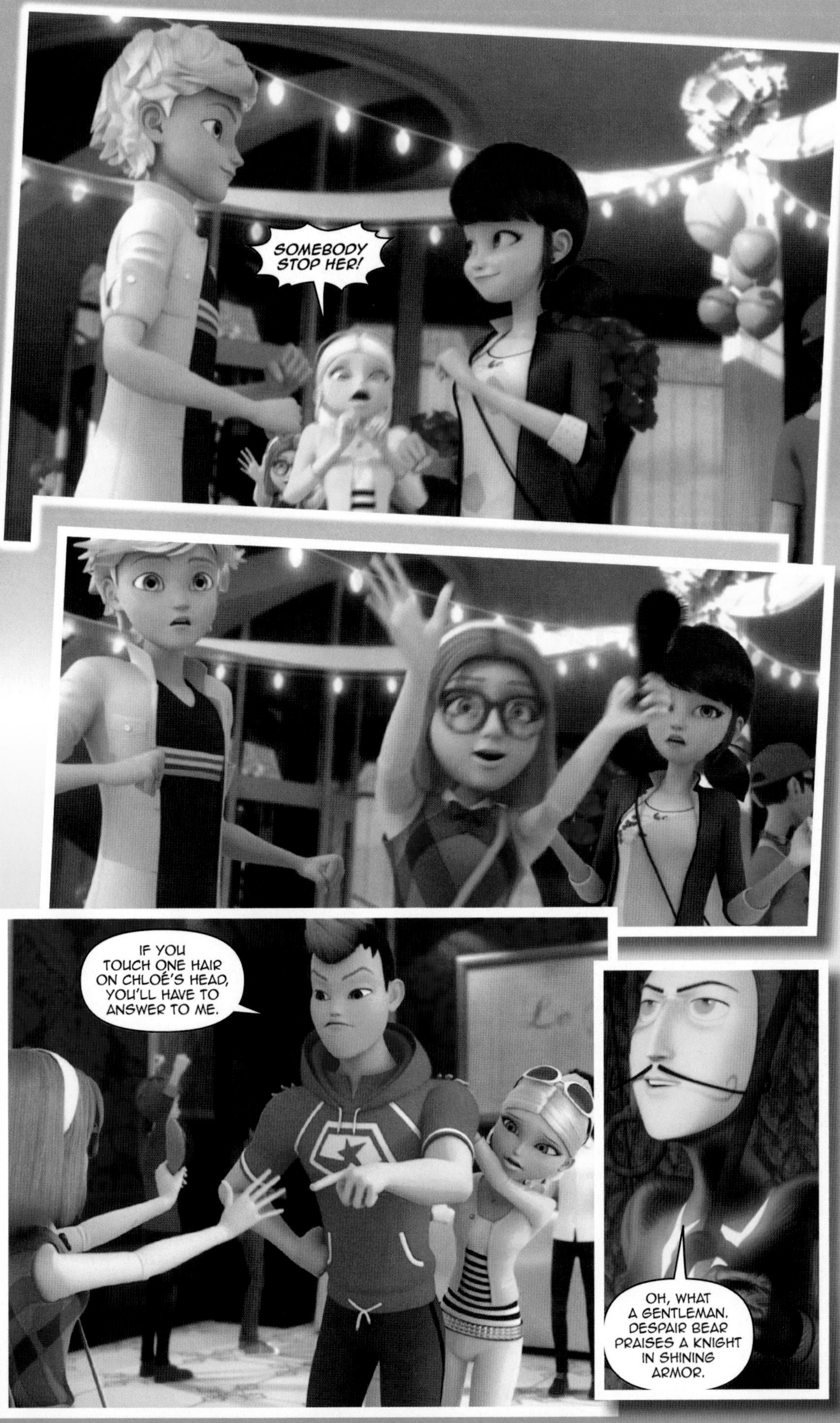
SOMEBODY STOP HER!
IF YOU TOUCH ONE HAIR ON CHLOÉ'S HEAD, YOU'LL HAVE TO ANSWER TO ME.
OH, WHAT A GENTLEMAN. DESPAIR BEAR PRAISES A KNIGHT IN SHINING ARMOR.

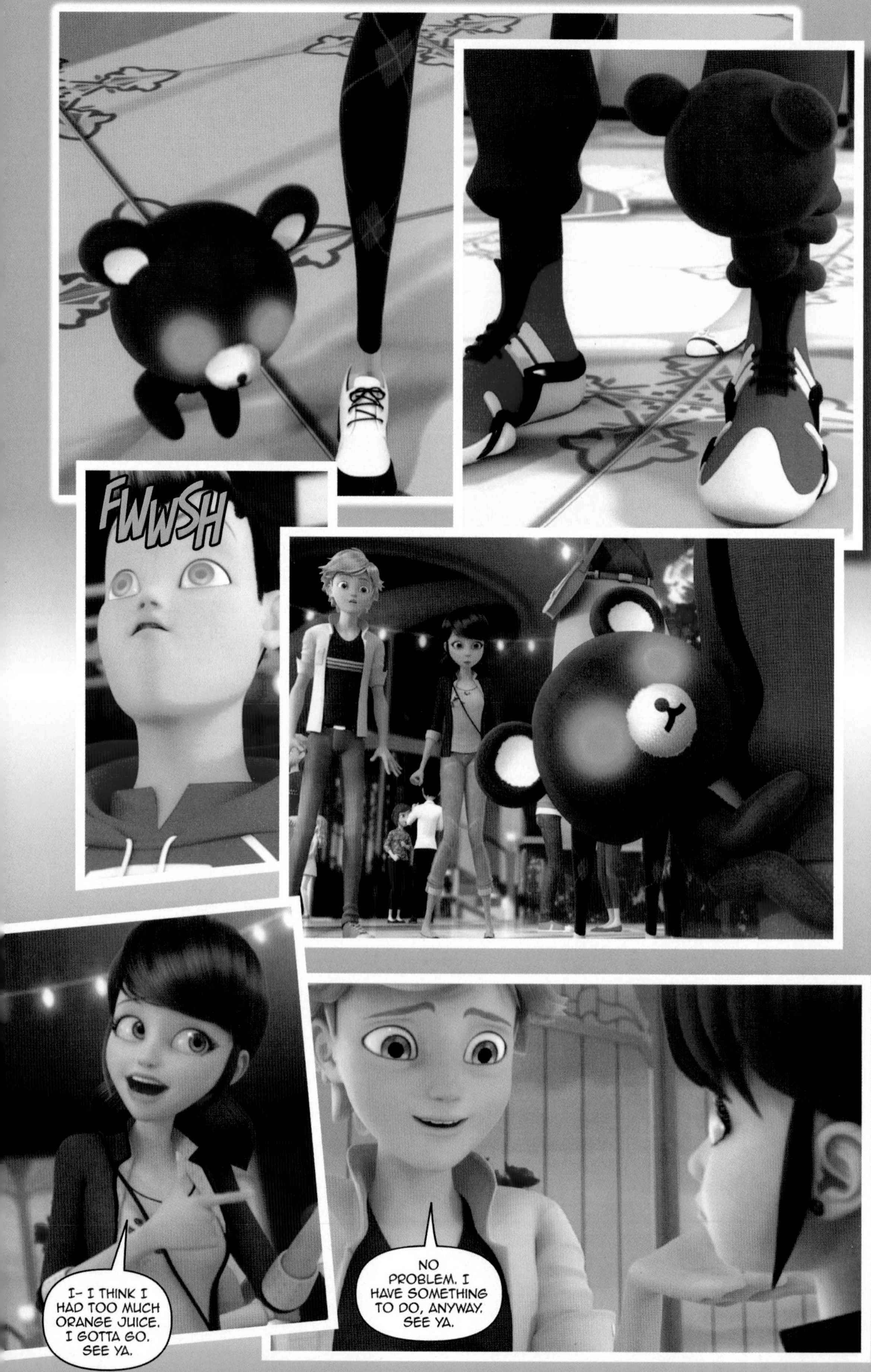
FWWSH
I- I THINK I HAD TOO MUCH ORANGE JUICE. I GOTTA GO. SEE YA.
NO PROBLEM. I HAVE SOMETHING TO DO, ANYWAY. SEE YA.

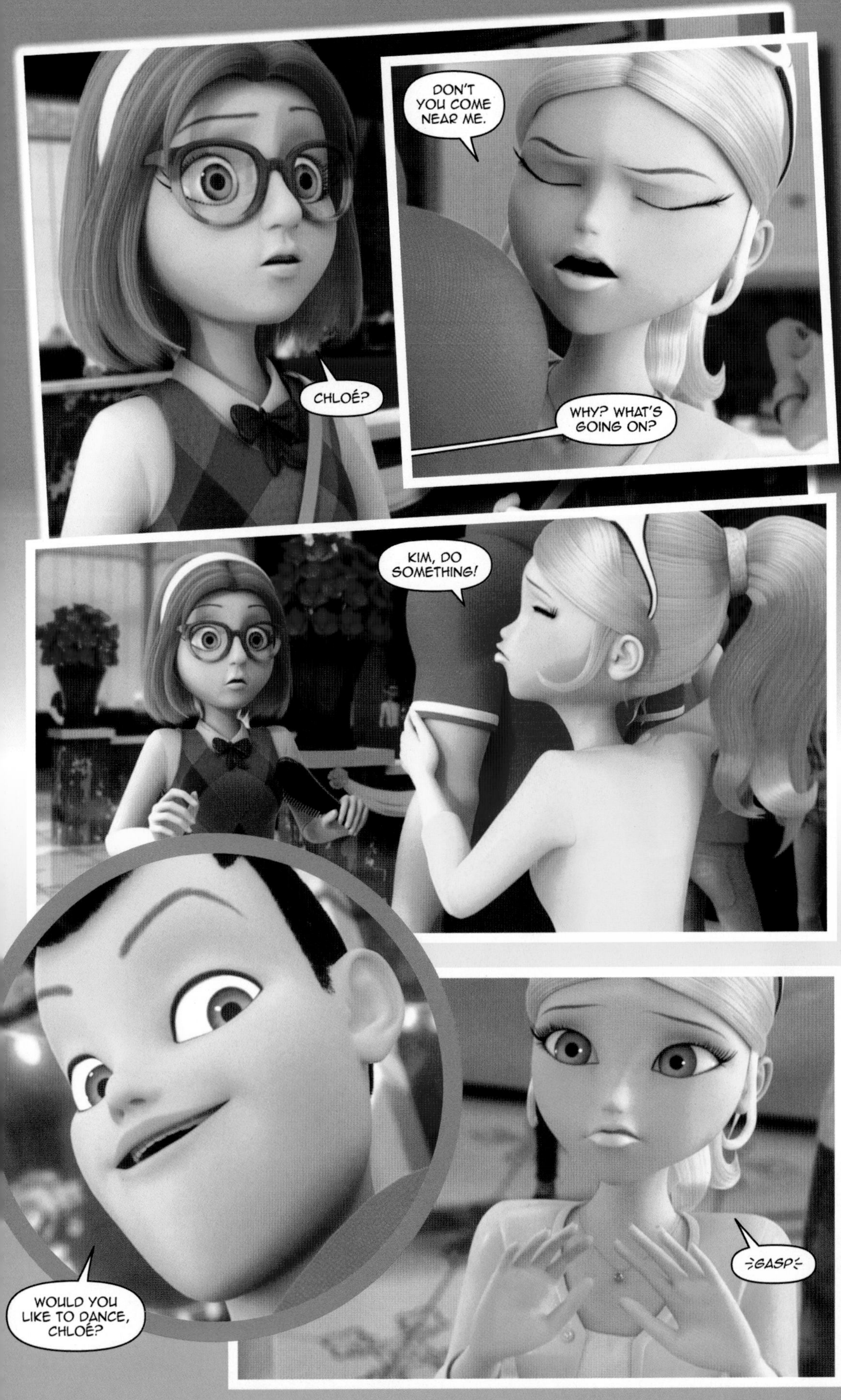
CHLOÉ?
DON'T YOU COME NEAR ME.
WHY? WHAT'S GOING ON?
KIM, DO SOMETHING!
WOULD YOU LIKE TO DANCE, CHLOÉ?
GASP

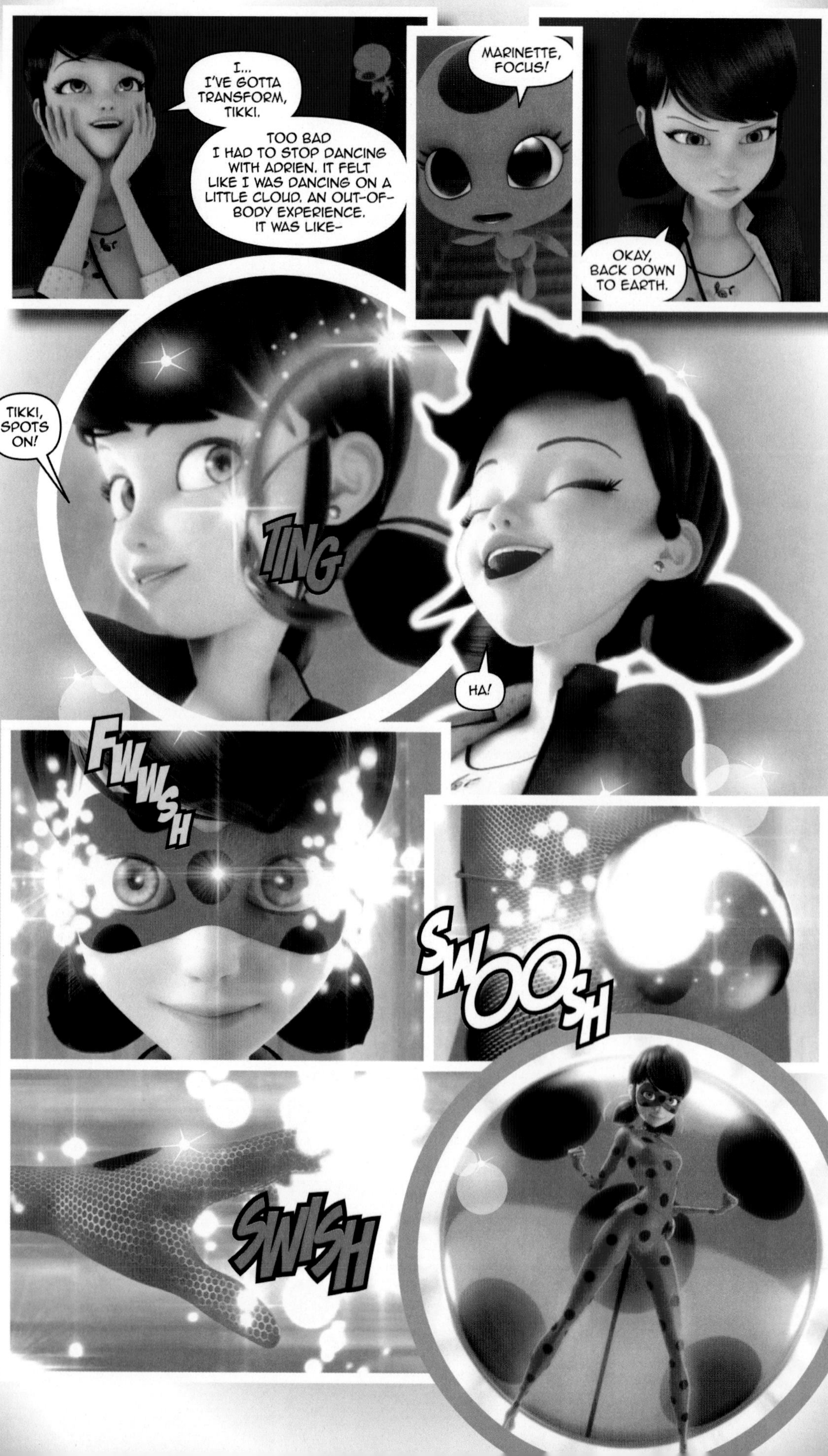
I... I'VE GOTTA TRANSFORM, TIKKI.
TOO BAD I HAD TO STOP DANCING WITH ADRIEN. IT FELT LIKE I WAS DANCING ON A LITTLE CLOUD. AN OUT-OF-BODY EXPERIENCE. IT WAS LIKE-
MARINETTE, FOCUS!
OKAY, BACK DOWN TO EARTH.
TIKKI, SPOTS ON!
TING
HA!
FWWSH
SWOOSH
SWISH

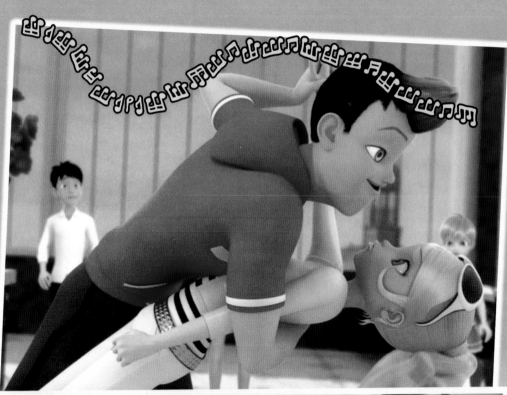

LET GO, YOU EVIL JERK. YOU'RE MESSING UP MY HAIR!

I HOPE YOU'RE HAVING FUN, CHLOÉKINS!

AH!

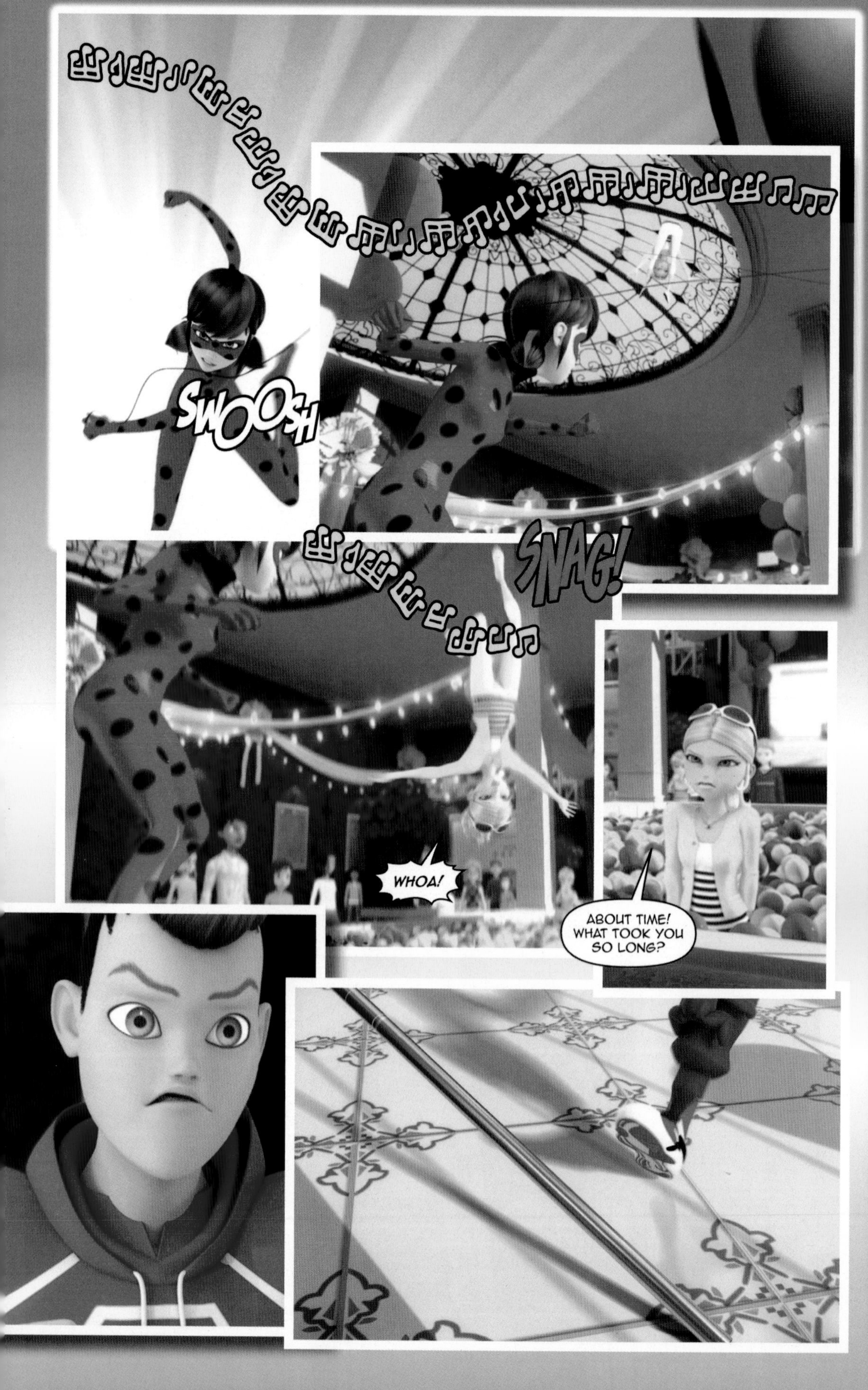
SWOOSH
SNAG!
WHOA!
ABOUT TIME! WHAT TOOK YOU SO LONG?

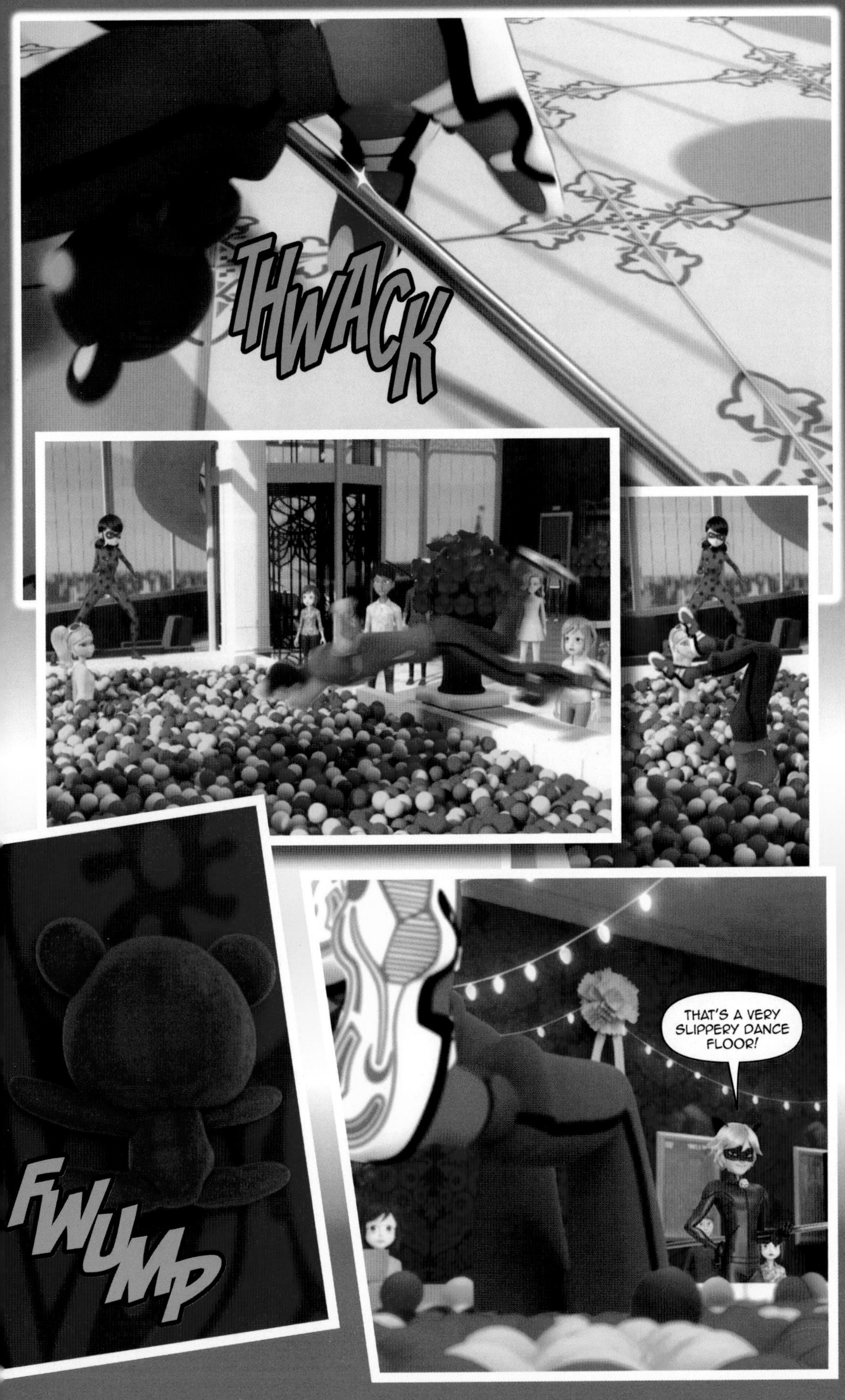
THWACK
FWUMP
THAT'S A VERY SLIPPERY DANCE FLOOR!

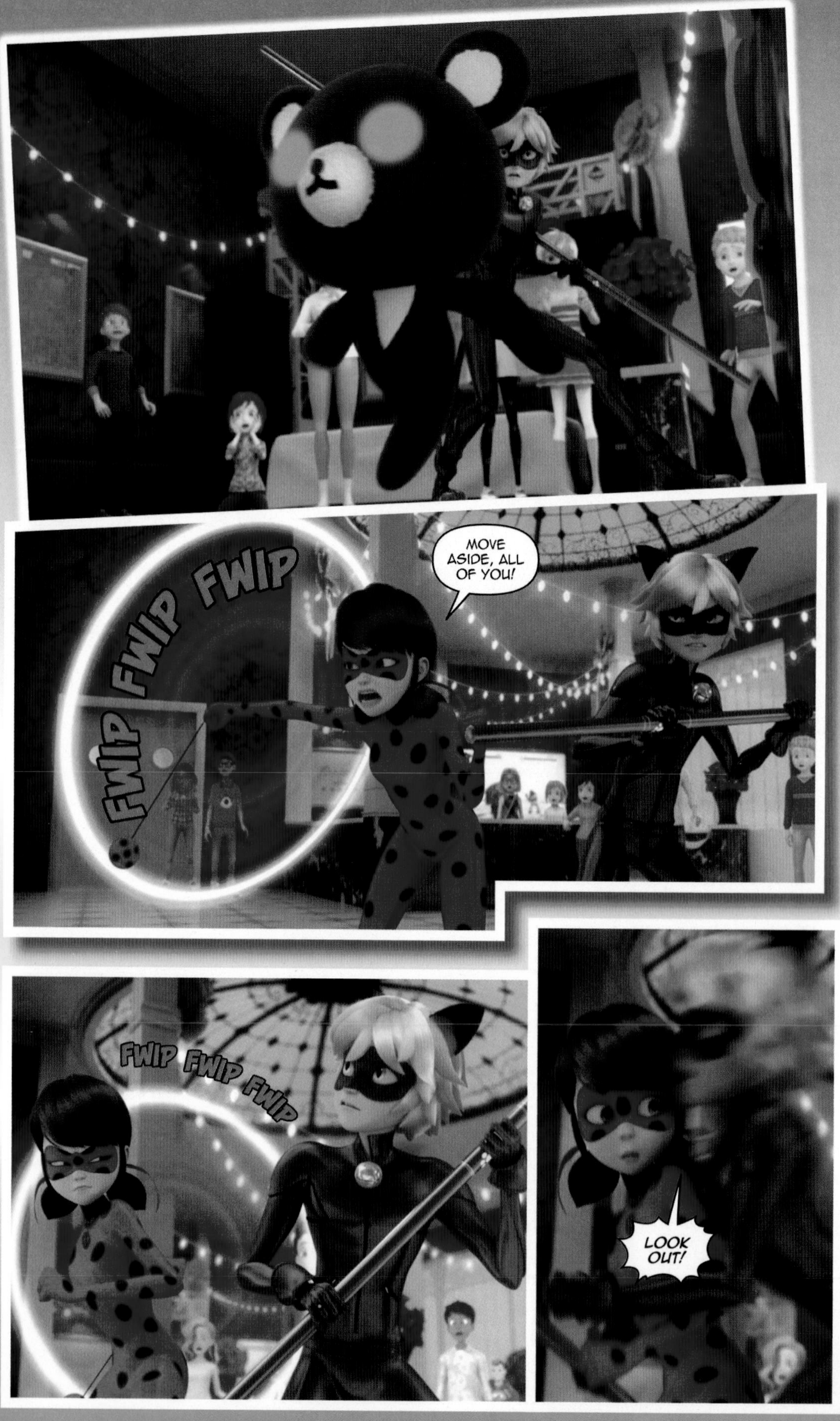

MOVE ASIDE, ALL OF YOU!
FWIP FWIP FWIP
FWIP FWIP FWIP
LOOK OUT!

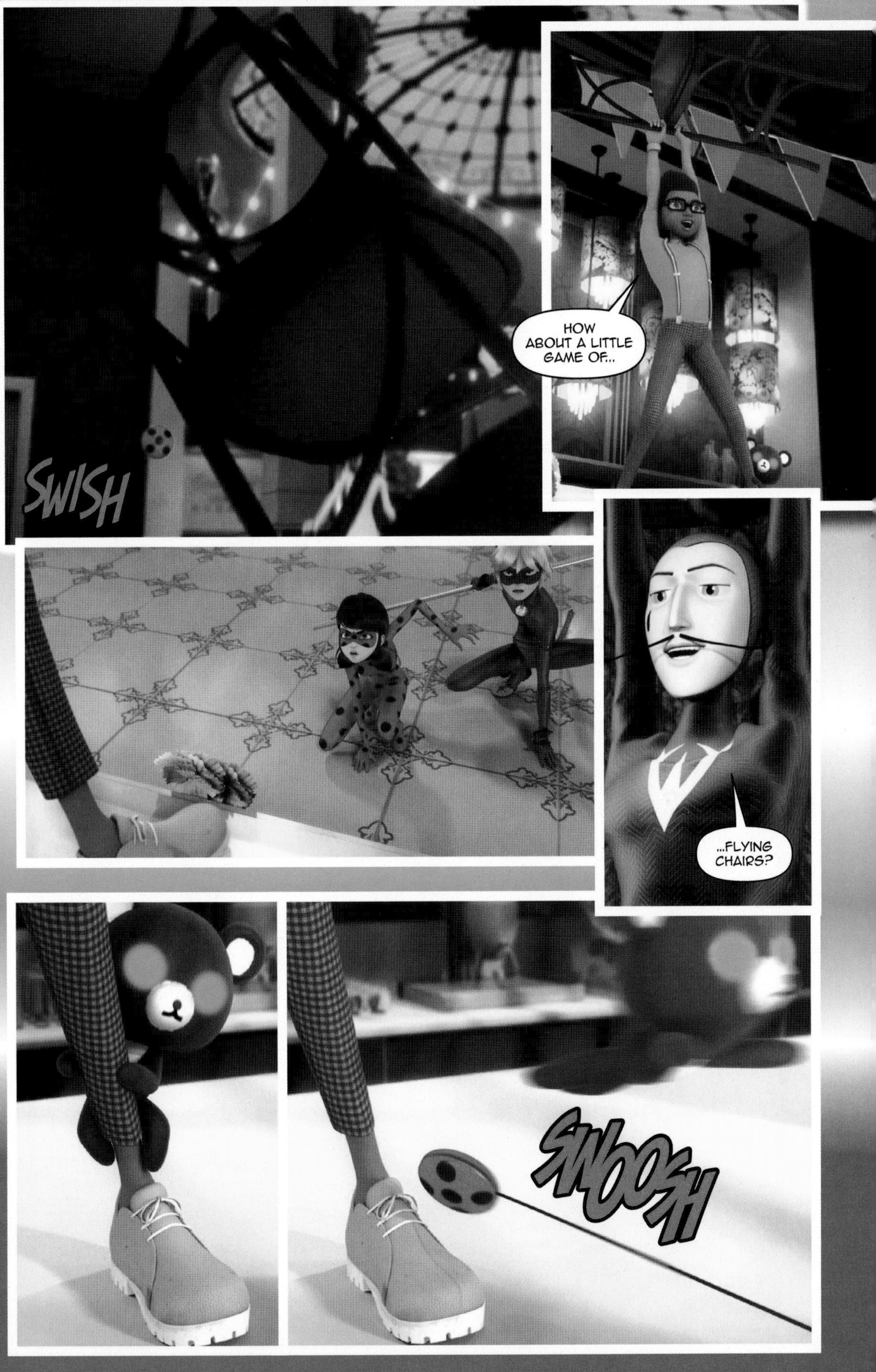
SWISH
HOW ABOUT A LITTLE GAME OF...
...FLYING CHAIRS?
SWOOSH

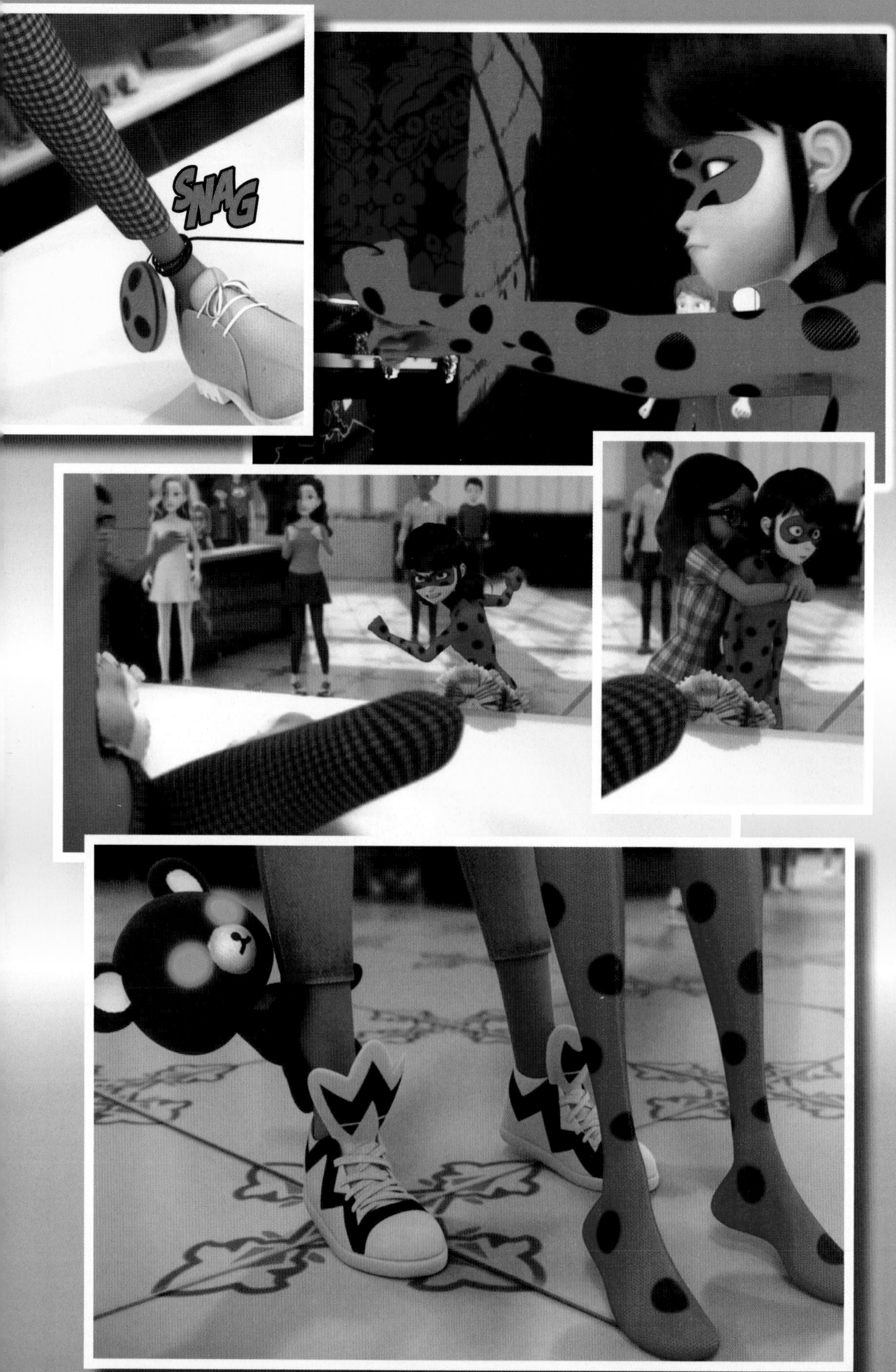
SNAG

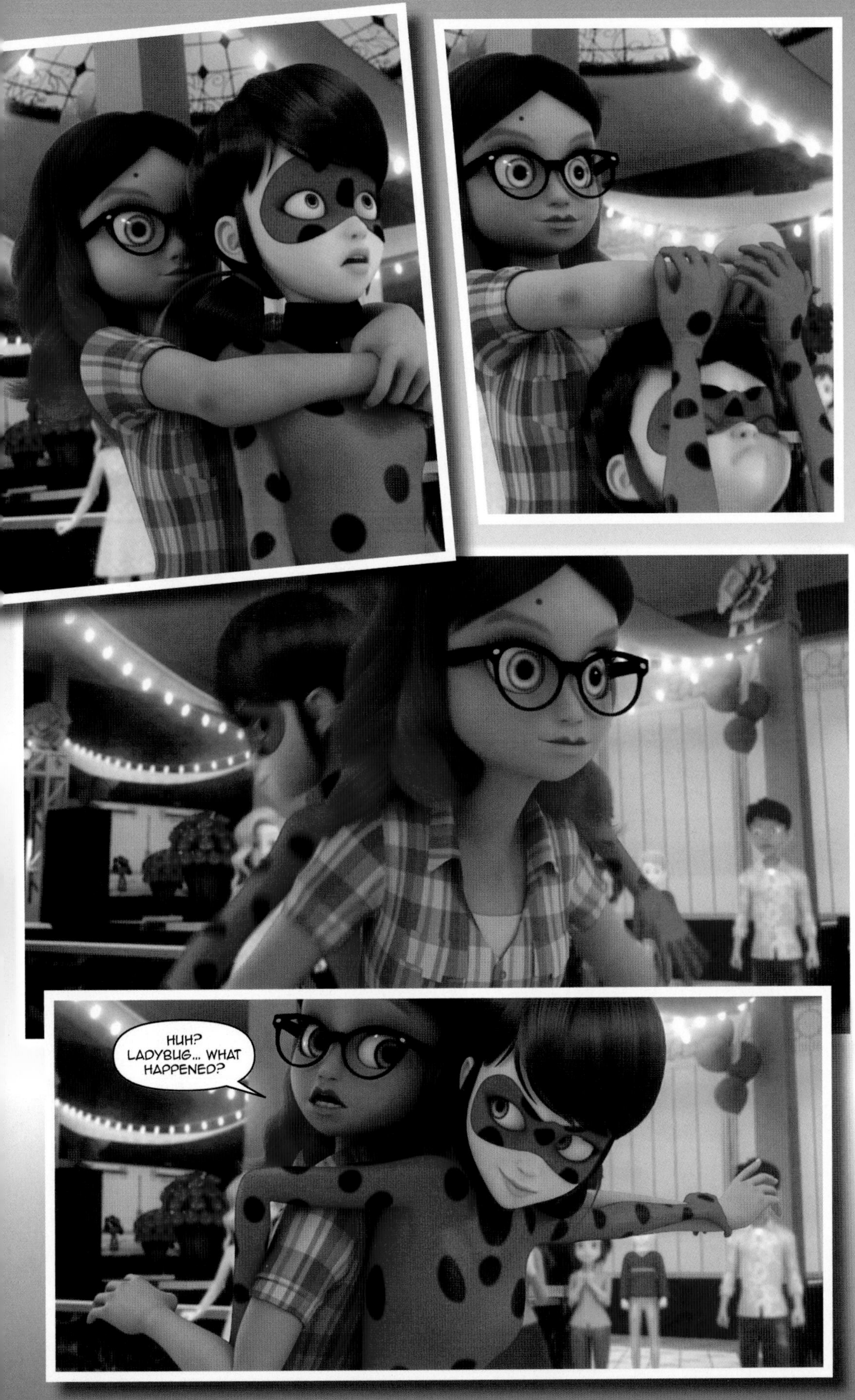
HUH? LADYBUG... WHAT HAPPENED?

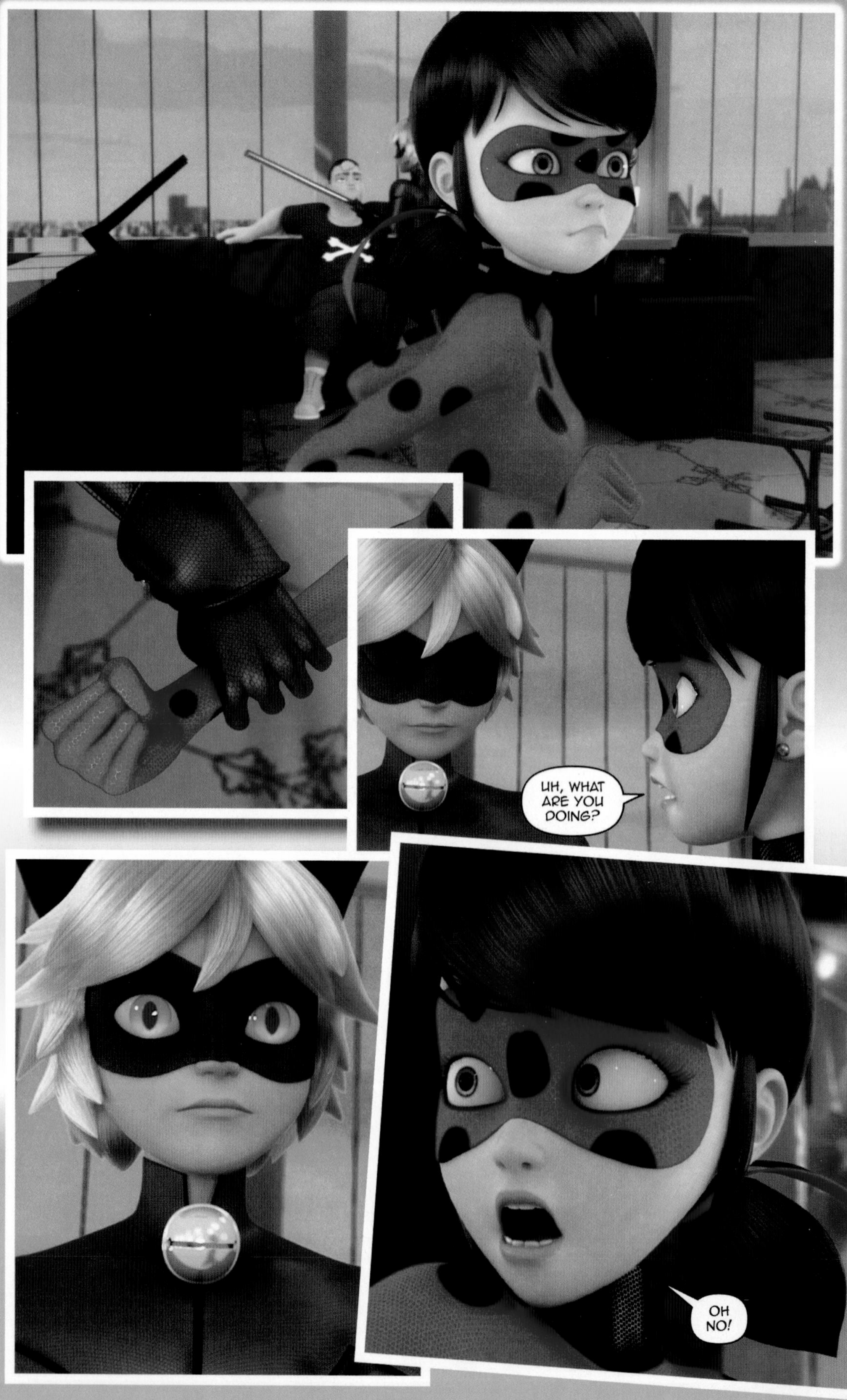
UH, WHAT ARE YOU DOING?
OH NO!

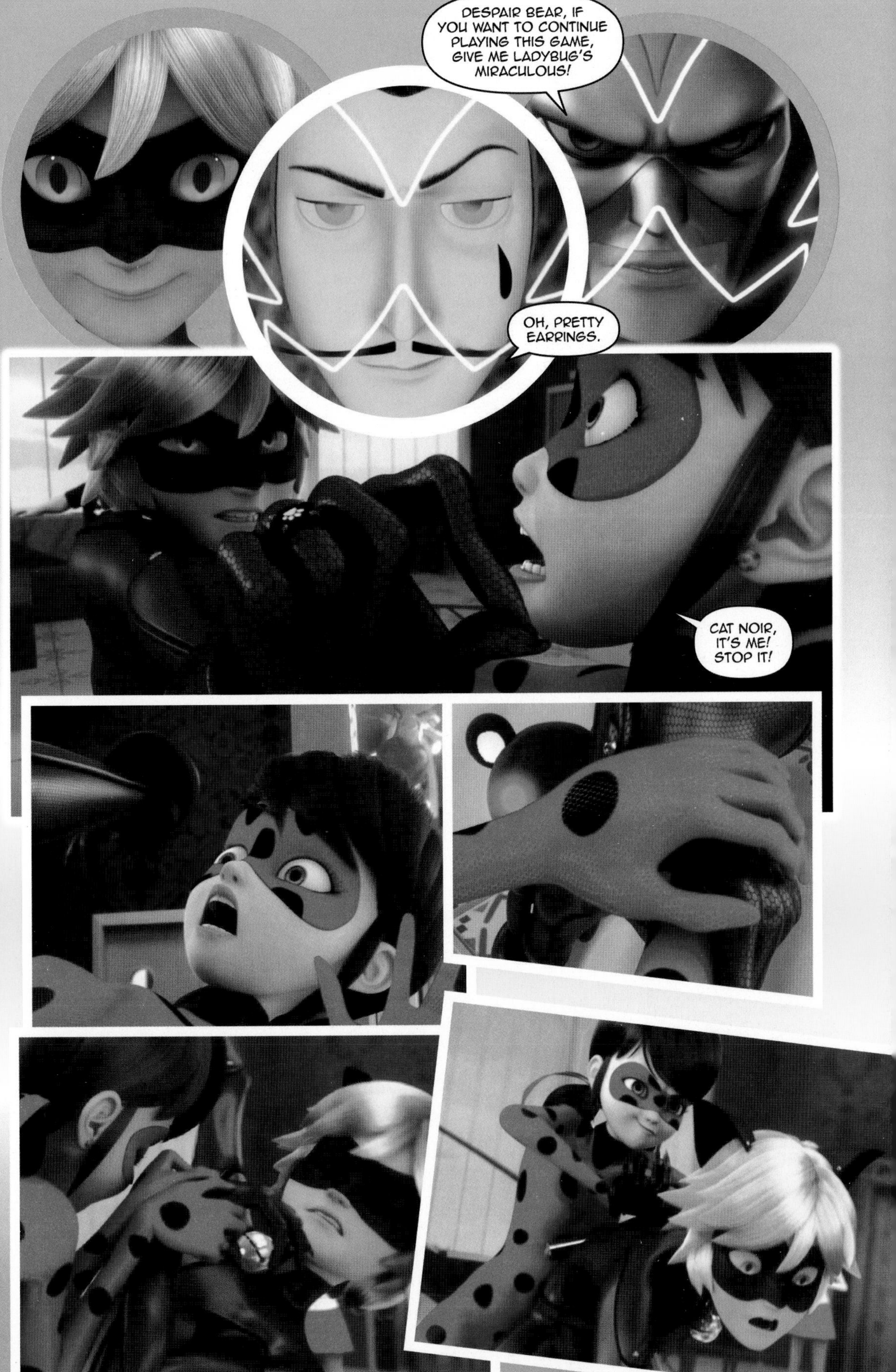
DESPAIR BEAR, IF YOU WANT TO CONTINUE PLAYING THIS GAME, GIVE ME LADYBUG'S MIRACULOUS!
OH, PRETTY EARRINGS.
CAT NOIR, IT'S ME! STOP IT!

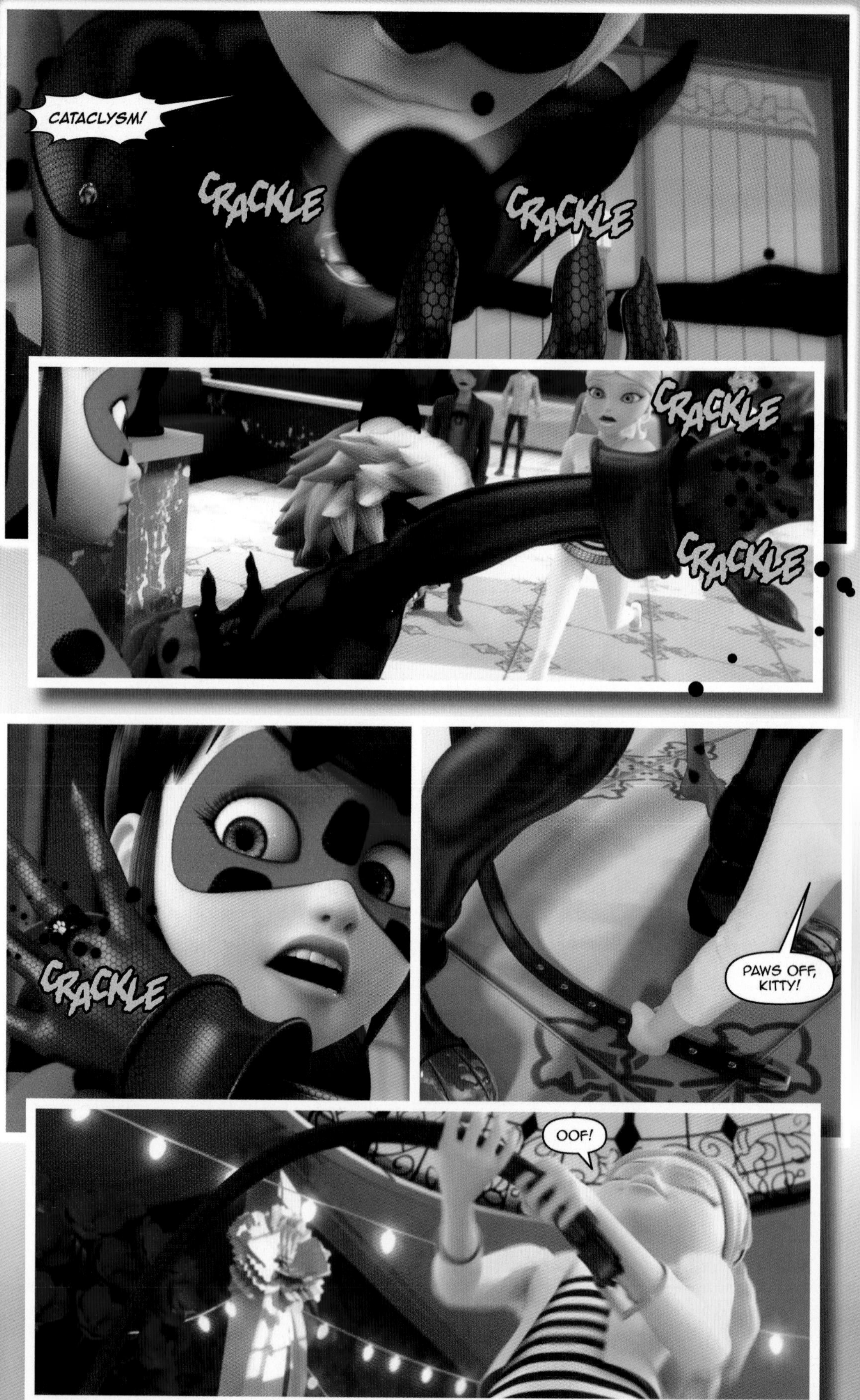
CATACLYSM!
CRACKLE
CRACKLE
CRACKLE
CRACKLE
CRACKLE
PAWS OFF, KITTY!
OOF!

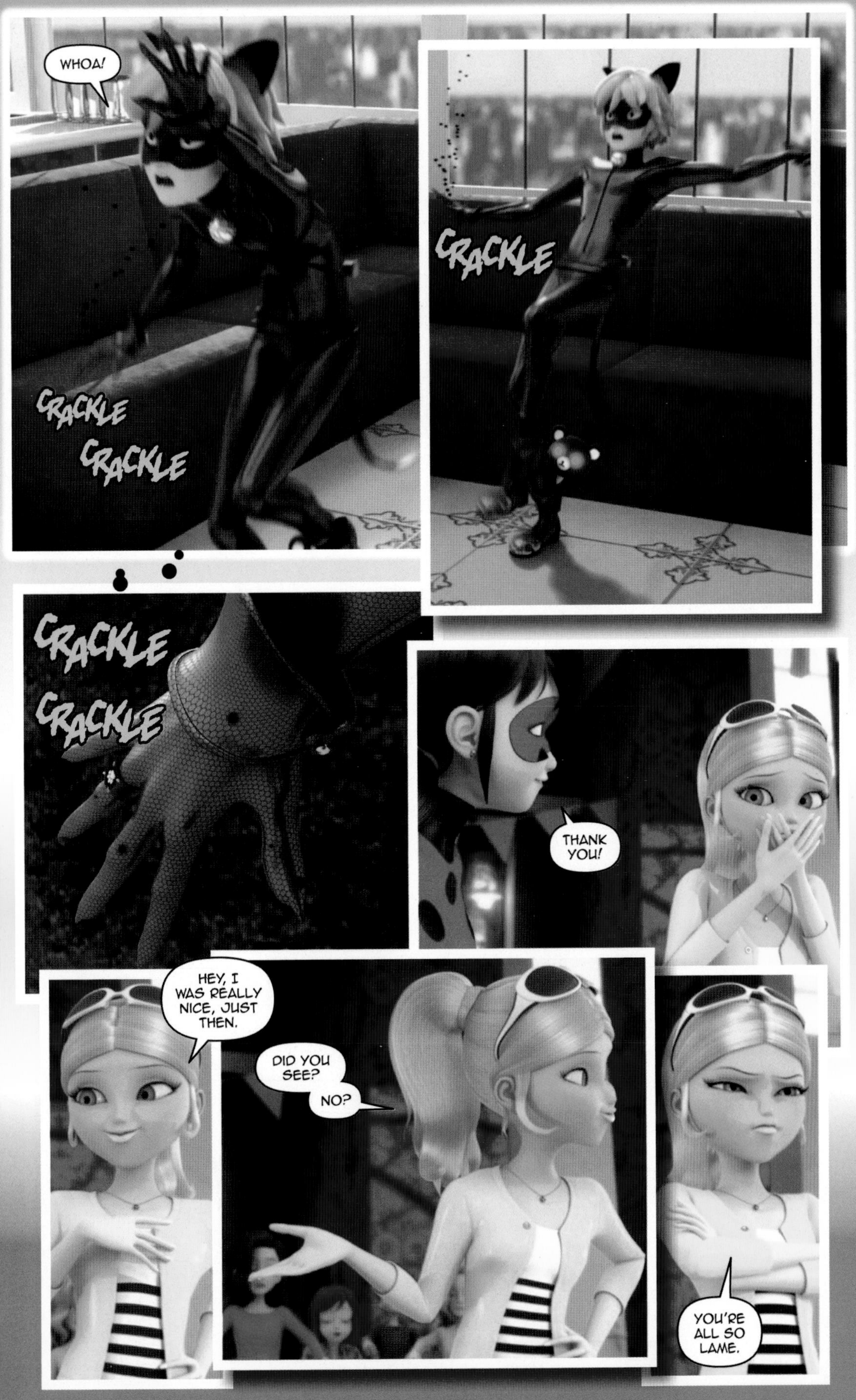
WHOA!
CRACKLE
CRACKLE
CRACKLE
CRACKLE
CRACKLE
THANK YOU!
HEY, I WAS REALLY NICE, JUST THEN.
DID YOU SEE?
NO?
YOU'RE ALL SO LAME.

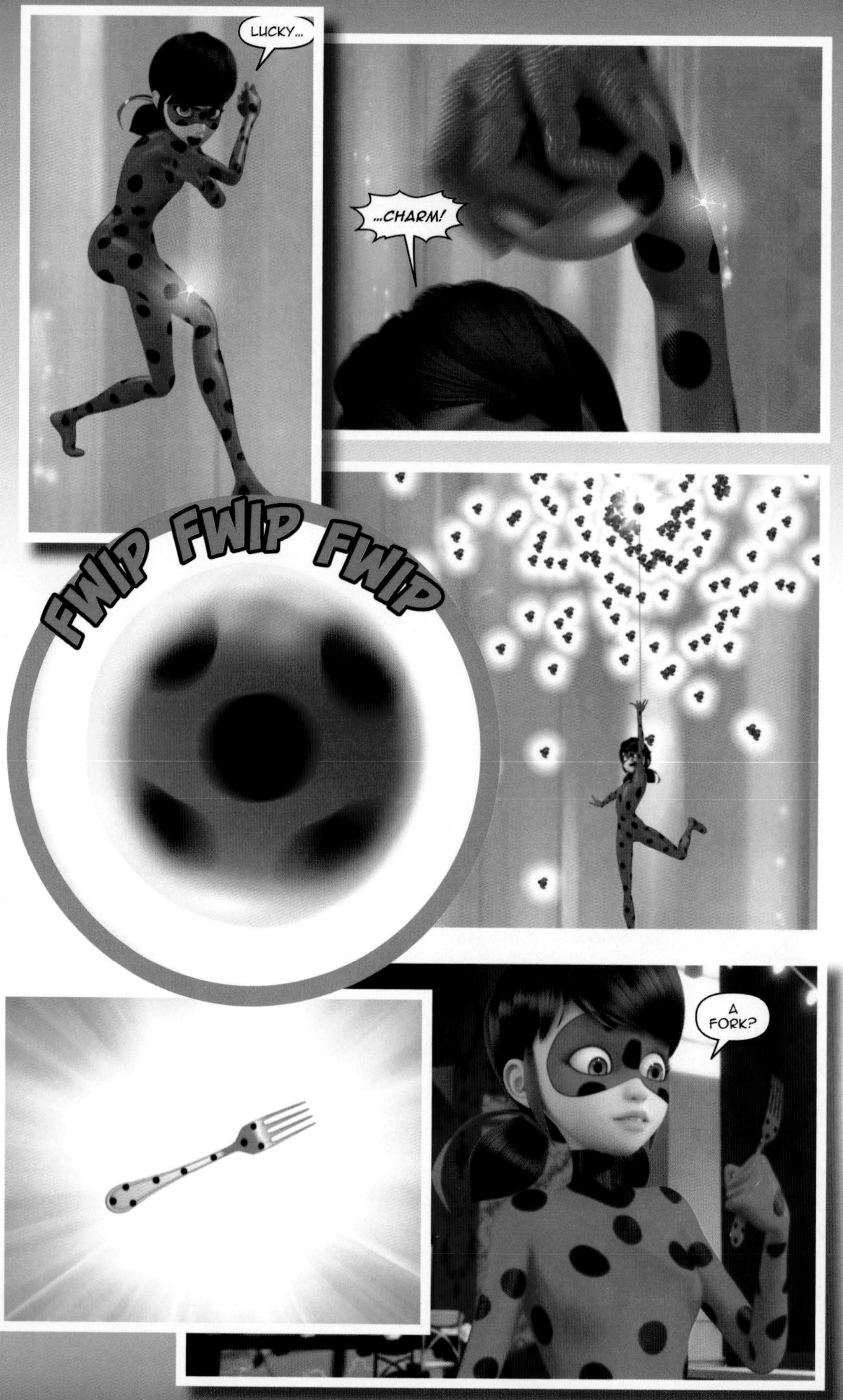
LUCKY...
...CHARM!
FWIP FWIP FWIP
A FORK?

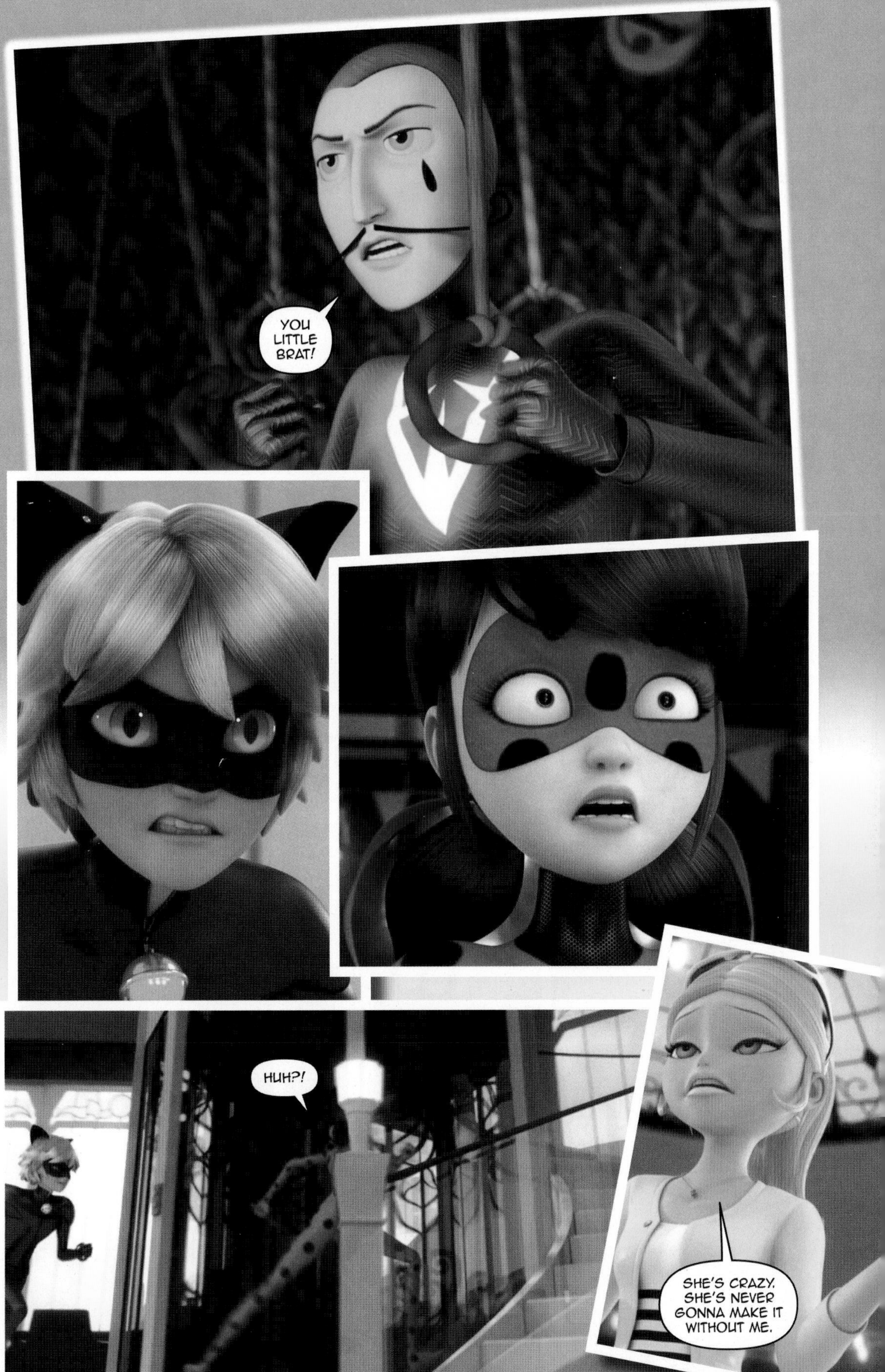
YOU LITTLE BRAT!
HUH?!
SHE'S CRAZY. SHE'S NEVER GONNA MAKE IT WITHOUT ME.

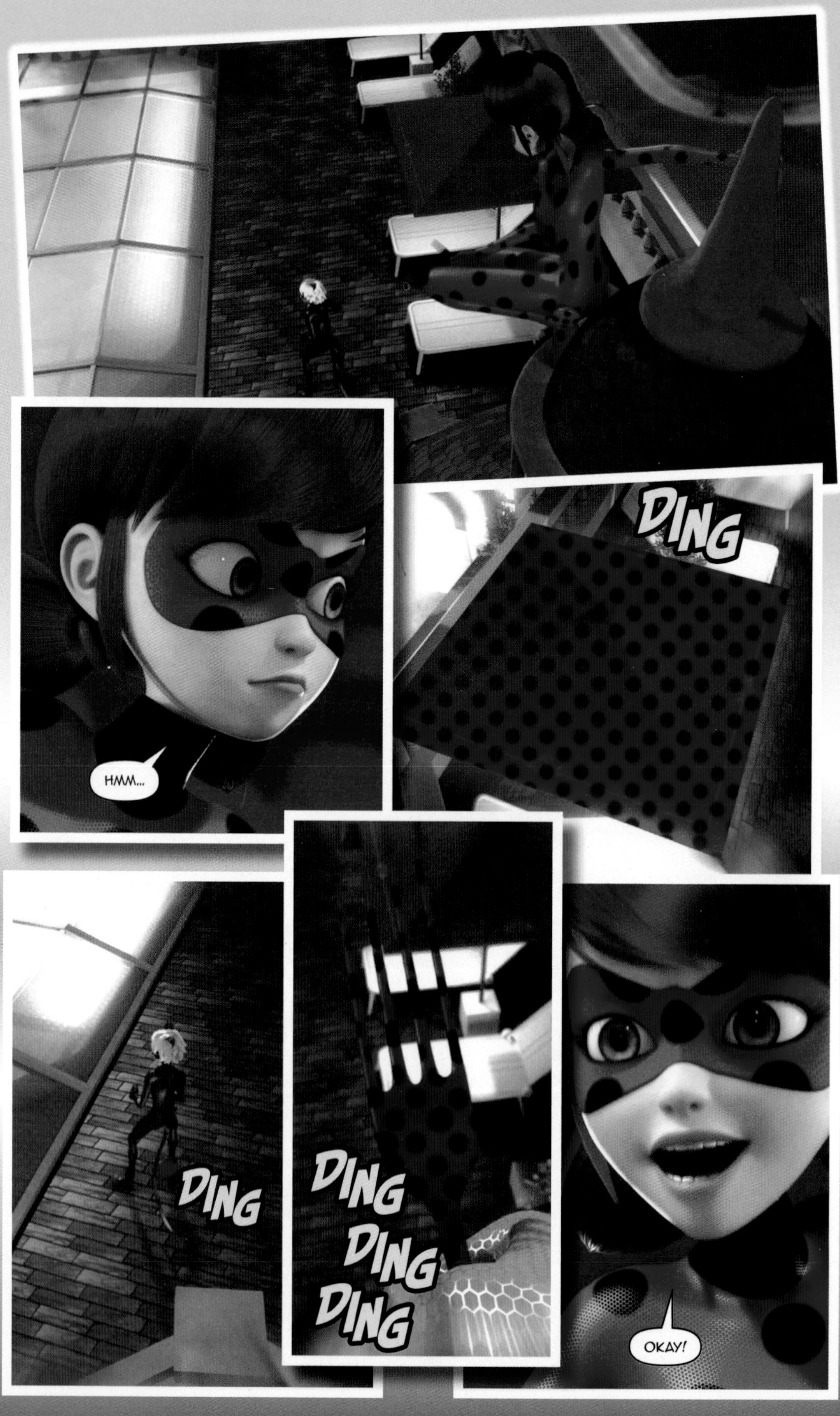
HMM...
DING
DING
DING
DING
DING
OKAY!

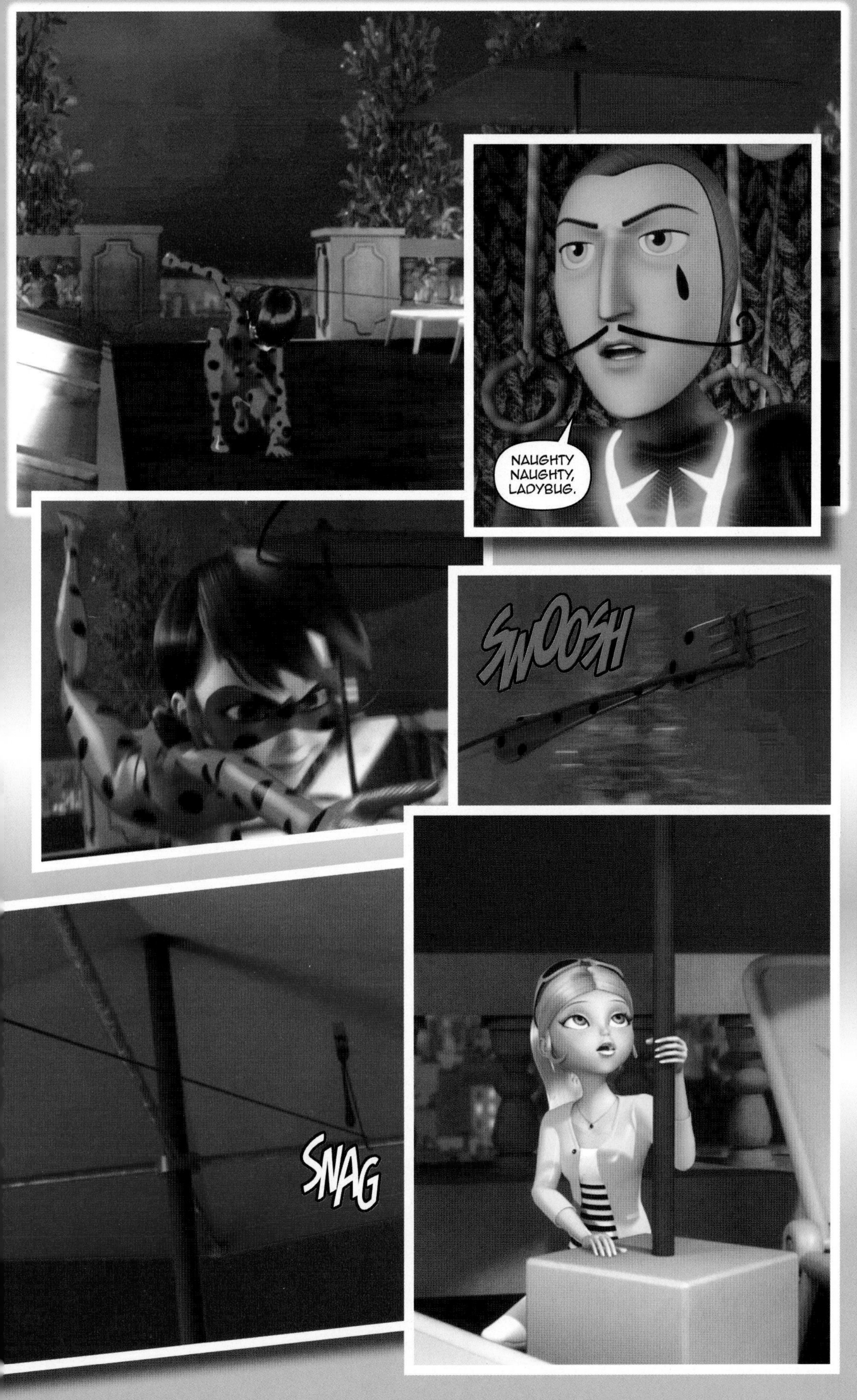
NAUGHTY NAUGHTY, LADYBUG.
SWOOSH
SNAG

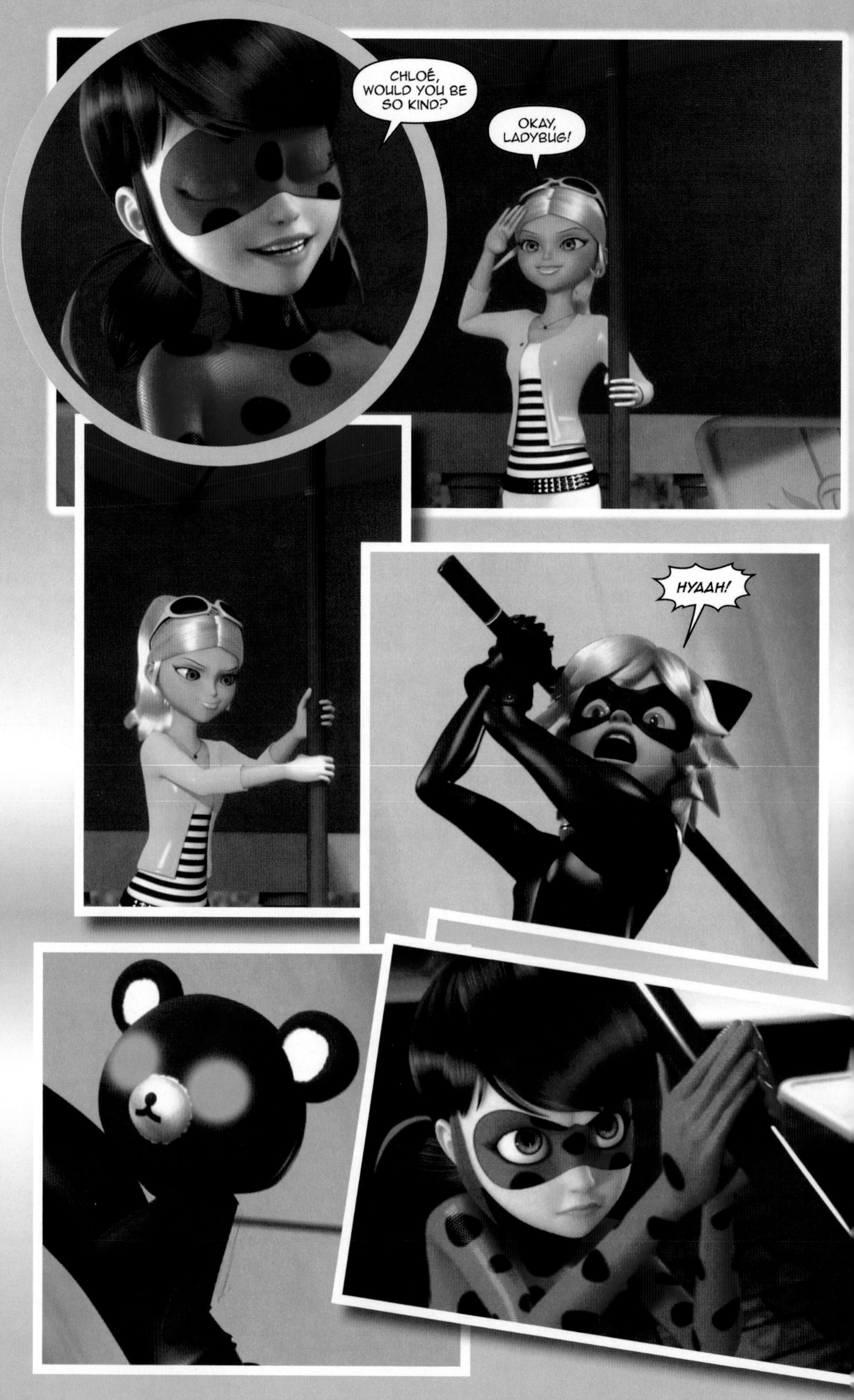
CHLOÉ, WOULD YOU BE SO KIND?
OKAY, LADYBUG!
HYAAH!

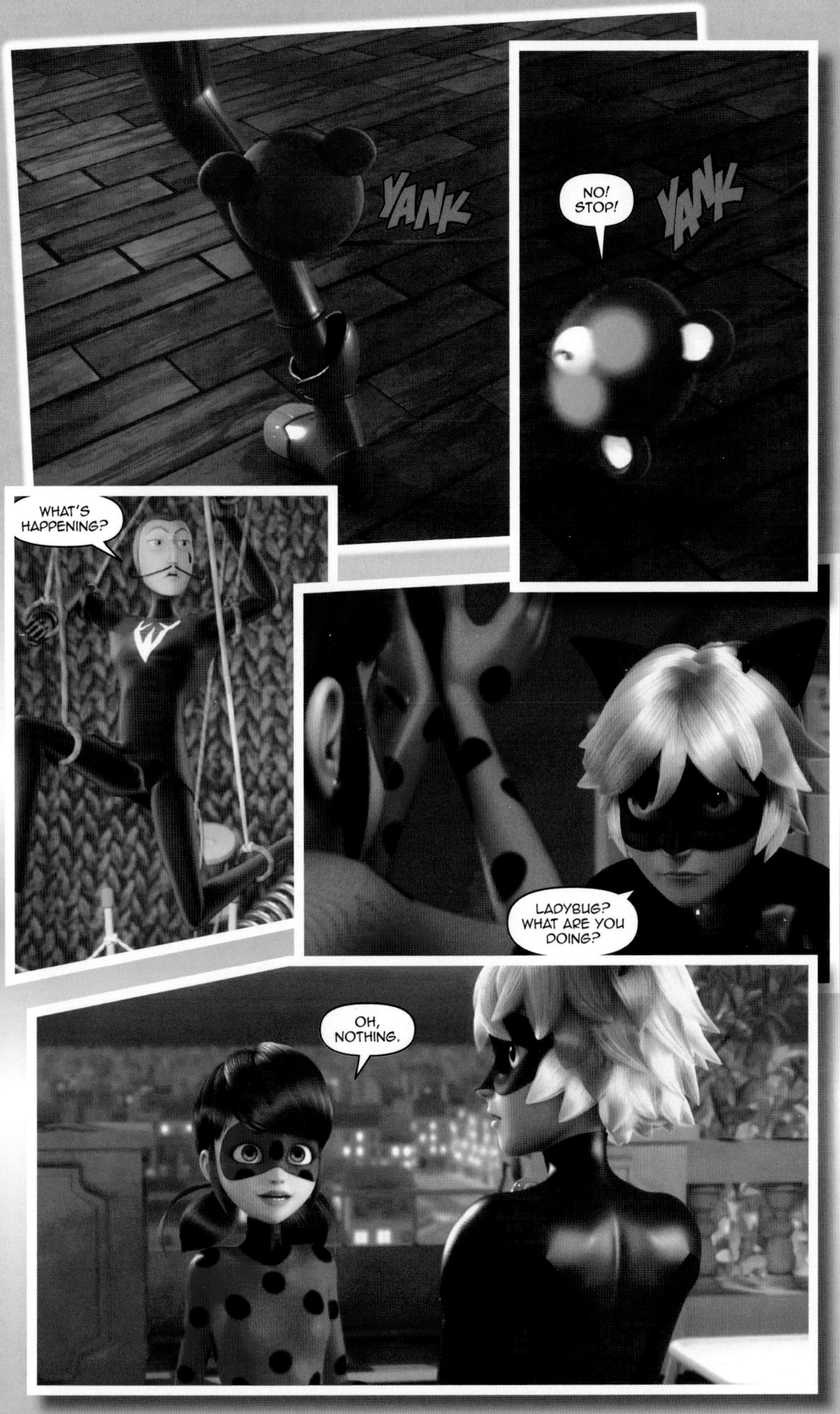
YANK
NO! STOP!
YANK
WHAT'S HAPPENING?
LADYBUG? WHAT ARE YOU DOING?
OH, NOTHING.

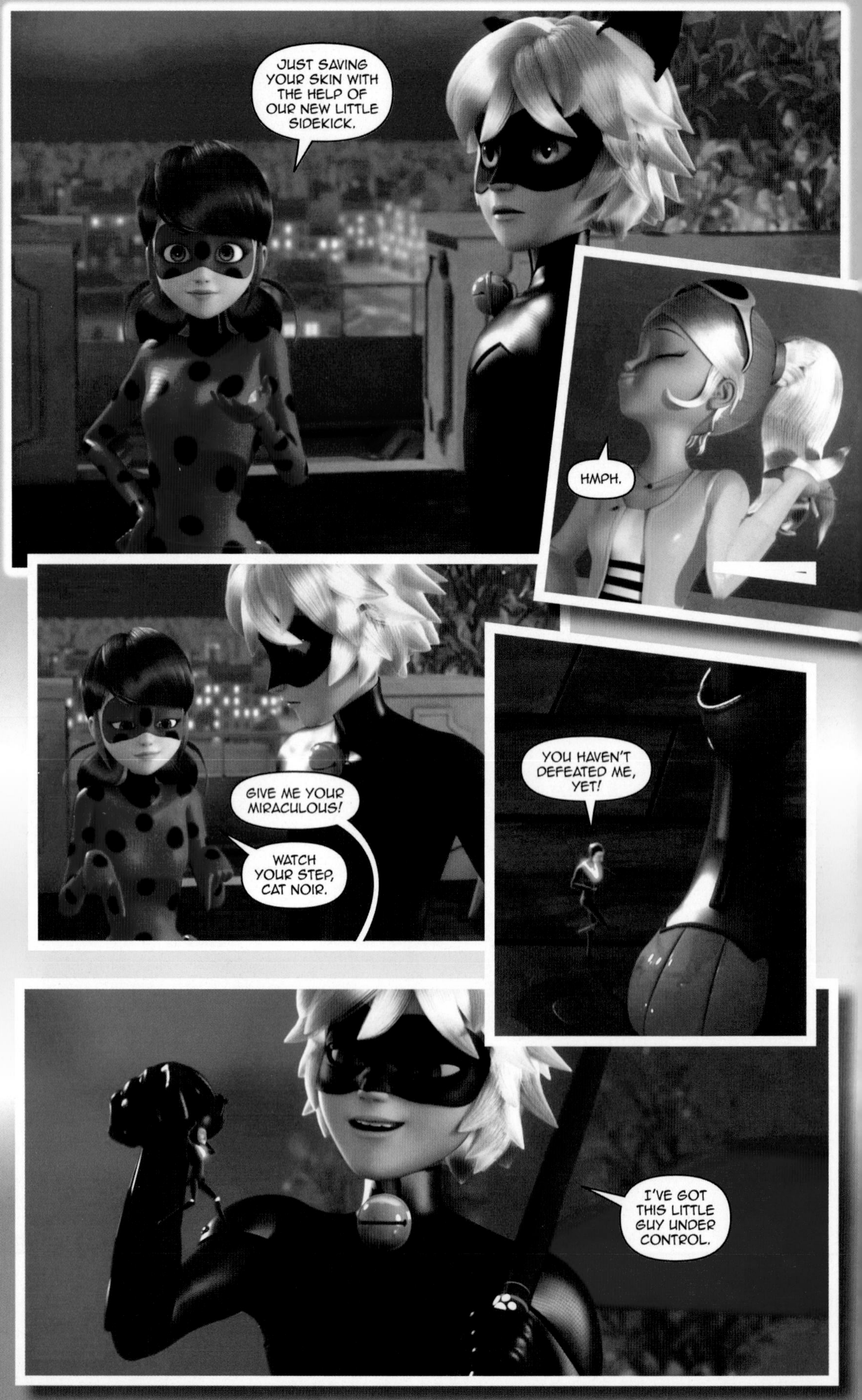

JUST SAVING YOUR SKIN WITH THE HELP OF OUR NEW LITTLE SIDEKICK.
HMPH.
GIVE ME YOUR MIRACULOUS!
WATCH YOUR STEP, CAT NOIR.
YOU HAVEN'T DEFEATED ME, YET!
I'VE GOT THIS LITTLE GUY UNDER CONTROL.

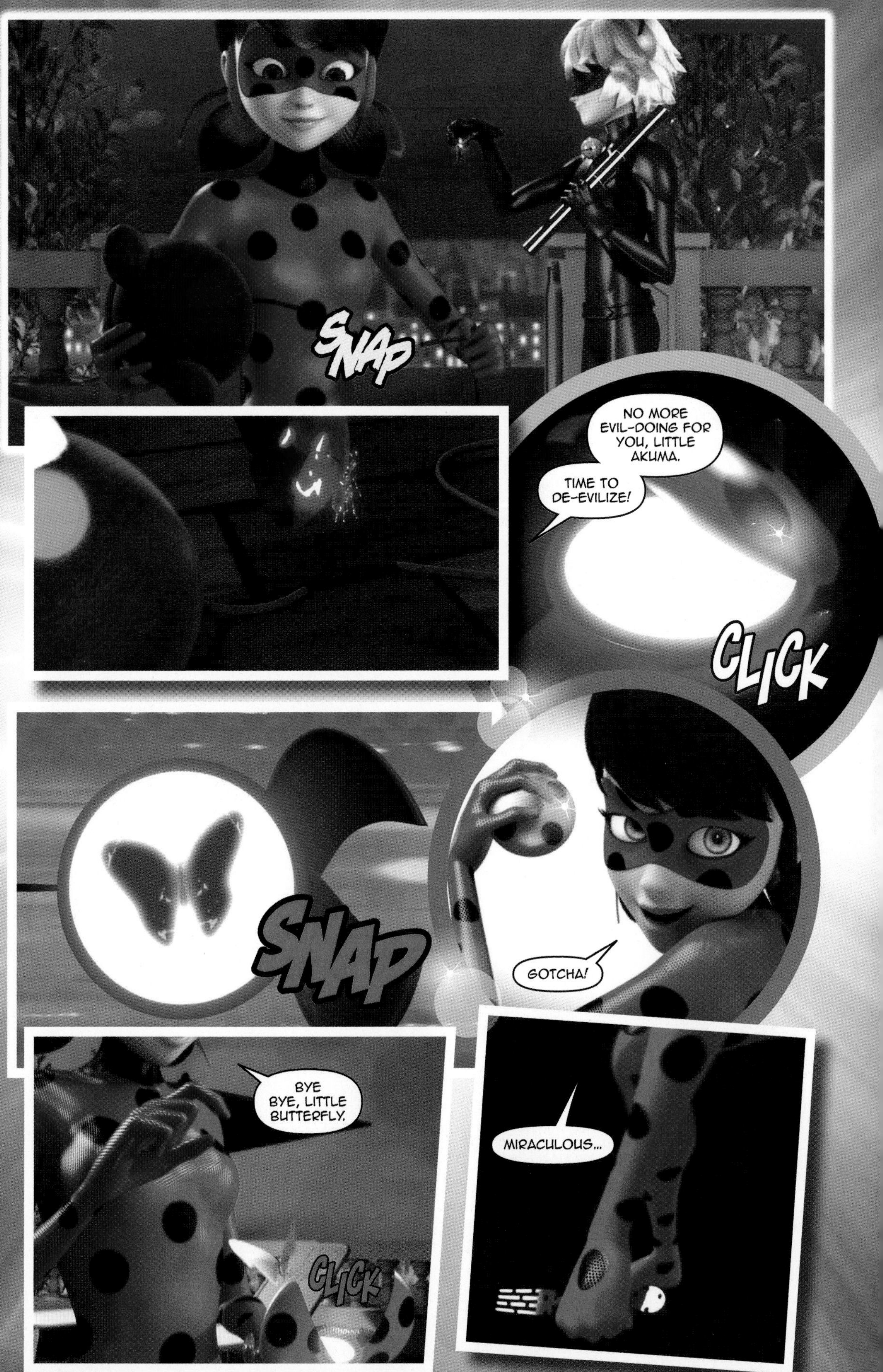
SNAP
NO MORE EVIL-DOING FOR YOU, LITTLE AKUMA.
TIME TO DE-EVILIZE!
CLICK
SNAP
GOTCHA!
BYE BYE, LITTLE BUTTERFLY.
CLICK
MIRACULOUS...

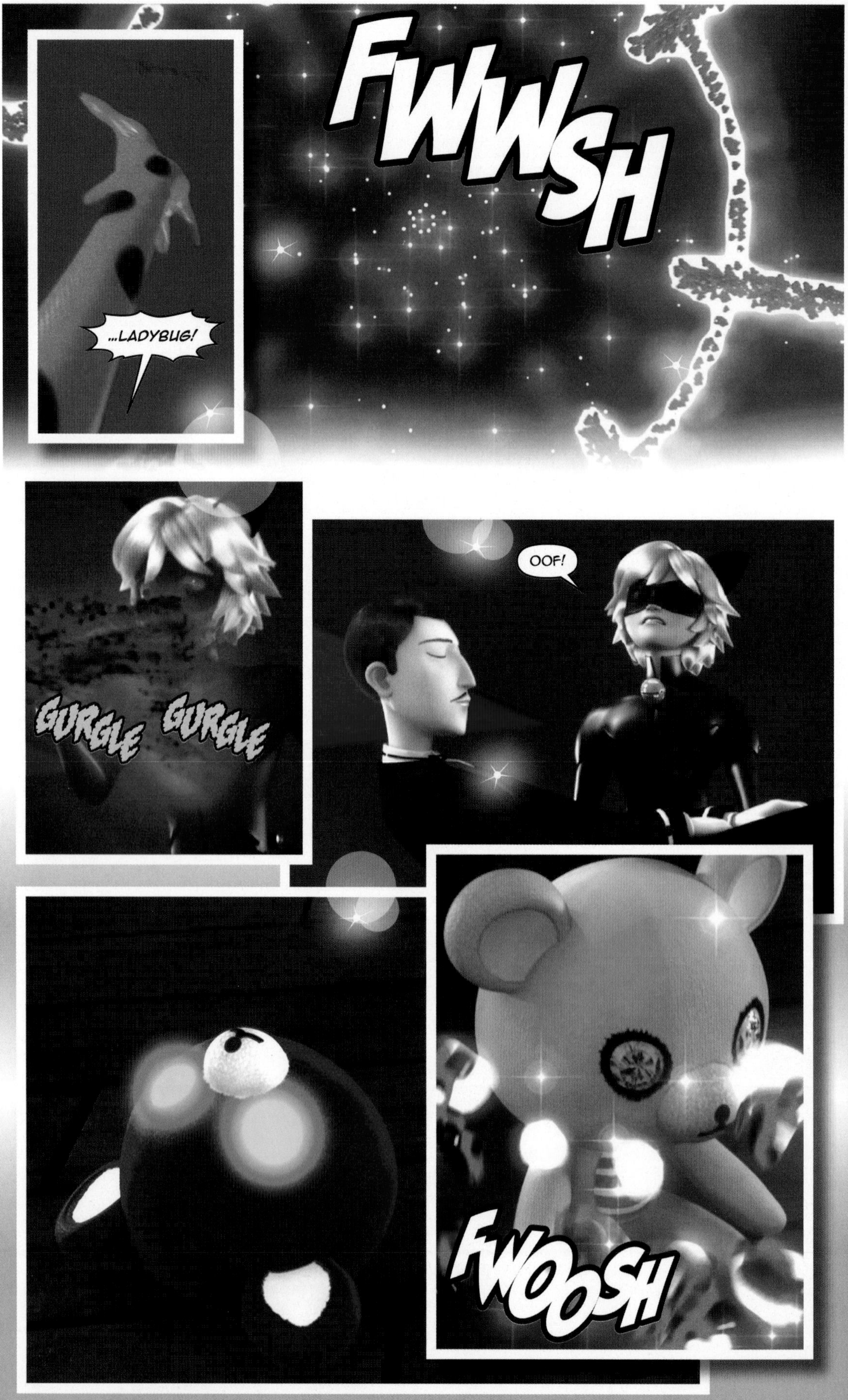
FWWSH
...LADYBUG!
GURGLE GURGLE
OOF!
FWOOSH

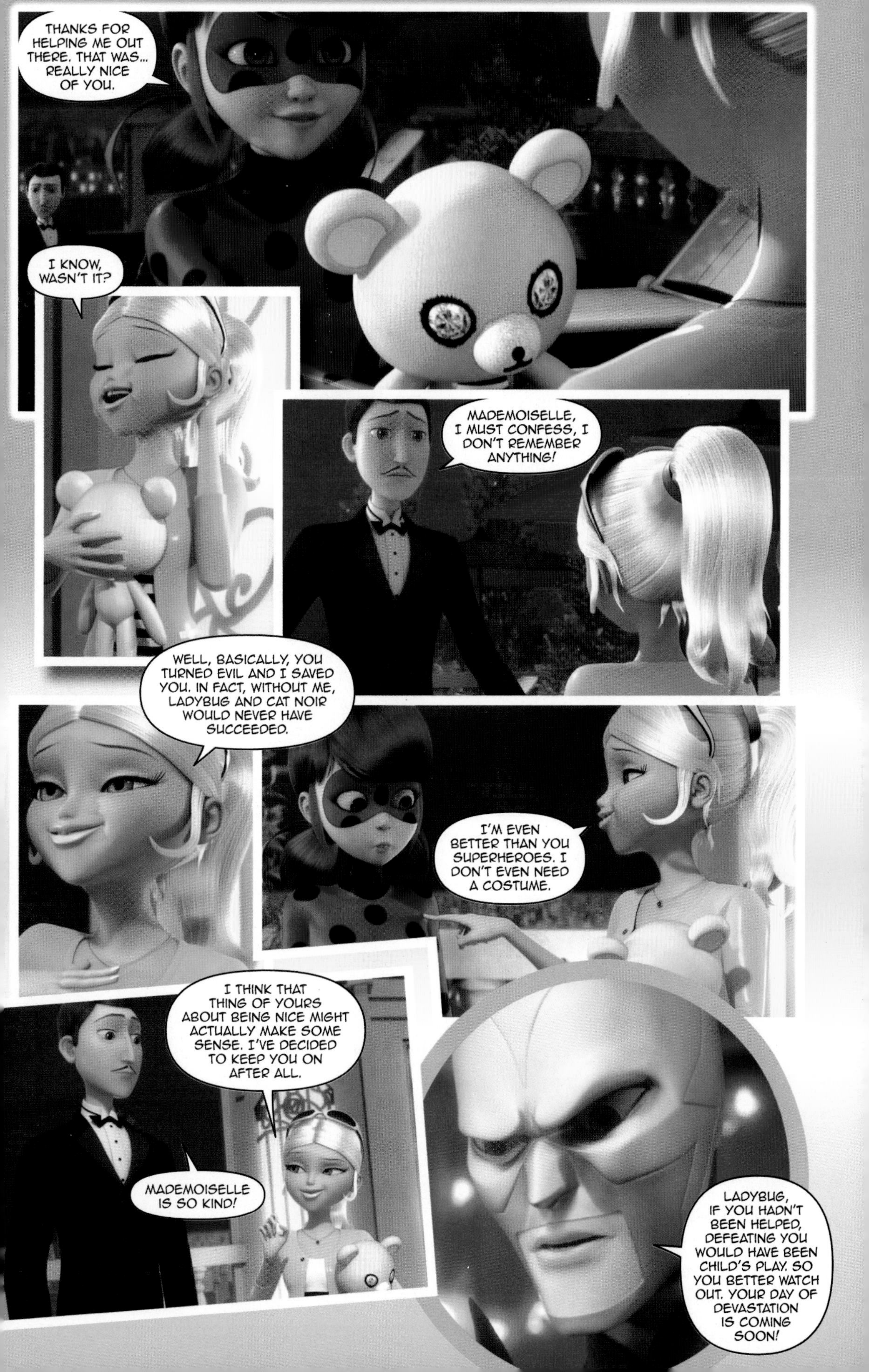
THANKS FOR HELPING ME OUT THERE. THAT WAS... REALLY NICE OF YOU.
I KNOW, WASN'T IT?
MADEMOISELLE, I MUST CONFESS, I DON'T REMEMBER ANYTHING!
WELL, BASICALLY, YOU TURNED EVIL AND I SAVED YOU. IN FACT, WITHOUT ME, LADYBUG AND CAT NOIR WOULD NEVER HAVE SUCCEEDED.
I'M EVEN BETTER THAN YOU SUPERHEROES. I DON'T EVEN NEED A COSTUME.
I THINK THAT THING OF YOURS ABOUT BEING NICE MIGHT ACTUALLY MAKE SOME SENSE. I'VE DECIDED TO KEEP YOU ON AFTER ALL.
MADEMOISELLE IS SO KIND!
LADYBUG, IF YOU HADN'T BEEN HELPED, DEFEATING YOU WOULD HAVE BEEN CHILD'S PLAY. SO YOU BETTER WATCH OUT. YOUR DAY OF DEVASTATION IS COMING SOON!

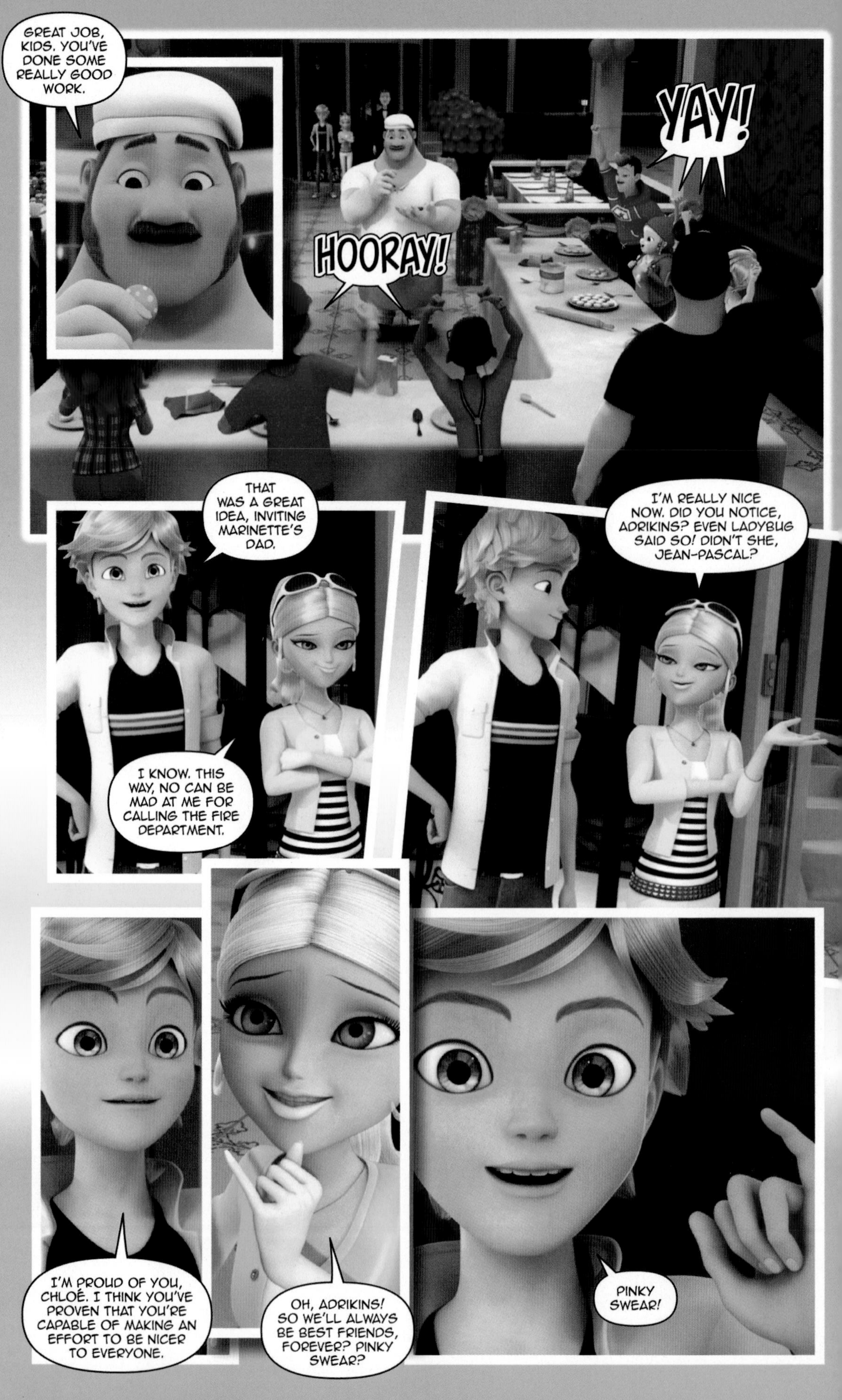
GREAT JOB, KIDS. YOU'VE DONE SOME REALLY GOOD WORK.
YAY!
HOORAY!
THAT WAS A GREAT IDEA, INVITING MARINETTE'S DAD.
I KNOW. THIS WAY, NO CAN BE MAD AT ME FOR CALLING THE FIRE DEPARTMENT.
I'M REALLY NICE NOW. DID YOU NOTICE, ADRIKINS? EVEN LADYBUG SAID SO! DIDN'T SHE, JEAN-PASCAL?
I'M PROUD OF YOU, CHLOÉ. I THINK YOU'VE PROVEN THAT YOU'RE CAPABLE OF MAKING AN EFFORT TO BE NICER TO EVERYONE.
OH, ADRIKINS! SO WE'LL ALWAYS BE BEST FRIENDS, FOREVER? PINKY SWEAR?
PINKY SWEAR!

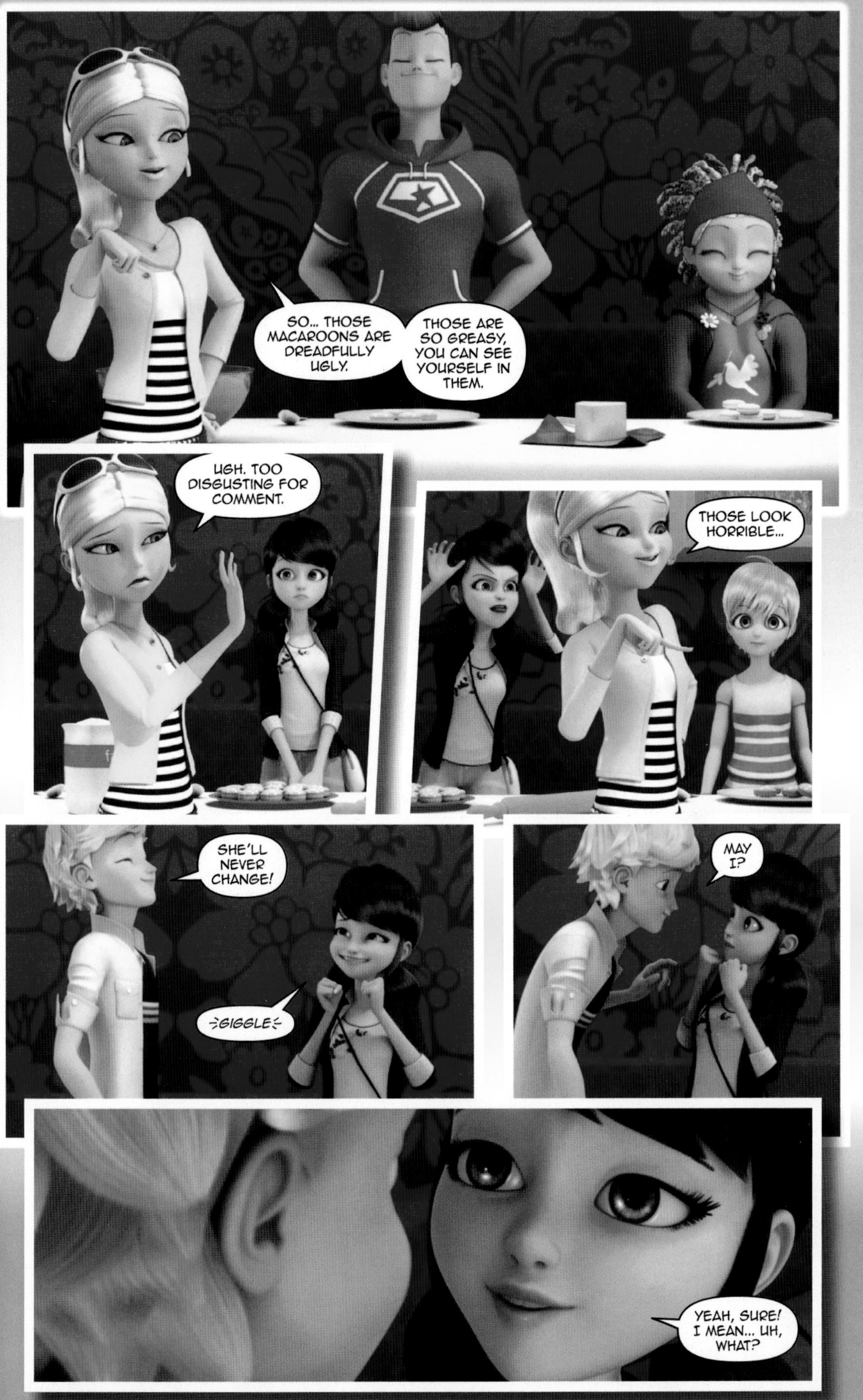
SO... THOSE MACAROONS ARE DREADFULLY UGLY.
THOSE ARE SO GREASY, YOU CAN SEE YOURSELF IN THEM.
UGH. TOO DISGUSTING FOR COMMENT.
THOSE LOOK HORRIBLE...
SHE'LL NEVER CHANGE!
GIGGLE
MAY I?
YEAH, SURE! I MEAN... UH, WHAT?

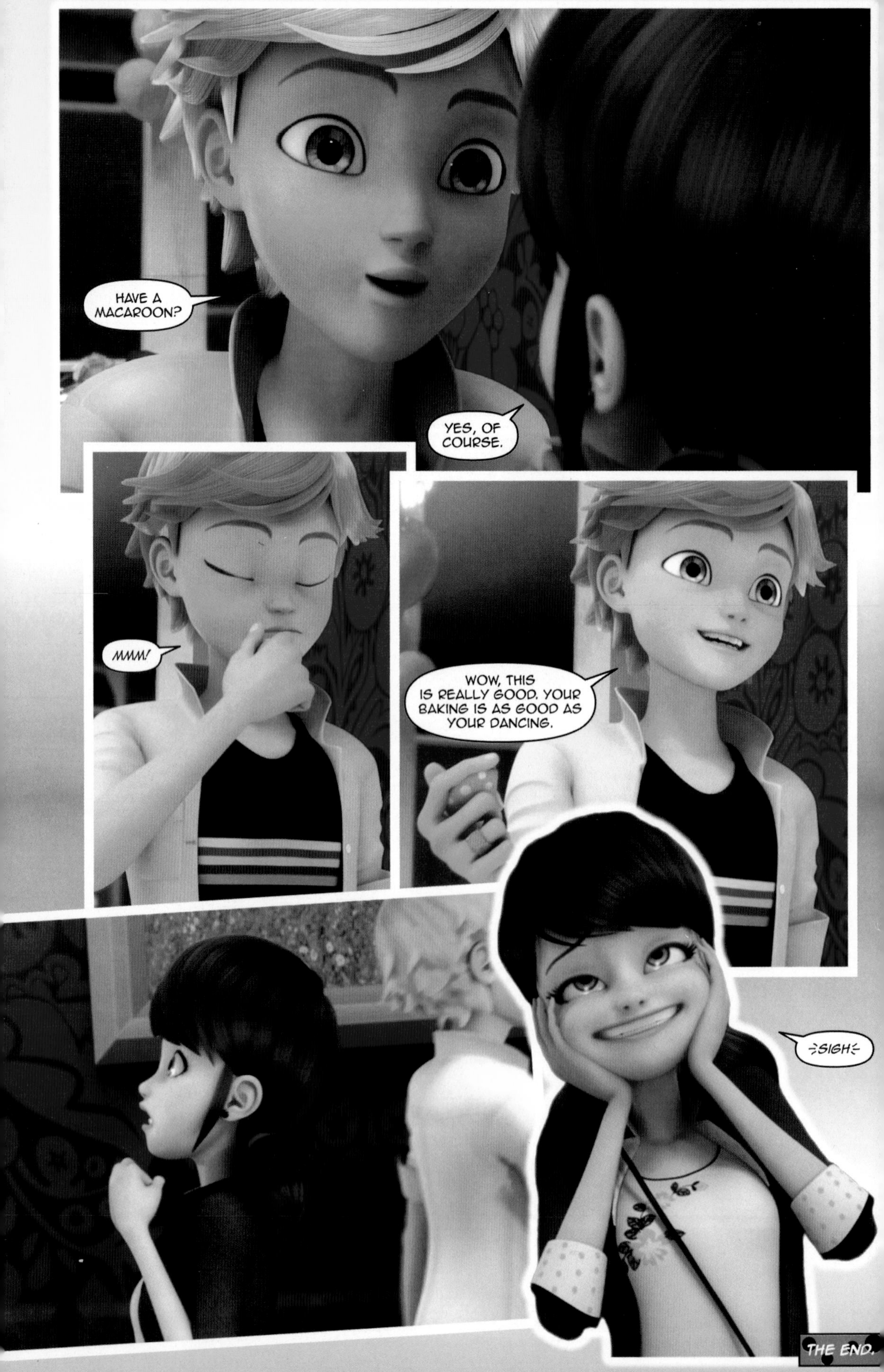

HAVE A MACAROON?
YES, OF COURSE.
MMM!
WOW, THIS IS REALLY GOOD. YOUR BAKING IS AS GOOD AS YOUR DANCING.
SIGH
THE END.

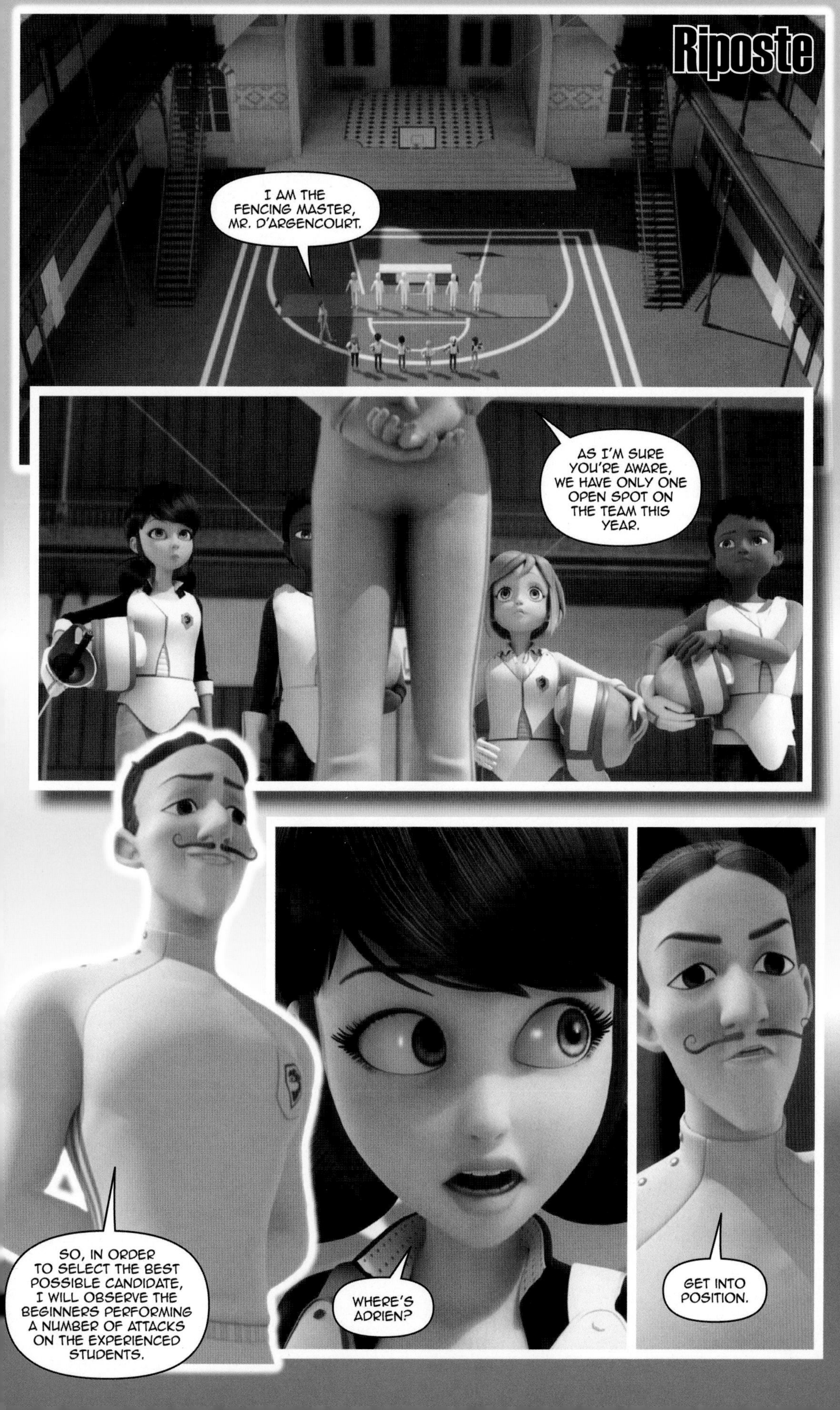
Riposte
I AM THE FENCING MASTER, MR. D'ARGENCOURT.
AS I'M SURE YOU'RE AWARE, WE HAVE ONLY ONE OPEN SPOT ON THE TEAM THIS YEAR.
SO, IN ORDER TO SELECT THE BEST POSSIBLE CANDIDATE, I WILL OBSERVE THE BEGINNERS PERFORMING A NUMBER OF ATTACKS ON THE EXPERIENCED STUDENTS.
WHERE'S ADRIEN?
GET INTO POSITION.

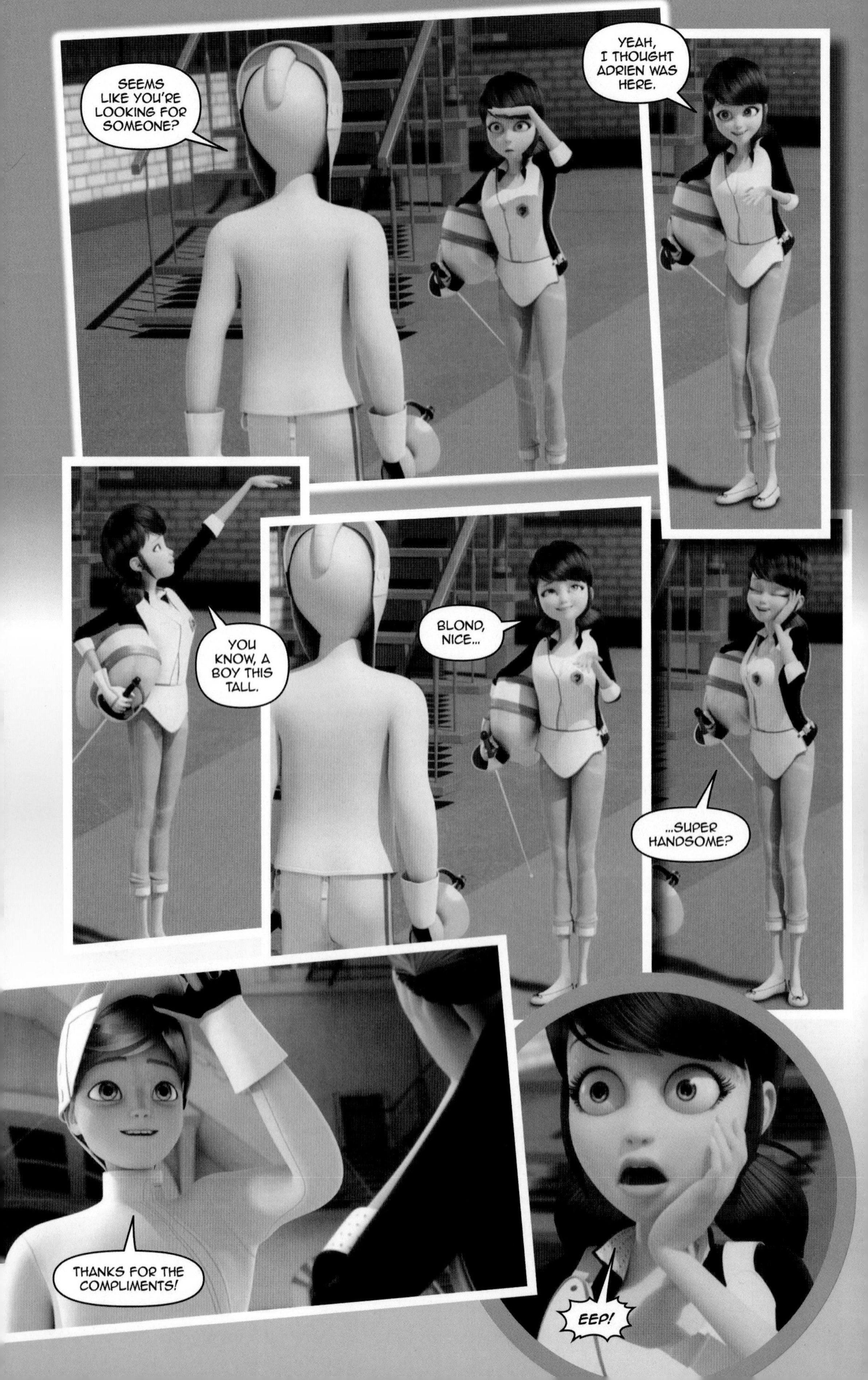
SEEMS LIKE YOU'RE LOOKING FOR SOMEONE?
YEAH, I THOUGHT ADRIEN WAS HERE.
YOU KNOW, A BOY THIS TALL.
BLOND, NICE...
...SUPER HANDSOME?
THANKS FOR THE COMPLIMENTS!
EEP!

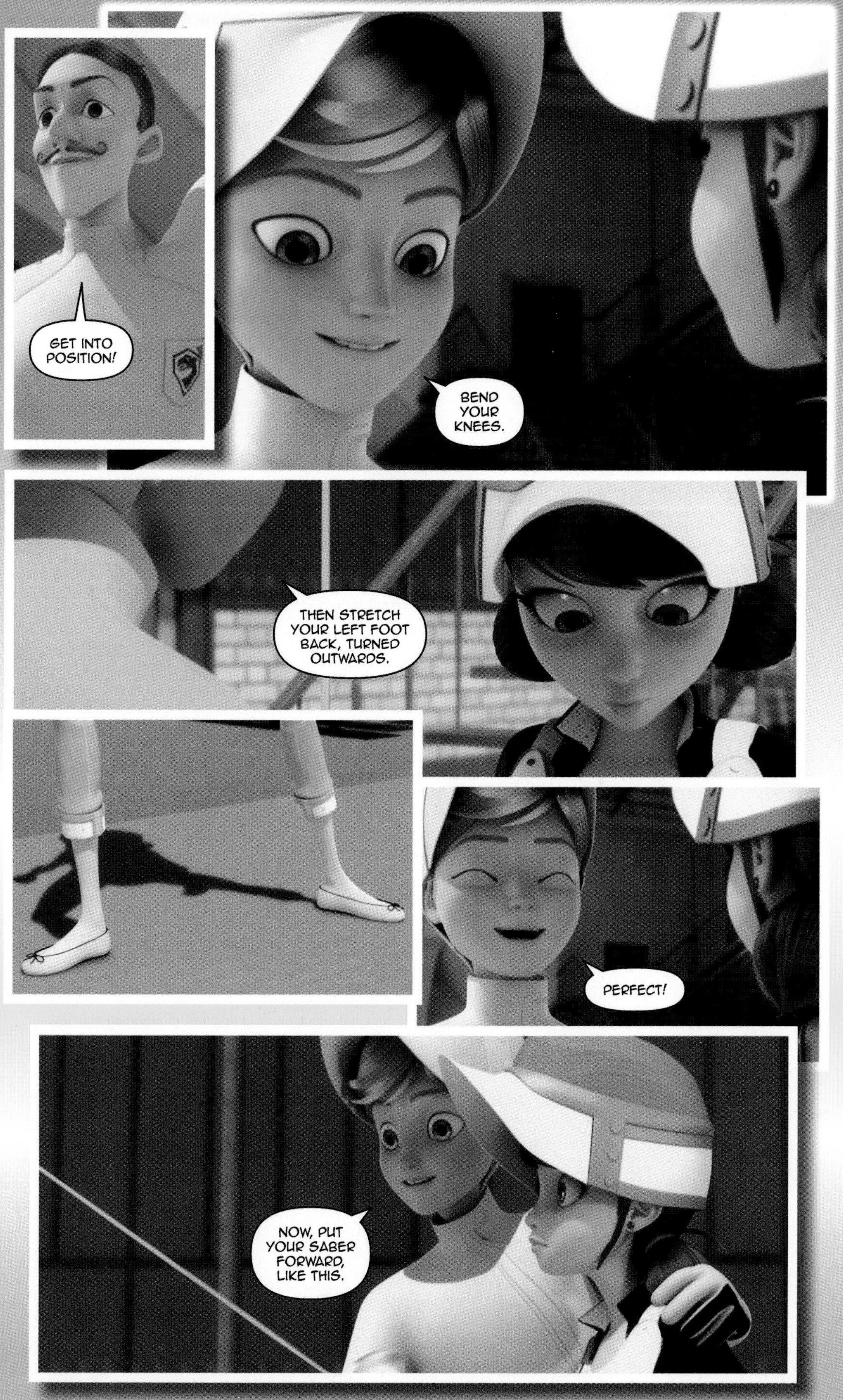
GET INTO POSITION!
BEND YOUR KNEES.
THEN STRETCH YOUR LEFT FOOT BACK, TURNED OUTWARDS.
PERFECT!
NOW, PUT YOUR SABER FORWARD, LIKE THIS.

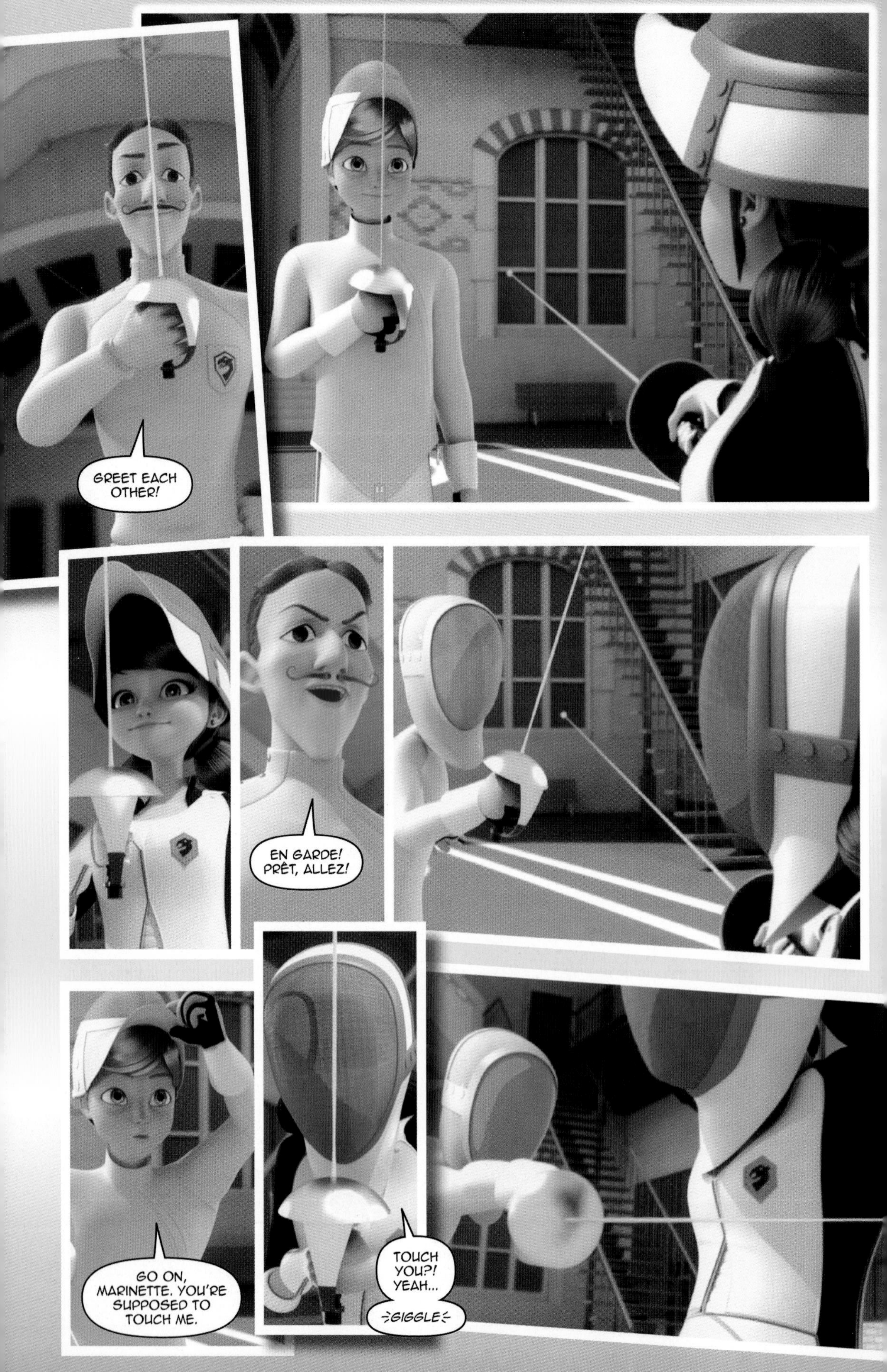
GREET EACH OTHER!
EN GARDE! PRÊT, ALLEZ!
GO ON, MARINETTE. YOU'RE SUPPOSED TO TOUCH ME.
TOUCH YOU?! YEAH...
GIGGLE

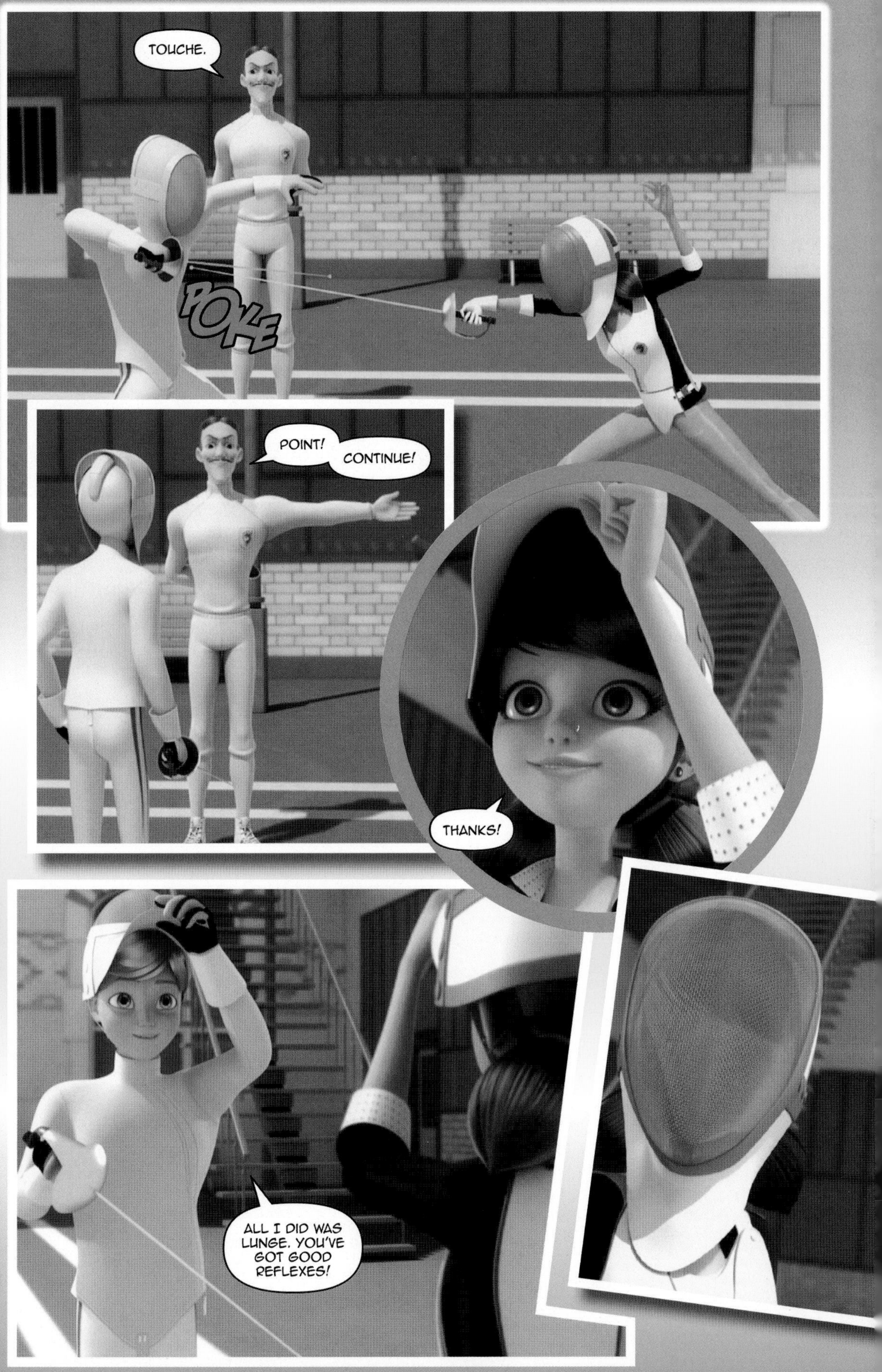
TOUCHE.
POKE
POINT!
CONTINUE!
THANKS!
ALL I DID WAS LUNGE. YOU'VE GOT GOOD REFLEXES!

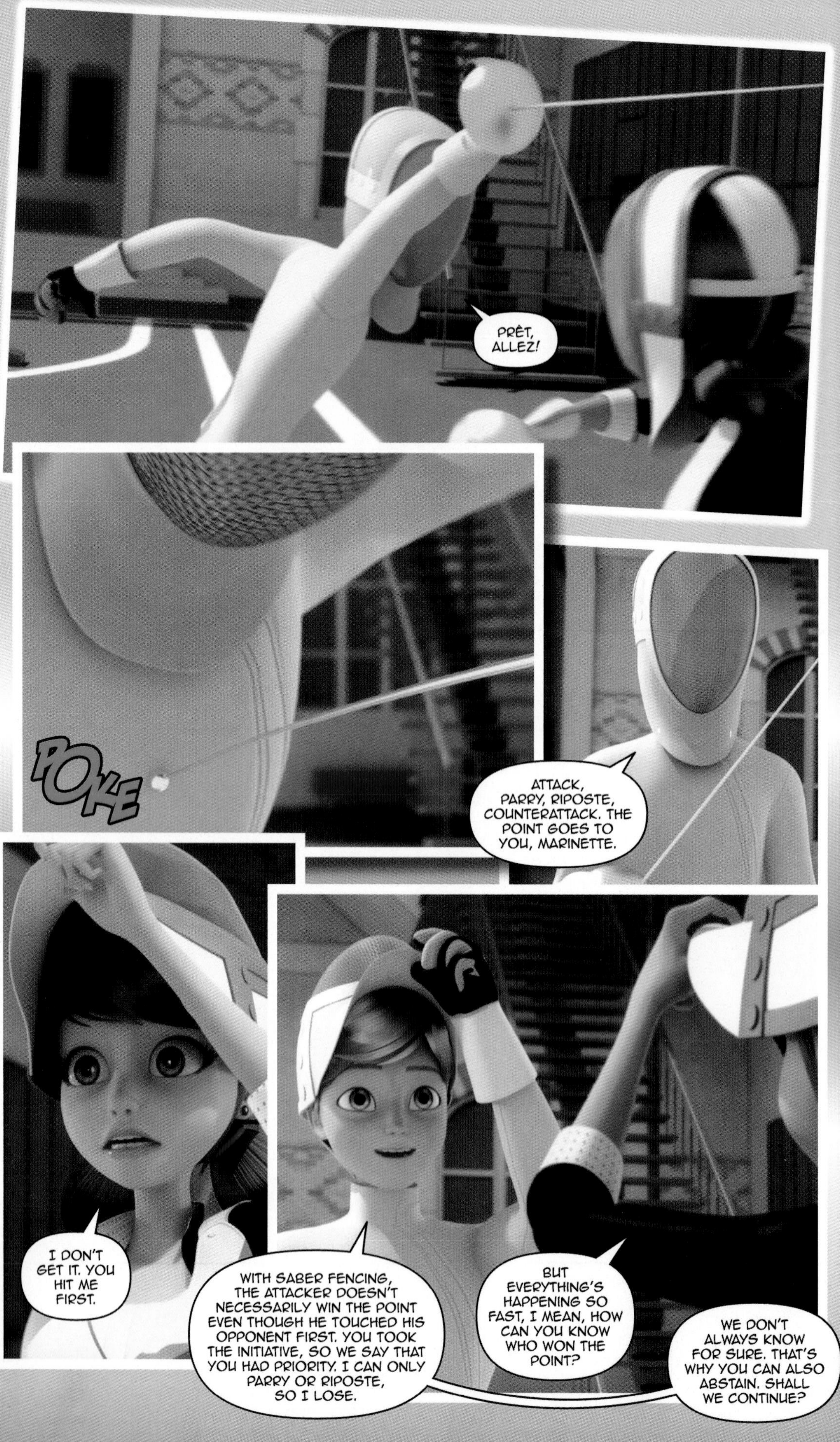
PRÊT, ALLEZ!
POKE
ATTACK, PARRY, RIPOSTE, COUNTERATTACK. THE POINT GOES TO YOU, MARINETTE.
I DON'T GET IT. YOU HIT ME FIRST.
WITH SABER FENCING, THE ATTACKER DOESN'T NECESSARILY WIN THE POINT EVEN THOUGH HE TOUCHED HIS OPPONENT FIRST. YOU TOOK THE INITIATIVE, SO WE SAY THAT YOU HAD PRIORITY. I CAN ONLY PARRY OR RIPOSTE, SO I LOSE.
BUT EVERYTHING'S HAPPENING SO FAST, I MEAN, HOW CAN YOU KNOW WHO WON THE POINT?
WE DON'T ALWAYS KNOW FOR SURE. THAT'S WHY YOU CAN ALSO ABSTAIN. SHALL WE CONTINUE?

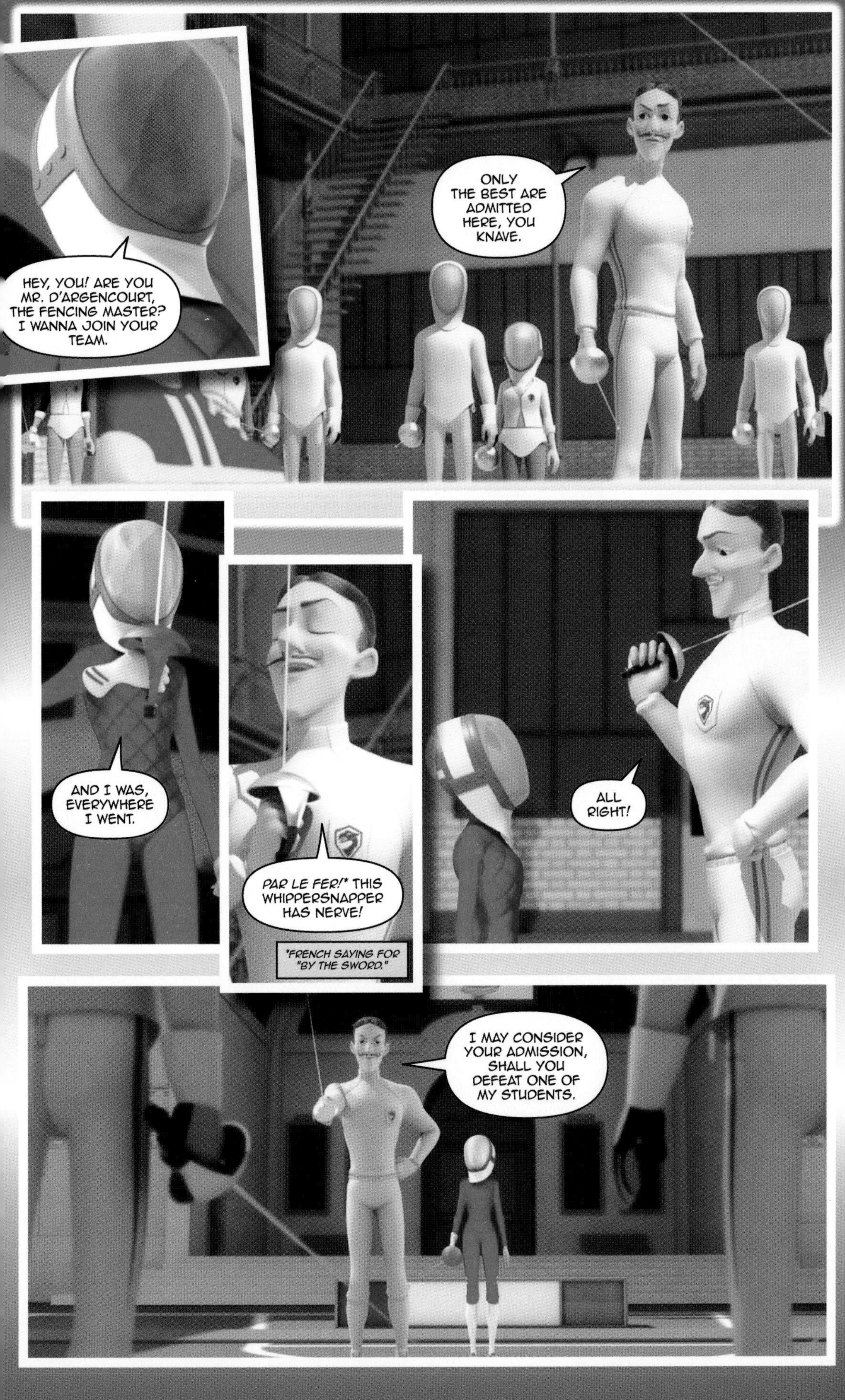
HEY, YOU! ARE YOU MR. D'ARGENCOURT, THE FENCING MASTER? I WANNA JOIN YOUR TEAM.
ONLY THE BEST ARE ADMITTED HERE, YOU KNAVE.
AND I WAS, EVERYWHERE I WENT.
PAR LE FER!* THIS WHIPPERSNAPPER HAS NERVE!
*FRENCH SAYING FOR "BY THE SWORD."
ALL RIGHT!
I MAY CONSIDER YOUR ADMISSION, SHALL YOU DEFEAT ONE OF MY STUDENTS.

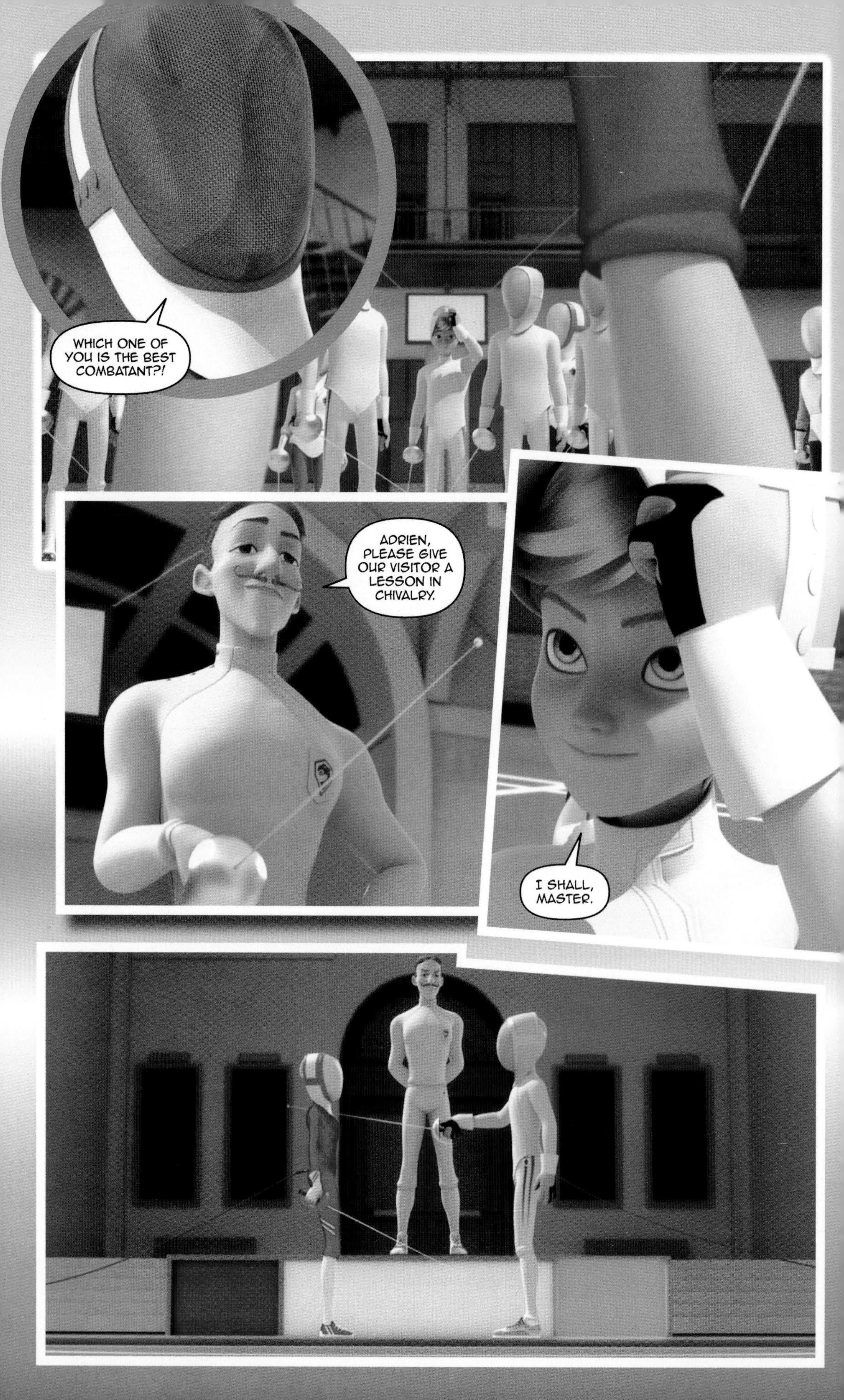
WHICH ONE OF
YOU IS THE BEST
COMBATANT?!
ADRIEN,
PLEASE GIVE
OUR VISITOR A
LESSON IN
CHIVALRY.
I SHALL,
MASTER.

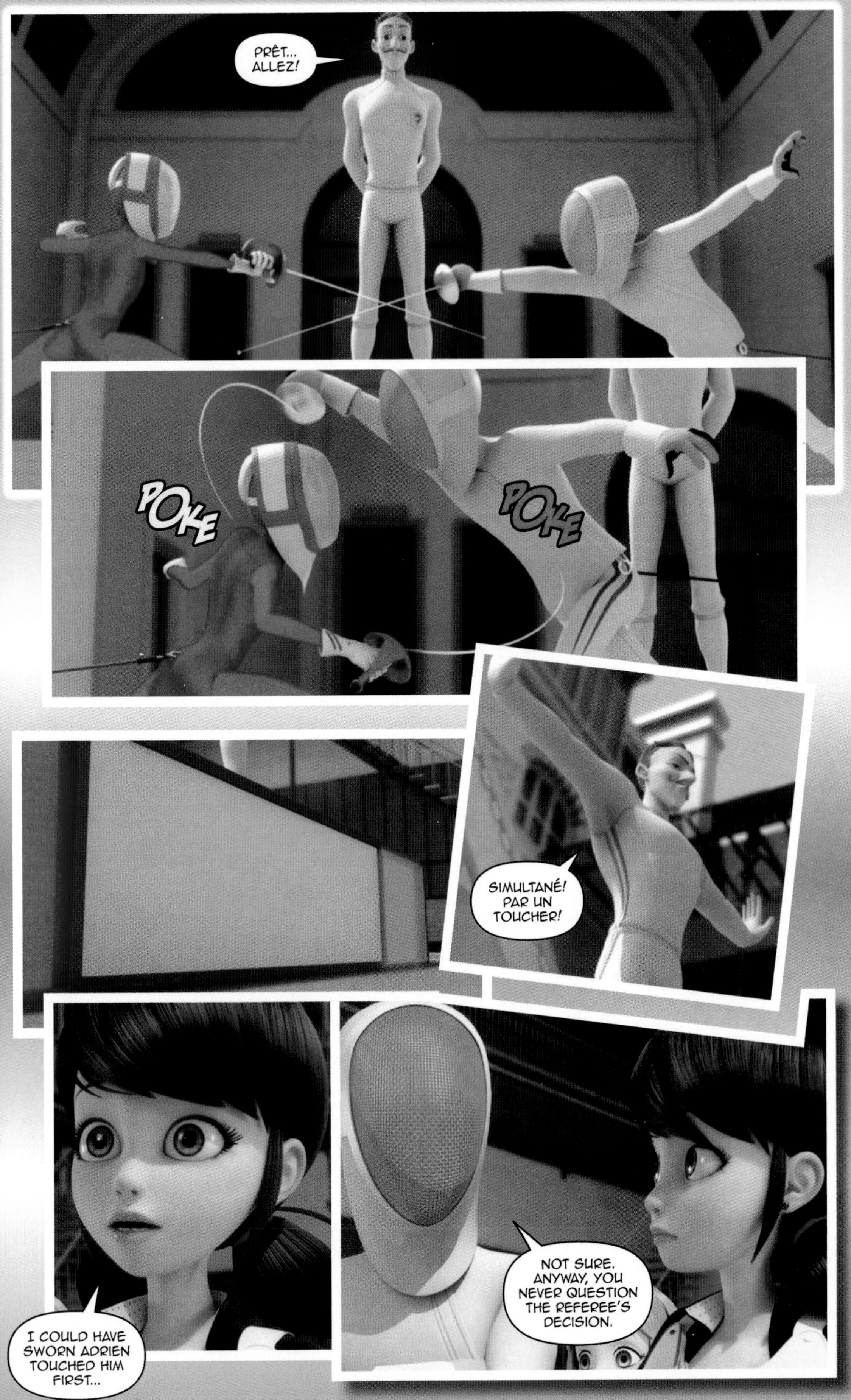
PRÊT... ALLEZ!
POKE
POKE
SIMULTANÉ! PAR UN TOUCHER!
I COULD HAVE SWORN ADRIEN TOUCHED HIM FIRST...
NOT SURE. ANYWAY, YOU NEVER QUESTION THE REFEREE'S DECISION.

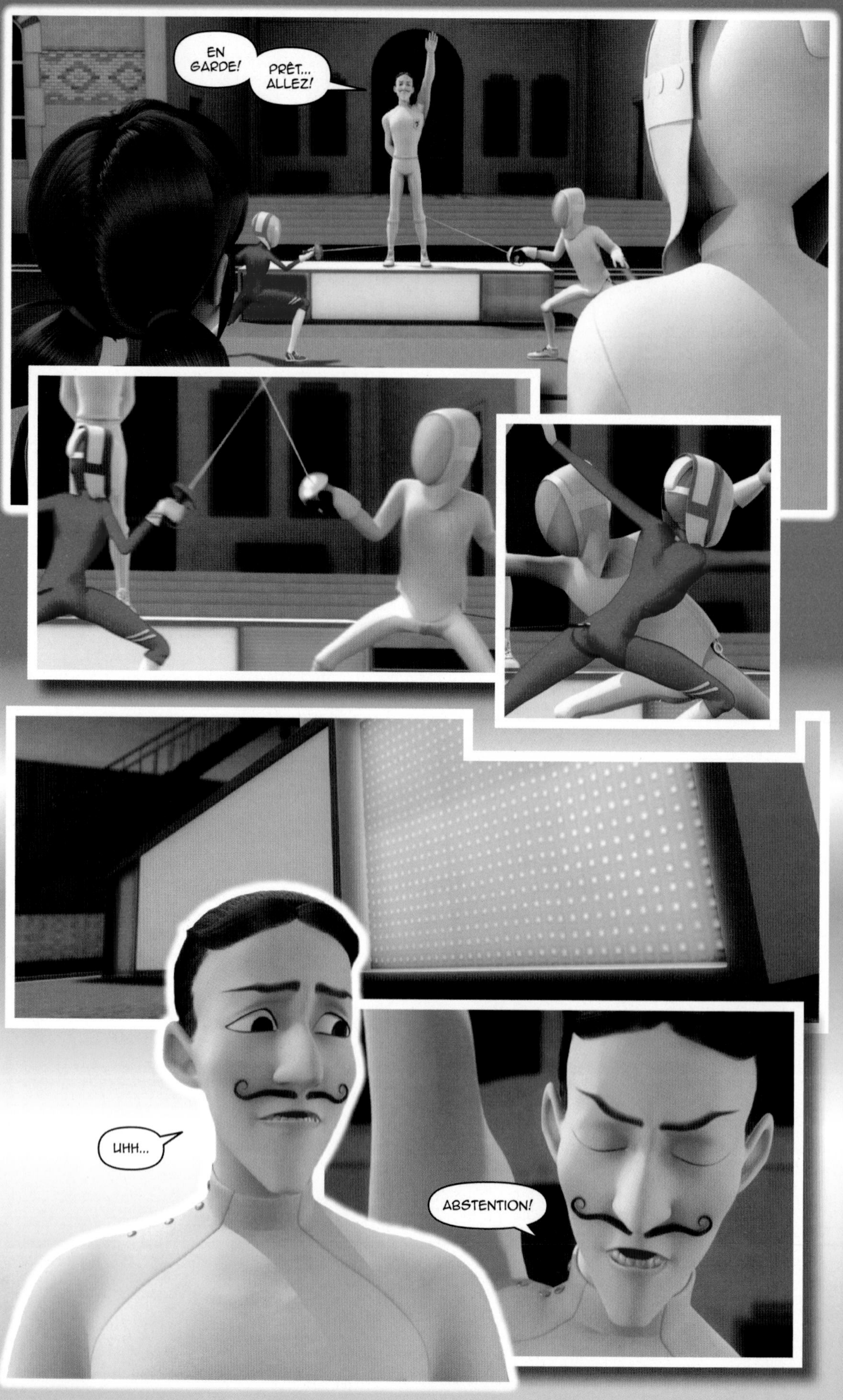
EN GARDE!
PRÊT... ALLEZ!
UHH...
ABSTENTION!

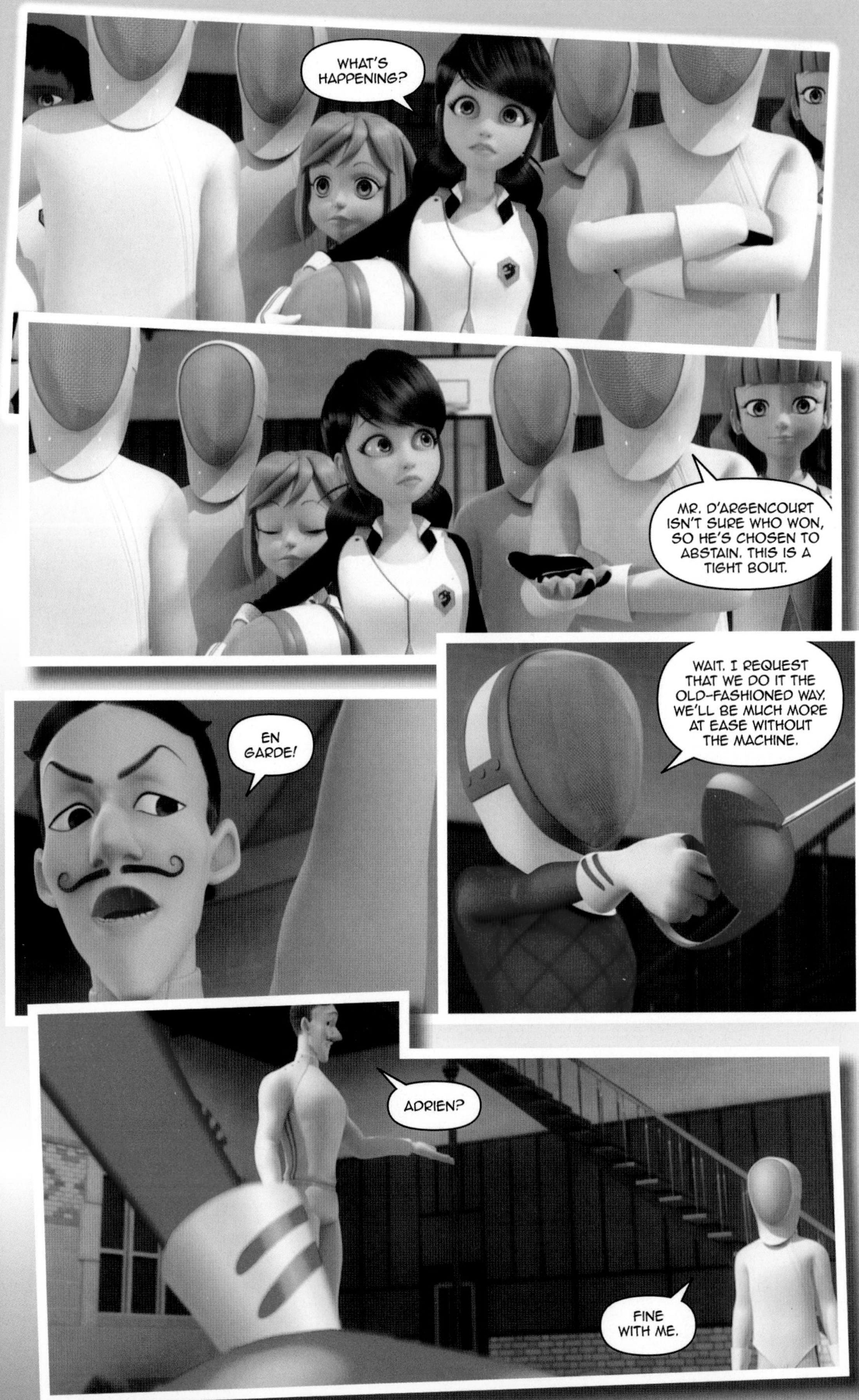
WHAT'S HAPPENING?
MR. D'ARGENCOURT ISN'T SURE WHO WON, SO HE'S CHOSEN TO ABSTAIN. THIS IS A TIGHT BOUT.
EN GARDE!
WAIT. I REQUEST THAT WE DO IT THE OLD-FASHIONED WAY. WE'LL BE MUCH MORE AT EASE WITHOUT THE MACHINE.
ADRIEN?
FINE WITH ME.

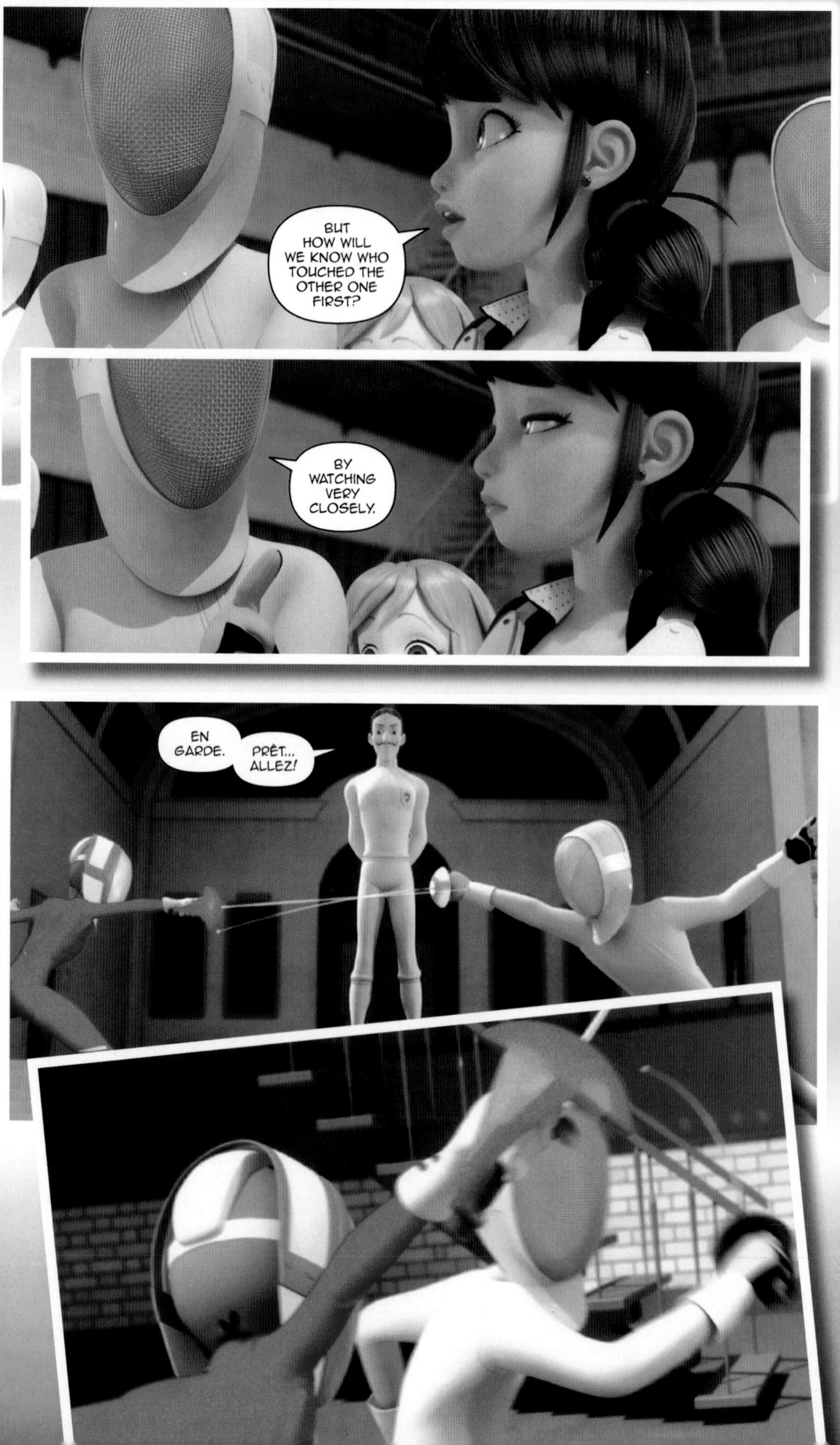
BUT HOW WILL WE KNOW WHO TOUCHED THE OTHER ONE FIRST?
BY WATCHING VERY CLOSELY.
EN GARDE.
PRÊT... ALLEZ!

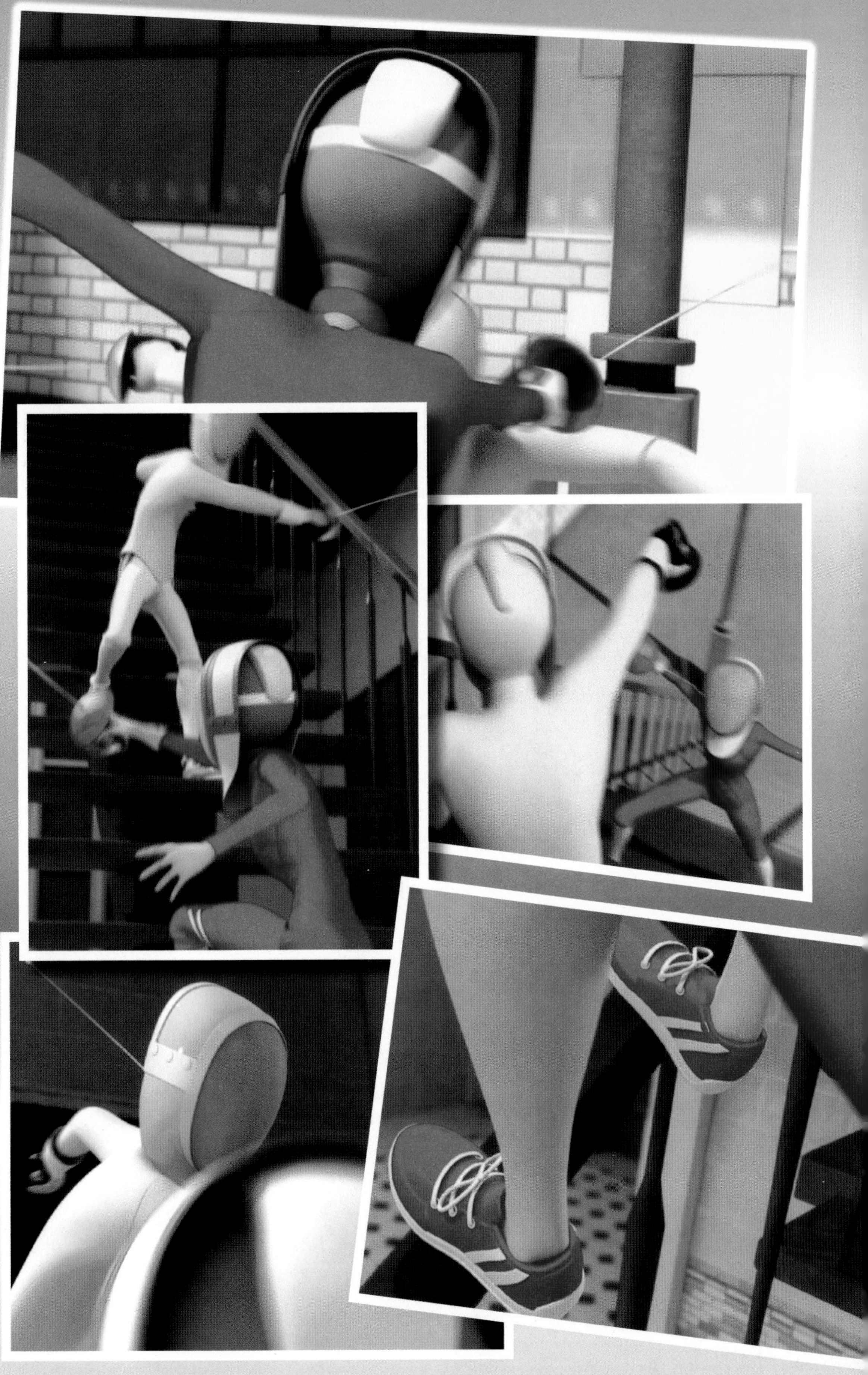

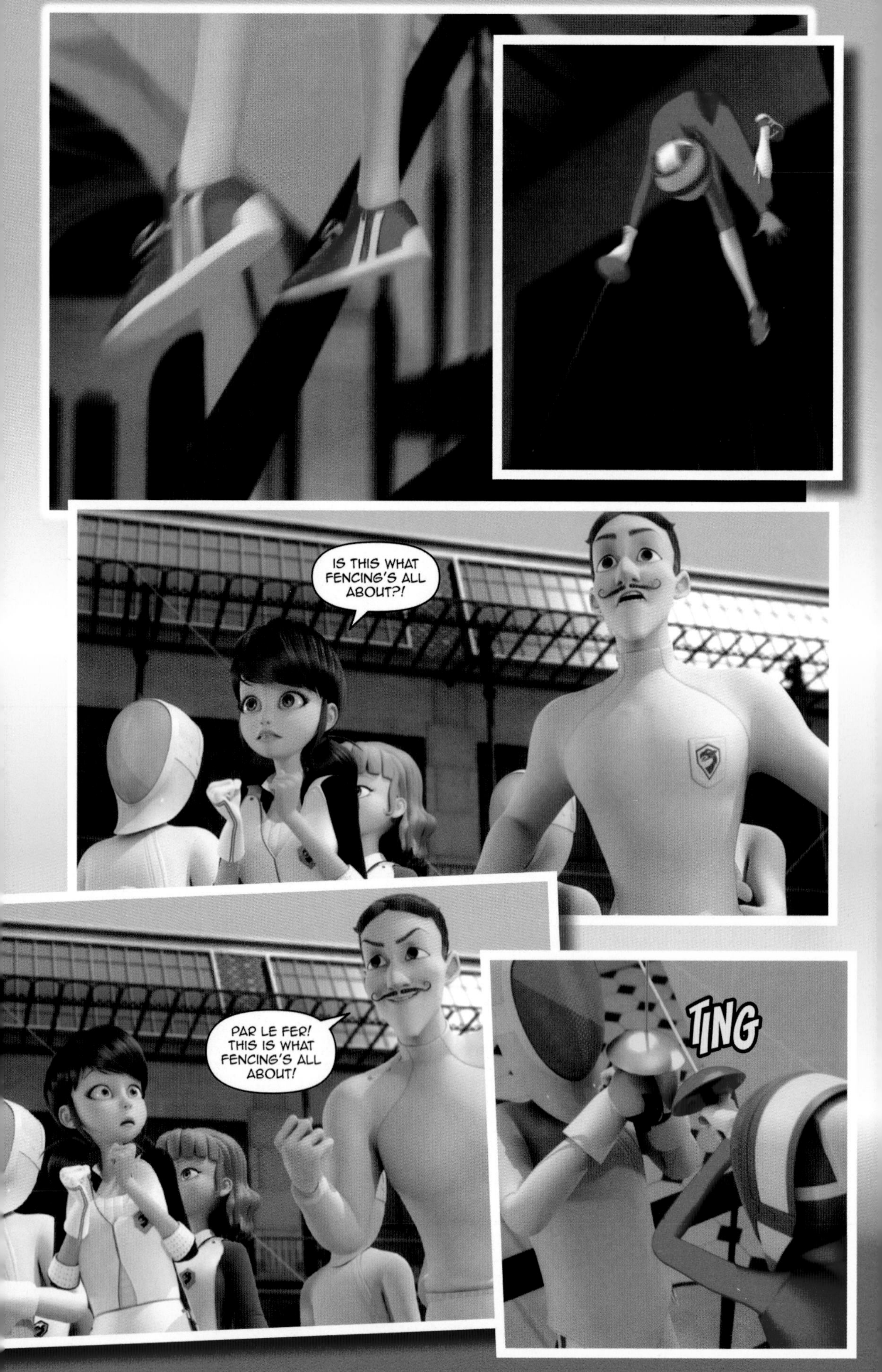
IS THIS WHAT FENCING'S ALL ABOUT?!
PAR LE FER! THIS IS WHAT FENCING'S ALL ABOUT!
TING

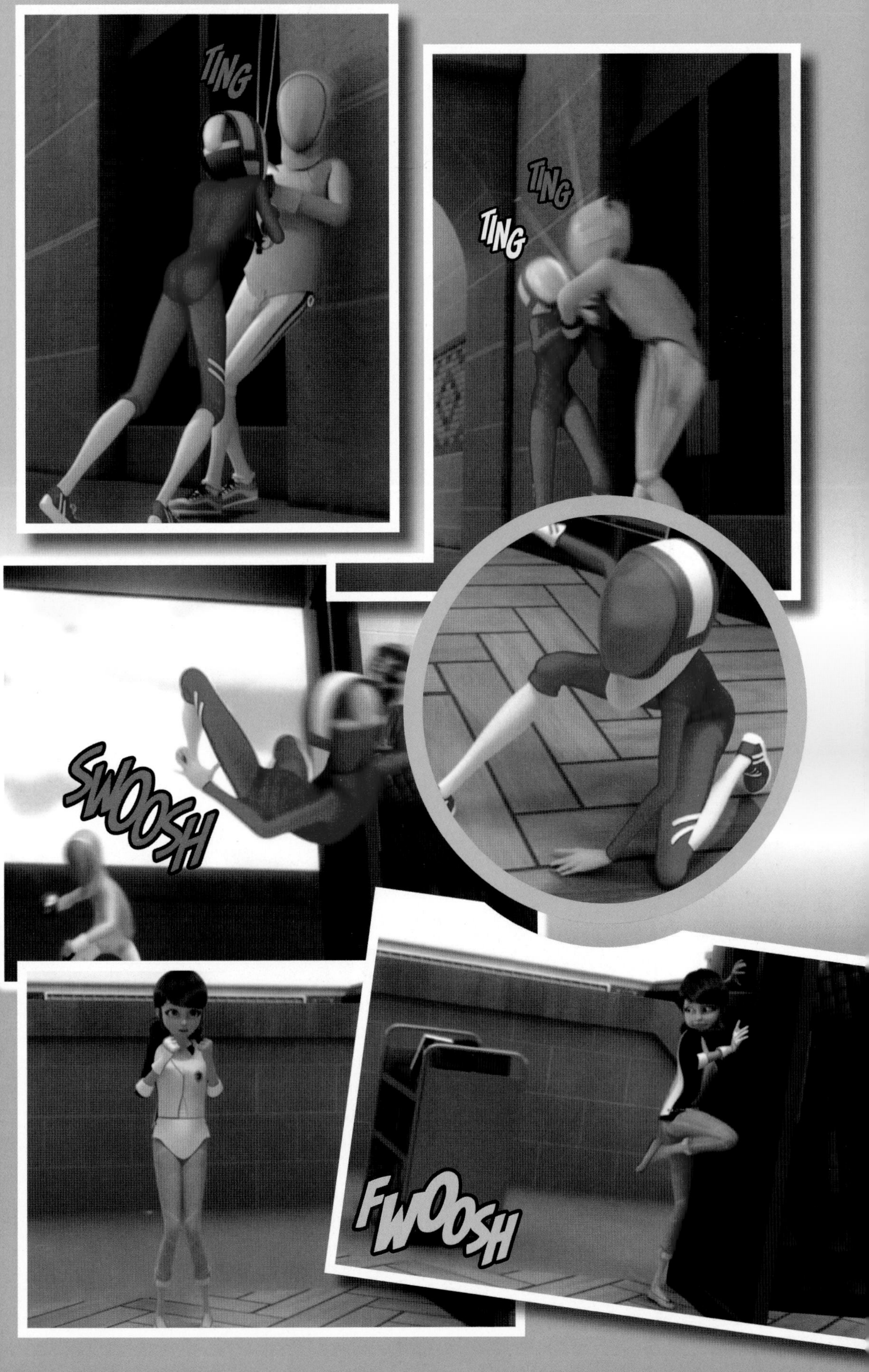
TING
TING
TING
SWOOSH
FWOOSH

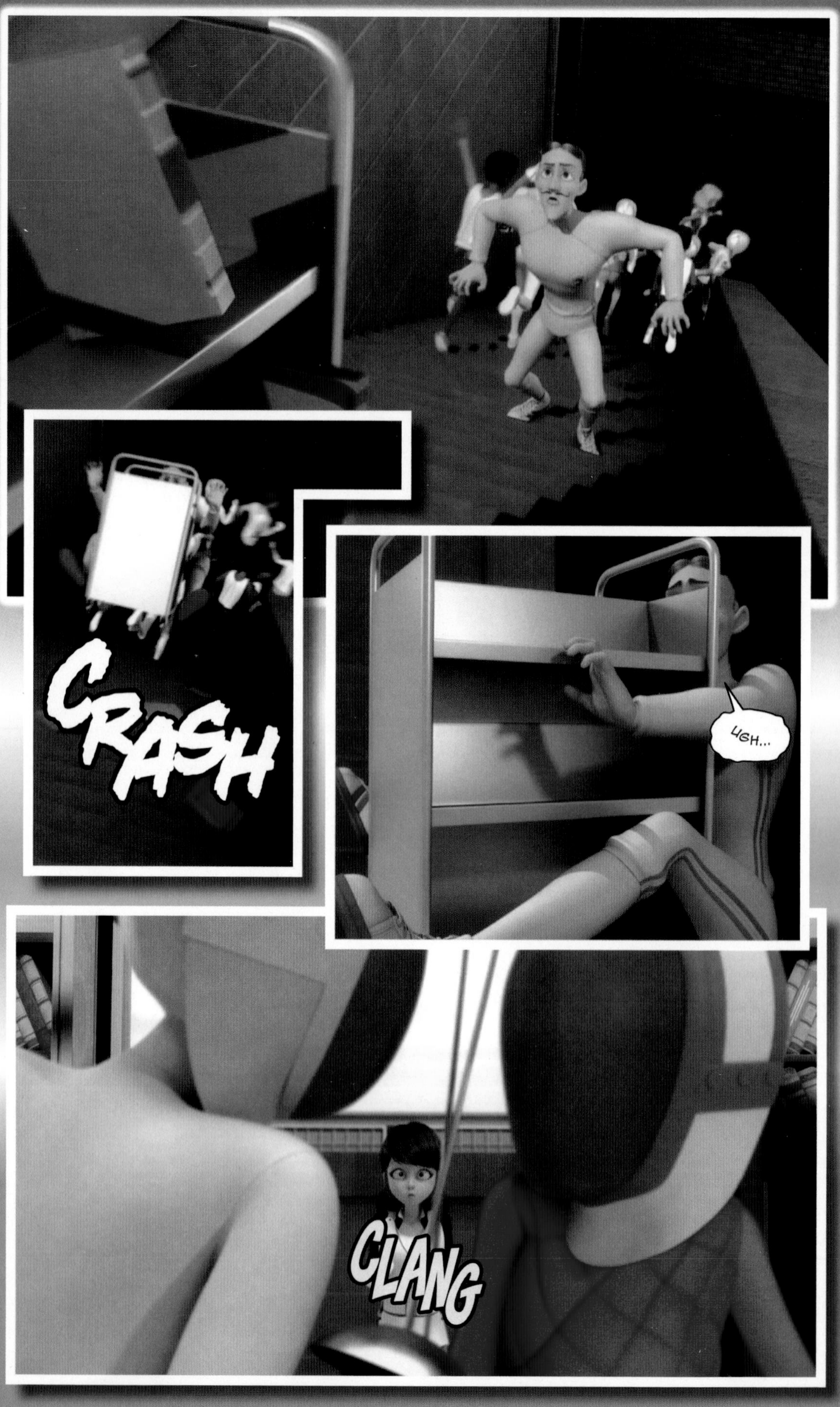
CRASH
UGH...
CLANG

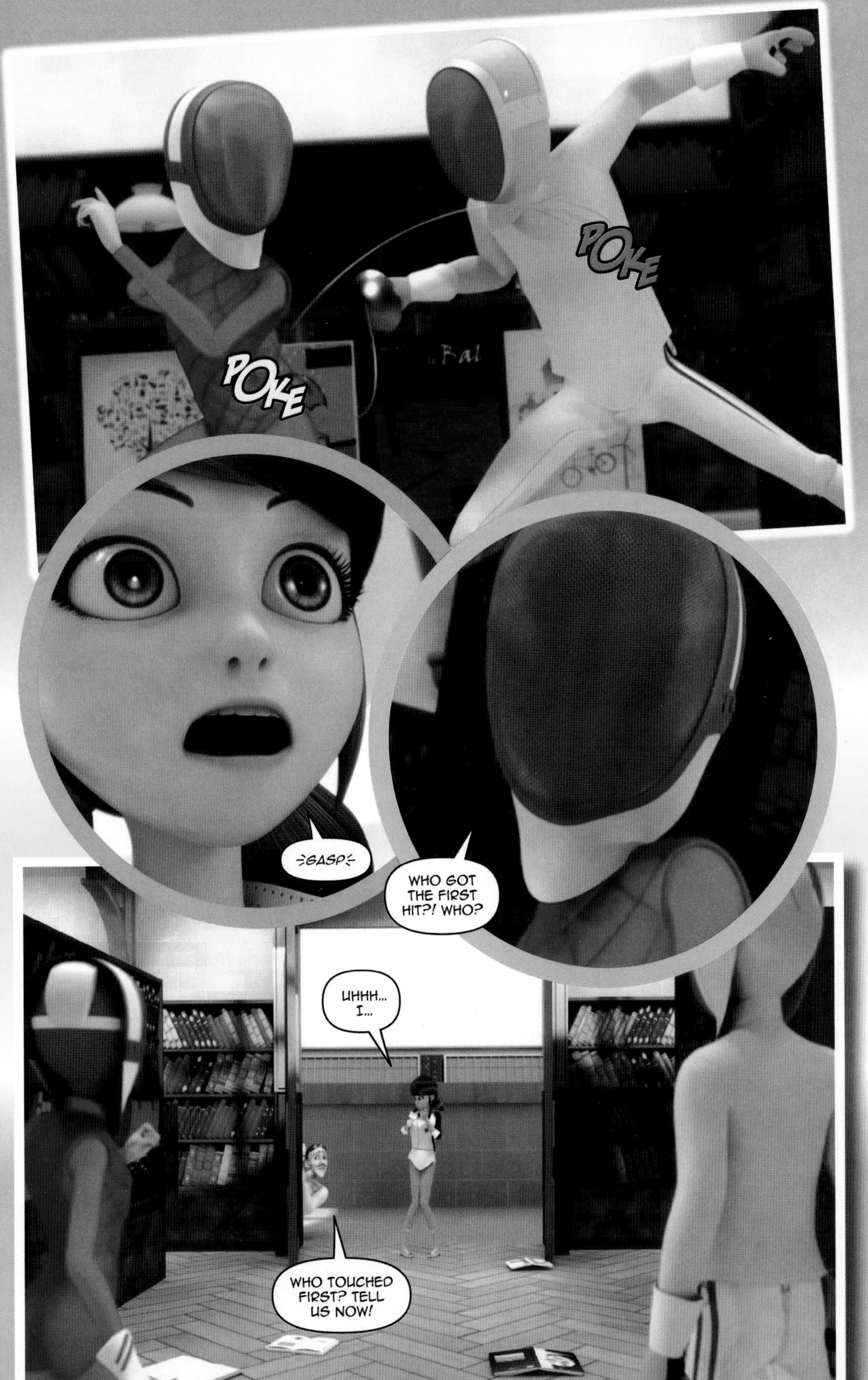
POKE
POKE
≈GASP≈
WHO GOT THE FIRST HIT?! WHO?
UHHH... I...
WHO TOUCHED FIRST? TELL US NOW!

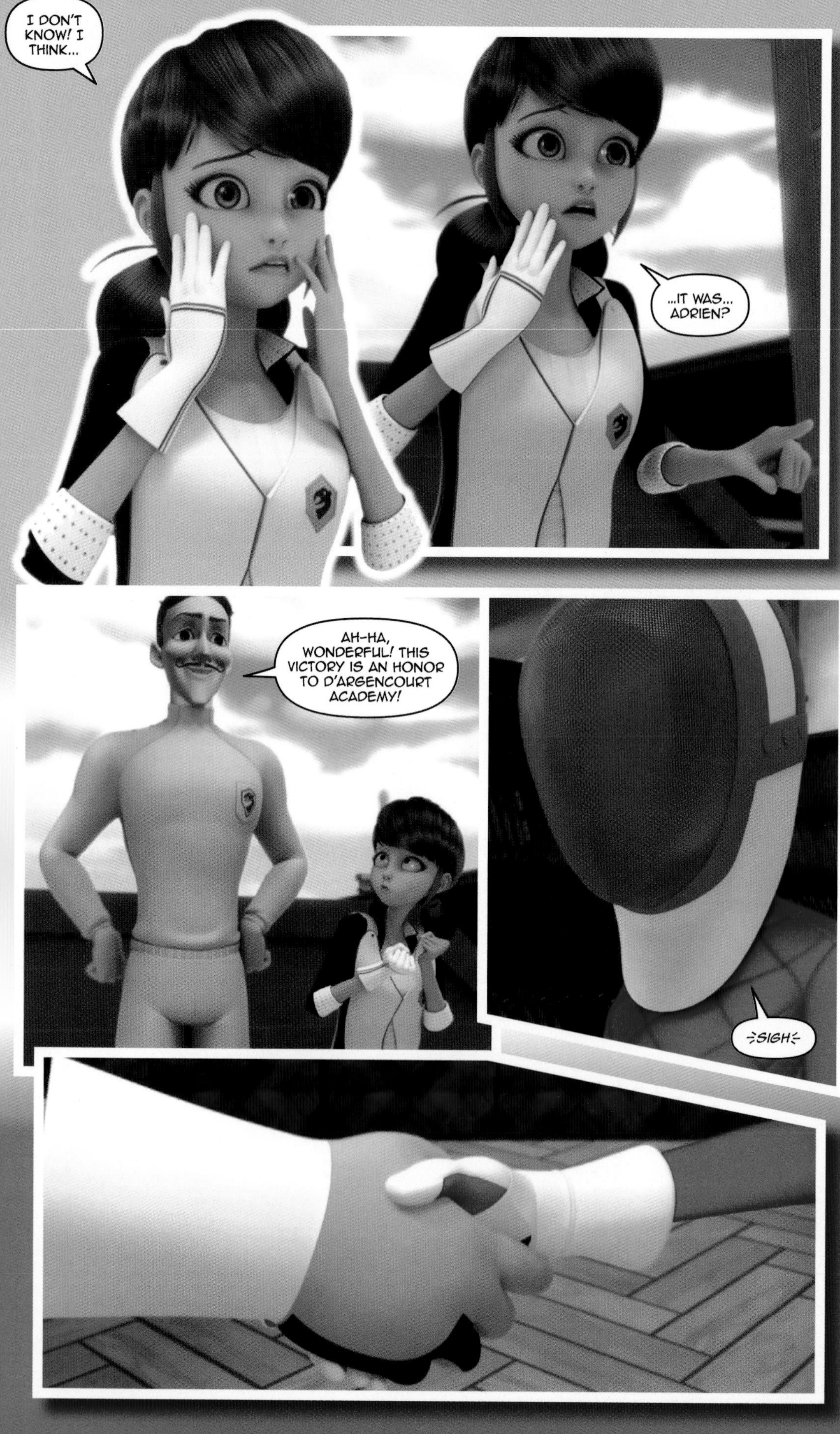
I DON'T KNOW! I THINK...
...IT WAS... ADRIEN?
AH-HA, WONDERFUL! THIS VICTORY IS AN HONOR TO D'ARGENCOURT ACADEMY!
SIGH

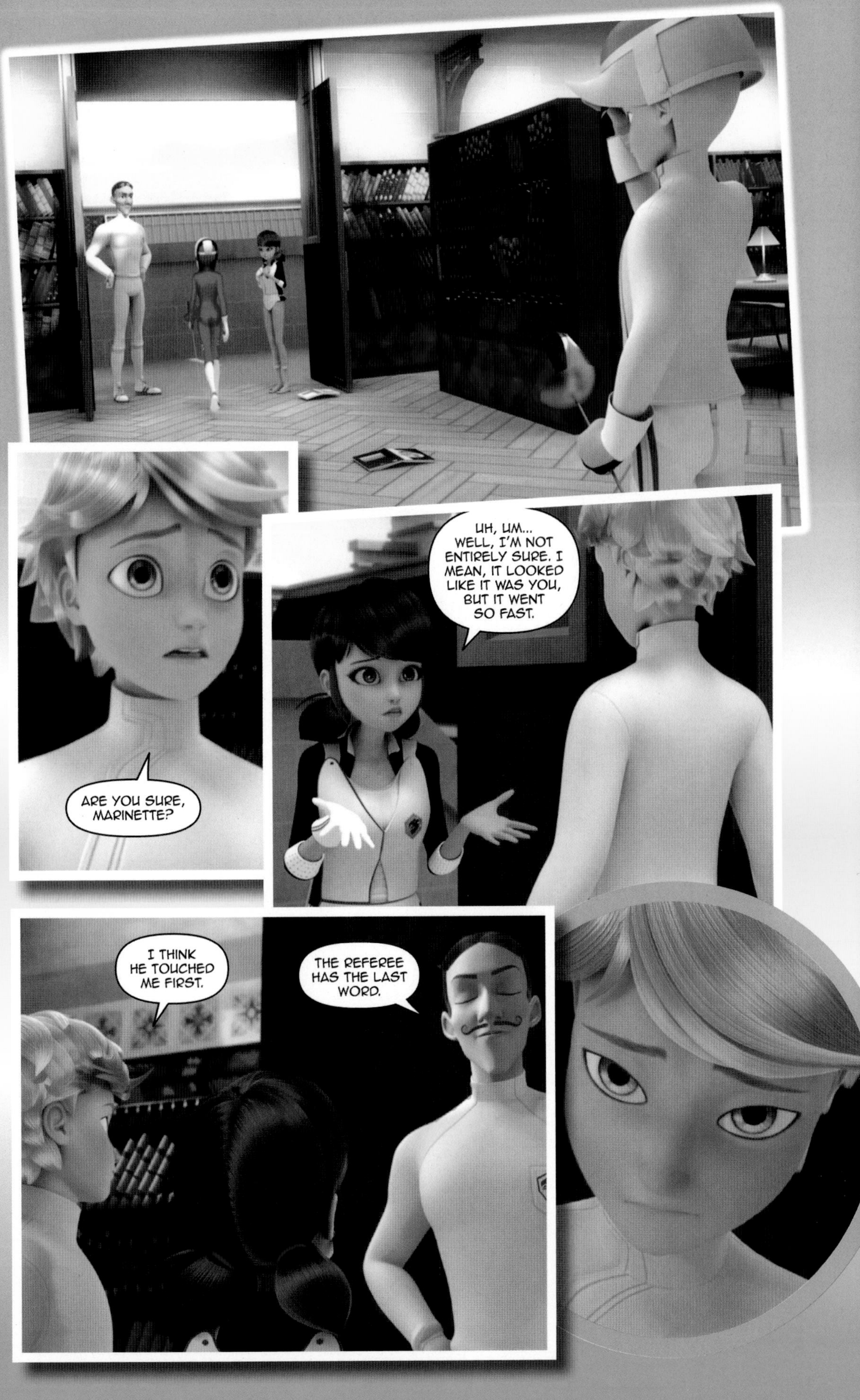
ARE YOU SURE, MARINETTE?
UH, UM... WELL, I'M NOT ENTIRELY SURE. I MEAN, IT LOOKED LIKE IT WAS YOU, BUT IT WENT SO FAST.
I THINK HE TOUCHED ME FIRST.
THE REFEREE HAS THE LAST WORD.

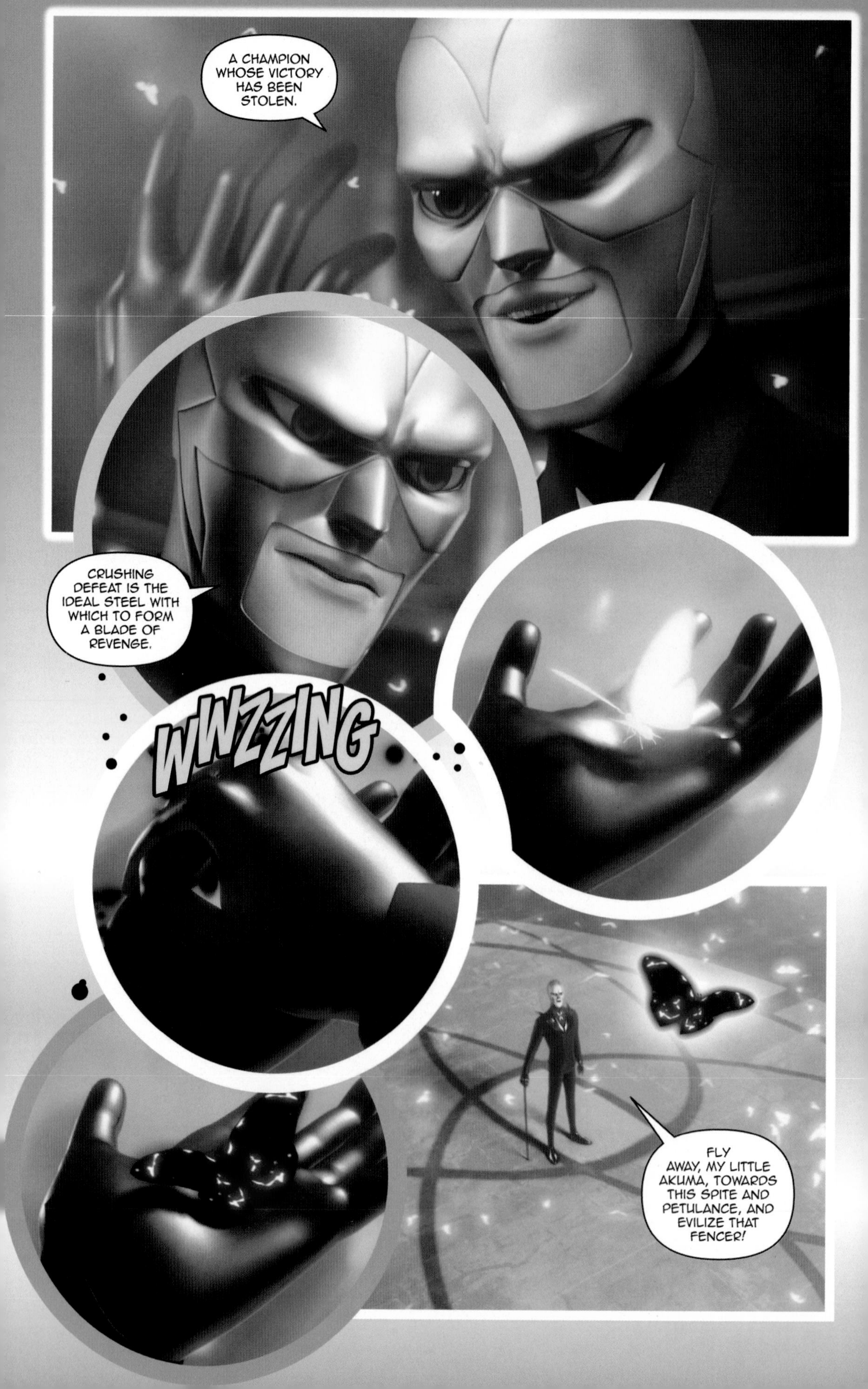
A CHAMPION WHOSE VICTORY HAS BEEN STOLEN.
CRUSHING DEFEAT IS THE IDEAL STEEL WITH WHICH TO FORM A BLADE OF REVENGE.
WWZZING
FLY AWAY, MY LITTLE AKUMA, TOWARDS THIS SPITE AND PETULANCE, AND EVILIZE THAT FENCER!

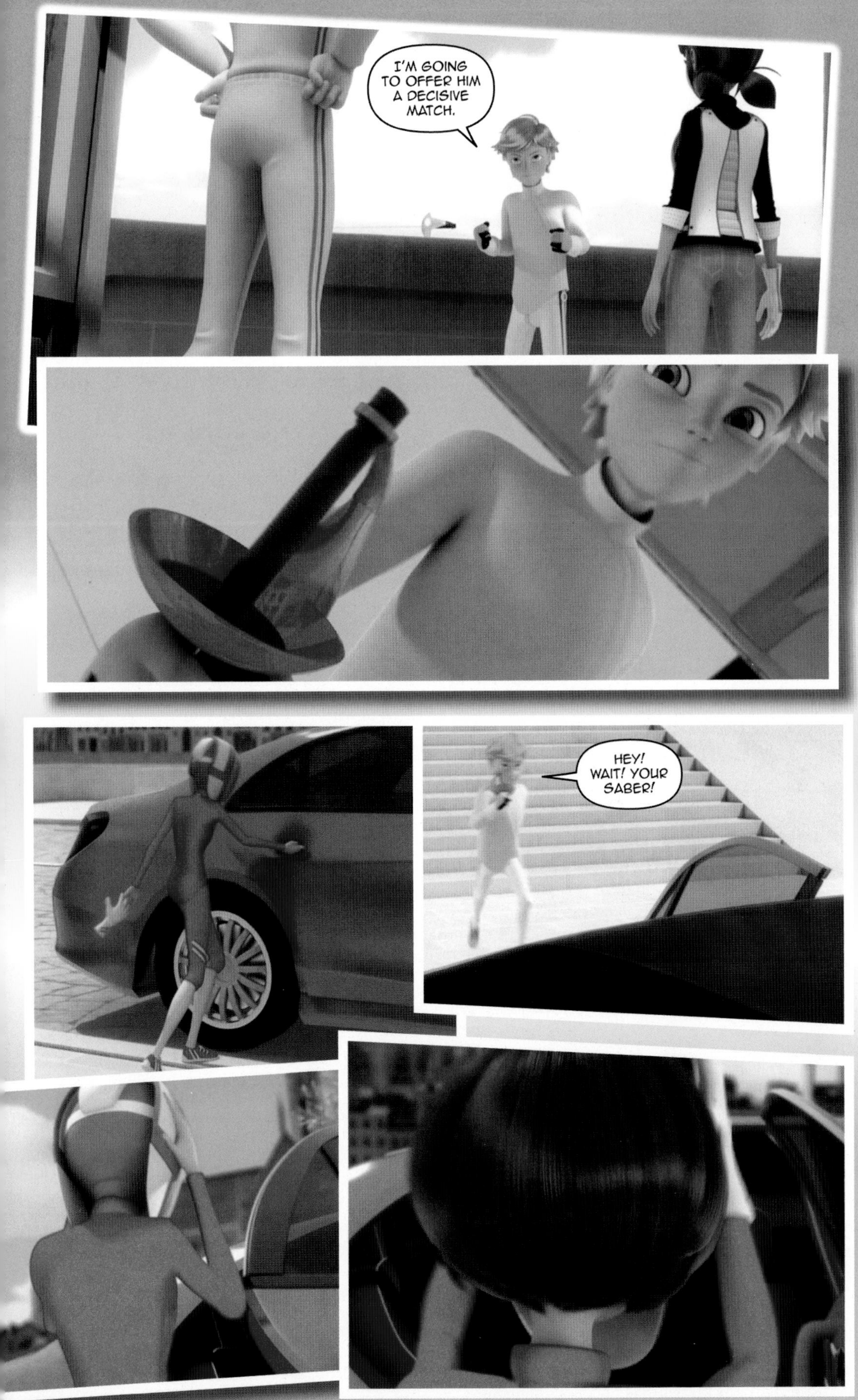
I'M GOING TO OFFER HIM A DECISIVE MATCH.
HEY! WAIT! YOUR SABER!

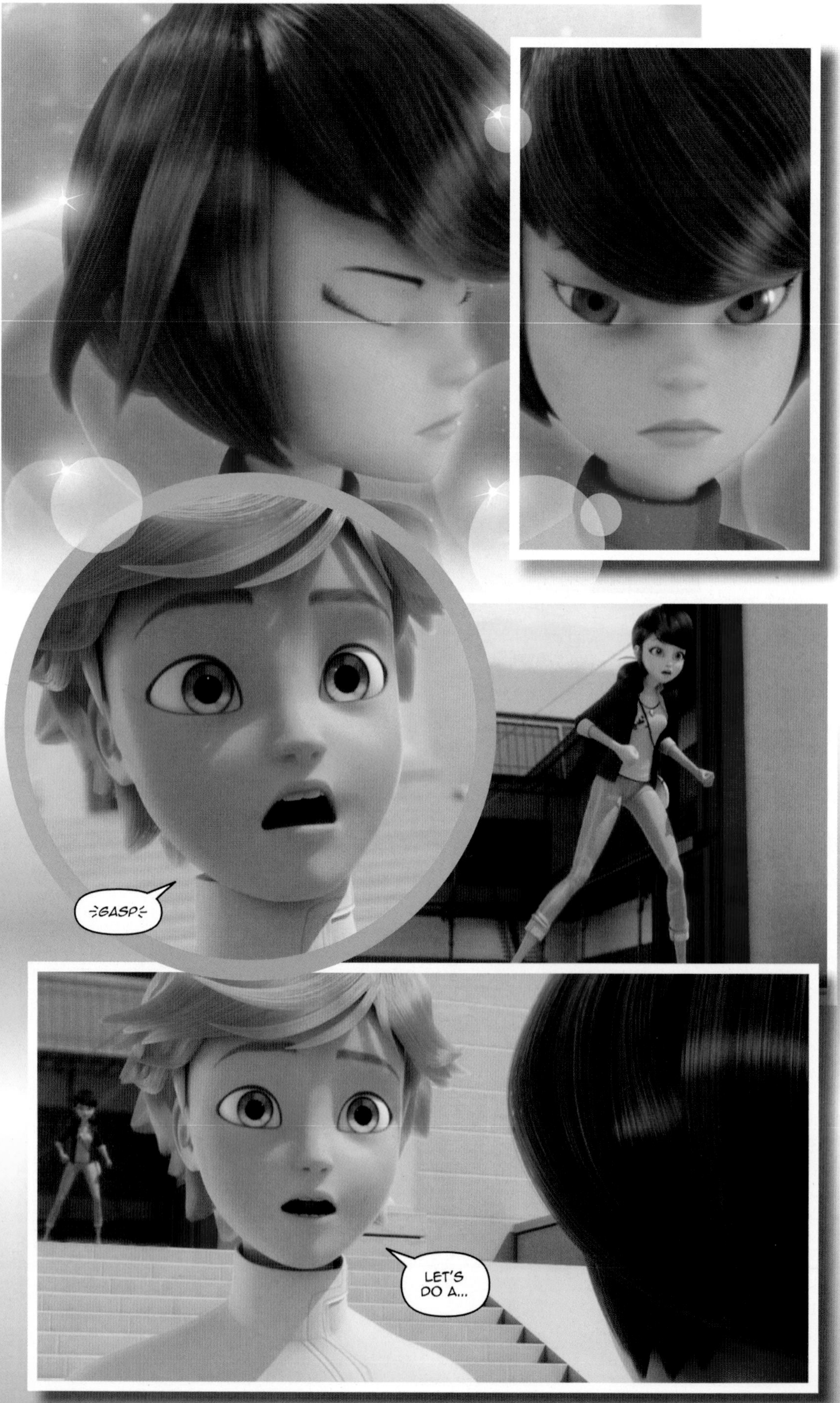
GASP
LET'S DO A...

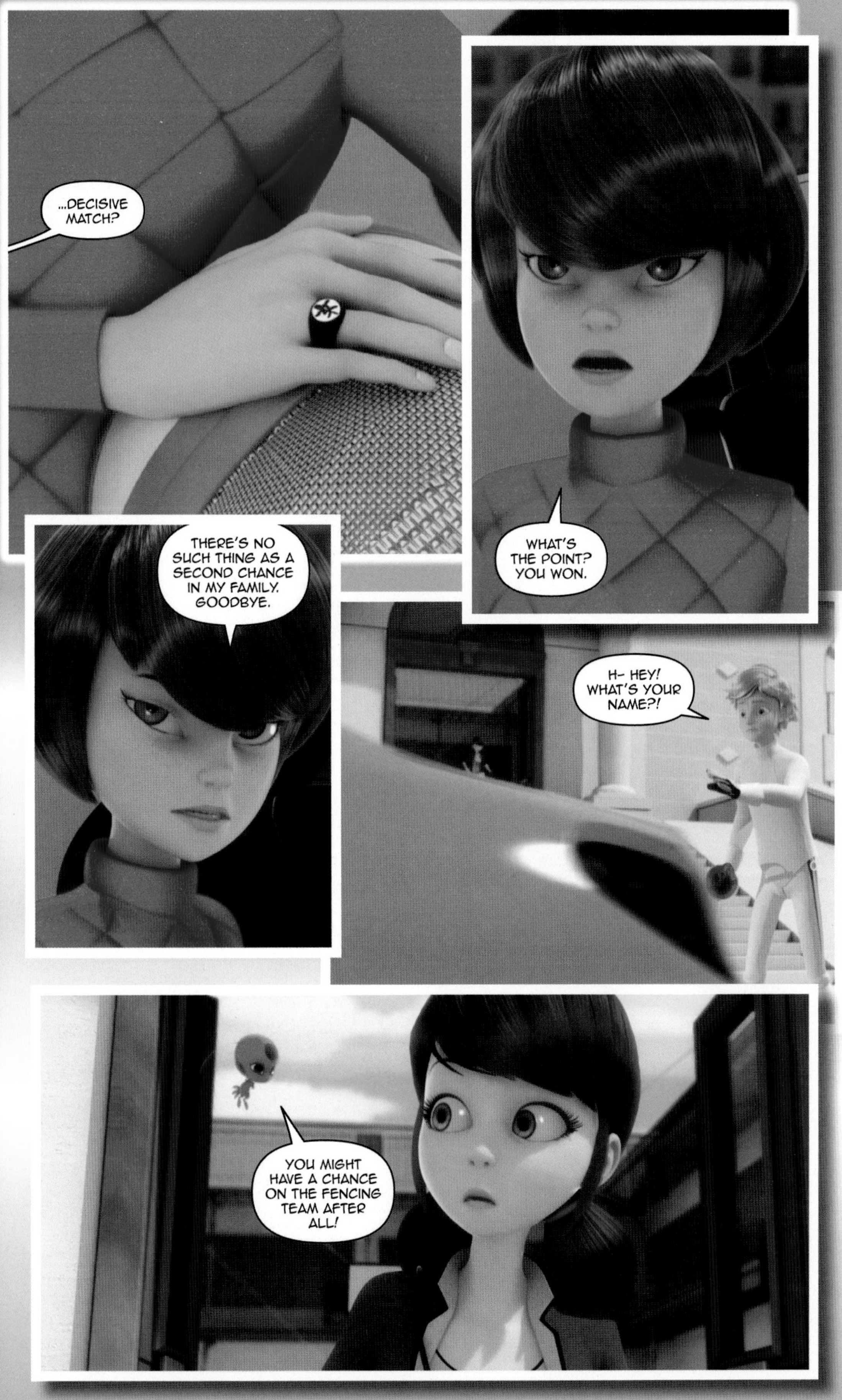
...DECISIVE MATCH?
WHAT'S THE POINT? YOU WON.
THERE'S NO SUCH THING AS A SECOND CHANCE IN MY FAMILY. GOODBYE.
H- HEY! WHAT'S YOUR NAME?!
YOU MIGHT HAVE A CHANCE ON THE FENCING TEAM AFTER ALL!

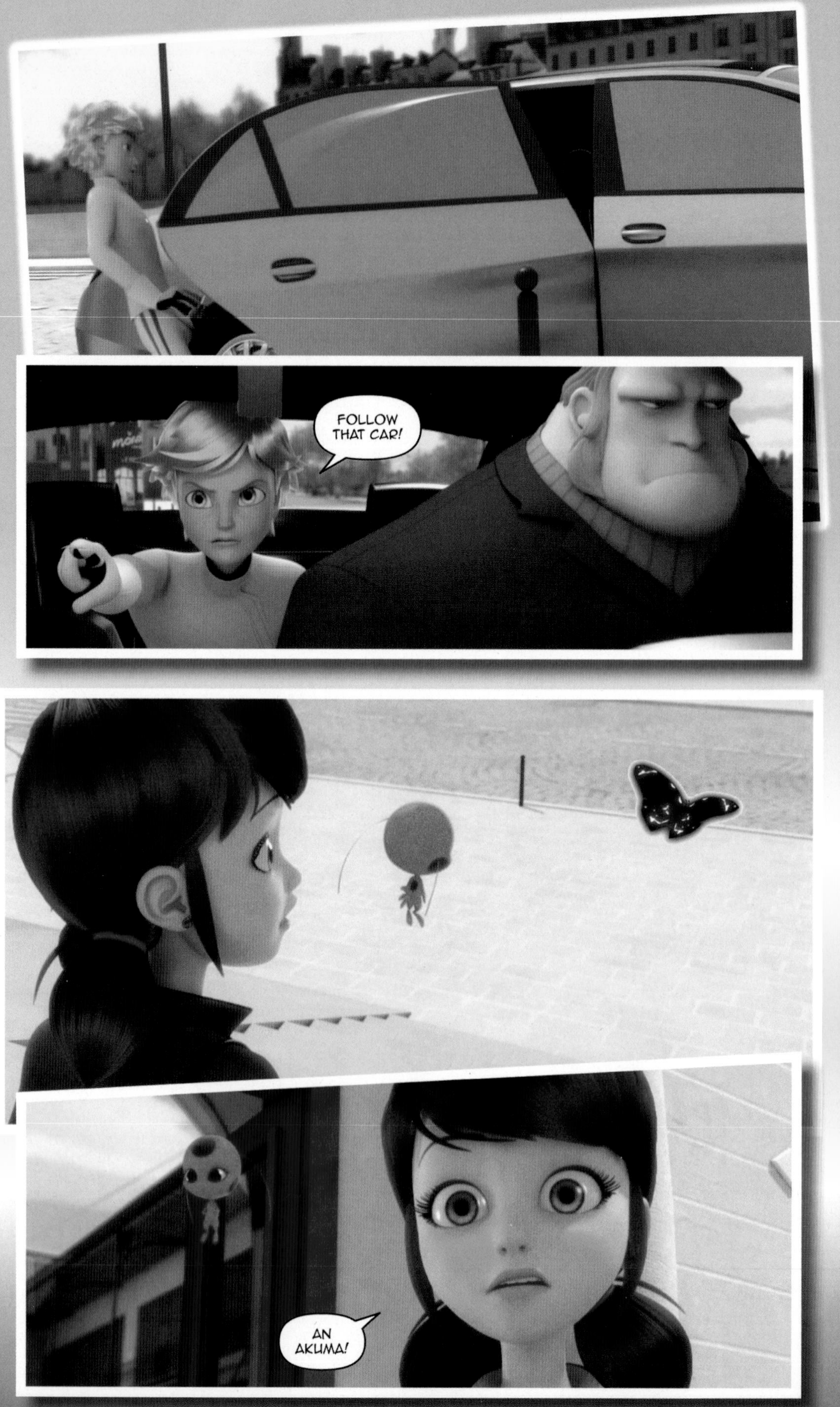
FOLLOW THAT CAR!
AN AKUMA!

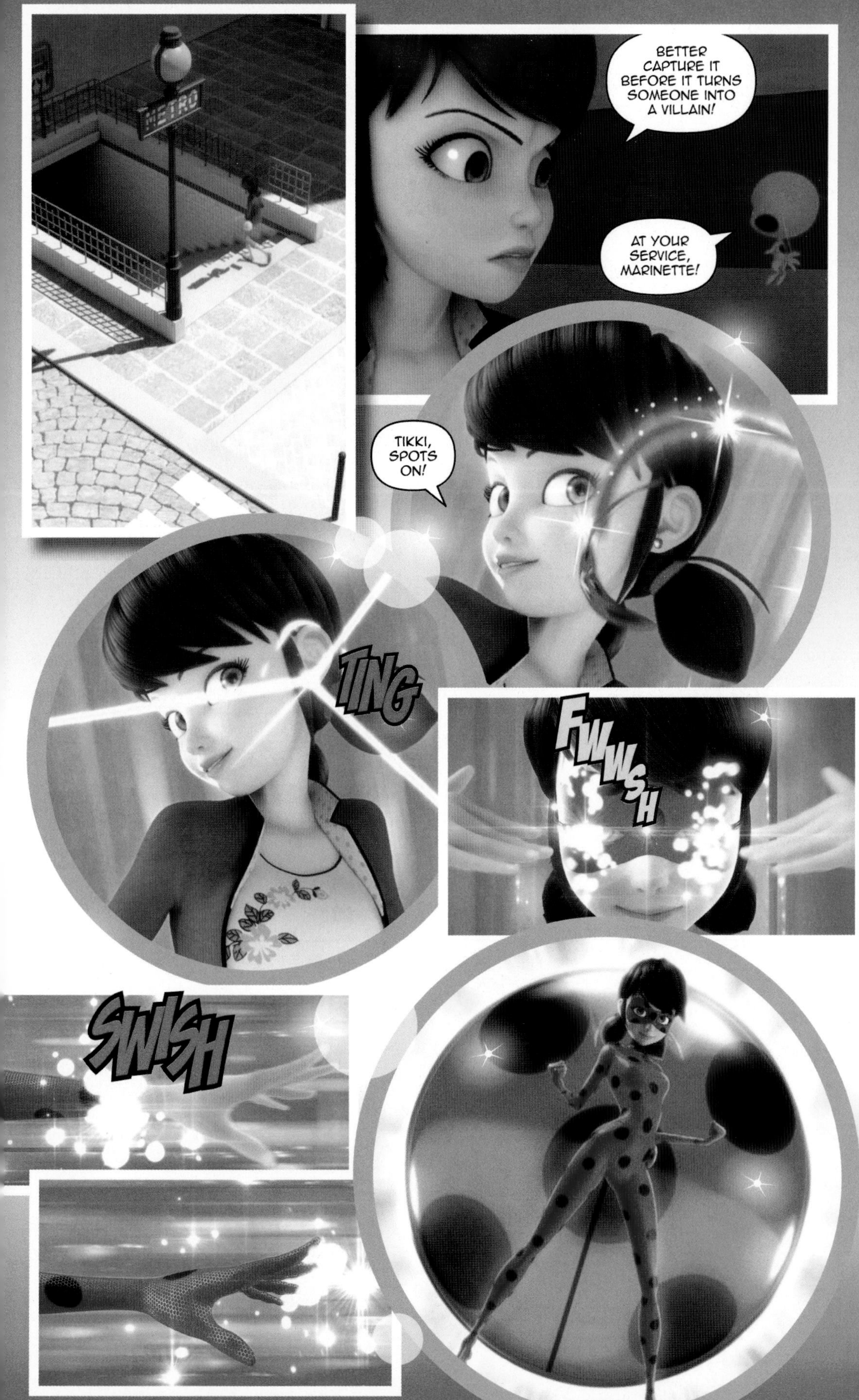
METRO
BETTER CAPTURE IT BEFORE IT TURNS SOMEONE INTO A VILLAIN!
AT YOUR SERVICE, MARINETTE!
TIKKI, SPOTS ON!
TING
FWWSH
SWISH

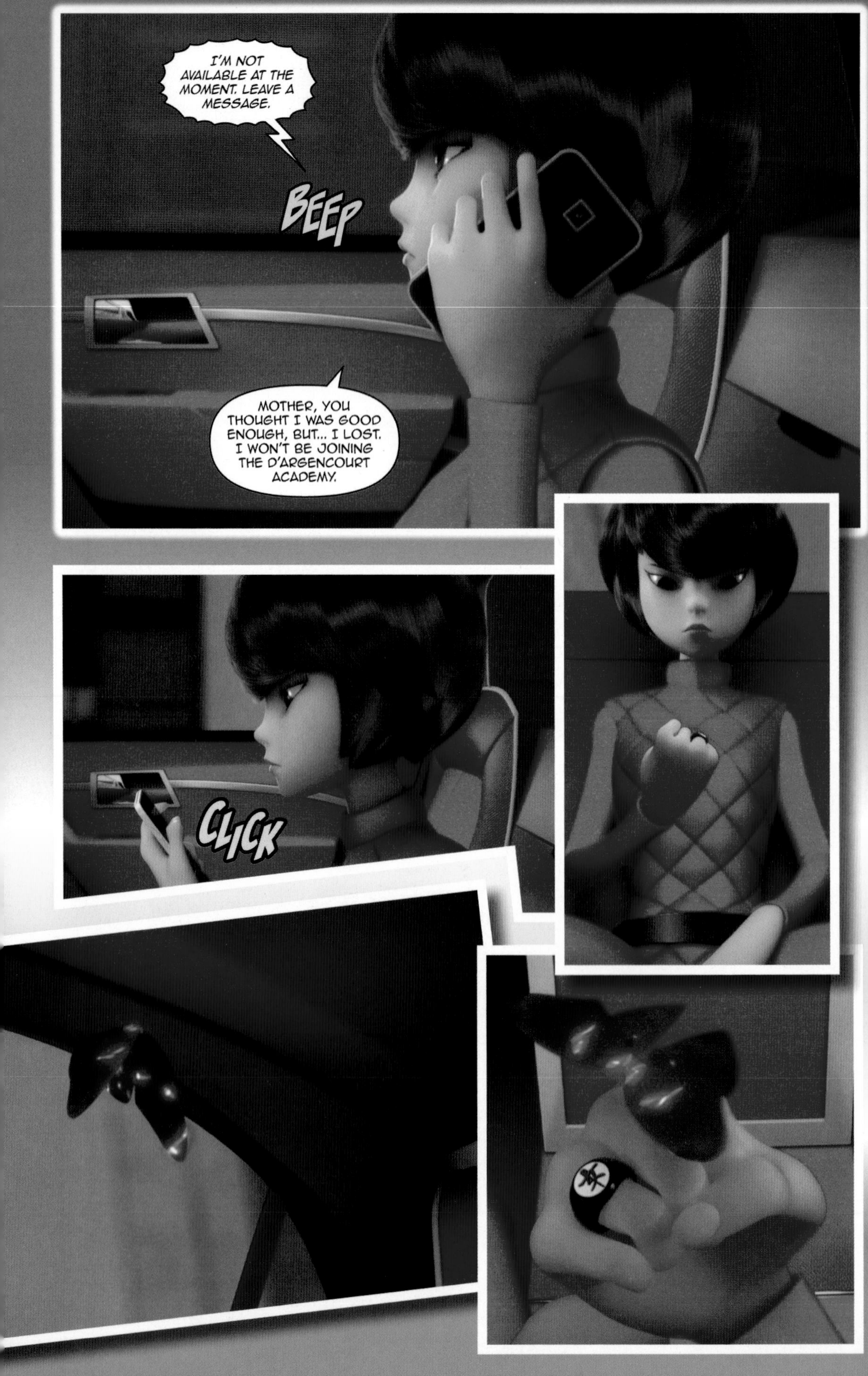
I'M NOT AVAILABLE AT THE MOMENT. LEAVE A MESSAGE.
BEEP
MOTHER, YOU THOUGHT I WAS GOOD ENOUGH, BUT... I LOST. I WON'T BE JOINING THE D'ARGENCOURT ACADEMY.
CLICK

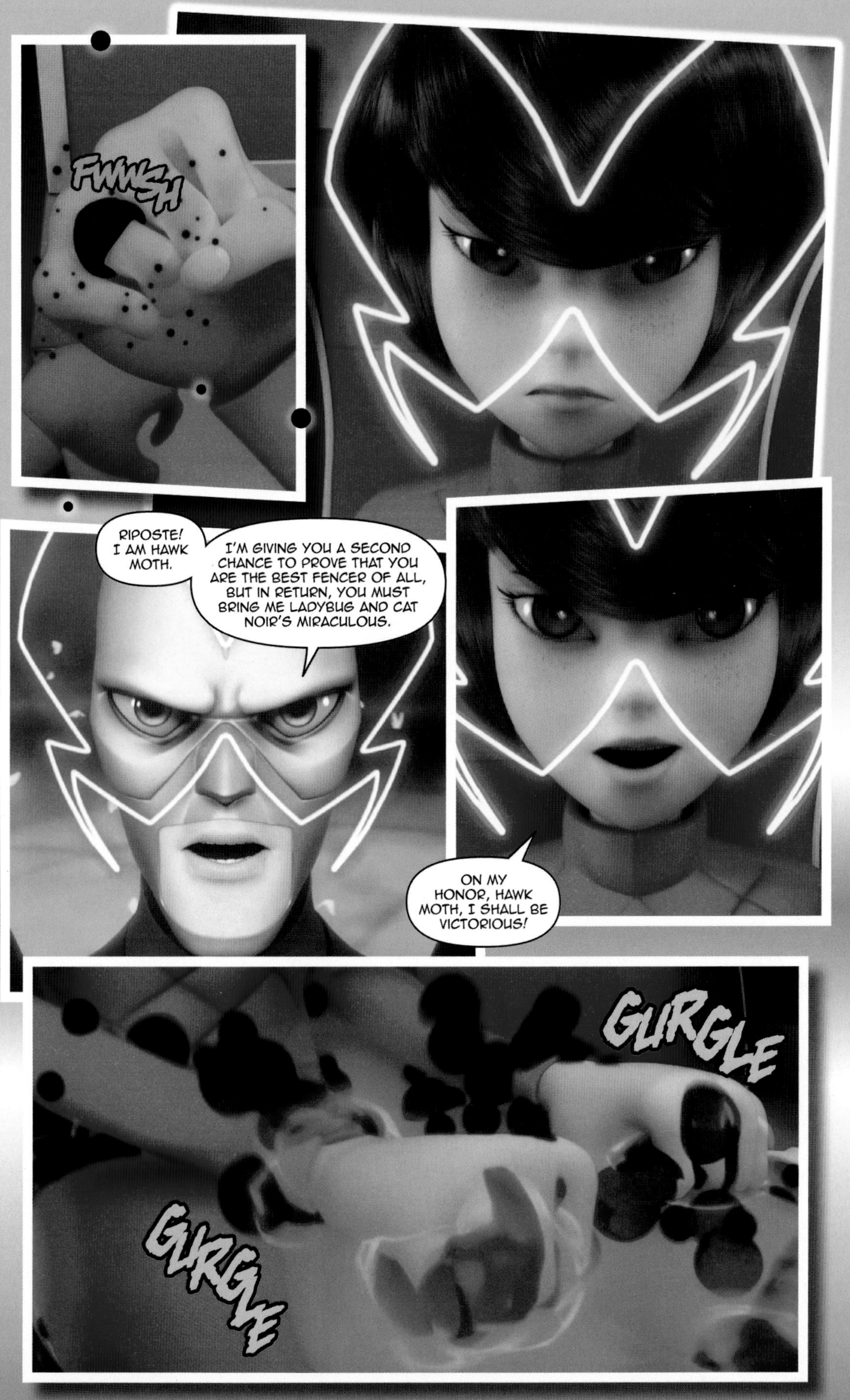
FWWSH
RIPOSTE! I AM HAWK MOTH.
I'M GIVING YOU A SECOND CHANCE TO PROVE THAT YOU ARE THE BEST FENCER OF ALL, BUT IN RETURN, YOU MUST BRING ME LADYBUG AND CAT NOIR'S MIRACULOUS.
ON MY HONOR, HAWK MOTH, I SHALL BE VICTORIOUS!
GURGLE
GURGLE

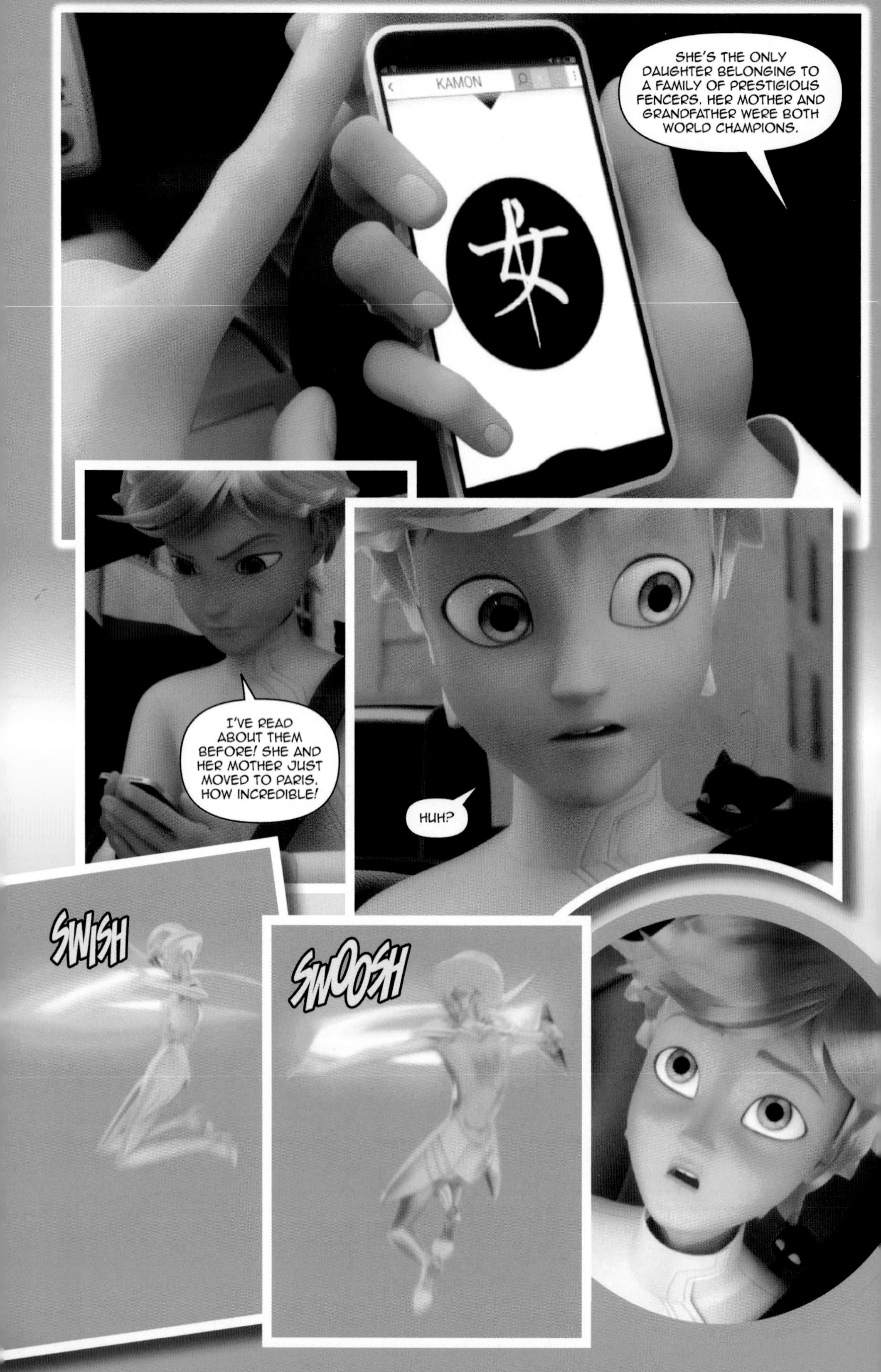
KAMON
SHE'S THE ONLY DAUGHTER BELONGING TO A FAMILY OF PRESTIGIOUS FENCERS. HER MOTHER AND GRANDFATHER WERE BOTH WORLD CHAMPIONS.
I'VE READ ABOUT THEM BEFORE! SHE AND HER MOTHER JUST MOVED TO PARIS. HOW INCREDIBLE!
HUH?
SWISH
SWOOSH

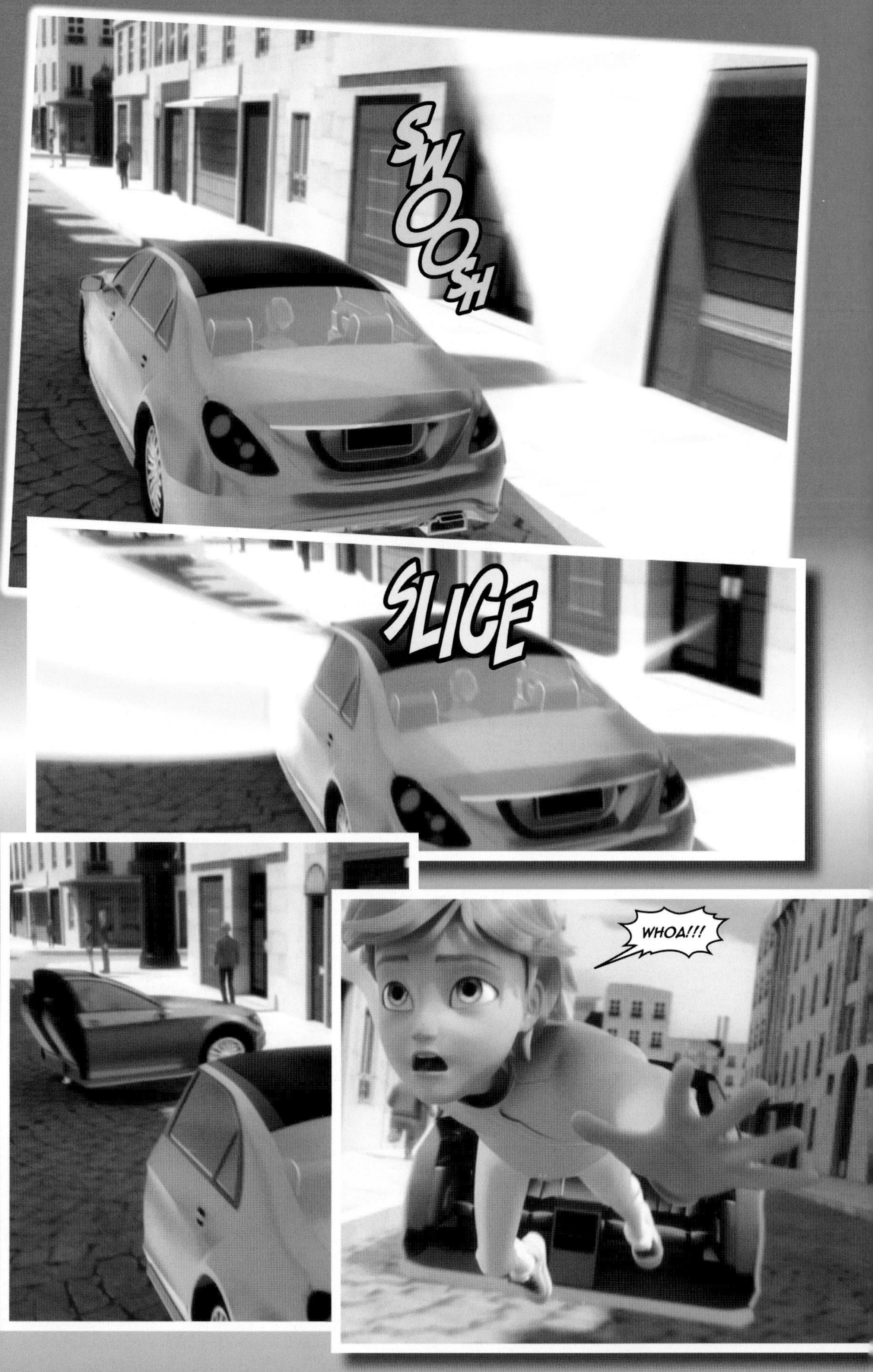
SWOOOSH
SLICE
WHOA!!!

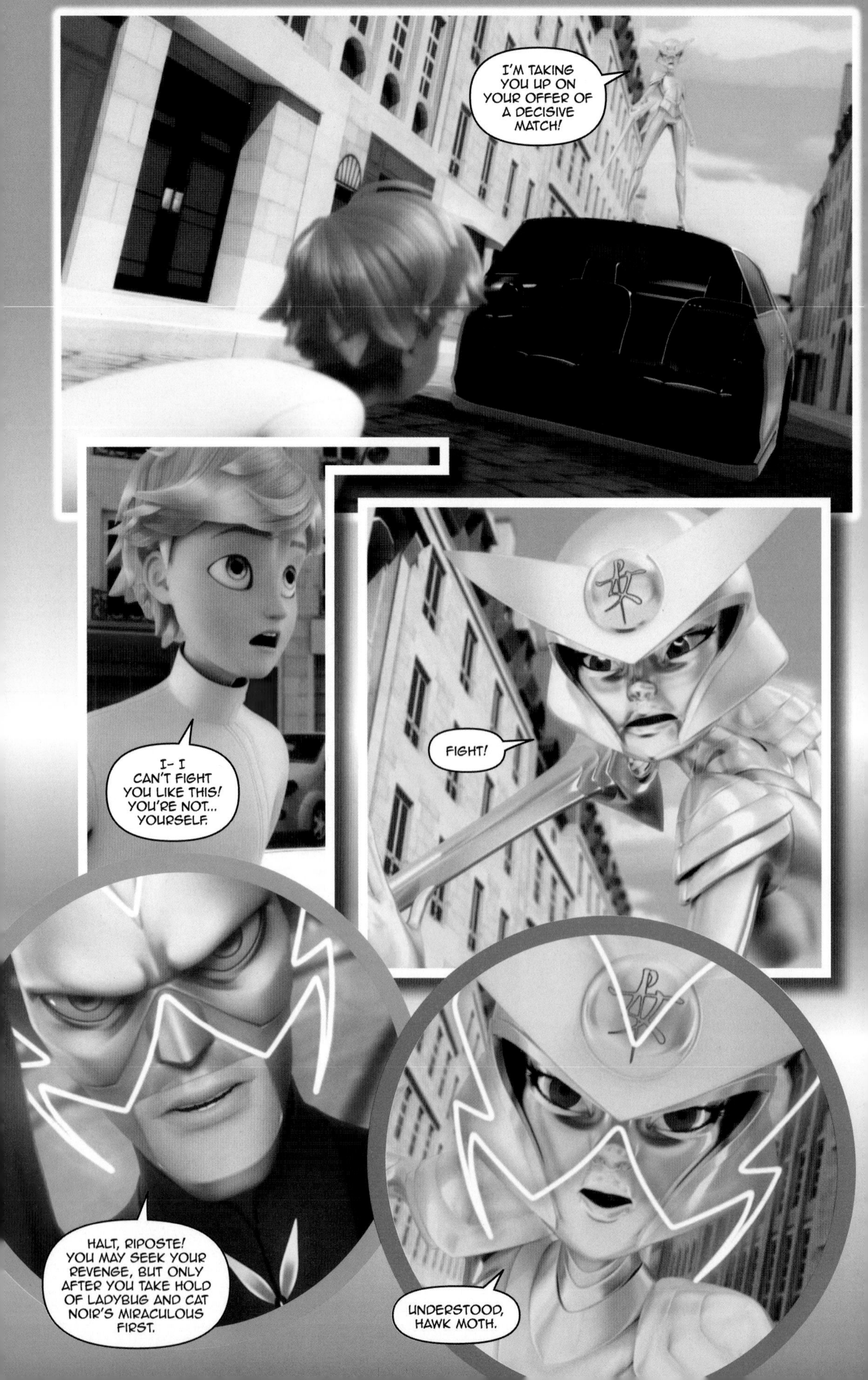
I'M TAKING YOU UP ON YOUR OFFER OF A DECISIVE MATCH!
I- I CAN'T FIGHT YOU LIKE THIS! YOU'RE NOT... YOURSELF.
FIGHT!
HALT, RIPOSTE! YOU MAY SEEK YOUR REVENGE, BUT ONLY AFTER YOU TAKE HOLD OF LADYBUG AND CAT NOIR'S MIRACULOUS FIRST.
UNDERSTOOD, HAWK MOTH.

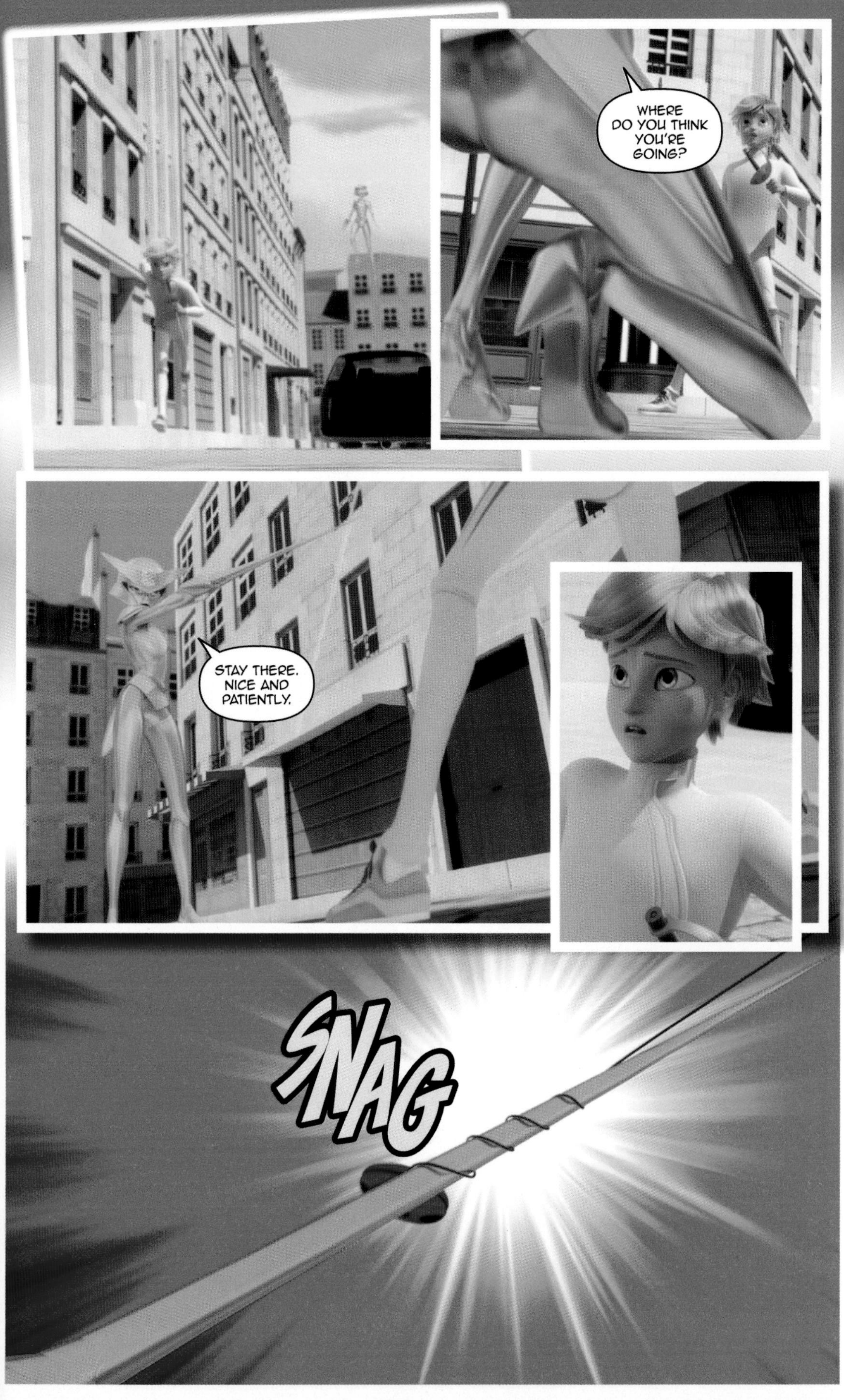
WHERE DO YOU THINK YOU'RE GOING?
STAY THERE. NICE AND PATIENTLY.
SNAG

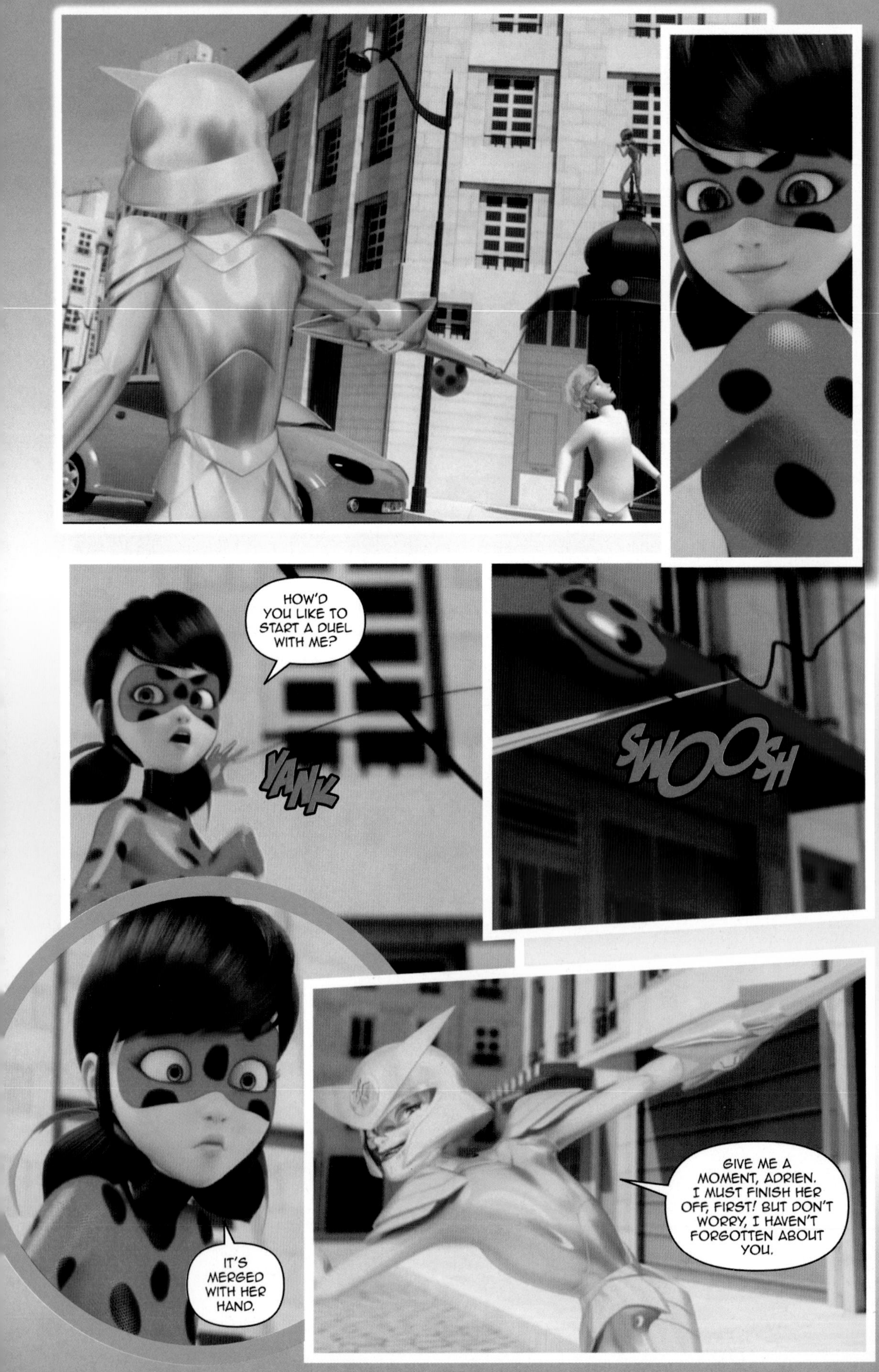
HOW'D YOU LIKE TO START A DUEL WITH ME?
YANK
SWOOSH
IT'S MERGED WITH HER HAND.
GIVE ME A MOMENT, ADRIEN. I MUST FINISH HER OFF, FIRST! BUT DON'T WORRY, I HAVEN'T FORGOTTEN ABOUT YOU.

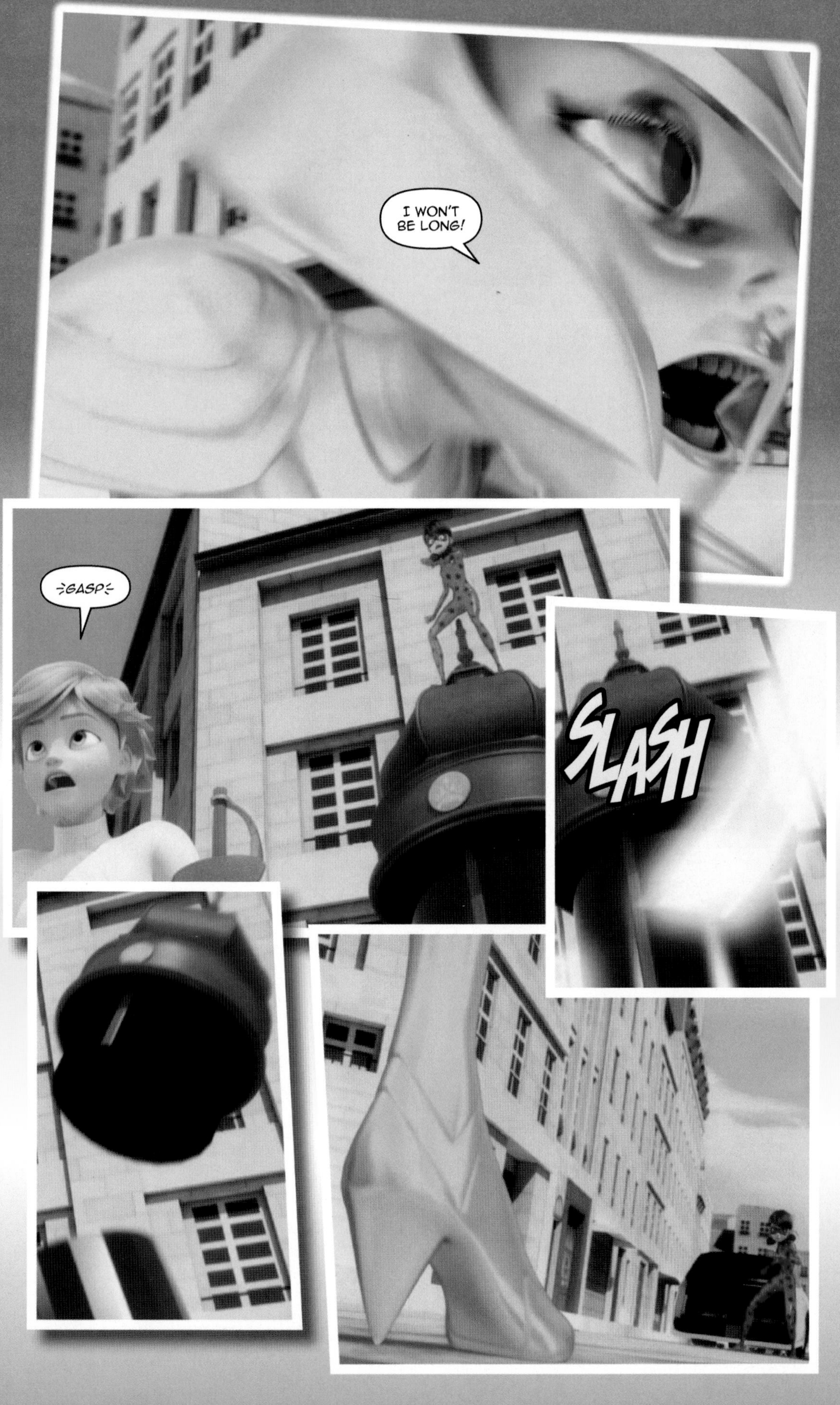
I WON'T BE LONG!
GASP
SLASH

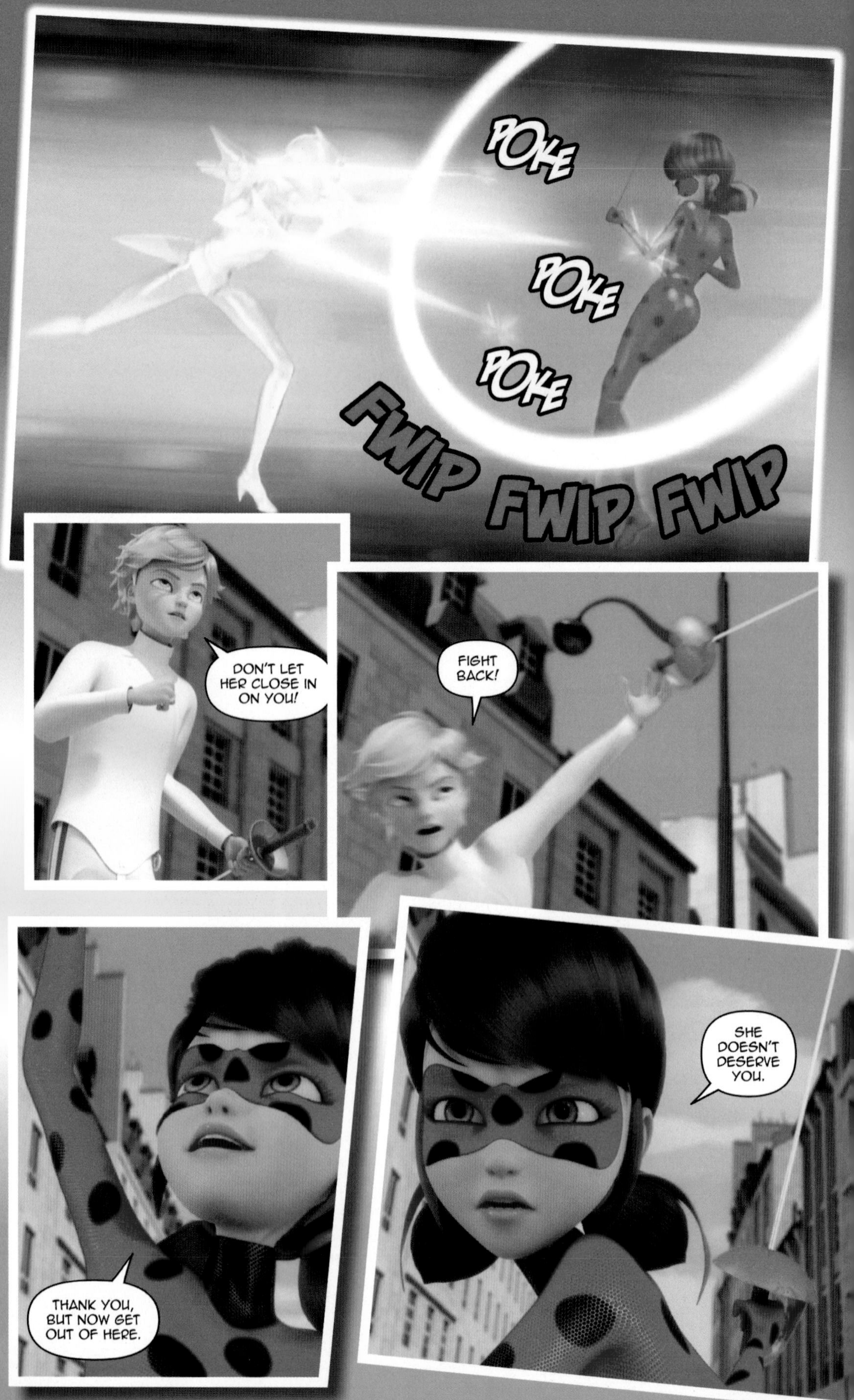
POKE
POKE
POKE
FWIP FWIP FWIP
DON'T LET HER CLOSE IN ON YOU!
FIGHT BACK!
THANK YOU, BUT NOW GET OUT OF HERE.
SHE DOESN'T DESERVE YOU.

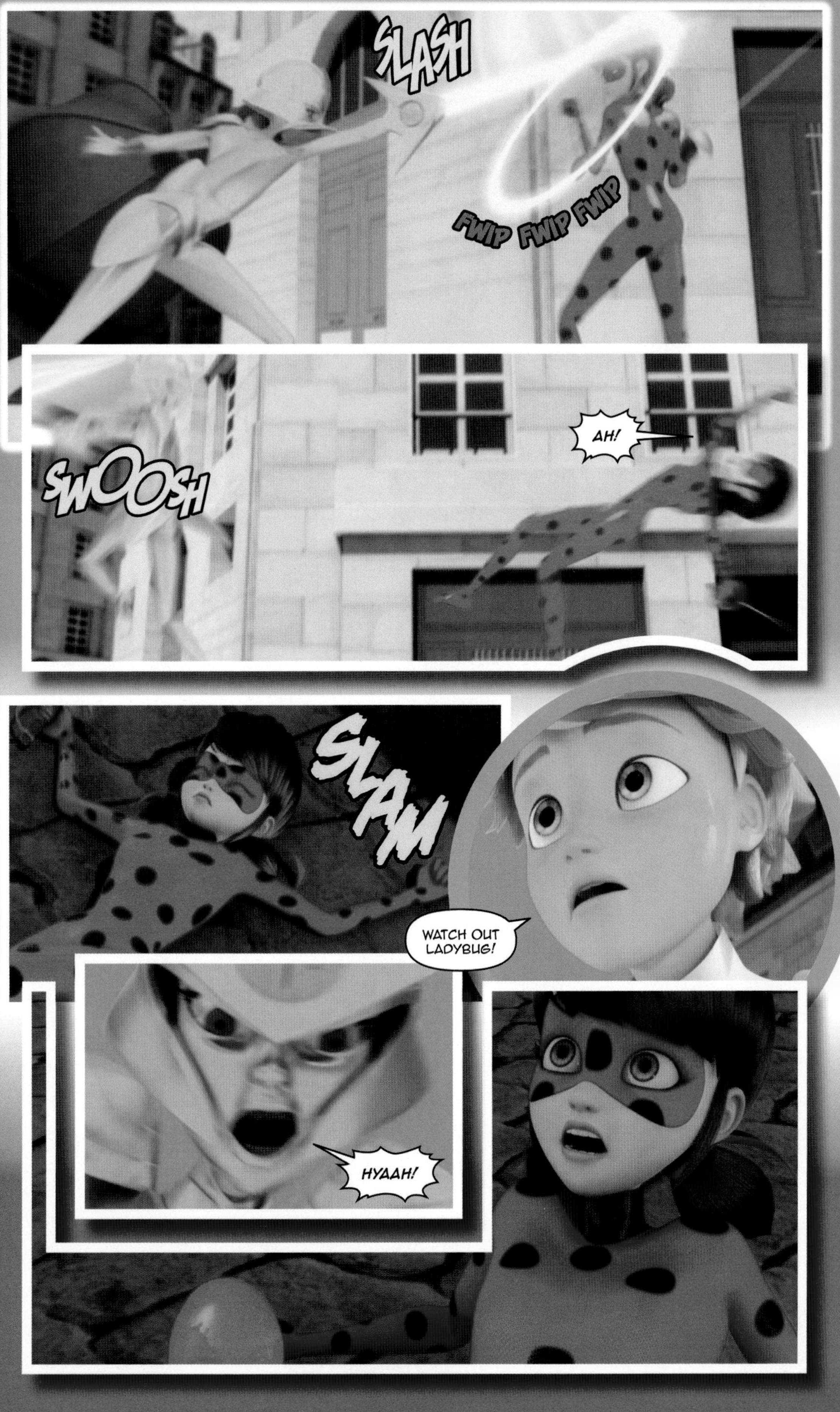
SLASH
FWIP FWIP FWIP
SWOOSH
AH!
SLAM
WATCH OUT LADYBUG!
HYAAH!

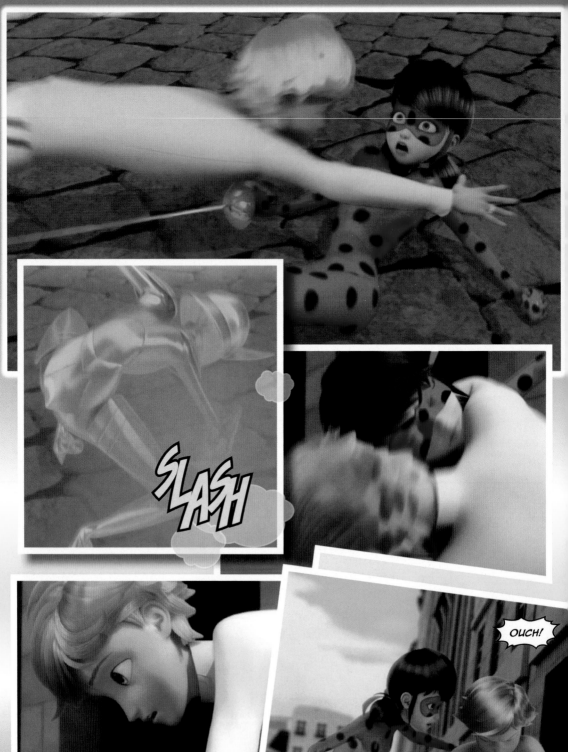

SLASH

OUCH!

ARE YOU HURT?

I'M FINE.

I NEED TO GET YOU AS FAR AWAY FROM THAT GIRL AS POSSIBLE.

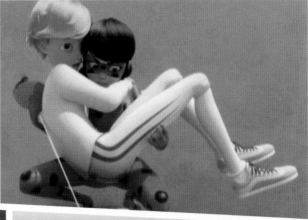

SOUNDS LIKE A PLAN.

WHAT KIND OF FENCING WAS THAT?

NOTHING LIKE I'VE EVER SEEN BEFORE.

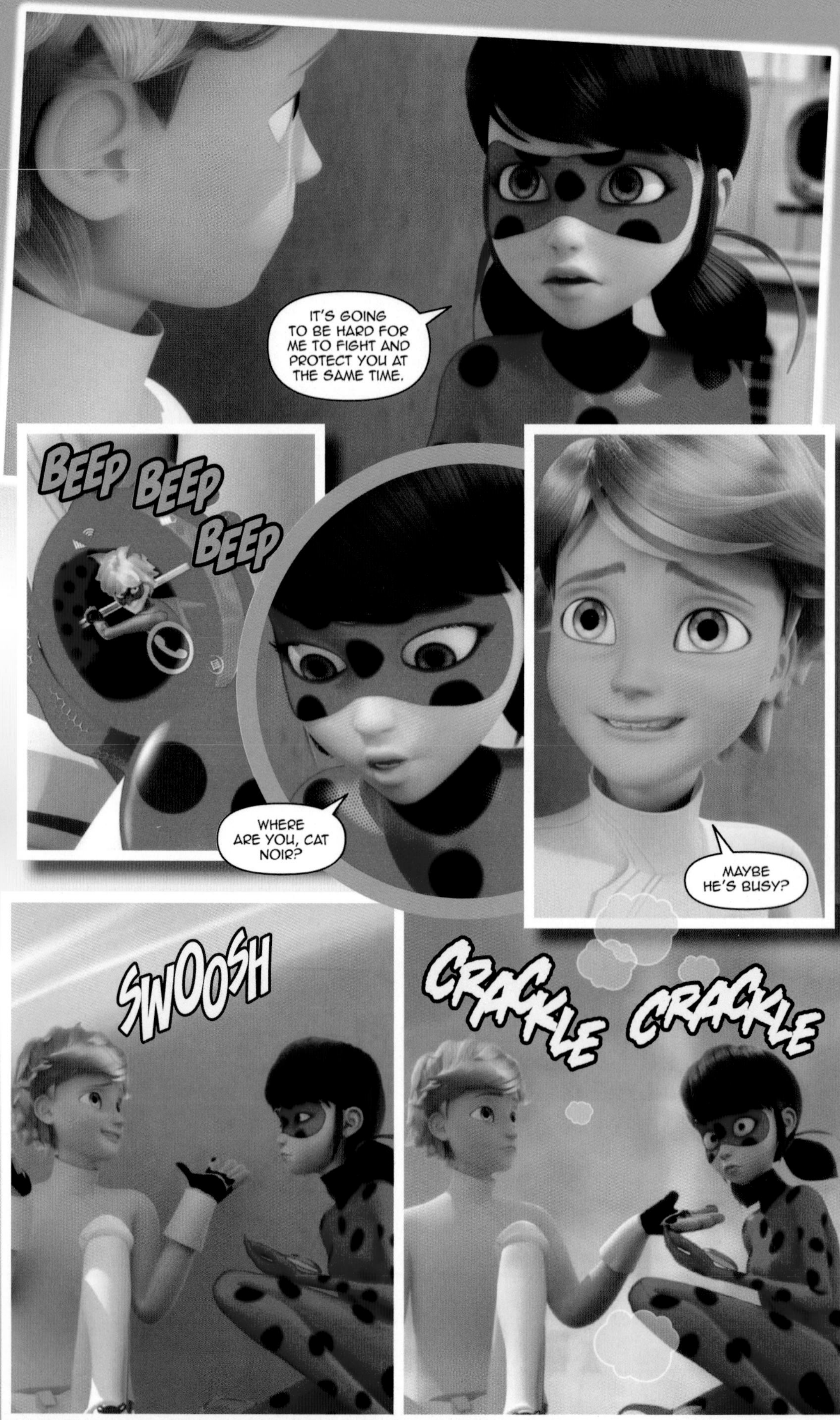
IT'S GOING TO BE HARD FOR ME TO FIGHT AND PROTECT YOU AT THE SAME TIME.
BEEP BEEP BEEP
WHERE ARE YOU, CAT NOIR?
MAYBE HE'S BUSY?
SWOOSH
CRACKLE CRACKLE

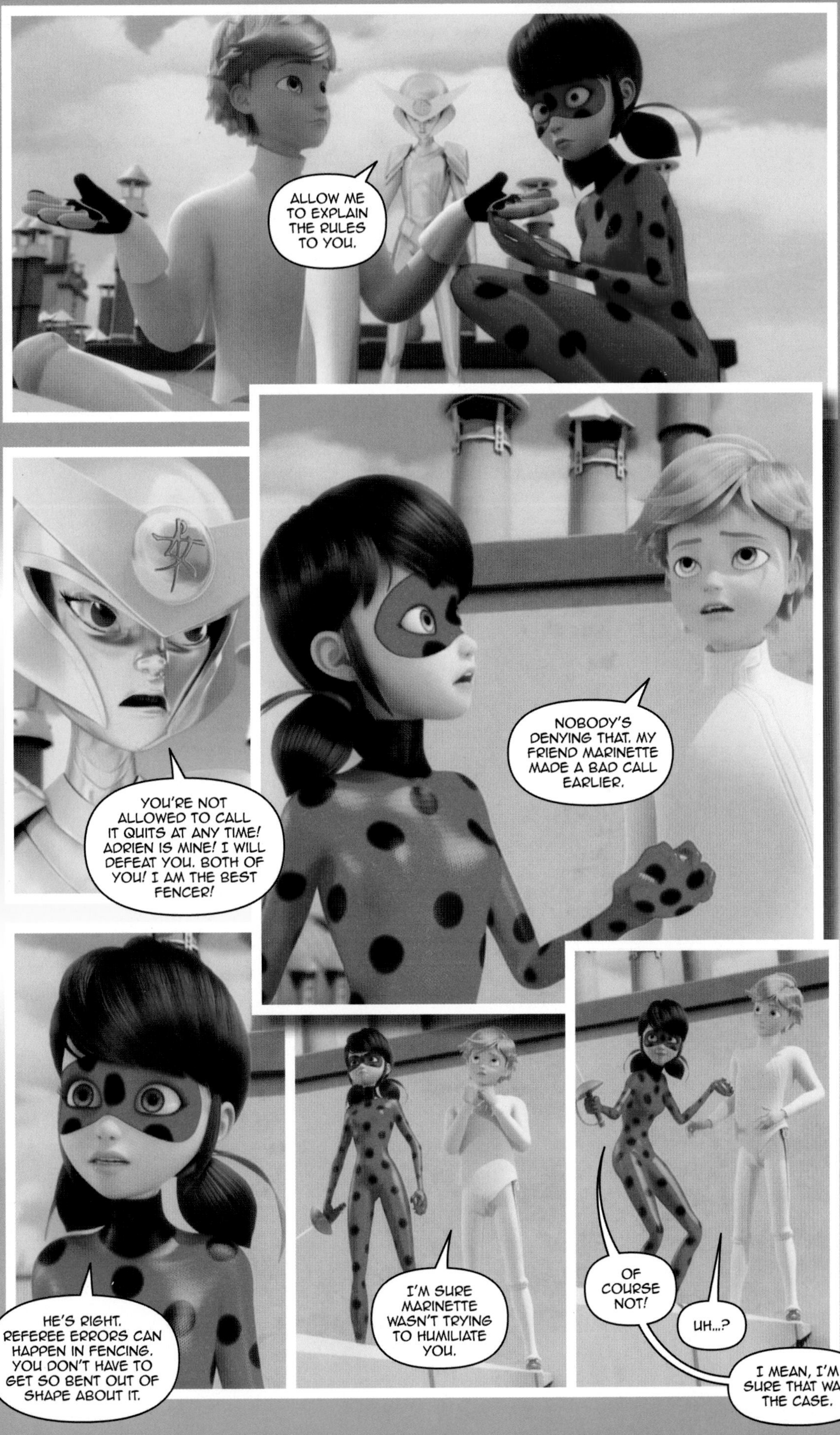
ALLOW ME TO EXPLAIN THE RULES TO YOU.
YOU'RE NOT ALLOWED TO CALL IT QUITS AT ANY TIME! ADRIEN IS MINE! I WILL DEFEAT YOU. BOTH OF YOU! I AM THE BEST FENCER!
NOBODY'S DENYING THAT. MY FRIEND MARINETTE MADE A BAD CALL EARLIER.
HE'S RIGHT. REFEREE ERRORS CAN HAPPEN IN FENCING. YOU DON'T HAVE TO GET SO BENT OUT OF SHAPE ABOUT IT.
I'M SURE MARINETTE WASN'T TRYING TO HUMILIATE YOU.
OF COURSE NOT!
UH...?
I MEAN, I'M SURE THAT WAS THE CASE.

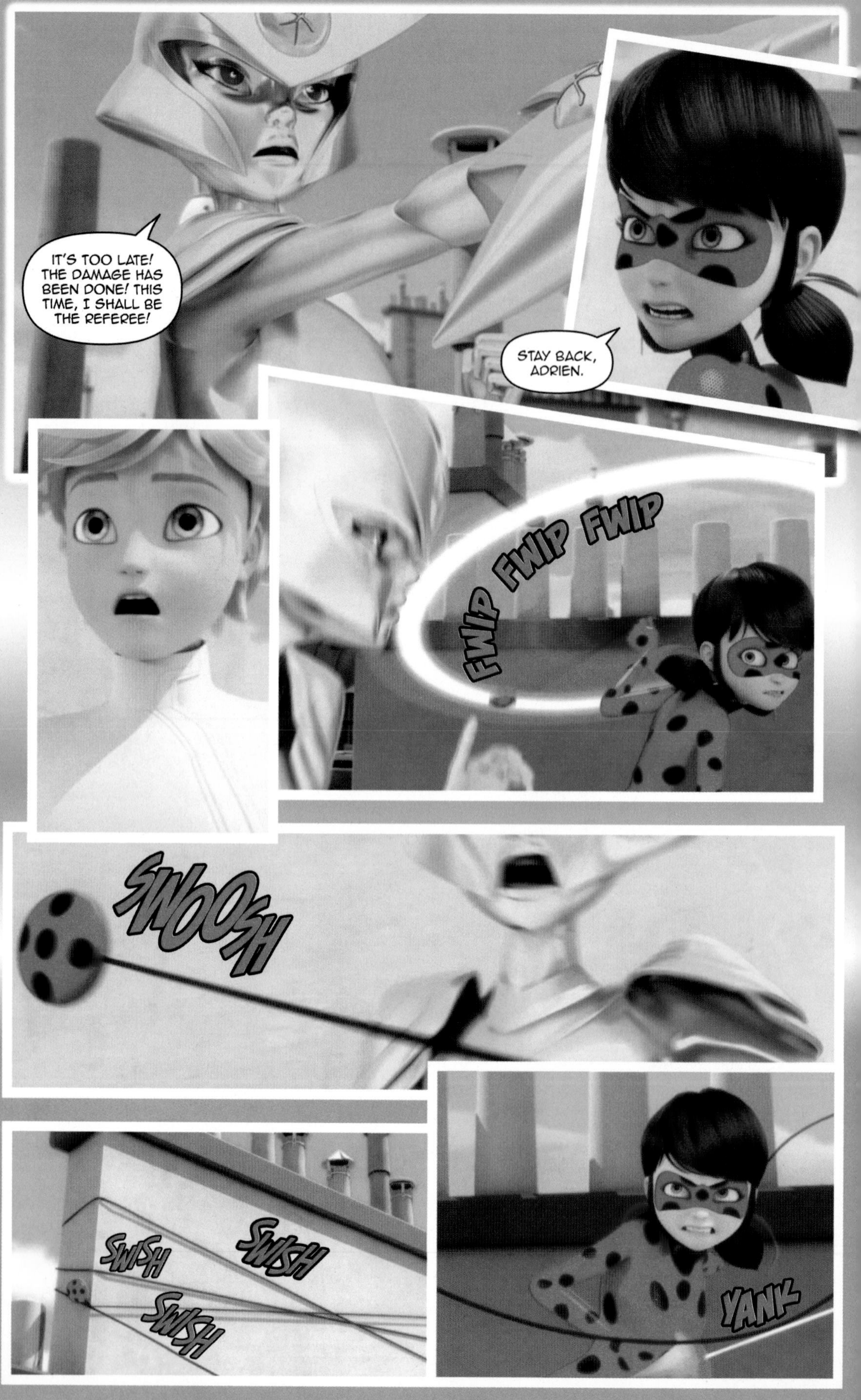
IT'S TOO LATE! THE DAMAGE HAS BEEN DONE! THIS TIME, I SHALL BE THE REFEREE!
STAY BACK, ADRIEN.
FWIP FWIP FWIP
SWOOSH
SWISH
SWISH
SWISH
YANK

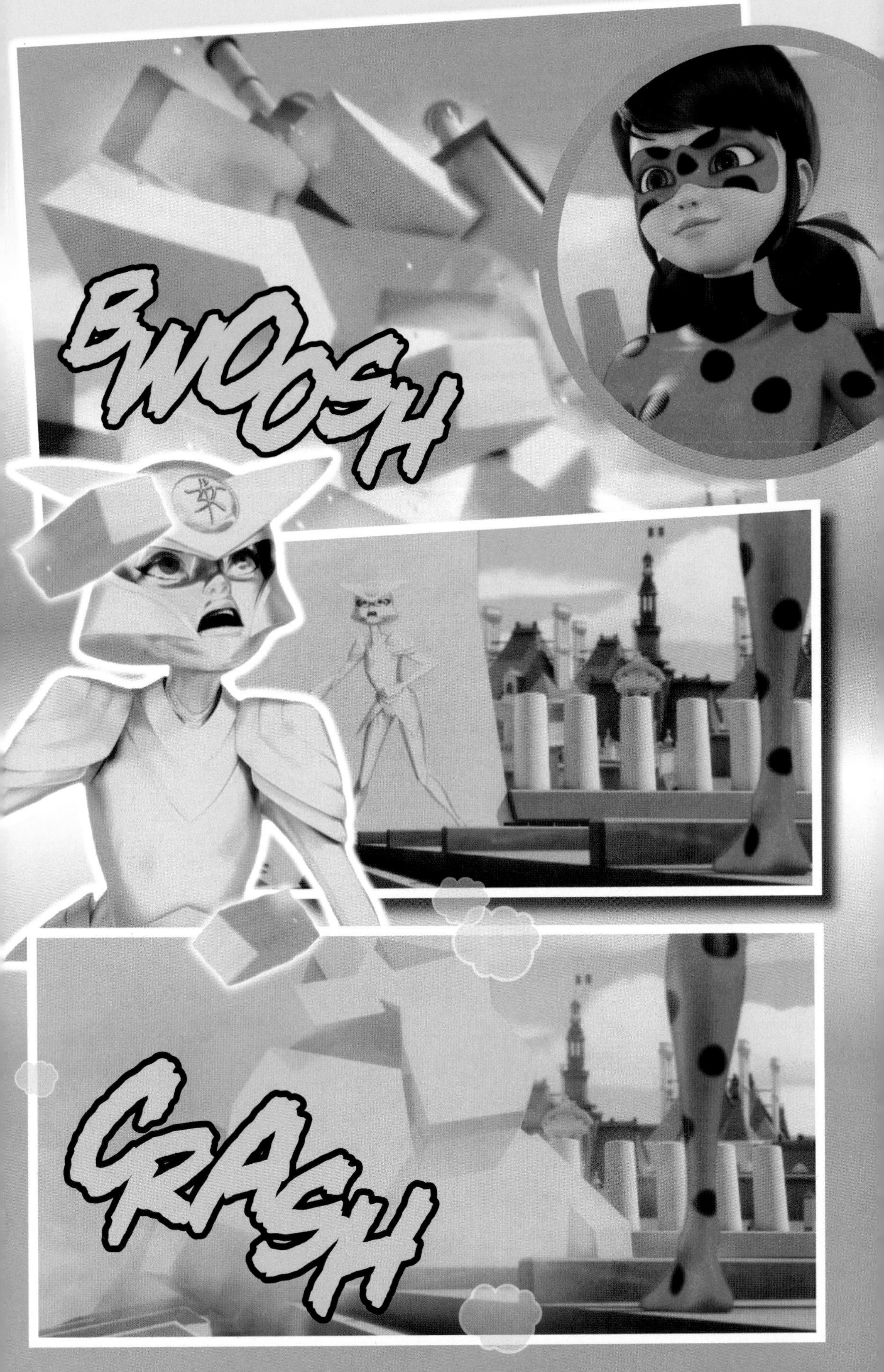
BWOOSH
CRASH

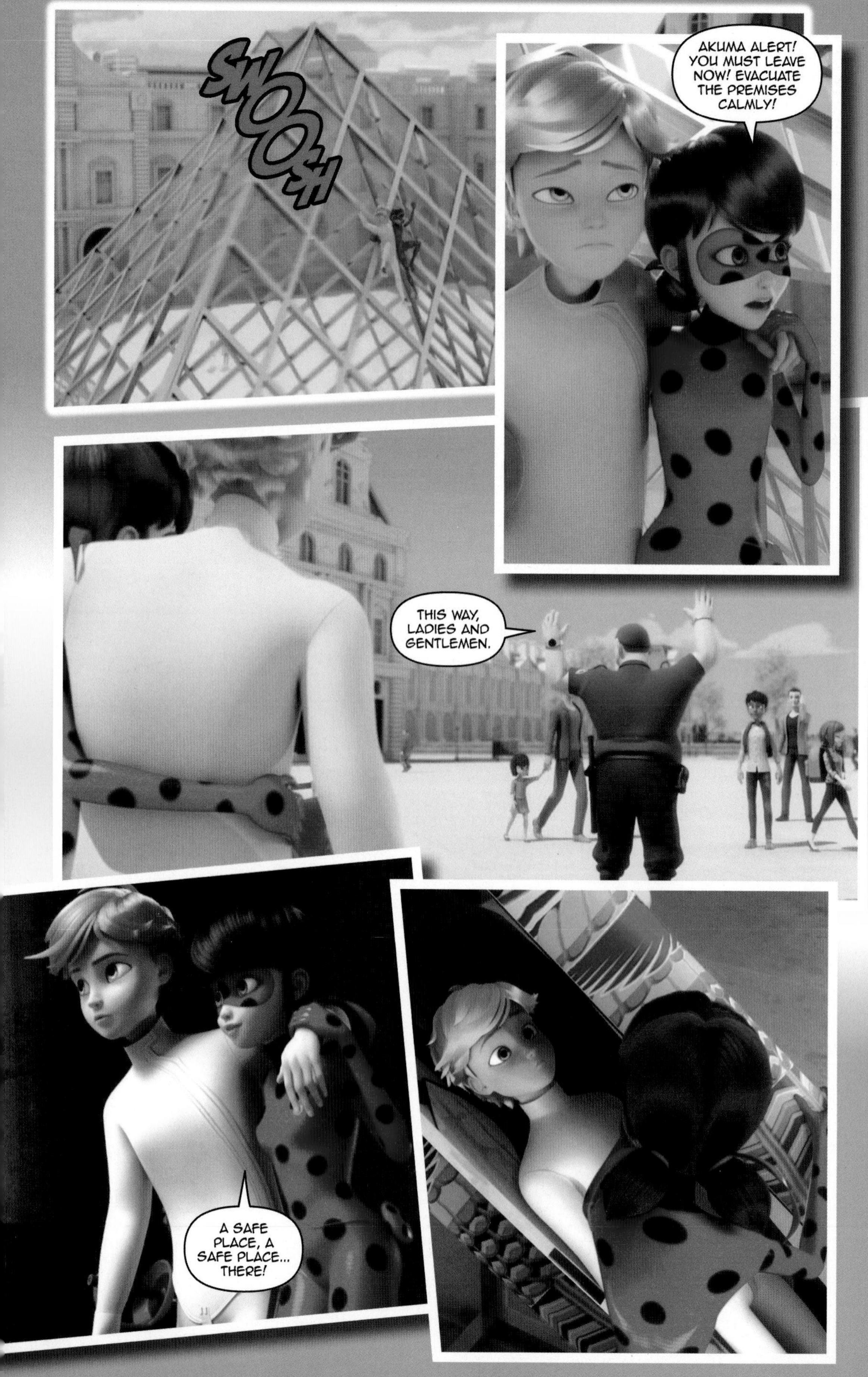
SWOOSH
AKUMA ALERT! YOU MUST LEAVE NOW! EVACUATE THE PREMISES CALMLY!
THIS WAY, LADIES AND GENTLEMEN.
A SAFE PLACE, A SAFE PLACE... THERE!

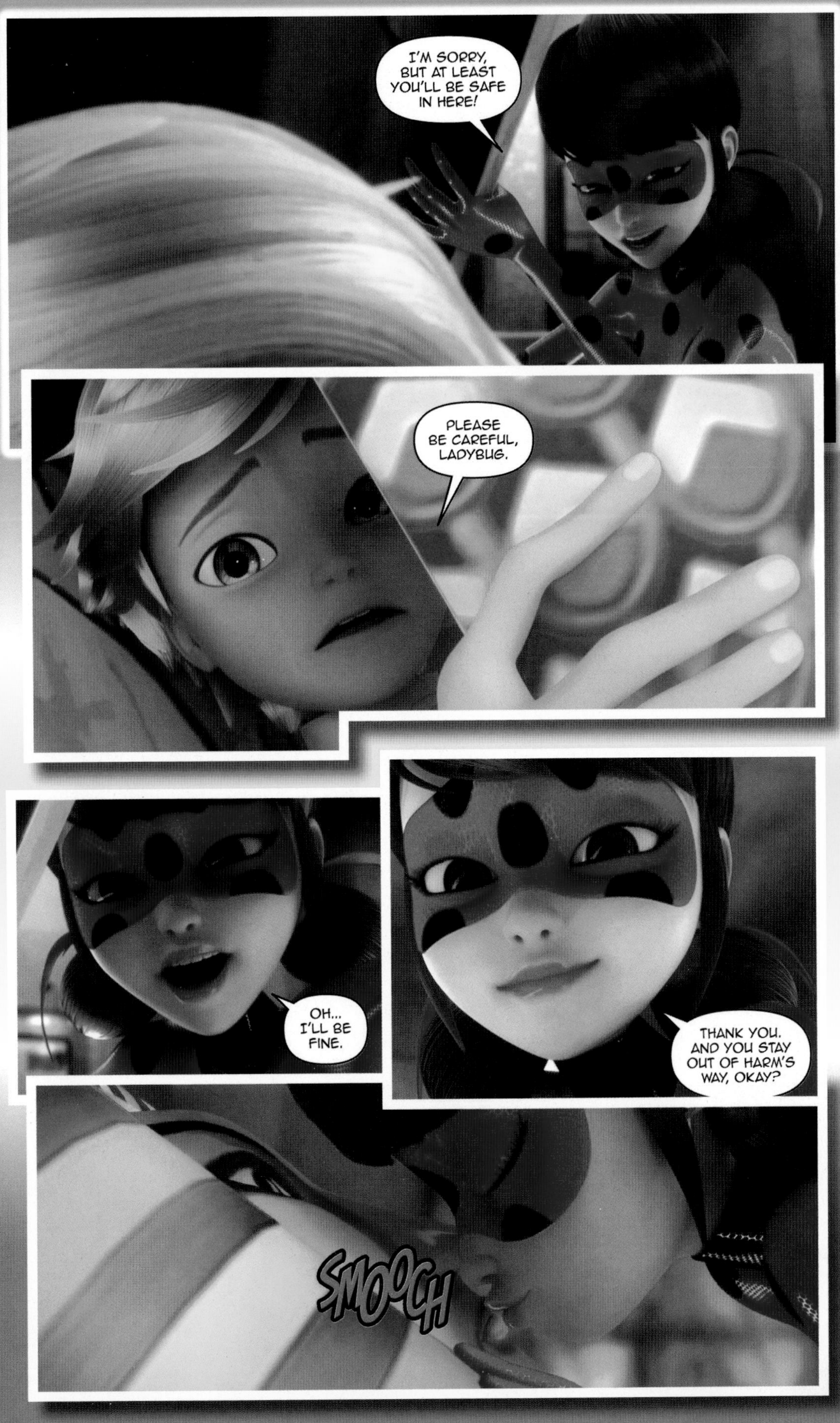
I'M SORRY, BUT AT LEAST YOU'LL BE SAFE IN HERE!
PLEASE BE CAREFUL, LADYBUG.
OH... I'LL BE FINE.
THANK YOU. AND YOU STAY OUT OF HARM'S WAY, OKAY?
SMOOCH

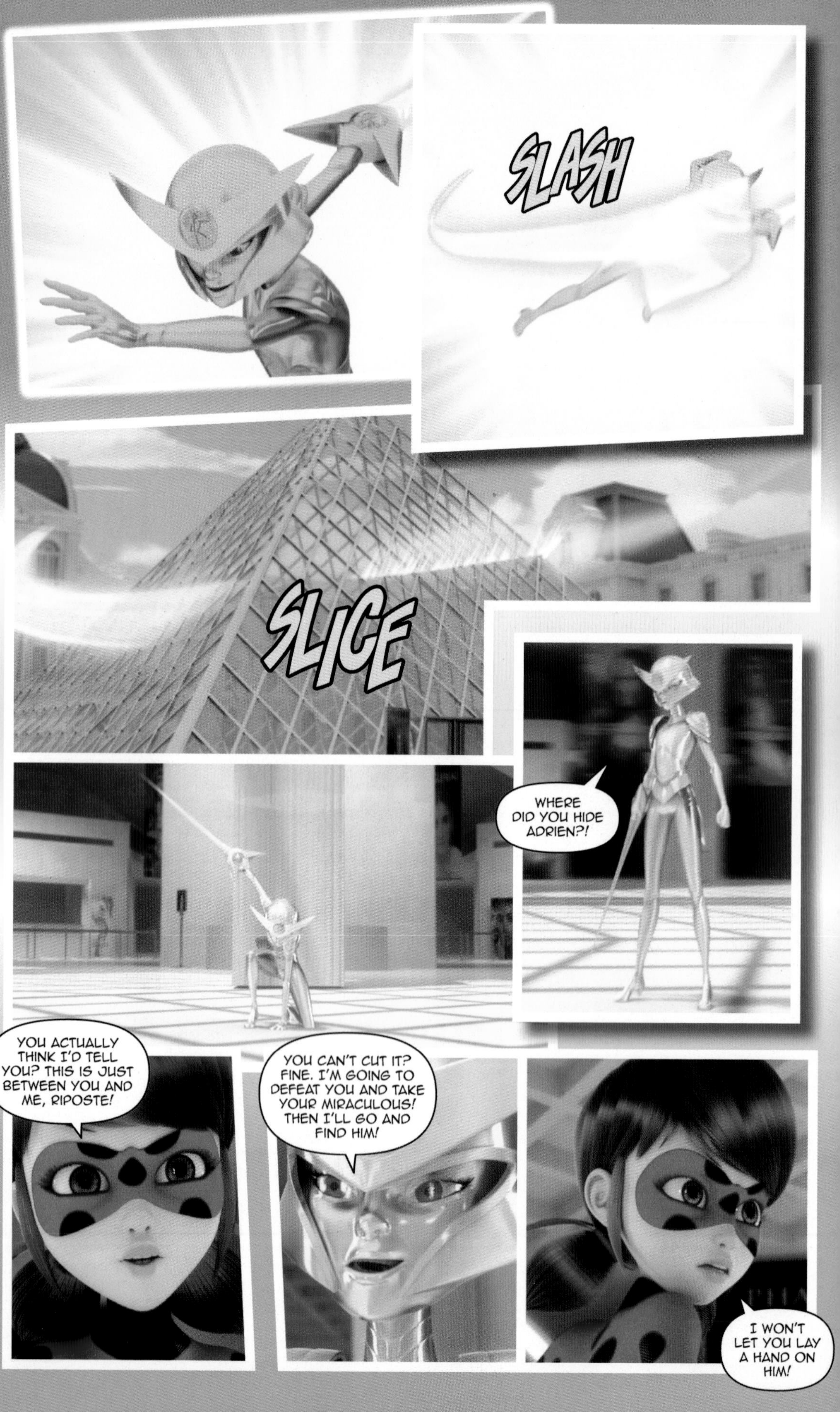
SLASH
SLICE
WHERE DID YOU HIDE ADRIEN?!
YOU ACTUALLY THINK I'D TELL YOU? THIS IS JUST BETWEEN YOU AND ME, RIPOSTE!
YOU CAN'T CUT IT? FINE. I'M GOING TO DEFEAT YOU AND TAKE YOUR MIRACULOUS! THEN I'LL GO AND FIND HIM!
I WON'T LET YOU LAY A HAND ON HIM!

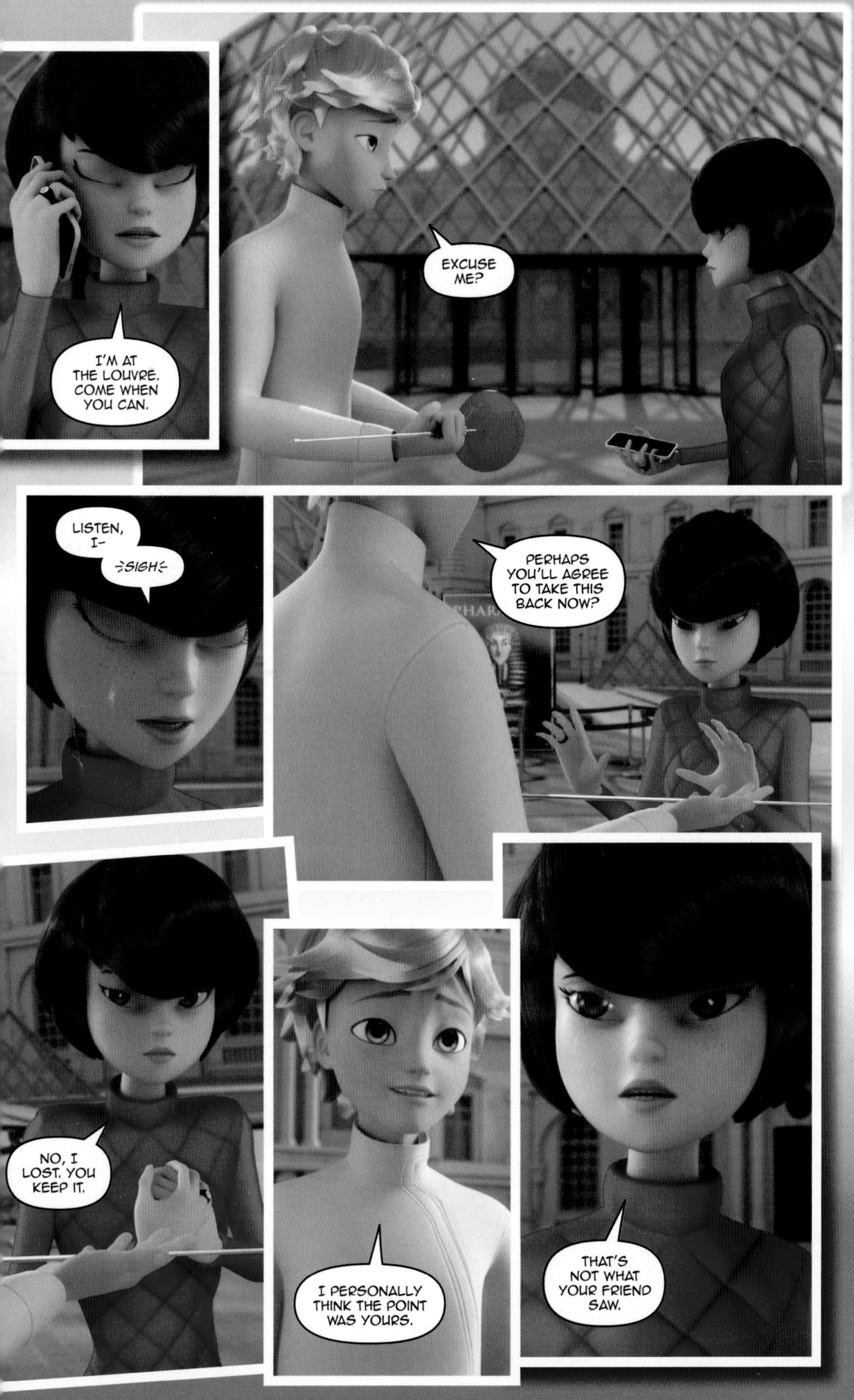
I'M AT THE LOUVRE. COME WHEN YOU CAN.
EXCUSE ME?
LISTEN, I-
-SIGH-
PERHAPS YOU'LL AGREE TO TAKE THIS BACK NOW?
NO, I LOST. YOU KEEP IT.
I PERSONALLY THINK THE POINT WAS YOURS.
THAT'S NOT WHAT YOUR FRIEND SAW.

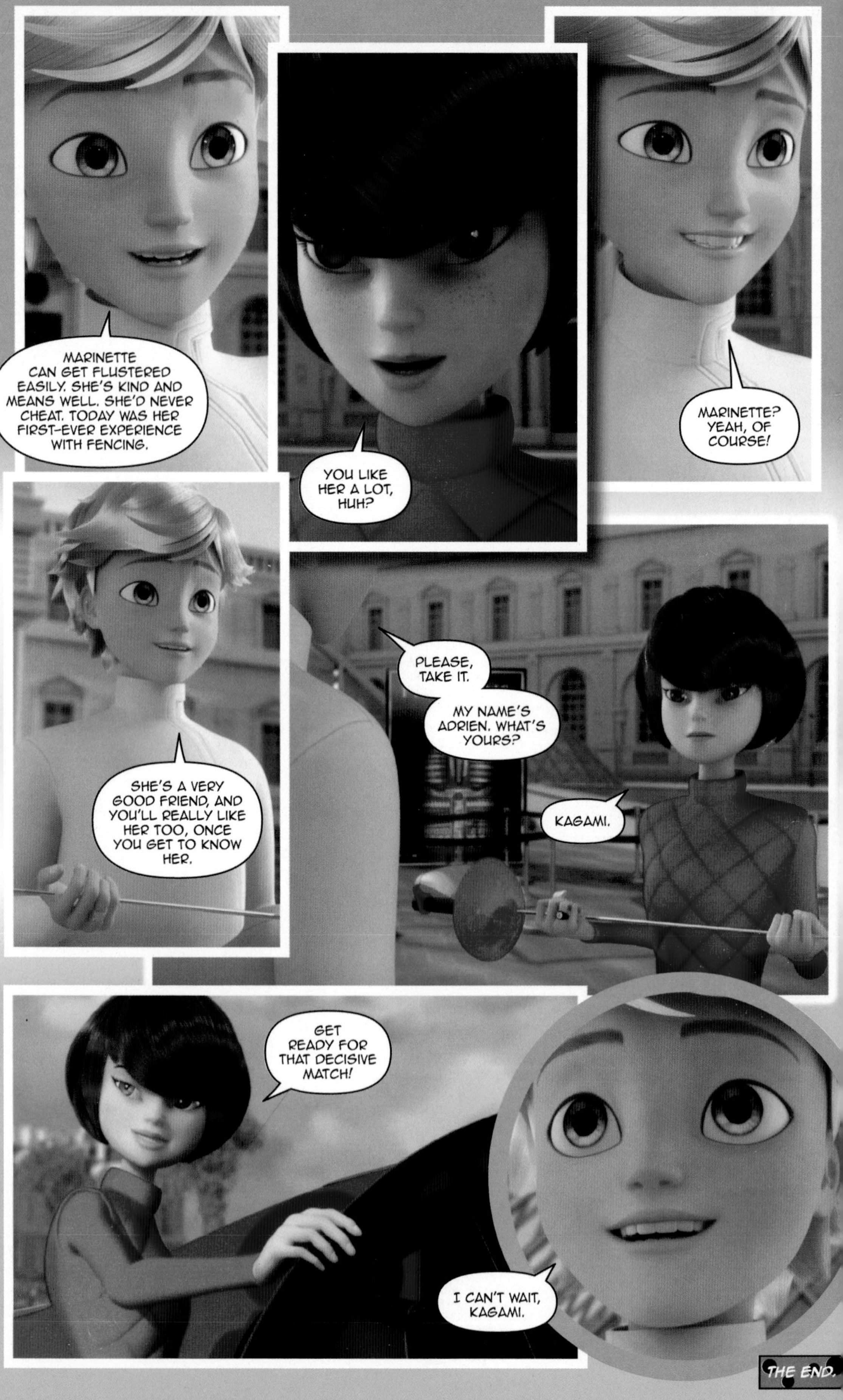
MARINETTE CAN GET FLUSTERED EASILY. SHE'S KIND AND MEANS WELL. SHE'D NEVER CHEAT. TODAY WAS HER FIRST-EVER EXPERIENCE WITH FENCING.
YOU LIKE HER A LOT, HUH?
MARINETTE? YEAH, OF COURSE!
SHE'S A VERY GOOD FRIEND, AND YOU'LL REALLY LIKE HER TOO, ONCE YOU GET TO KNOW HER.
PLEASE, TAKE IT.
MY NAME'S ADRIEN. WHAT'S YOURS?
KAGAMI.
GET READY FOR THAT DECISIVE MATCH!
I CAN'T WAIT, KAGAMI.
THE END.

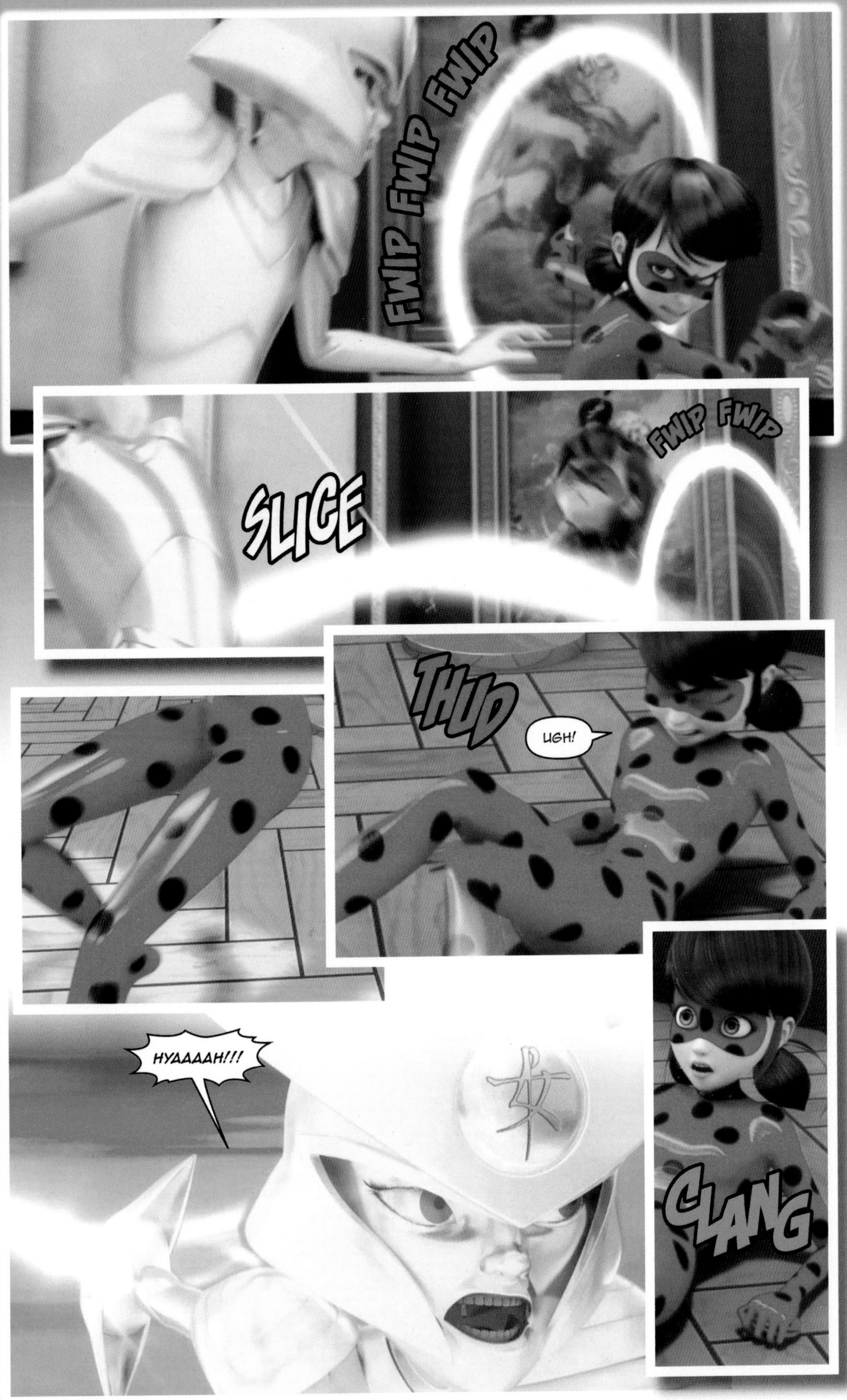
FWIP FWIP FWIP
FWIP FWIP
SLICE
THUD
UGH!
HYAAAAH!!!
CLANG

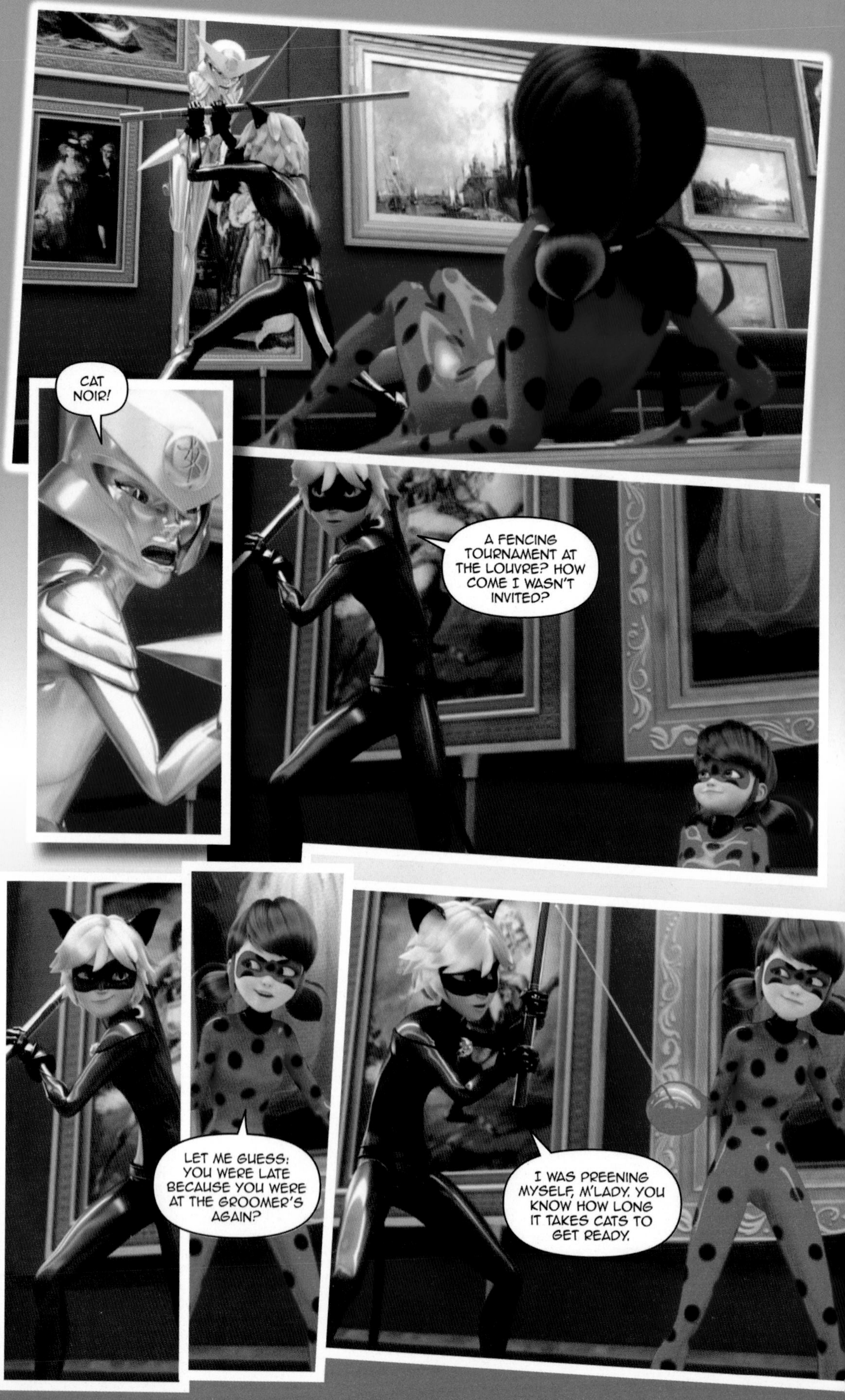
CAT NOIR!
A FENCING TOURNAMENT AT THE LOUVRE? HOW COME I WASN'T INVITED?
LET ME GUESS: YOU WERE LATE BECAUSE YOU WERE AT THE GROOMER'S AGAIN?
I WAS PREENING MYSELF, M'LADY. YOU KNOW HOW LONG IT TAKES CATS TO GET READY.

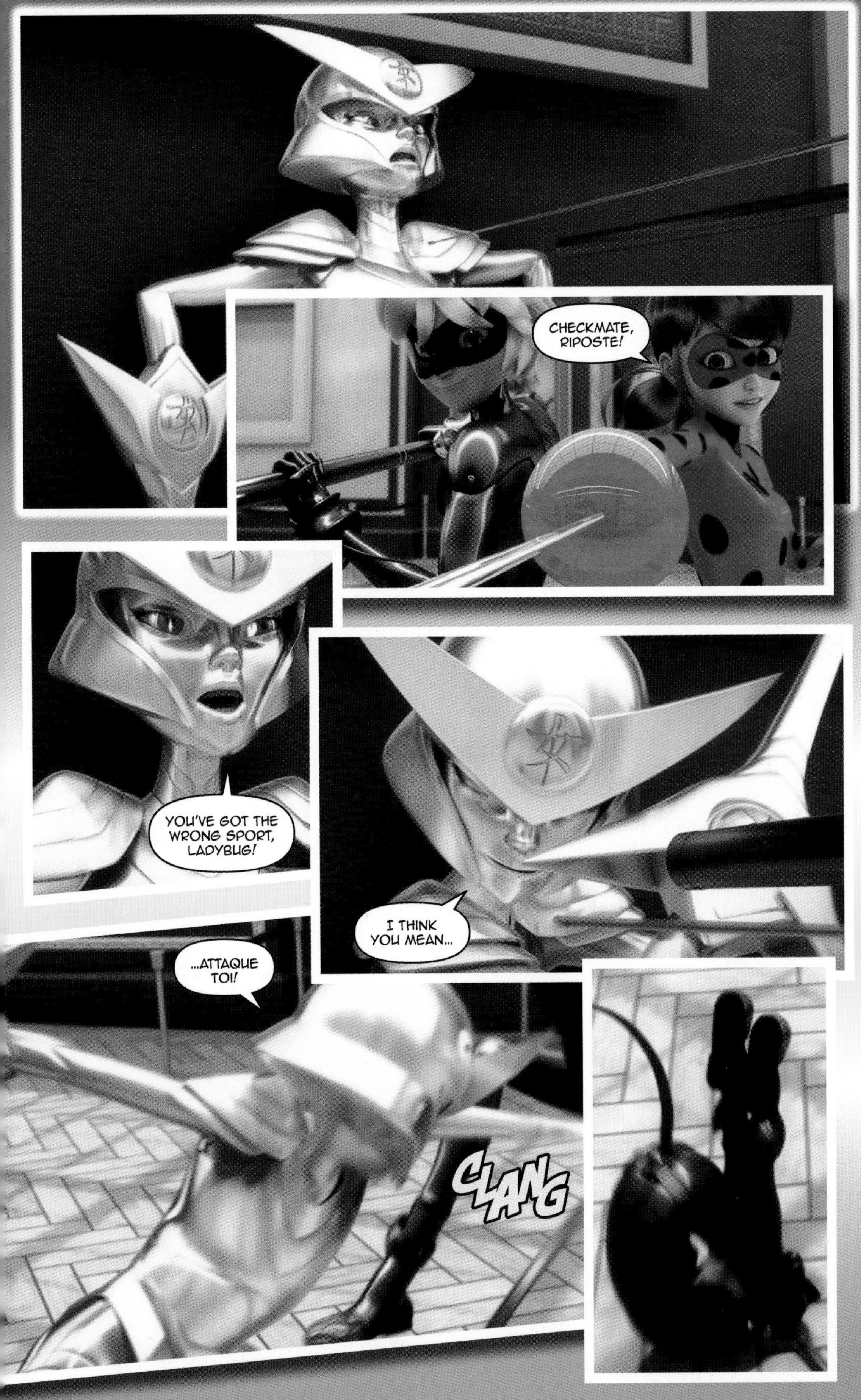
CHECKMATE, RIPOSTE!
YOU'VE GOT THE WRONG SPORT, LADYBUG!
I THINK YOU MEAN...
...ATTAQUE TOI!
CLANG

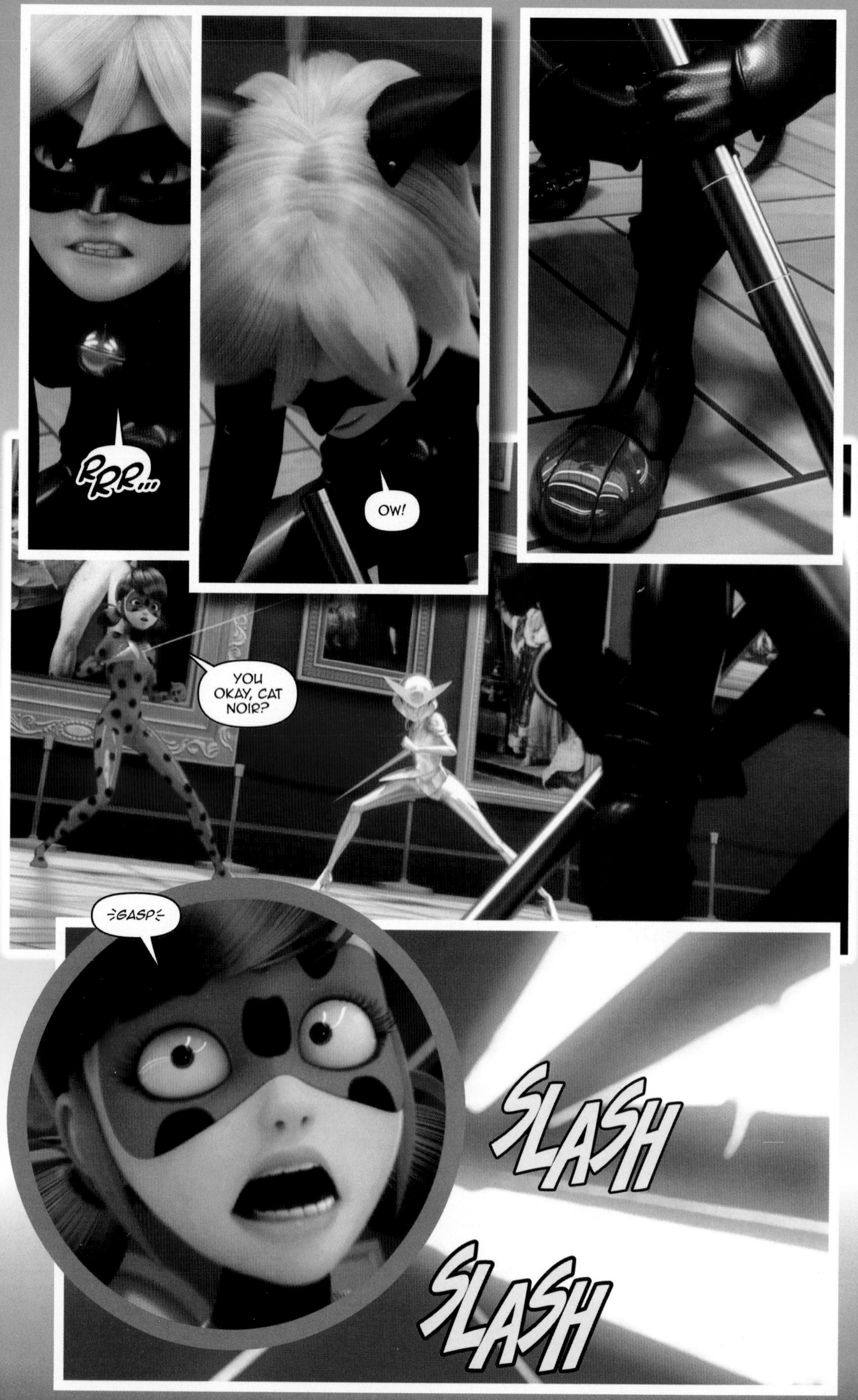
RRR...
OW!
YOU OKAY, CAT NOIR?
GASP
SLASH
SLASH

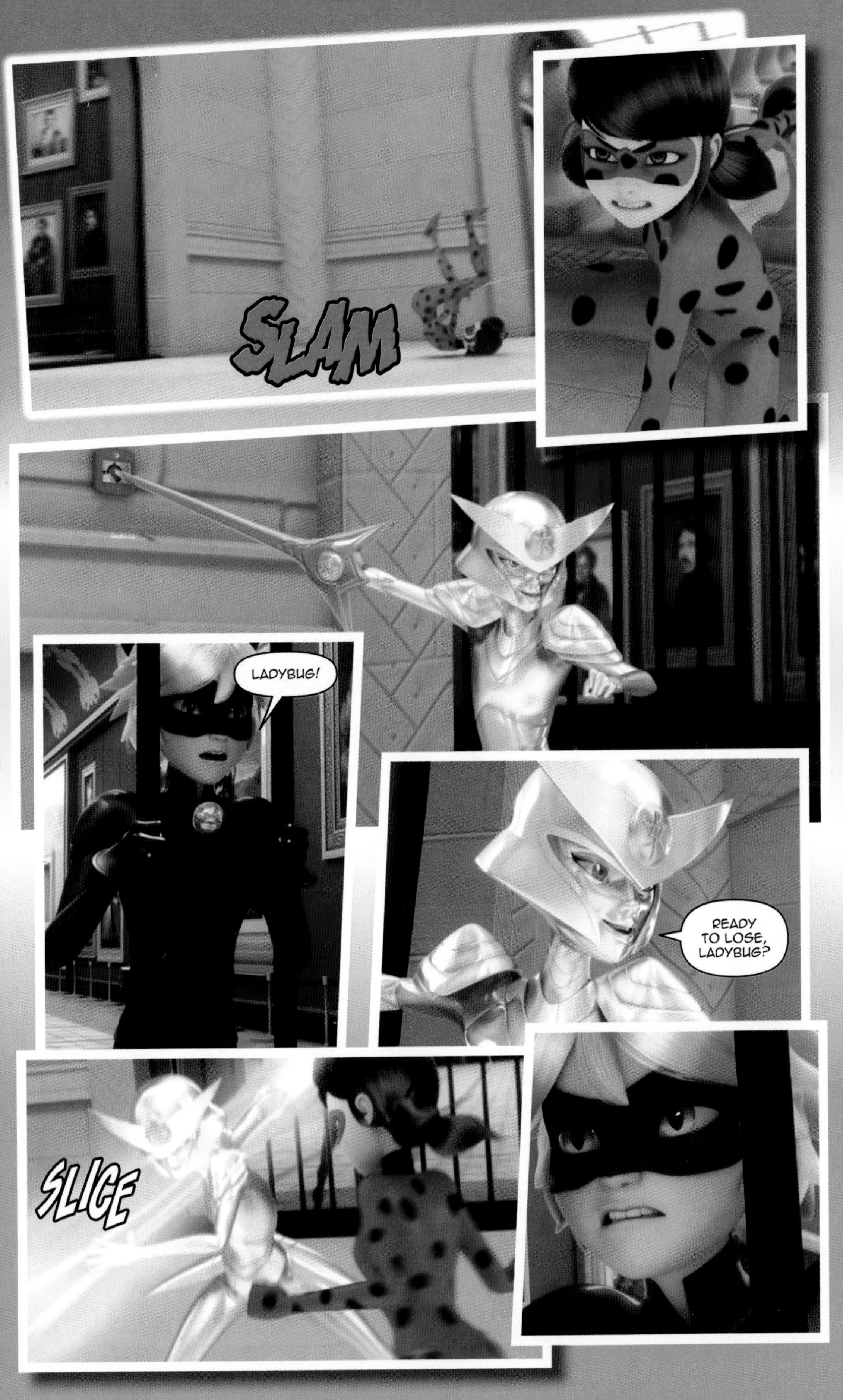
SLAM
LADYBUG!
READY TO LOSE, LADYBUG?
SLICE

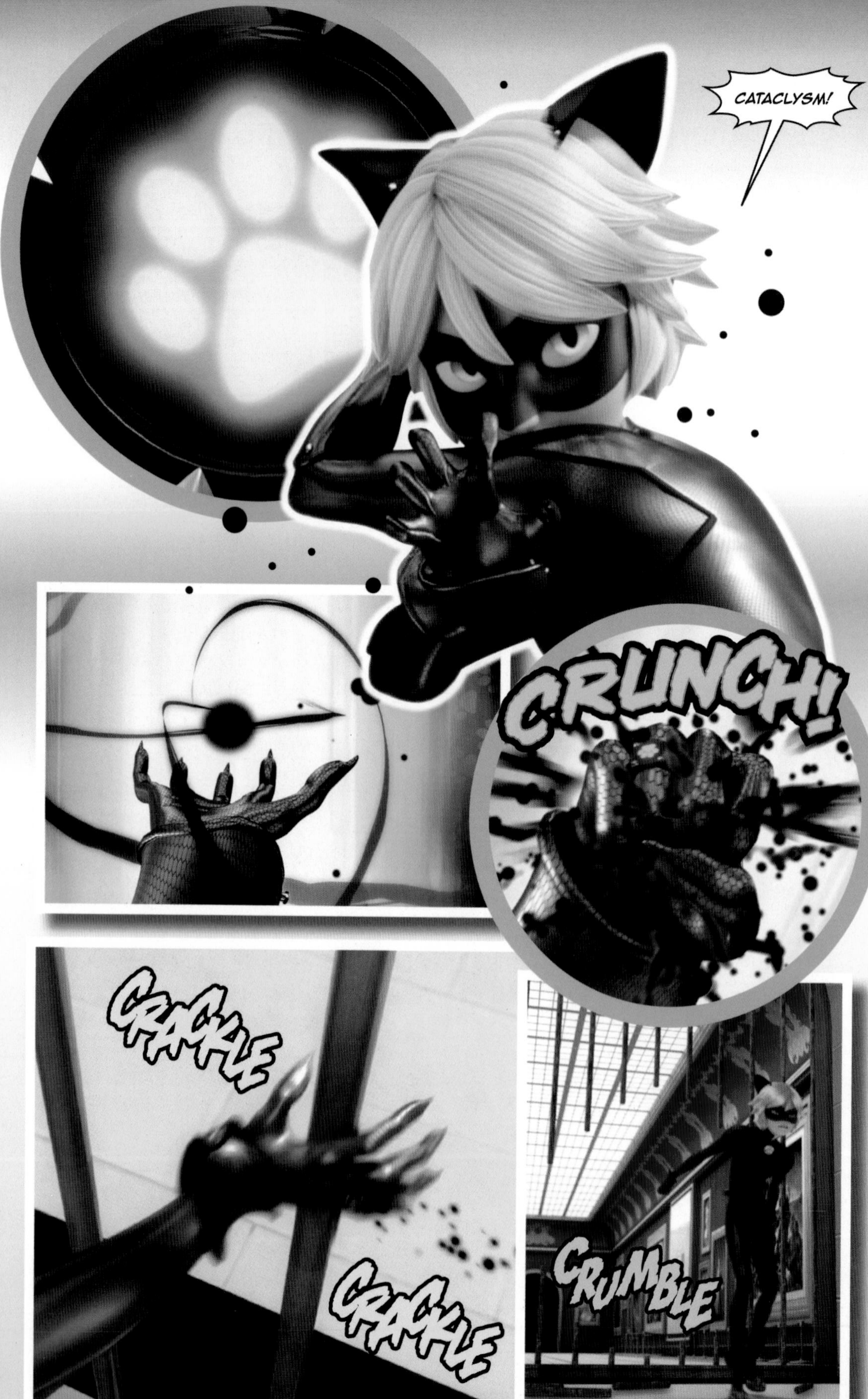
CATACLYSM!
CRUNCH!
CRACKLE
CRACKLE
CRUMBLE

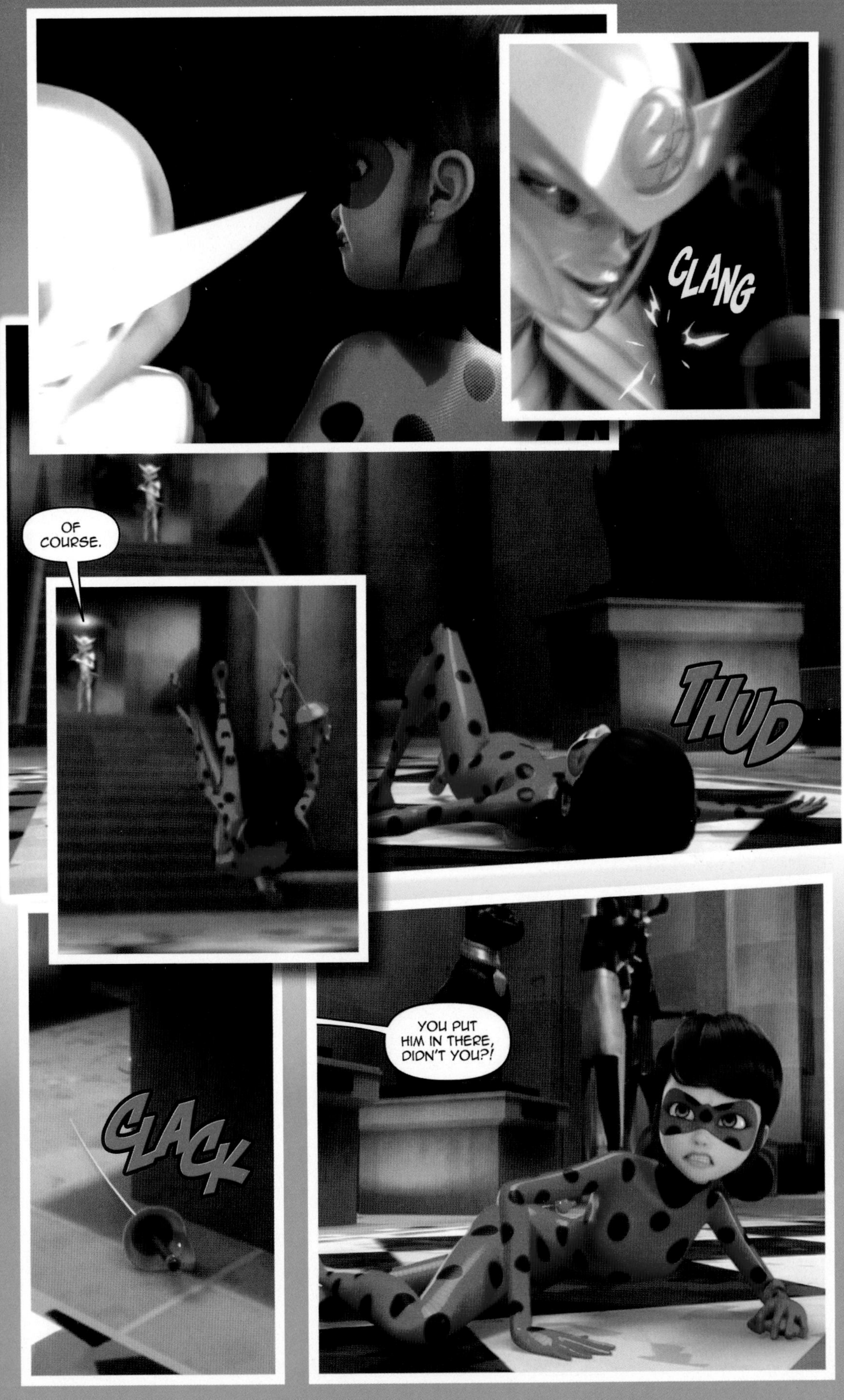
CLANG
OF COURSE.
THUD
CLACK
YOU PUT HIM IN THERE, DIDN'T YOU?!

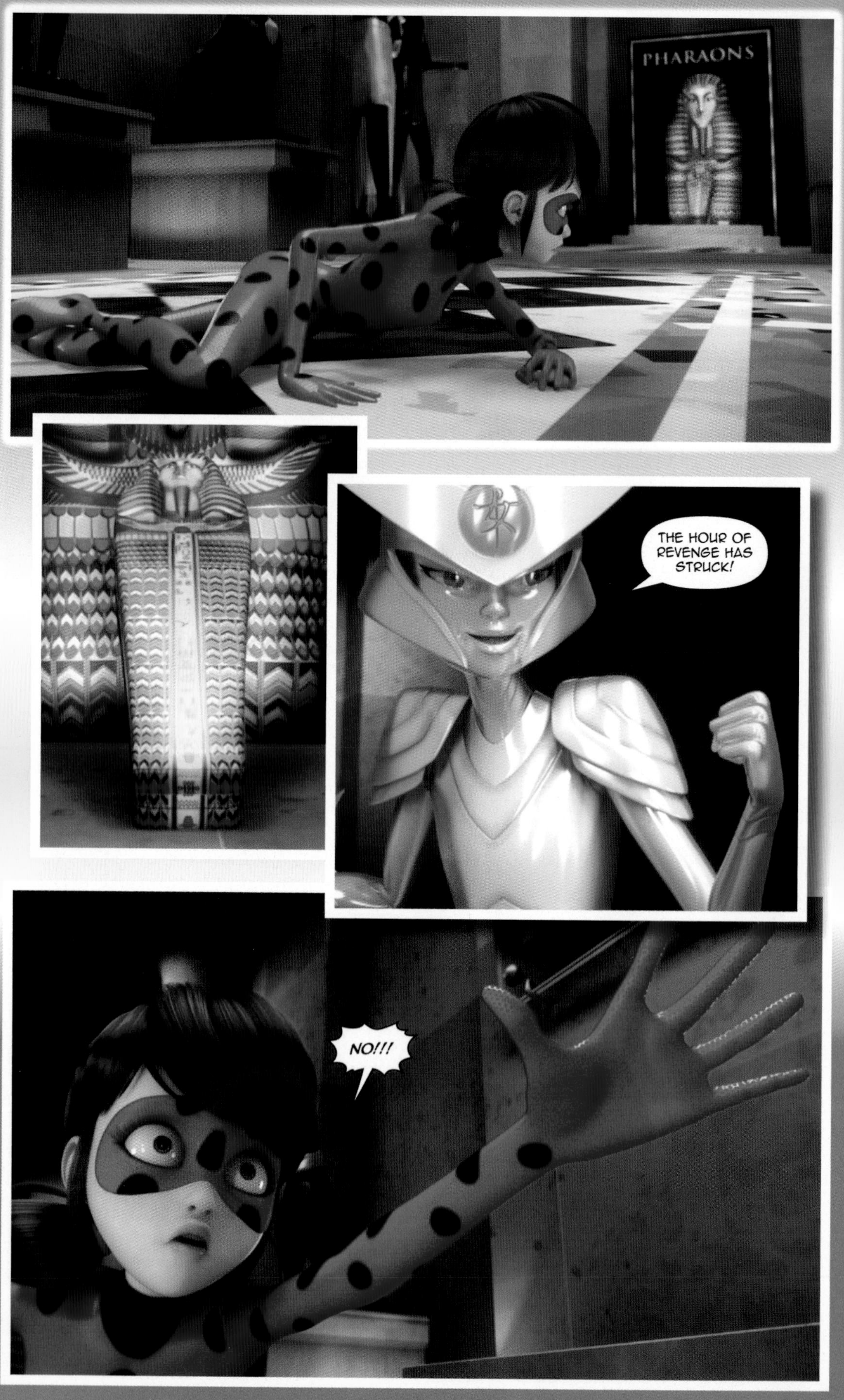
PHARAONS
THE HOUR OF REVENGE HAS STRUCK!
NO!!!

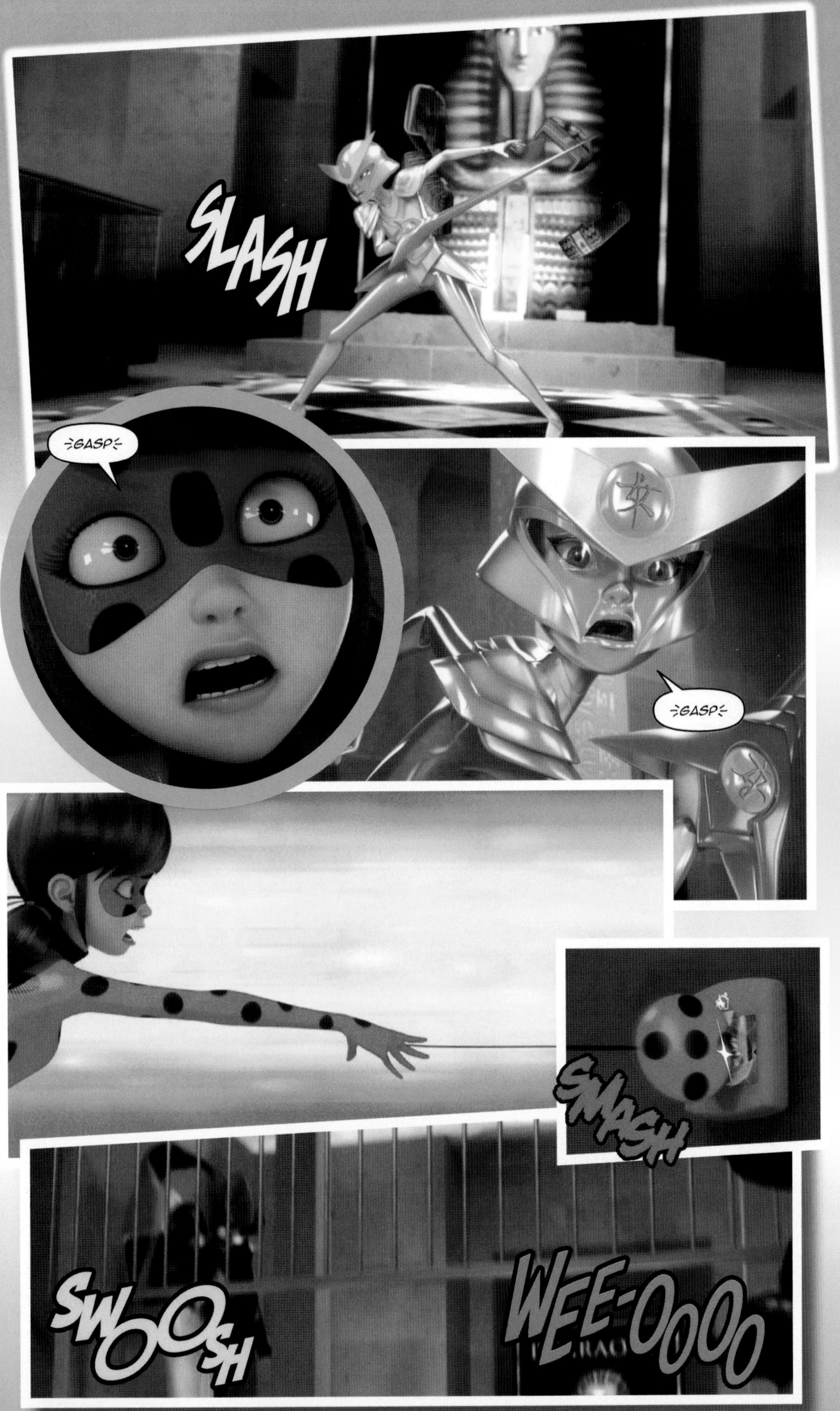
SLASH
GASP
GASP
SMASH
SWOOSH
WEE-OOOO

WEE-OOOO

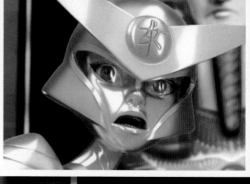

HE'S GONE!

UH... WHO?

FWIP-FWIP FWIP

FWIP

RIPOSTE IS TRYING TO GET REVENGE ON ADRIEN AGRESTE! I HID HIM INSIDE THE SARCOPHAGUS!

MAYBE HE WAS FEELING A LITTLE... CLAWS-TROPHOBIC?

LET'S LOOK FOR HIM TOGETHER, LADYBUG. AND FINISH THIS MATCH!

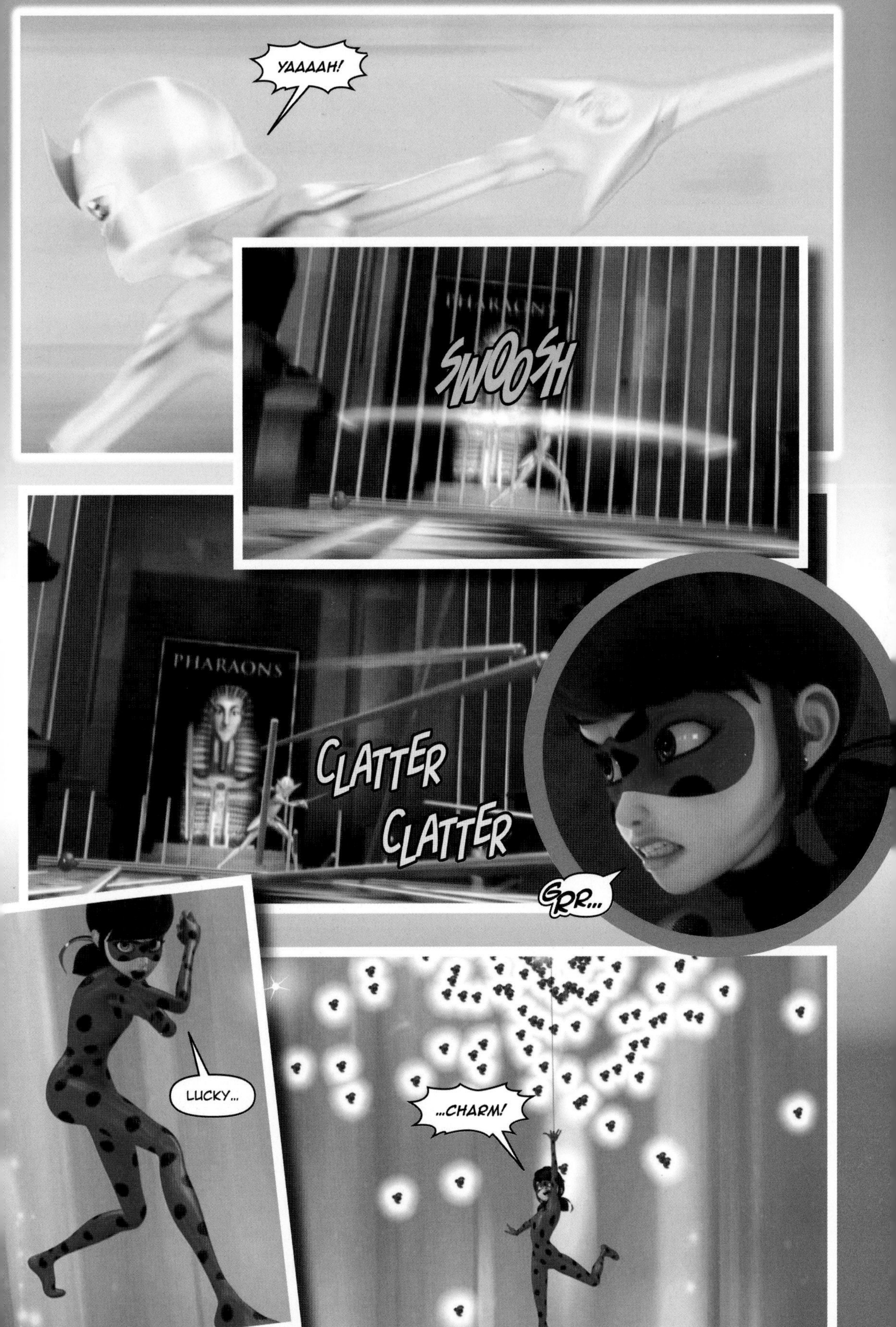
YAAAAH!
SWOOSH
PHARAONS
CLATTER
CLATTER
GRR...
LUCKY...
...CHARM!

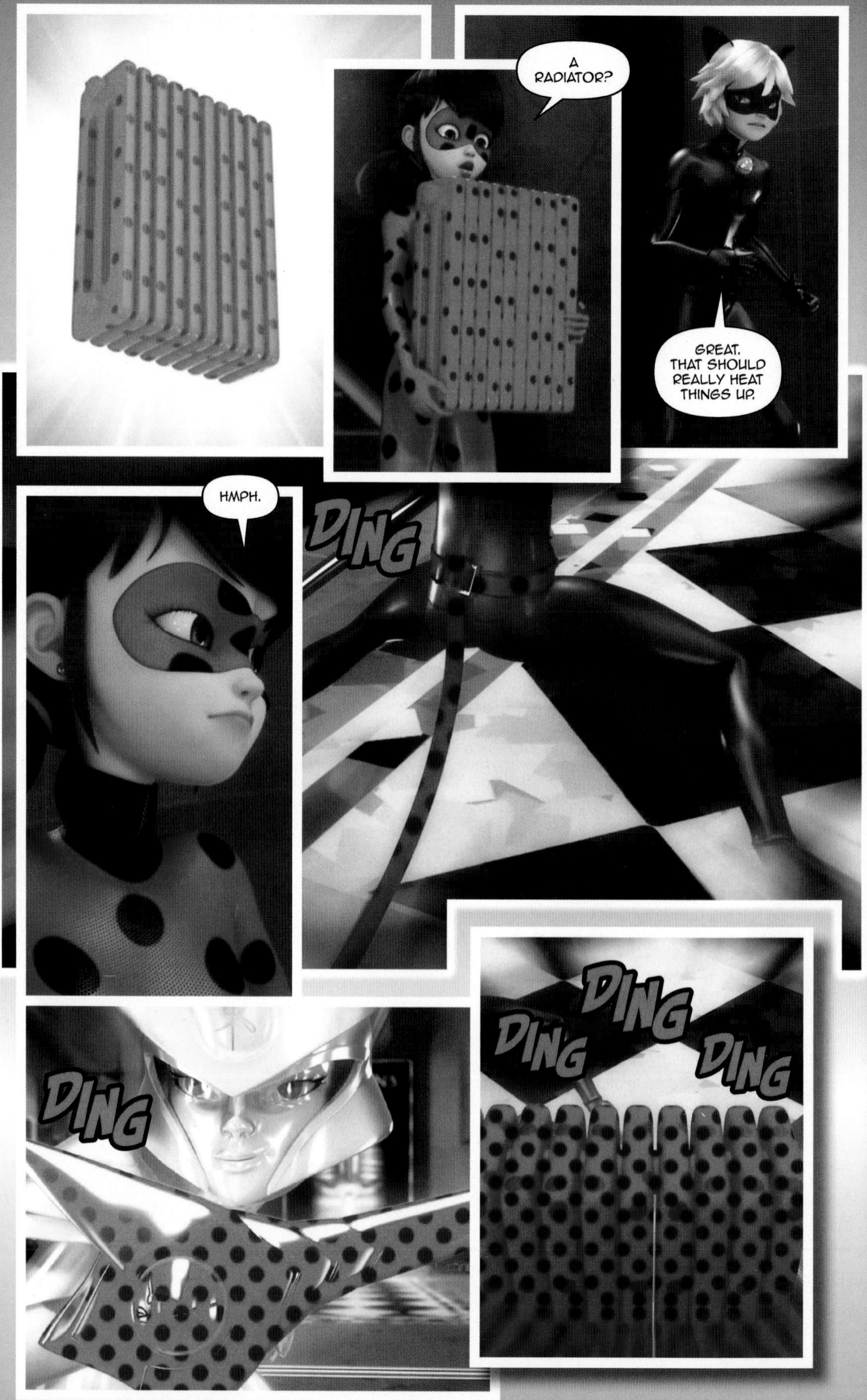
A RADIATOR?
GREAT. THAT SHOULD REALLY HEAT THINGS UP.
HMPH.
DING
DING
DING
DING
DING
DING

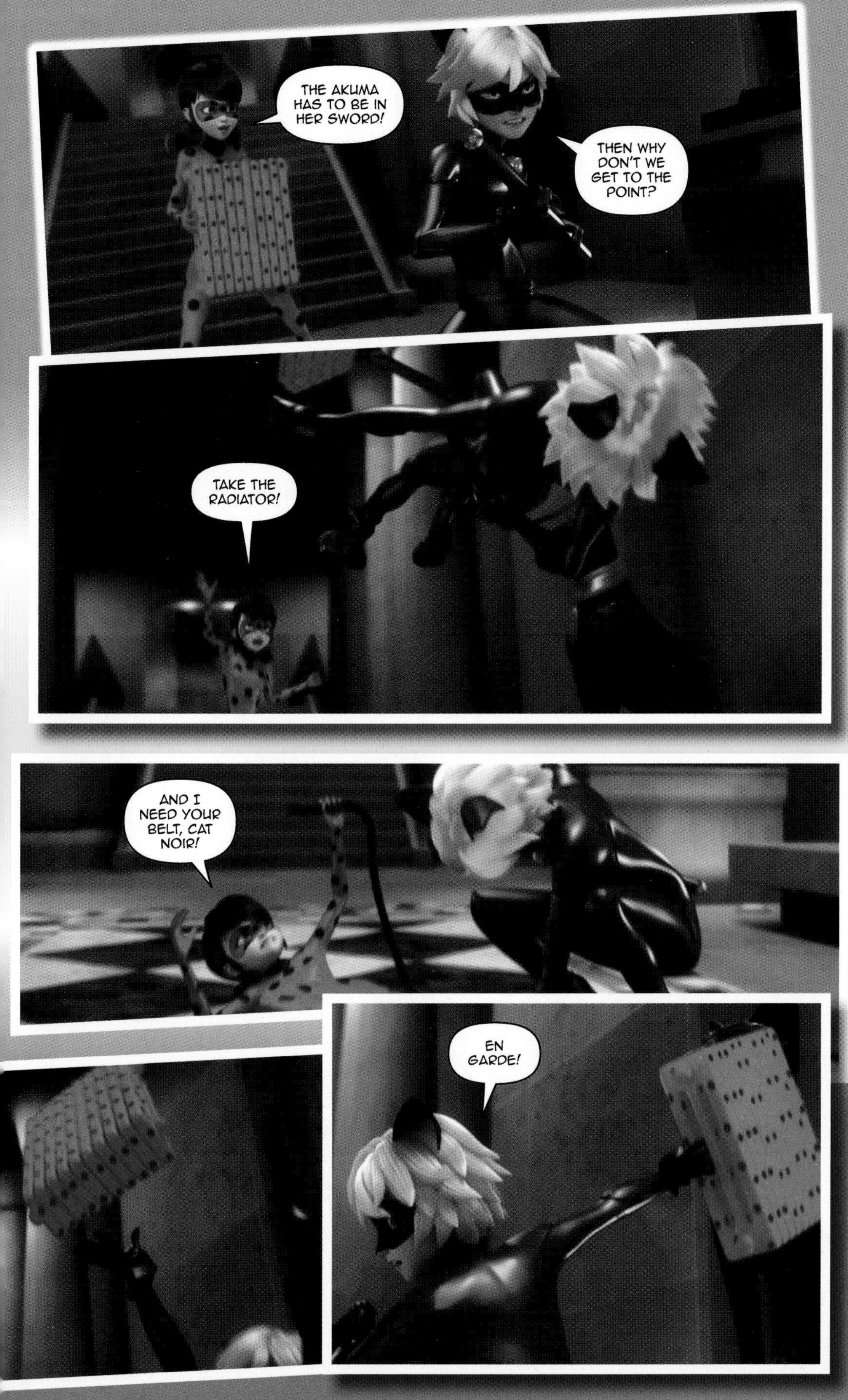
THE AKUMA HAS TO BE IN HER SWORD!
THEN WHY DON'T WE GET TO THE POINT?
TAKE THE RADIATOR!
AND I NEED YOUR BELT, CAT NOIR!
EN GARDE!

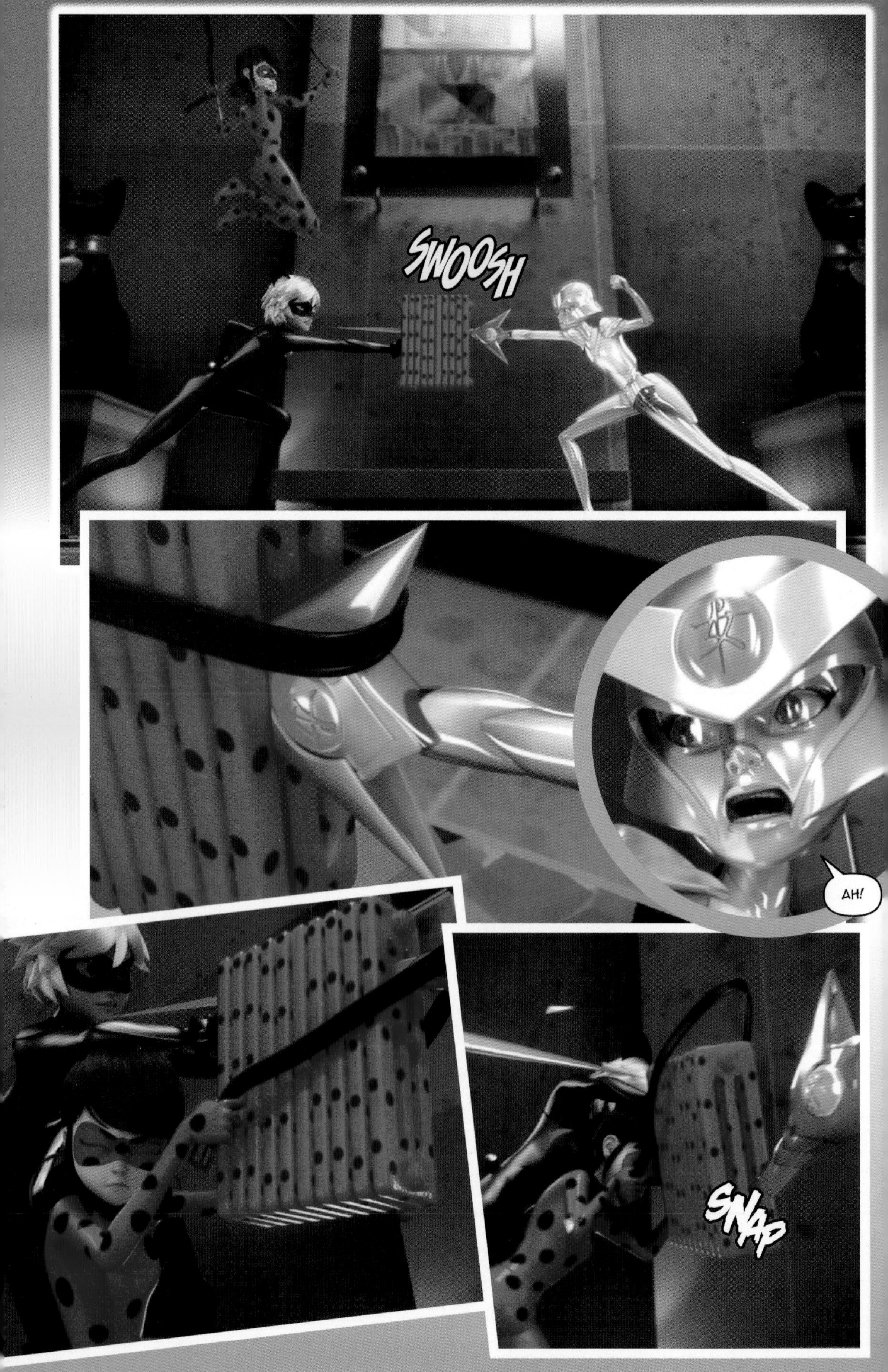
SWOOSH
AH!
SNAP

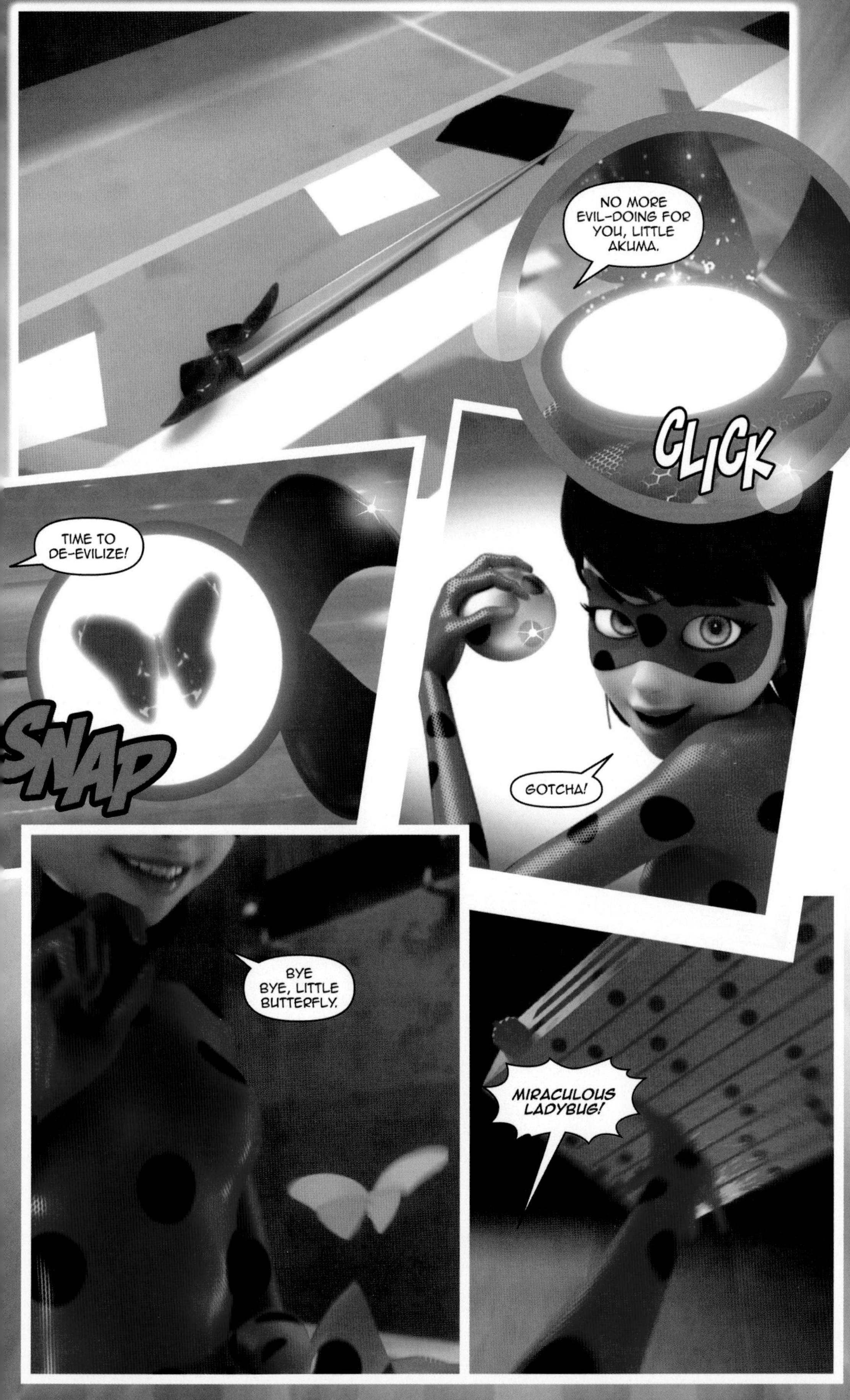
NO MORE EVIL-DOING FOR YOU, LITTLE AKUMA.
CLICK
TIME TO DE-EVILIZE!
SNAP
GOTCHA!
BYE BYE, LITTLE BUTTERFLY.
MIRACULOUS LADYBUG!

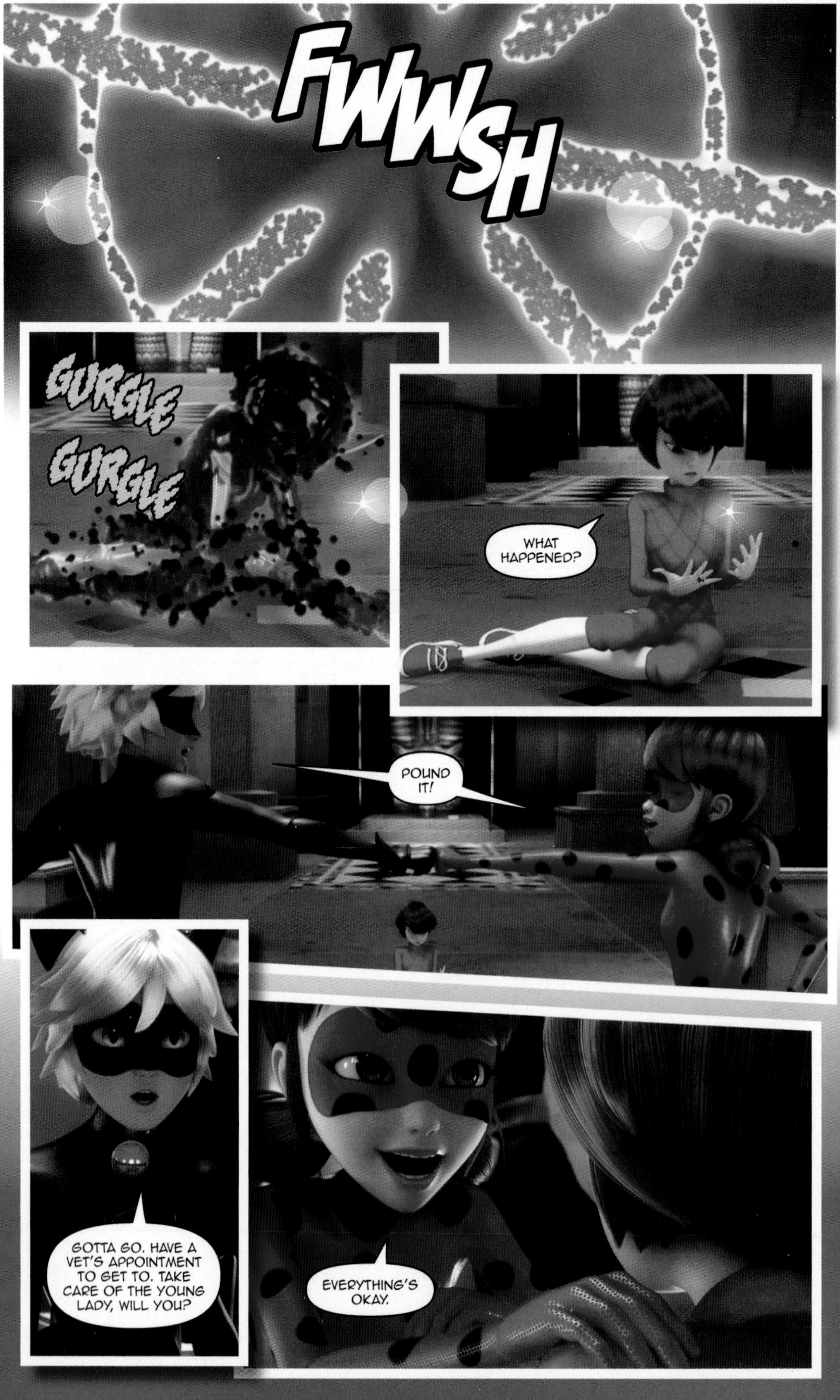
FWWSH
GURGLE
GURGLE
WHAT HAPPENED?
POUND IT!
GOTTA GO. HAVE A VET'S APPOINTMENT TO GET TO. TAKE CARE OF THE YOUNG LADY, WILL YOU?
EVERYTHING'S OKAY.

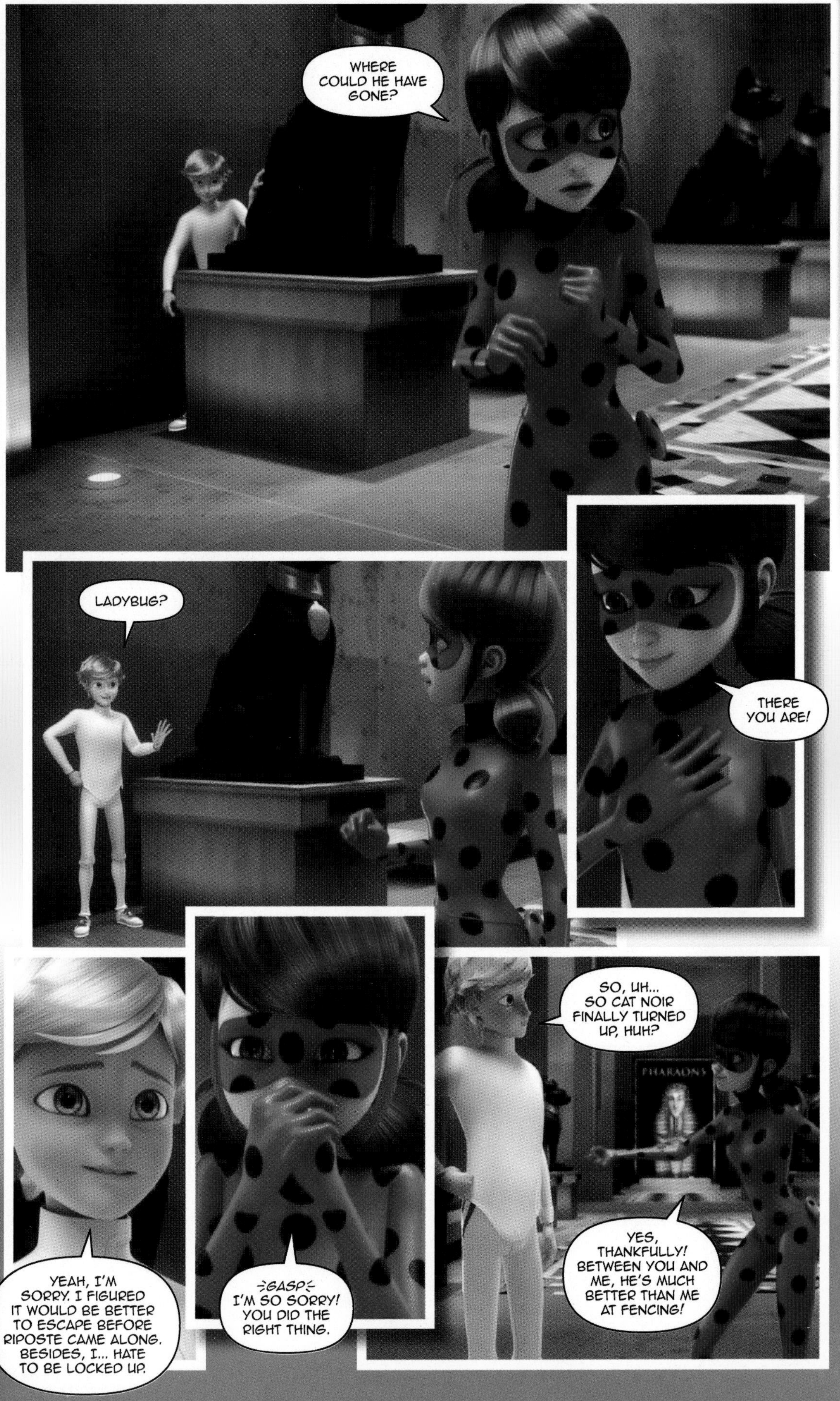
WHERE COULD HE HAVE GONE?
LADYBUG?
THERE YOU ARE!
YEAH, I'M SORRY. I FIGURED IT WOULD BE BETTER TO ESCAPE BEFORE RIPOSTE CAME ALONG. BESIDES, I... HATE TO BE LOCKED UP.
GASP
I'M SO SORRY! YOU DID THE RIGHT THING.
SO, UH... SO CAT NOIR FINALLY TURNED UP, HUH?
PHARAONS
YES, THANKFULLY! BETWEEN YOU AND ME, HE'S MUCH BETTER THAN ME AT FENCING!

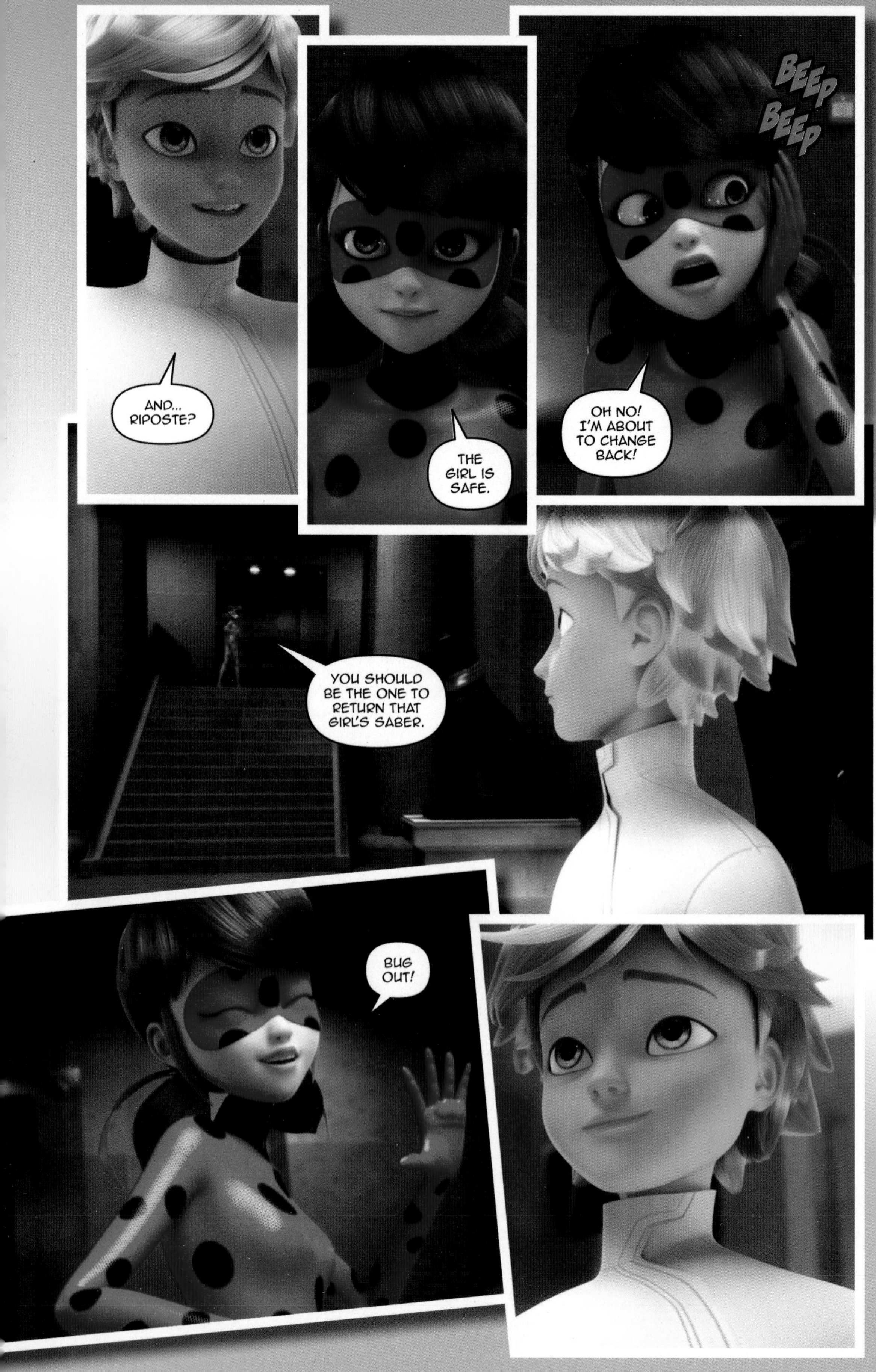
AND... RIPOSTE?
THE GIRL IS SAFE.
BEEP BEEP
OH NO! I'M ABOUT TO CHANGE BACK!
YOU SHOULD BE THE ONE TO RETURN THAT GIRL'S SABER.
BUG OUT!